LOVE ME LATER

LIBBY RICE

ISBN: 0990353613
ISBN-13: 978-0-9903536-1-4

This is a work of fiction. Names, characters, places, and incidents are the product of the author's imagination or are used fictitiously. Any resemblance to actual events, locales, or persons, living or dead, is coincidental.

Gateway Publishing Ltd.
P.O. Box 1414
Golden, Colorado 80402

Cover design by Viola Estrella
Edited by Kathie Middlemiss

DEDICATION

For Tom, who made it possible for me to write. In that, you gave me everything.

ACKNOWLEDGMENTS

As they say, it takes a village, and this book was no exception. From the very beginning, so many offered their valuable time and advice. I'm truly at a loss for how to express my gratitude to all the people who read and made this book better: Amy Denim, Erin Bradmon, Julie Sheridan, Lindsey Donakowski, Viola Estrella, Jen Maitlen, Larie Brannick, Lorna Bryan, Kimberley Anderson, Spice Jones, Krista Hwang, and Judy Adams.

I owe so much to the lunch crew, filled with women who've blazed trails in both traditional and self-publishing: Thea Harrison, Courtney Milan, Jenn LeBlanc, and Elise Rome. Thank you for your willingness to share all you've learned with a newbie who redefines the definition of inquisitive.

Viola Estrella deserves special thanks (and a case of red wine!) for all she did to mentor me over the last two years. Not only did Vi volunteer to be one of my first beta readers, she introduced me to my agent, designed my gorgeous cover over at Estrella Cover Art, and answered endless questions about "the biz" along the way. You're the original badass, Vi.

My agent, Elizabeth Winick Rubinstein, provided valuable insight into this book and my publishing choices. While I ultimately decided to embark upon an indie career, I am so grateful for her intellect, her honesty, and her guidance.

So many others, literally too many to list, provided moral support and a "get back on the damn horse" when the waters got rocky. To all my friends with the Colorado Romance Writers, I salute you! I count myself lucky to be part of such a vital, supportive organization. And to my "non-writing" friends and family, who didn't bat an eye when I embarked on this lark and have remained steadfast in their belief in my ultimate success, thank you for being such wonderful people.

And, finally, I could write sonnets to my husband, Tom. Not many husbands would appreciate their spouse's decision to chuck lawyering in favor of writing. You made sacrifices for my books, and you've made them with a smile and said, "I love you, and I always will."

Ditto.

The course of true love never did run smooth.

William Shakespeare

CHAPTER 1

December—New York City

The tunneling entrance of the club opened to a packed arena and a blinding wall of light. Blood, sweat, and testosterone hung heavy in the stale air, shrouding two roped-off contenders in an invisible layer of menace. The fight had started.

Scarlet tracked the boxers with an untrained, but keen, eye. In the midst of sinking to her space on the scarred aluminum bleacher, she stopped, arrested by what she saw in the ring two rows down.

One man had blond hair, the other black, a color so dark it gleamed with a bluish tint under the fluorescent glare. The blond certainly deserved his heavyweight distinction, but next to the darker brute, his pale limbs appeared almost fine-boned. The striking contrasts didn't end there. Both men pummeled each other without reserve, yet the dark-haired fighter struck with less desperation, more calculation. From the other, she sensed a tendency to throw out every move in his repertoire, one after the other, until a fist connected.

"Utkatasana?" The question arrived with butchered pronunciation and a low chuckle that dragged Scarlet from her slack-jawed musings. She and Lissa had come to the fight to ogle her friend's new interest. From Lissa's description—"tall, dark, and rough"—Scarlet knew exactly who the man was, and she certainly couldn't fault Lissa's taste.

"As a matter of fact," Scarlet said, looking left to catch Lissa's smirk. "I always drop a quick chair pose before a boxing match. All the cool kids do."

Except she'd never been to a boxing match and was pretty sure that other than Lissa, none of the Harry-Winston-wearing, charity-hosting socialites she knew would be caught dead in a dingy fight club in Brooklyn,

1

perfect yoga form or not. Tennis was more their style. Especially when played quietly and accompanied by one of those announcers who screamed in a whisper.

Their loss. Or so she told herself. In truth, she didn't think those women found the confines of wealth lonely or isolating, whereas she fit in at the top about as well as she did here, where men fanned money in the air, taking impromptu bets on the violence unfolding for their entertainment, while Scarlet tried to casually blend into her seat.

"Where'd you meet him?" Scarlet thrust her chin at the dark-haired Adonis who now danced beyond his opponent's reach. With each movement, the muscles of his arms and torso flexed and relaxed with the fluidity of an evening tide, dark eyes burning with quiet determination. At least it would be a short fight.

"Not him," Lissa replied with a dismissive clip, ducking to rummage through her purse. "I met mine in sculpture class." She glanced up. "Looks like I should ask yours to model."

Scarlet got stuck on "Not him." As in, not hers and possibly available. She wouldn't be violating the cardinal rule of girlfriend-hood if she hunted the soon-to-be winner down after the fight and proposed. The radical thought stuck in her chest, pushing her heartbeat from a semi-manageable trot to a full-scale gallop.

Lissa shot her a fascinated look. "Re-heely, stop licking your lips. He's not a snack."

"No." Scarlet coughed into a fist, letting herself smile. "I'll be his." Already gleaming with sweat, dark head bent low, the man was delicious, the perfect spice for a stifled life if she dare reach high.

"Touché," Lissa answered with a wide grin. Then, bold as she pleased, Lissa reached out and tugged at the square bodice of Scarlet's dress. Scarlet jerked back, but the material inched downward under Lissa's tenacious attention, revealing a flash of flesh.

Squirming away, Scarlet yelped, "What are you doing?" And batted at Lissa's questing fingers, wrestling for control over the thick brocade bodice.

Lissa shrugged. "We want He-Man's focus to shift right"—light taps pegged the apex of Scarlet's cleavage—"here."

Heat crawled from Scarlet's hairline downward. "No, we really don't." With a final wrench, she righted the dress and turned back to the fight. One look told her she hadn't been the only one distracted by the skirmish. An aggressive gaze had swiveled her direction from inside the ring. She'd known his eyes would be dark, but like his hair, they were black, chips of midnight that examined her with the same single-minded calculation he used to size up his opponent in the ring. Before she could muster even a faint nod in acknowledgment, his thickly fringed lids dipped, then jerked toward his shoulder with the rest of his head, absorbing what looked to be a killer blow to the jaw.

Of course Lissa didn't miss the exchange. "You alone in that apartment tonight?" She slid Scarlet a sly look, wetting her lips.

Scarlet's stomach dropped in quick, clenching rebellion, whether from Lissa's question or the lost glance, she couldn't say. "Just me, Liss." Her words sounded overly bright to her own ears. She'd spoken to her father once since arriving from Stanford for the winter break. A hundred bucks said Tripp Leore wouldn't venture within a thousand miles of New York City for the holidays, leaving her the sole inhabitant of six-thousand square feet of Manhattan high-rise.

Alone put it mildly.

Feeling the need to justify her answer, to seem a tad less pathetic, Scarlet added, "But Dad left a present." A one-sentence note on the counter had announced the car waiting in her underground parking space. Maserati. Red. Hers. The typed narrative had conveyed the gist, everything except, maybe, "Merry Christmas."

Each year brought a gift more extravagant than the one before it. Beginning with a Russian sable jacket the December her mother had died, and continuing every holiday since, the presents had proven costly, yet impersonal, luxury items to be paid for by her father, but selected by an assistant. One Christmas without her dad had turned to two, then five, now ten. Time had morphed from longing for his presence into anger over his absence and, finally, into acceptance of the status quo. These days, Scarlet took the presents and tried to enjoy them, never confusing money for love.

The arena erupted around them, and Scarlet jumped up to see her future husband power drive a right hook into his opponent's jaw. The man wobbled on his feet before sliding slowly to his knees and face planting on the canvas.

The referee's hands hurtled skyward. "Knockout!" He grabbed Husband's wrist for a victory revolution, giving the crowd its frenzied fill.

Scarlet remained standing when her man ducked under the ropes, escaping without a backward glance. She wiggled her fingers, but plastered damp palms against her thighs, refusing to reach for his retreating form. A familiar glow settled in her chest, then spread upward. Want. Different than the trivial, acquisitive desires she'd been exposed to for most of her life— for a trip, a trinket, a haute-couture gown. The low burn spoke of what she actually needed—affection, closeness, passion. All the things she'd been taught never to demand.

An optimistic smile tugged at the edges of her lips. Scarlet had found her sport.

******

Ethan folded himself onto an indoor picnic bench in a dive Mexican place in none other than Little Italy. He sat on prize money for the rent, and across from a stunning blonde for pure pleasure. His post-fight mood had been light, and he'd been persuaded to join a couple other boxers heading into Manhattan with two beautiful, and apparently rich, coeds.

The aroma of seared onions and green chili wafted from the kitchen, and his growling stomach balked at the wait for a plate of cholesterol. Patience came easy, though, with the unbeatable scenery. He let his gaze track lazily across the table. A bit of frippery? Yes, but Scarlet Leore dazzled all the same.

"Where'd you learn to fight?" she asked.

Ethan heard the question but decided it was likely directed at someone else.

"Ethan, right?"

Nope. She definitely spoke to him.

"Chicago." He swallowed a mouthful of Corona. Eight hundred miles stretched between him and home. Not nearly enough.

Scarlet drummed her hands against the table and then pointed at him in a clear invitation to elaborate. When he didn't, she dug in. "Did you box in school?"

Tenacious little thing. Ethan habitually avoided questions about the life he was in the process of leaving behind, but he was equally uneager to see her turn that gorgeous face to the guy sitting to her left. So he improvised. "Still in school." A skinny wallet had dictated a late educational start. "And no, not at *Kingsborough*. Community colleges don't generally have boxing programs, Empress." He'd never been the Columbia type.

She grinned, momentarily sidetracked. "Empress?"

"I figure you blew past princess around the third grade." The dress, the flawless hair and makeup, the car she'd been lucky to park outside—and would be even luckier to retrieve in one piece—all of it pointed to a life as someone's queen. She made him wish he could afford the upkeep.

"*I* think you might be right," she conceded with a conspiratorial wink. "So where'd you learn?"

He surprised himself with an honest answer. "At home." Not knowing how to say more without saying too much, he bit his tongue, refusing to add, "*On the blood-stained carpet under my mom's old couch.*"

Unfazed, Scarlet waited patiently, calm and expectant, obviously ready for an uplifting tale. The story didn't go that way.

"My dad was a hitter." He dropped the bomb casually. Her expression remained passive, but her shoulders hitched a fraction closer her ears.

Gripping the table, he stretched through the length of his arms. "I learned to hit back." He owed much of that journey to an inner-city boxing club. Other aspects of his training could be called... freelance.

Sudden irritation spiked at what his Barbie of a dinner companion had coaxed him to reveal. He let his eyes roam from the top of her shining head to her well-displayed breasts and back again. She exuded old-school sex. The costly vintage dress and outrageous jewels conjured up images of the glamorous pinup girls of a bygone era. Women didn't look like her anymore. Too many dieted down to nothing before purchasing globular breasts of the man-made variety. She appeared to be a utopia of *au natural.* And he *liked* it.

Her back shot straight, and she reached behind her. In a blink, a black cardigan covered her assets.

His stomach, already grasping, clenched at the loss. "Think a woman like you would like a street fight, where the loser bleeds in the gutter until he gets up and drags himself home?"

She stiffened despite the cheerful conversations buzzing around them, and her once-coaxing voice dropped in open challenge. "A woman like me?"

Flawless. "Rich. Spoiled." He took another long pull from his beer. "Ever seen a street fight, Empress? If you do, nix the earrings."

Her flirtatious smile faded, replaced with a wary look. One hand rose to skim nervously over a huge diamond stud flashing at her ear. She looked to have an idea about where he might take the conversation, and she wasn't willing to go along. But she surprised him when she said breezily, "Quite the tough guy, huh? A fighter out of necessity and all that? Never had a thing handed to you and resent people who did?"

His eyes narrowed. Few people mocked him. And Scarlet had recently seen him beat a man unconscious for money. Her words stung, a little because of the sheen of disdain that threaded through the thinly-veiled joke, but mostly because she was right. *Well, well . . .*

She ignored his look and went on. "I suppose that makes you smarter, more worthy than someone like me? Because I was born wealthy, I'm stupid? Lazy? Dangerous in some way?"

No, he thought, obviously not stupid. And her brand of head-to-toe perfection couldn't be lazy. But *dangerous* put it mildly.

Already fascinated, it only got better as she decided to give him a run for the money he didn't have. She stretched languidly and pulled the cardigan off her shoulders. Then she leaned forward—far forward—over the table. Her golden eyes were a couple shades darker than her hair, and she smelled like anything but onions and green chili.

"Tell me," she whispered, heat simmering in her appraising gaze. "Other than being poor and able to hit really, *really* hard, why are you so special?"

Ethan stared back. The answer was simple. He excelled at doing *a lot* of things really hard.

Scarlet's taunt had ended just as their food arrived. Before they could be interrupted, Ethan leaned in to meet her. She didn't pull back, and his lips brushed her diamond earring when he said softly, "Wouldn't you like to know."

"Scarlet"—her friend slid a margarita between them—"Su amiga no get carded."

Scarlet. He liked hearing the name said aloud, a siren's name as tempting as the rest of her. Except for that smart mouth…

The thought died when he decided her mouth tantalized, too. She ate leisurely, with a sensual ease he supposed all rich kids were taught. Forget the burrito, he wanted to see her suck oysters straight from the shell, then lick an ice cream cone drizzled with strawberry sauce.

The way people ate said a lot about their nature. This rich man's daughter wasn't cold.

And that was pre-dessert. When she sucked the sopaipilla sugar from the tips of her fingers, he scrubbed his face, threw a twenty to the table, and extended his palm in her direction.

"Let me take you home."

******

Scarlet eyed him in speculation. "What kind of 'take me home' are we talking?"

"The multiple choice kind. You get whatever you want."

Intriguing. He didn't seem the type to rush, let alone into a woman he held in mild contempt. An *empress* like her.

Yet she slid her hand into his grip, a compulsion to get close overriding any doubts. Perhaps she felt compelled to play reckless. Or maybe she was driven to place herself in the hands of a man who offered her something of value.

Like time.

They rose from the table, his thumb discretely circling her palm. Wisps of heat trailed upward, at once arousing and endearing. She ought to pull back for at least appearance's sake. But she didn't. Instead, she let him lead her away from the sanity, or at least the safety, of her friends. On the street, they headed straight for the Maserati. Two hours ago, the car had been nothing but a reminder of emotional distance. Now it seemed thrilling as all hell.

The ride was smooth and quiet. Ethan slid behind the wheel, revved the engine, and glided into the night. A complete chameleon, he looked and acted like he slipped into the extraordinary every day.

Parked in her underground space, he leaned across her seat and pulled the passenger handle. On withdrawal, his shoulder grazed her chest. He didn't acknowledge the subtle caress, so she kept quiet, resisting the urge to arch forward in search of an actual grope.

Swinging one leg from the car, she twisted back. "The earrings were my mother's." They were a living memory she rarely left home without.

Ethan had already unfolded himself from the car. At her words, he dropped to a crouch, meeting her gaze across the seats.

She lifted a hand to tug a stone. "They're talismans for luck. For strength." For the ability to enjoy life and spread warmth like her mother had. When he didn't respond, she rolled her head back to examine the ceiling. "You said to lose them if I ever see a street fight."

He leaned in. "You never will, so—"

"These rocks are like your attitude. I mean, they remind me who I am and provide the ultimate mask." The earrings told the world she was nothing more than a pretty bauble, expensive and meaningless. They told her she was strong and resilient and, at least once, loved. Ethan's cynic warned the world away, but maybe his harsh exterior provided mere camouflage.

His expression remained impassive, revealing nothing. "You surprise me, Scarlet."

Calling her "Empress" had been fine until he said her name, long and slow like chilled maple syrup. His mouth, she decided distractedly, might be his best feature. Full lips curved over white teeth in patterns that injected everyday words with undeniable power. They let her in while his eyes locked her out.

When she stepped from the car, he was there, and she let him clasp her hand and guide her to the elevators. Fumbling for the key card in her bottomless purse, she worried she'd gotten in over her head. Awareness of the man who stood large and solid next to her, at once disarming and enigmatic, raised the skin on her arms into a thousand tiny bumps.

She came to a hard stop at the split doors. "Here we are."

Ethan's lingering smile fled. "We're in a garage, Empress, standing at an elevator."

Scarlet regarded him for a weighty moment. "Penthouse," she explained, pointing up. "Private elevator. This, essentially, is my door."

He stepped closer, and a nervous chill chased down her neck. For all her feeble attempts at rule-breaking, her life invited solitude. She lived behind walls, walls in the form of guarded buildings, alarm systems, and close confidants from her limited social stratosphere.

"So what'll it be," he murmured, eyes on her mouth.

She cleared her throat, refusing to step away, yet wringing the handle of her bag with two fists.

"Scarlet," he said in that low voice big men use to soothe frightened animals, barely moving forward, but advancing all the same. "Relax."

"Please, don't say that." First of all, she couldn't obey. Worse, commanding her to simmer down, no matter how gently said, only pointed out that she clammed up at the mere hint of intimacy.

He backed her up with his body, then hunched over her smaller frame, bracketing her rear against the seam between the elevator doors. "All right. Should we get it over with?"

"A kiss?" she breathed. *Yes, kiss.*

He leaned in, and she felt heat seep from his tense thighs and stomach. "If you insist."

His dark head lowered a fraction, and she let her suede bag crumple to the dirty concrete. Splaying her hands against the cold metal at her back, she willed him to touch her, to never pull away. A soothing caress skated from her shoulders to her wrists, prying her hands loose and settling them at his hips. Then his arms fell to his sides, not pinning or restraining in any way.

He stroked his tongue silkily over her bottom lip until she opened and let him in. When she did, he didn't rush to take all she offered. No, he dipped in for a taste, then another, gradually deepening the kiss in a maddening show of restraint.

Afraid he might stop, she worked her hands up his torso until they wound around his neck. With a groan, his tongue met hers in long, deep caresses, each one offering another sweet hint of flavor, like a lollypop dipped into her mouth over and over again.

Sensation dissolved the strength in her knees, and she leaned into him for support. When she thought the kiss might end, he took more, went deeper. Finally, with a light suck on her tongue, he lifted his head and peered down at her.

She detected a flash of surprise, maybe even frustration, in the flare of his eyes and the tight pitch of his lips. He hadn't expected to like kissing her, at least not so much.

Uncertain whether she could stand, let alone walk into the elevator when it dinged, she held on and let him gradually pull back. Before he stepped away, he moved steadying hands to her shoulders. Then he bent to retrieve her purse, pressing the strap and her key fob into her palm, deliberately closing her fingers with a squeeze.

"Up you go," he whispered.

CHAPTER 2

Scarlet stared out her bedroom window on the forty-sixth floor, ignoring the caterwauling coming from the closet where Lissa scoured for items to take to the upscale Goodwill in Greenwich Village. Scarlet didn't mind the noise, especially since Christmas week had passed in pained silence. Her father hadn't called. Neither had Ethan.

She'd texted a holiday hello to both men on the morning of the twenty-fifth. To one, the gesture had been dutiful. To the other, hopeful.

So much for garage kisses and elevator dreams.

After ten minutes of massacred country songs, Lissa stopped singing and started issuing demands. A muffled, "You're going," sounded from the closet.

"Nah," Scarlet replied absently. Ethan's brush-off had kyboshed her plans to attend a second fight.

Lissa marched out of the closet and handed over a flyer showing a grainy, black-and-white Ethan facing off against an unknown competitor. "He's fighting Gerard Chamber." Lissa delivered the news with a conspiratorial hush. "The two are evenly matched. Nemeses really—"

Scarlet tried to sound dry, totally disinterested. "I see you've become a boxing expert in no time."

"Fast learner." Lissa paused dramatically, then continued in her best voice-of-authority-with-no-actual-clue. "Look, Ethan's become something of a wonder on the local circuit. Except against this guy. There've been draws. Disqualifications. Gerard hasn't bitten off any ears, mind you, but he goes for low blows."

Scarlet studied the ad. The dueling headshots managed a menacing cast despite the cheap, lime-green card stock.

Leaning over, Lissa tapped Ethan's picture with a tapered nail. "If you're mad at Ethan—"

Scarlet couldn't hold back an indelicate snort. "I'm not—"

"—then this is the fight to see. There's a chance he'll take a beating."

"Like I want him to lose?" *Oops.* She so wanted him to lose. Wasn't humility good for the soul?

"Of course not." But Lissa's look didn't match her assurances. She knew exactly how full of shit both of them were. "I'm saying *I* want him to lose for not calling. If you think it, you're a bitch. If I do, I'm a good friend."

Scarlet folded the paper into a meticulous square, making sure the corners aligned perfectly before slipping it into her pocket. The last fight had been so one-sided. Titillating, certainly, but watching Ethan work could be even better. She nodded, and Lissa grinned like she always did after Scarlet gave in.

Five hours later Scarlet sat with her ass glued to a familiar metal bench, watching as Ethan's visibly-exhausted challenger staggered between blows. The pit of her stomach fell away when Ethan faltered, stumbling forward into an awkward crouch before lurching to his feet in the face of yet another glancing hit. She let her eyes drift closed, blocking the sight she shouldn't have been surprised to see. After all, she'd been warned.

Ethan and Gerard did appear physically equal, both about three inches over six feet with the taut leanness of born-and-bred fighters. Like dueling wrecking balls, each man flayed himself against a body similarly strong. Gerard swung wildly while Ethan bobbed and weaved out of reach. In turn, Ethan's punches went wide, a fraction of a second too late, leaving him swiping the air in Gerard's wake. The two weren't merely matched in strength. They moved the same, exhibiting equal speed and stamina, staging an enduring brutality.

At an opening, Ethan renewed his offensive, each blow landing in a targeted path of destruction. Sweat streamed from the gleaming black hair cropped close to his temples, and Scarlet detected a twice-a-day shaver beneath the dark stubble already shadowing the harsh line of his jaw. Roped musculature surged with each swing, flexing beneath the blue veins that tracked the definition of his chest and arms.

His lips distorted, no doubt from the mouth guard and his pained grimace, but the ferocity paid off. Each hit pounded Gerard closer to the canvas. Knees bent, Gerard's hands fell to visibly trembling quads. His head bowed in sluggish concession, and Scarlet tasted the first drizzle of Ethan's victory.

Her thighs tensed, ready to propel her body forward with the winning blow.

Beat by beat, Gerard pushed off his legs, tunneling the top of his head into Ethan's sternum. Holding Ethan at bay with his torso, Gerard slammed heavy fists against Ethan's ribs. When Ethan reared back to reset their position, Gerard arced his body upright, clipping Ethan beneath the chin and snapping his head against his shoulders with enough force to give Scarlet whiplash in the stands.

The referee bounded forward, hands in the air and mouth to a whistle he blew in impassioned gusts.

Lissa coughed, "Bullshit," into her shoulder. "Did you see that? Totally intentional."

A corner man shoved Ethan onto a low, ringside stool and dabbed at the blood that trickled from his mouth. After several minutes, Ethan still gripped the ropes, head angled awkwardly with a glazed, faraway look. The referee blew the whistle again, shouting, "No contest," to the hissing crowd.

Gerard slumped into his corner, gloves discarded at his feet. He sucked water from a squeeze bottle in rhythmic bursts. Five gulps in and the bottle joined the gloves.

Rising up, Gerard adopted a demeanor akin to what Scarlet would expect in a bar fight, not a prizefight that was minutes over. He plowed through the referee, barreling forward in a surge of energy that Ethan observed with unnatural calm. Despite the apparent effectiveness of Gerard's earlier cheap shot, Ethan stood, suddenly looking willing and able to settle the score.

The referee dove after Gerard but only managed to crash against his back and shove him chest-to-chest against Ethan. For a second, Ethan stood frozen, almost as if in indecision. Then a hard gleam entered his eyes, and Scarlet saw the slightest of nods, an acknowledgement of some internal promise of retribution. Choice made, Ethan's palm landed against Gerard's neck and pushed. His hand inched upward, fingers clenching against the straining muscles of his opponent's throat. Gerard's heels lifted, barely skimming the mat as Ethan dragged him in a slow arc that ultimately jammed Gerard's ass against Ethan's rope post. Cornered and cut off, Ethan lifted Gerard higher, then rose to his toes, whispering in the other man's ear. A three-second secret passed before Ethan let him fall.

Gerard's crumpled form didn't budge when Ethan slipped away amid fanatical applause.

Scarlet's head spun at seeing Ethan shift speeds so casually. A week ago, he'd feigned disinterest before a kiss that smoked the soles off her shoes. Tonight, she'd have sworn to his injury until he lifted over two hundred pounds of muscle by the scruff to deliver a message.

Which facets of Ethan were real? Last week's boredom at the restaurant or the brief moment of tenderness in the garage? Tonight's wounded warrior or the hulking avenger?

The sheen of Ethan's robe dulled with each retreating step down a dim, tunneling hallway. He passed another fighter she couldn't quite make out, though a passing fist bump said the incomer was a friend.

"Woo-hoo!" Lissa chanted, jumping from her seat when her new man, Matt, left the shadows and entered the arena. Not only was Lissa willingly listening to rap. She was undulating—actually dancing—to a pseudo-rhythmic rendition of several choice words like "bitch," "whore," "tramp," and "blowjob." The song didn't even rhyme.

Unable to compete, Scarlet let her attention stray. The lights didn't brighten the dinginess of their surroundings or lift the low ceilings. The ring-side stands were packed, mostly with men, too many sporting stained wife beaters and leering grins. Young and female and well-dressed suddenly seemed out of place, too exposed.

As Matt prepared to duck into the ring, the referee hauled Gerard's slumped form upright. Left to stand on his own, Gerard leaned briefly against the ropes before unfurling to his full height. A tentative move took him in the direction of Ethan's retreat, but rather than take another step, he pivoted in a slow turn that brought him face-to-face with Scarlet's section of the stands. Bending low, Gerard executed a genial bow the audience met with half cheers, half jeers. When he rose, all the showmanship had drained from his rough-hewn features, replaced with a look that promised revenge.

Pursing slightly, his lips formed a chilling pretense of a kiss that Scarlet would swear he aimed at her.

******

"I'm out," Scarlet said from her seat in the stands. "My ass can't handle another greasy meal. And Ethan doesn't dig me." Given the sad but obvious lack of mutual attraction, she preferred to spare herself another bout of unrequited lust. Scarlet Leore rose above stalking, *mostly*.

Lissa scanned Club Rancor's interior on their way to the entrance. "Wrong." She raised her arms in a flurry of tremulous jazz hands. "You're headed back to Palo Alto to subsist on tofu and radishes for the next five months." Her hands dropped. "Screw calories and screw Ethan."

Scarlet didn't *subsist*. Not when it came to good food. Or clothes. Or shoes. Or hair care products. Or... "If only you weren't a pathological liar," she said on a fatalistic sigh, slanting Lissa a worn look. "And if only I *could* screw Ethan."

They'd exited the front door and huddled under the club's awning. With the wind howling around their little cluster, Scarlet made her break. "But I can't, so I'll call when I get—"

"Can't what, Empress?" Scarlet heard Ethan's low voice behind her. *Right* behind her. She shuddered, suddenly noting the heat against her back. How long had he been standing there?

She turned too fast and looked up, face flaming and mind blank. "Whaa? I can't eat you, er, with you. I mean, I can't eat"—she circled her hand to indicate the group that had gathered—"with *all of you* tonight."

Bottomless black eyes drew her focus to the fact that he smelled... edible. No strong aftershave, no cologne, just soap and world-class pheromones. Shiny strands of hair gleamed from an earlier shower, and she could practically taste the chunk of peppermint candy he worked with his tongue. Amazing how a guy in nothing but a sweatshirt and jeans could noticeably warm the freezing air around them.

His hands rose to rest on his hips. "That so?"

"Yes." She kept her breathing shallow, refusing to suck in the sweet mintiness washing over her face. "But I've"—*savored? relished?*—"enjoyed watching you."

Ethan didn't respond. He simply stared down at her, slowly crunching that candy cane. Then he smiled, not a wide grin, but a knowing one. And she knew *he knew*. Knew he was warming her from the inside out, melting her down like a star-struck groupie.

Seizing on a distraction, she spoke of the first thing that came to mind. "What happened in the ring tonight?" Voice pitched low and quiet, she made it personal, focusing on a reddish bruise that darkened the skin beneath his chin. "I mean after the fight ended, when Gerard wouldn't leave?"

Ethan's eyes registered a moment of surprise at her question. Again he remained silent, but this time he brought a hand to the tips of her hair, his movements unhurried and sensual. Sensation prickled over her scalp as his stroking continued, emulating a head massage. Scarlet relaxed into the gentle pulls and soon tipped her head back to provide easier access to the fall of her curls, luxuriating in the touch that both soothed and stimulated.

When she thought he wouldn't answer, he began to speak. "Guys get involved in things they can't handle. Chemicals they can't always control." The comforting strokes on her back stopped. His tone went light and brittle. "Either that, or he's had one concussion too many."

She could never let go so easily. "What did you say to him?"

The stroking began again, this time in circles over the whole of her back. In tandem, he pressed a warm fingertip to her cool bottom lip. Anger countered the gentle touch, seething behind his narrowed gaze, and she realized Ethan hadn't let anything about the fight go. "Boxing matches have rules I follow. Post-fight cheap shots... don't. I clarified the difference."

Tendrils of unease threaded around her throat, choking the easy flow of breath. Like his palpable fury, the subtle threat wasn't directed at her. Yet his easy rise to violence shook her first-class ideals. In her world, people didn't hit or strangle or kick. Not once had a slammed door echoed through the penthouse. Her kind fought with silence and indifference, the chilly reception that functioned like a slap in the face. She didn't know how to speak Ethan's language.

He'd been right to blow her off. Paths like theirs could never meet in the middle. Flushed heat boiled beneath her scarf, and she forced herself to ease away, stepping off the curb and wandering backward in the direction of her car.

Round two to Ethan.

******

"If only I could…" Ethan had heard the words distinctly on approach and was gunning for a literal interpretation, one similar to last week, when she'd been a melting treat on his tongue, sweet and giving and, he now knew, prone to linger.

He quashed the thought, pulling his focus from her retreating back and trailing blindly behind the rest of the group. He'd heard Scarlet's name before last week, but it'd taken a bout of locker-room talk to put two and two together. Her father was Tripp Leore, a well-known real-estate magnate. Stories hedged at long-standing feuds between Tripp and other prominent businessmen on the New York circuit. The guy seemed like a cold bastard who didn't mind shitting in his backyard.

Tripp had married Scarlet's mom after his star had risen. Ethan knew only that breast cancer had taken Cora Reed over a decade ago, and strangely, that little ditty had been Gerard's prefight contribution over the catcalls coming from the showers. He'd cryptically talked of never forgetting million-dollar asses or attitudes.

Ethan nodded in silent, grudging commiseration, lamenting the fact that poor men who pandered to rich women rarely got off the ground.

Flexing his jaw, he rubbed at the bruise that proved exactly what a disruption Scarlet would be. When he'd sensed her during the fight—a sting of awareness sliding over the skin—his focus had shifted. Being in a ring with a guy trying to beat the shit out of him hadn't changed a thing. He'd broken stride to search her out, opening him to the heaviest hit he'd taken in weeks.

"Interesting." The sardonic observation drifted over Lissa's shoulder before she turned to face him, walking backward at a leisurely pace. Her glance worked him over like a pellet gun buffeting every inch of his body. But when her eyes met his, her narrowed gaze said she hadn't seen anything worth the price of admission. "Manly, too," she sniped. "Or not."

He shoved his hands in his pockets. "You obviously have a point—"

"And smart. What a prize." She rolled her eyes at that bit of inflammation. "You've let a woman who wears Carolina Herrera to prizefights wander away. In the dark. Alone."

Lissa's meaning sank deep, farther and faster than he would have preferred. He saw himself letting Scarlet flee into the night, allowing her that brazen farewell in the face of his fake indifference, both of them ignoring what they really wanted.

Despite the reasons to steer clear—fights to win, degrees to get, a company to launch—need flashed beneath his skin, a pulsing realization that stiffened his body and slowed his steps.

A fraction of the judgment lifted from Lissa's gaze. "Like I said, manly *and* smart."

Mindless talking had eaten up blocks that could have been spent seeing Scarlet to her car. Home. Anywhere private. A long line of women, starting with his own mother, had quietly called him overprotective.

He'd made peace with the title, saw it as a compliment. Jerking to a stop, he spoke to the others over Lissa's head. "I'm out. Not hungry." Before anyone gave voice to their knowing smirks, he turned and jogged the other direction.

Scarlet was about to join the ranks of the overprotected.

******

A gust of Atlantic wind bristled over Scarlet's exposed legs, and she shivered through a dose of longing for her college condo on the West Coast, all sunbaked tile and terracotta warmth. She sped up, moving as fast as her three-inch heels could navigate the patches of inky ice glinting on the sidewalk. One block down and another to go. As she clipped along, clenching her pepper spray in a bloodless fist, she chastised herself for being careless, muttering inane observations about the area in an effort to fill the silence. The empty words simply misted into the ether.

Panting, she considered removing her shoes for a mad dash. Instead she slowed, then went still, listening to make sure her heels didn't mask sounds she needed to hear.

The street appeared empty. Nothing but stoic warehouse fronts, their corrugated doors flickering in the light of a few buzzing street lamps. No movement. Not a hint of sound. She hadn't thought it possible for New York City to fall silent. The calm only bred agitation.

Relief bloomed at the sight of familiar red paint. She sucked in the deep breath her shallow rasps hadn't allowed and skated across the parking lot, grappling for her driver's-side door, congratulating herself on the simple, but rare, act of walking to her car unaided.

Heavy footfalls sounded out of the eerie quiet. Before she could react, a rough shove between the shoulder blades slammed her chest first against an old Ford pickup parked in the next space. Rough edges dug into her ribs.

A gloved hand spun her around, and she gazed up into the blinding beam of a flashlight. Disoriented, Scarlet saw nothing beyond a glowing orb rimmed with absolute blackness.

But she could hear, and worse, she could feel. The man leaned in close and spoke in a gritty, unrecognizable whisper. "Throw the fucking vegetable spritzer." She soundlessly ditched the pepper spray. "The bag, too." She tossed again.

Gripping the slick, oily edges of her courage, it dawned on her to struggle… to call out. *Fight. Go for the eyes.* Had Lissa and Matt and—please God—Ethan, walked this way?

The guy must have sensed her mental rally because he reached up and squeezed her jaw below the ears, using the leverage to crack her head against the frozen window of the truck, hard. "Good girl," he said, compressing her small face in his hand. "What else?"

What else? The light above focused in and out… in and out, through a lens she couldn't control. She blinked, then forced a squint. Still nothing.

The pain in her face receded to a terrible numbness before he shifted his grip to her chin and forcibly turned her face to the Maserati. "See the pretty car, *Empress.* What else?" His free hand went to her pockets, skimming over her hands before jerking a bracelet from her wrist.

Empress. "Ethan?" she choked. "Don't." Tears leaked from beneath closed lids. *Not him.*

"Not used to this, are you, Empress? You're used to the win, like me." His voice was guttural. "Perhaps this time you've strayed too far from Daddy's penthouse."

He grazed a fingertip along the shell of her ear. The almost-gentle caress was her only warning before a sharp, malicious agony flooded the side of her face. She cried out. Her mother's diamond earring moved into her blurred peripheral vision. It shimmered with a trace of blood that gleamed in the glow of the flashlight. Muscles locked, her every nerve ending awaited his next move. The sting came fast when he ripped the other locking stud to freedom.

Whimpering in the aftermath of the excruciating pain, she kept her gaze downcast, staring dully at the familiar jeans in the murky fringe of light. Like before, Ethan's too-light attire didn't prevent him from putting off waves of heat. Only now, his warmth didn't comfort.

That kiss. The embrace beneath the awning. They'd been worse than lies.

Though the light never faltered, his hand again momentarily left her face. This time, harsh steel took its place. Saying nothing, he slid the flat side of a freezing blade across her cheek and down her throat. Then, slowly, he began to slice the buttons along the seam of her coat.

Scarlet clenched, bracing for the violation that would come next. But Ethan didn't cut away any more clothing. Once the buttons were gone, he used his knife-hand to nudge the edges of her coat outward. Scarlet relaxed imperceptibly. *Too soon.*

"This will hurt, Empress," he said softly. "A little pain to show I always win."

He kissed her cheek as the knife punctured her party dress and kept going... slowly... until it bottomed-out deep within her lower abdomen. Working an airless scream, Scarlet almost convinced herself the adrenaline would mask the pain, but a clenching misery hit as he extracted the blade with jerky movements.

She murmured Ethan's name one last time before her world slipped away.

******

Gone.

Relief eased Ethan's balled fists when he didn't see Scarlet or her Maserati in the lot. *Probably halfway back to paradise by now.* Yet a vague sense of foreboding remained.

Despite her absence, he loped forward across the expanse of lined pavement, which was empty save an old pickup and a beat-up Toyota sedan. Nothing out of place. At the other end, he turned his tired ass around, heading for the subway.

He saw her hair first. A bright stream of blonde, too beautiful to touch the filthy pavement, streamed out beneath her shoulders. She lay crumpled on her side beneath the passenger door of the truck he'd ignored.

Like a shot, he charged for Scarlet's prone form. A few steps out, he bent and scooped up a petite canister. Rolling the cold metal in his palm, he recognized a lipstick-sized mace spray. He winced, feeling the aluminum give in his fist. Like her, the package was shiny and colorful and, unfortunately, fragile. Purple, of all things.

Shoving the spray into his pocket, he crouched next to her, blood pounding at his temples. Icy sweat froze over the long slide down his face, becoming part of the frigid landscape.

She might be fine, a run-of-the-mill carjacking, and she hit her head.

But her little body curled into itself. Reaching out, he hovered a hand over her slumped form, then pulled away. Bruises marred the pale skin of her face and jaw, but otherwise he couldn't gauge her injuries. *Too much black.* Keeping his touch feather light, he brushed along her chest and stomach, the only side he could access without shifting her torso.

Jesus. Blood-stained fingers wavered in front of him. A lifetime of transferring the fear in his mother's eyes to the coward who'd put it there, and he'd let this ethereal beauty go it alone. He might as well have done the damage himself.

He tucked her coat inward to block the wind. "Hold on, Empress." She couldn't hear his strained plea, but the appeal gave him hope, let him pretend she'd grant his wish. Fumbling for his phone, he managed to dial 911, clutching her chilled fingers while he talked to dispatch.

Huddling beside her, he wrenched himself under the truck to curl around the slope of her spine in a silent offer of warmth. Of comfort. And he waited, the whole time stroking the sunshine of Scarlet's blonde curls and praying to a God he didn't believe in that she'd be okay.

CHAPTER 3

June—New York City

Nine years later...

Water and conditioner sluiced over wet lace. Glancing to her chest, Scarlet smoothed a palm over her breasts to rinse any remaining soap from the bra stretched across her skin. Steam molded the delicate lingerie to every curve, though at six a.m. on a Tuesday morning, the sight was hers alone.

And she barely looked.

Stepping from the shower, she reached for a plush towel and dried herself, underwear and all. Only after she'd secured the towel around her dripping hair did she peel out of the drenched bra-and-panty set, casually revealing a set of angry scars that marred the otherwise smooth skin of her abdomen. She knew they were there but didn't waste a glance. With a flick of the wrist, her underthings landed in the sink, and she donned a dry thong beneath a soft, terry-cloth robe. The act of changing had become a precise science. She managed the transition from sopping wet to dry and robed in thirty seconds every time.

Ritual complete, she wrung the water from the sodden lilac lace and flung it over the drying rack that never got stowed. *One day,* she chanted on an internal promise, *I'll be ready.* When that day came, she wouldn't need clothes in the shower. She'd feel safe without them.

A half hour later, she skidded to a halt in the front lobby. No night watch. Scarlet shifted her weight as she contemplated her building's security desk. Seth should have been at his post pawning his wife's stale muffins. His jovial greeting was conspicuously absent, leaving her without the armed lookout she paid good money to have present and ready. Stepping closer to

Seth's counter on shaky legs, she surveyed the space in a subtle sweep.

Get ahold of yourself. The ever-present knowledge of work languishing at the office forced her to shake it off, and she pressed forward and out the coded entrance despite the unwelcome reminder that one guard could be distracted. *Two* security personnel on round-the-clock duty would be better, but that luxury exceeded her pay grade.

Plus, smack in the middle of Chelsea, and tucked between blocks of pulsing urban history, her modern complex won on location and ambiance. Her father had built it. He'd also sold it, years before she'd begun calling the address home but only months after she'd quit calling him Dad. Season upon season of entrusting her safety to the same set of walls left the building feeling more like family than brick and mortar. She'd stay no matter how often the guard went missing.

"Morning, Miss. Leore."

Seth might be AWOL, but Andy manned the steps, ever reliable in his pomp and circumstance. He provided a last line of defense, even if he was a seventy-year-old doorman armed with nothing more than a crisp suit and a red bowtie. "Morning, Andy. How goes it?"

"Quite lovely," he said in his false British upper crust. "And you?"

She mustered her best rendition of Middle America. "Swell," she quipped. "*Quite* swell, I mean."

The amendment brought out a paternal headshake. "It's till tomorrow then, isn't it?"

"That's a promise."

Joining the sunrise hustle on the street, Scarlet lifted her head and shoulders, physically shifting into lawyer-mode. She strode down the sidewalk like any other confident, but sleep-deprived, New Yorker looking for a latte. With a breath of rancid steam rising from a gutter grate and a quickstep around a present left by a city-dwelling dog with a lazy owner, she reminded herself she *was* any other businesswoman on her way to work. N-o-r-m-a-l.

Mentally tallying the day's to-do list, she pondered the logistics of conference calls at nine and eleven, with a noon business lunch at a restaurant located six blocks from her office.

Take the eleven o'clock on my mobile and wrap the meeting while sprinting down the street in heels?

Most days she loved her life. Some days she was merely thankful for a job. Still others, she had trouble keeping up and wondered how she could ever maintain the pace. But she'd had the best education money could buy, and she'd inherited her father's business acumen. *Fine with me, Daddy. You can keep the rest.*

Scarlet slid into her office chair at ten past seven, her eyes blurring at the number of e-mails she'd received overnight. *Sixty-seven.* Sixty-seven e-mails between six o'clock on Monday evening and seven o'clock on Tuesday morning.

Today brought messages from patent attorneys on site at a medical disposables company in Singapore. Her client was interested in incorporating Pacific Limited's more innovative products into its own systems. But Pacific was demanding fixed-price purchase agreements when raw-material costs were trending downward. She'd advised her client to consider acquiring Pacific, along with its intellectual property, so the company could independently manufacture Pacific's technologies without bothering with, well, Pacific.

"Gut and trump," she liked to call it, leaving "mergers and acquisitions" to nicer people.

Complexities weaved through her inbox like a patchwork quilt, aspects of the larger problem only revealing themselves as she considered each additional message and added its secrets to the collage.

She checked the time—eight thirty in the New York offices of Jahn Tremane & Spellman. Perhaps she could still catch someone in Singapore. Although late in Asia, her people might be reachable. *They* didn't find it impossible to resist the city's sky-high mega malls in their meager free time. She'd never understand that kind of dedication.

Scarlet gulped her latte, absorbing the best of the bad news trumpeting from her computer screen. Pacific had been forthcoming with documents, but the paperwork didn't convey what she'd hoped.

Slumped over her keyboard, the monotonous ring of her office phone broke through her frustration. When she reached for the receiver, her fingernail caught the facet of a diamond at her ear. She jerked, and her hand balled into an instinctive fist. Without realizing, she'd been worrying the stone. Again. Unlike the presumably chop-shopped Maserati, her mother's earrings had surfaced at a small auction house a few months after her attack. Now she loved them too much, as if inanimate objects could be guardians or friends.

Scarlet knew the association wasn't rational, but when her mother's heirlooms had been returned, she'd felt like her relationship with Cora Leore—that shining beacon of remembered perfection—had also survived the trauma. She couldn't say the same for her living parent. In the aftermath of her stabbing, her father had made a short trip to the city, just long enough for a stop at the hospital and the office of the chief of police. After Ethan Blake had been arrested with all due haste, Tripp had disappeared again, leaving months of long-distance strain in his wake.

Scarlet hadn't seen her father in person since he'd left her to the mercy of the morphine drip.

Loosening her fingers, she answered the ring seconds before the call went to voice mail.

Lissa's banter sounded over the line. "I'm flea-marketing for inspiration. Just found the perfect T-shirt. Says, 'Friends don't let friends go to Yale.' I think it actually has your name written on the tag."

"Do they have one that says, 'Friends don't let friends major in art or art history' or 'Hi, welcome to Jerry's Artarama, would you like a basket for your supplies today?'"

"Straight to hell."

"Only because you'll need a wingwoman."

A bark of laughter, then, "Pick you up at seven?"

Scarlet said one final word as her arm arced back toward the phone's cradle. "Sharp." Then she was back to game on.

The impending hours of mayhem would eventually dispose with the day. At some point, she'd sprawl over her couch and wait. At a knock, she'd jump up and rush the door. There'd be Lissa, standing by for takeoff. Like so many times before, Scarlet felt a wave of appreciation.

Most of her evenings out began with greeting Lissa, or another personal escort, across the gleam of the security chain. If an escort wasn't possible, she hired a private car. As a last resort, she called a cab and found a chaperon to accompany her straight to the yellow door.

And then there was the collection of underwear hanging in her bathroom like Tuesday was laundry day. Only hand-washing for the delicates, of course.

All the security requirements demanded time and money, but the burning need for a round-the-clock guard—and worse, wishing there were two—broke the bank.

Her hand crept back toward the diamond. When her rent came due this month, she'd be selling another piece of jewelry to cover it.

******

Ethan padded to the kitchen, casting a worn grimace on the gourmet space. When had the gleaming granite and stainless steel stopped imparting a sense of satisfaction? For years, even the smallest luxury hadn't been lost on him. Now he took his palatial surroundings, including the beautiful woman in his shower, for granted.

Mixing eggs and aged gouda, he mechanically assembled omelets for two. As the scent of gooey, melted cheese and frying eggs permeated his surroundings, he could only dread the pending confrontation with Miranda. He would offer breakfast. She would refuse.

None of them ever ate. His murmured compliments didn't disabuse them of the notion, but in reality, he wanted *healthy*. He wouldn't take a woman to a dinner he didn't want her to eat or prepare her a meal he didn't want her to enjoy.

Miranda joined him as he slid their golden breakfast from the pan. Wearing a short satin robe that showcased the smooth perfection of her long legs, she cast a pensive eye toward the food before reaching for a mug of coffee. Black, of course. Against his will, his mind's eye pictured curving hips and high breasts, the kind of lush figure that couldn't thrive on caffeine alone.

He sighed, digging in to both breakfasts. Once, he'd taken his chances with a woman like that. The result had been an unjust, but no less agonizing, stint in a notorious prison.

Relationships after Scarlet had taken on a decidedly impersonal cast. Each decrease in his emotional barometer was met with an increase in the physical "perfection" of his next girlfriend, as though his subconscious understood that less body fat and more augmentation were safer choices for a guy who didn't want to care.

Lately, though, the string of sterile exchanges left him cold. Ethan loathed disappointing a beautiful woman by ending their several-week fling, but neither was he prepared to maintain a liaison that existed merely for show. She got press as the starlet on his arm, along with gifts and confidence. He gave and received fleeting physical pleasures, nothing more.

He cracked his jaw on another impossible thought. Opening and closing his mouth to release the tension, he pictured last Sunday's brunch—Bloody Marys and eggs Benedict all around. Two bloodies in, a well-heeled family had rolled in with twins, literally trundled through the café with a stroller the size of a Volkswagen. He'd found himself ogling the kids, his desire for more than work and sex and boxing assuming the face of those two babies and their doting parents.

With a grim expression to match his thoughts, he started in with Miranda, hoping to let her down easy.

Less than an hour later, she slammed out of the apartment, leaving him with an overwhelming sense of relief. And an extra omelet. *C'est la vie.*

The sappy urges fled with the bang of the door. He grabbed a battered NYU sweatshirt and was on the street in less than two minutes. The high life may have desensitized him to indulgence, but he'd never take his freedom—the *physical* ability to stand and walk out if and when he liked—for granted. Amazing how he relished knowing his doors and windows only locked from the inside.

Ethan wound his way west and then north on Lexington Avenue, not stopping until he stood under the cerulean blue of Grand Central Station's astronomical mural. There, he found a spot against the buffed stone of the main concourse, where he leaned back and watched, his manner and posture casual.

With the jeans and sweatshirt and ball cap, he was rarely recognized despite the ever-increasing number of magazine articles and television interviews. He did his best to retain a degree of anonymity, allowing him to melt into the city and watch other nameless people.

Ethan eyed the concourse, nonchalant, no camera in sight. Whether for business or pleasure, train passengers immersed themselves in their personal experiences. They embarked and disembarked, in both work and play, with a feeling of obscurity that let them sink into their authentic selves. The people they were when no one was watching.

A living city of stimulus.

A middle-aged man strode past. He wore a dark trench, the standard MBA coat. Ethan spied the leather strap of a briefcase slung across his chest. The man talked on a mobile phone pressed between his ear and shoulder while he hammered at the touchscreen of another device with his fingers. An *Atavos* smartphone, no less.

Good choice—Ethan-made and Ethan-manufactured.

Multitasking got the best of the man at the end of the concourse. He slammed into a young woman who rushed into the terminal from the other direction. Both phones went flying, and the woman was thrown off the points of her high heels. She reeled backward and slammed into the wall.

The man dove for his phones, not the woman. Only after he'd secured his electronics did he take a moment to apologize or to see if the lady had been injured. She accepted his proffered hand, rubbing the back of her skull as he steadied her on her feet. When she looked up in mild reproach, Ethan froze. He jerked his gaze away before returning for another look.

Not her. For a moment, the blond hair and delicate calves that tapered to designer-shod feet had strung him tight. But no, Scarlet Leore wouldn't be caught dead in a common train station, and this woman's features, while pretty, were too coarse—the nose a tad wide and the lips a smidgen thin. Attractive, but not his idea of perfect.

Ethan shook his head in a rapid-fire thought dump, trying to tamp the rage that rose every time Scarlet invaded his thoughts. There were certain things he didn't do anymore. He didn't cut his own hair. He didn't wash his clothes in the sink. And he didn't think, wonder, or worry about Scarlet Leore. She'd lost those privileges around the time she'd accused him of assault, robbery, and attempted murder, which meant that when a distracted commuter happened to trip her pseudo-look-alike in a train station, he didn't break the guy's arms and leave him writhing on the tile.

On second look, the man was probably a lawyer—the gadgets, the coat, the briefcase. He looked a bit like the public defender who'd extracted Ethan from an island prison nine years ago. Back then, the young Ron Michael had come across as an *occasional* gunner, with big glossy lawyer-teeth and a breezy here-today-gone-tomorrow smile. He'd so fit with the lawyer-on-a-billboard set, the image had stuck. In the throes of fury and panic, Ethan hadn't been able to pinpoint whether Billboard had become a public defender out of a deep-seated belief in the right to competent counsel or out of a tight legal market and the want of a job. But Ron's initially lackadaisical attitude had gradually shifted. With time and an inhuman reserve of patience, Ethan and Billboard had pieced together the unexpected reality of Scarlet's attack.

Another had eventually taken Ethan's place inside that cramped cell.

Scarlet had descended with an immediate apology. He shouldn't have been surprised when she'd tried to plaster over her "mistake" with dollar signs. Trembling, her voice small and almost afraid, she'd handed him a check and waited for him cave in to her artifice. But Scarlet Leore had sat before a grand jury and pointed the finger at him. No amount of money could erase that kind of wreckage.

One look at her proposed payoff and vitriol had poured out of him like acid from a drum. With each word, her face had paled another shade, until he'd exhausted the anger and the futile need to fight back against a woman and a system that had mangled his plans to rise from the gutter. His last image of Scarlet was one of shock, a diminished liar sinking to her seat and re-pocketing a check that was supposed to have paved her way, as usual. The intervening years had passed without another glimpse of her fragile, yet deceitful, facade.

Bending his mind's path by sheer dint of will, Ethan pulled his thoughts from Scarlet's destruction and returned to the debacle at the end of the terminal. He knew exactly why a man, who had accidentally mauled a gorgeous blonde, would rescue his phones before the woman. All of life moved through one or the other of those devices. The guy couldn't afford to lose them. They *were* him.

Ethan pictured a product that would simplify the stranger's balancing act, letting his attention bounce around the cavernous hall. Some stopped to review the train schedules, and others plowed head-down through the chaos. A student sat in the corner, bobbing her head to the ear buds connected to her phone, while she traced an index finger across the screen of a tablet perched on her lap. Nearby, a young professional gripped a wireless headset wrapped around one ear, yelling louder with each attempt to be heard.

The technologies meant to simplify life now ran it ragged.

Consumers needed one device to simultaneously manage multiple phone numbers and accounts, one product to integrate the processing and memory capabilities of a computer with the password-protected firewall features of a sophisticated network.

One device to do it all. *Atavos's next giant.*

Pushing away from the wall, Ethan wound his way back through the concourse, up the curving marble staircase, and through the maze of shops and restaurants on the upper floor. As he strolled, he continued to observe, but now his thoughts tripped over logistics.

Atavos had grown rapidly. The conglomerate was divided into a number of business groups. His new brainchild—*One*—would go to the mobile solutions group, Parlann Technologies.

Ethan reached for his own phone, dialing his second-in-command. After Ron Michael had helped prove the truth that had won Ethan his freedom, Ron had pulled an about-face on criminal defense. From that day forward, the two of them had worked side-by-side to build Atavos. The same man who'd extracted Ethan from the cell block had accompanied him to the pinnacle of the business world. Today, Ron acted as Atavos's general counsel and president of the Parlann division.

Ethan's smile dawned after the first ring and grew wider at hearing Ron's harried, "Now what?" chime in after the second.

His and Billboard's time had come again.

******

Scarlet cocked her head far to the right, then to the left. She stifled an urge stand on her hands for another look at Lissa's largest painting to date. The image morphed slightly with each vantage point, more a story than a still. With little logical underpinning and no attempt to reproduce an illusion of visible reality, Lissa had created a work of art that personified her spirit, an exquisite departure from the mundane. In Scarlet's opinion, her best work yet.

The gallery-and-frou-frou-dinner scene provided an endless array of client-entertainment options. Tonight proved no exception. The air of the Gray Halls Gallery sizzled with energy. Art patrons and serious collectors hovered around each of ten paintings displayed against a blood-red backdrop. Perhaps this would be the show to ignite Lissa's career.

Scarlet strolled the room, cataloguing snippets of praise from the types of people who could afford Lissa's work, men and women—many on obvious dates—who'd dressed midweek-cocktail, dripping in jewels that exceeded the cost of a mid-sized sedan.

"True art is incomprehensible…"

"Breathtaking. A subtle fusion of chaos with order…"

"…rather than any implied meaning or message, we're encouraged to consider the visual qualities of the work. It's so direct and incisive in its dissection of the mind…"

"A stunning achievement. You know, Ms. Blanc has been on the rise…"

"…a lucent mirror of our collective subconscious…"

Scarlet circled around to Lissa, hyper-aware of her stag status and keen to share the moment with another living being. As she approached, she noted a certain bruising of the air surrounding her friend. The graceful lines of Lissa's neck were frozen, and her hands clenched and unclenched at her sides.

Lissa faced an extraordinarily attractive man. In distressed jeans with disheveled blond hair, the man looked like a Tommy Bahama model, only *all grown up.* Lissa's proximity to a gorgeous male was par for the course. The weird part lay in the rigidity of her shoulders and stance.

Scarlet eased forward, rising slightly on her toes to avoid a telltale heel-click when Lissa's retort flamed in the sterile room. "You've called my work drivel. D-r-i-v-e-l." Without moving so much as a hair, she added, "*Scarlet,* do tell me why I should hear this asshole out."

Scarlet reared back, caught in the act of spying and on the fence about whether to answer or plead the fifth.

Cool eyes met hers over Lissa's shoulder, "Yes…, Scarlet, is it? Let's hear why your friend might want to listen."

Let me count the reasons. Cole's reserve reminded Scarlet of a long-ago night in a Mexican restaurant in Little Italy, when a tantalizing man hadn't wanted to, but hadn't been able to resist, devouring *her* with his eyes. If things hadn't gone so wrong, she still believed they might have gone fantastically right. She wouldn't let Lissa pull a Scarlet and fuck up that kind of attraction.

He wants you from the Louboutins up, Liss. And every woman deserves that. Even me.

Cole's gaze stilled, a smear of ice covering the blue depths beyond. "I suppose if that doesn't convince her, nothing will."

Huh? Looking around, Scarlet realized her thought had tumbled out. In words. Every last embarrassing one of them. *Yes. Way. Mustgetoutmore.*

Lissa turned, ever so slowly, until Scarlet stood in the line of fire. Now she would die by Lissa's hand, a casualty of an art show gone wrong. All over a bit of vicarious yearning. Pressing the backs of her hands to her flushed cheeks, Scarlet focused on a nearby placard. The distraction didn't work.

"Really?" Lissa said dryly. "We're getting you a date."

The taunt pierced Scarlet's armored detachment. *Strike getting out more. Stay in and get laid.* She'd give "come early, come often" whole new meaning.

Cole cut in—*thank God*—all nonchalant confidence. "I received a grant, a large one." He paused, though Scarlet secretly didn't think he needed the effect. "That means funding, marketing, name recognition, and an end to all… this."

Lissa's teeth clenched, and she seethed, "Don't say anything you'll regret."

He looked around lazily, unimpressed, as if regret were impossible. "You'll paint *reality* as I've photographed it, not abstract." He shrugged, and Scarlet got the distinct impression the man wasn't nearly as detached as he'd have them believe. Then he added, "Perhaps it's time. Hmm?"

Cole didn't need to ask Scarlet twice. "Lissa," she said, all sweetness and light, or at least as innocuous as her inner eavesdropper could manage, "you have to do it." *The time for missed chances is over. For me, too.*

Lissa bristled. "Where're we going?"

We. Scarlet smiled at the slip.

Cole's eyes went unfathomably dark for a guy getting his way. "To my estate in Colorado for training. Then to the wilds of India, city girl." He slipped his card between Lissa's fingers. "Don't forget your shots."

As Cole worked his way toward the door, shaking hands and greeting the people—mostly women—who'd begun cluster nearby, they both stood still, staring at the sea of bodies that parted in his wake.

Finally, Lissa turned her head, and Scarlet saw terror-tinged excitement gleaming in those almond eyes.

And she knew. "You're going." In Scarlet's fevered imagination, the gamble would bring her friend success, acclaim, adventure. With a wave of optimism, she realized Lissa's life verged on change because she refused to let fear win the day.

Perhaps it was time to follow suit.

******

Ethan reached toward the glass encasing his office high above the city when he smelled his assistant behind him. He knew Susan neared every time he started contemplating whether he'd died and been reincarnated as a gingerbread house. Turning, he leaned against the window in an effort to escape the cloud of perfume that followed his assistant wherever she went. She smoked three packs a day. All the sweet cologne in the world wasn't erasing that simple fact. It just made her reek like a smoking scone, heavy on the vanilla. He grimaced, keeping his thoughts to himself. *Maybe another day.*

Gesturing toward the far wall, she asked, "New pictures?" Susan didn't do friendly. But today she made an effort at conversation.

He pointed to the corner. "My mother's on the left. She finally agreed to move to the city from Chicago." He'd gotten antsy, so he'd sent a full-time caretaker to his mom's doorstep in Wauconda, Illinois. The young, pretty nurse had presented a card on arrival. "Happy Monday, Mom," Ethan had written. "This nice lady could be *part-time* if you lived much, much closer." The implication hadn't been lost on his mother. Keen on her independence, she'd called the moving company, also provided in the card, within the day.

"The others?"

"Came with the frames." He frowned at the stock photos. The pasty wedding and boating scenes provided decent business ice-breakers. His fake niece made a beautiful bride, and his imaginary nephew showed promise at yacht racing.

"You want to do this standing up?" he asked.

"Never," she replied, her tone bland. "We'll sit, like the civilized person *I* am."

Holding his somber expression, Ethan swept a hand toward a sitting area situated in the corner of his office, where comfortable lambskin chairs and a matching couch beckoned for a nap. "Ladies first."

She didn't move. "Mr. Michael is here." A sly smile threatened behind the set line of her mouth. *So much for playing nice.* "He's been waiting approximately fifteen minutes."

So Billboard camped in the lobby while Ethan played hostage to his diminutive assistant. *I should fire this woman.*

But he wouldn't. Like Billboard, Susan had been with him since the beginning, and she'd probably be with him till the end. Susan acted the bitch, but she was also brilliant, discrete, and loyal. A prime example of what he demanded—the best.

Plus, an ugly divorce and two rowdy boys would turn anyone mean. Both young men were in college now, but the reprieve hadn't lightened her demeanor. The dragon, apparently, meant to linger.

He returned her loyalty with an astronomical salary and, to her face, playing the hard-ass. It gave her another challenge to power through with a stiff upper lip. Her specialty.

Susan handed him a shiny binder with an inch of paperwork tucked inside. The first page read, "*One*—Supplier Scouting—Hong Kong." While Susan would happily keep Ethan from other pursuits, she never wasted his time. "You're scheduled for breakfast in Hong Kong on Monday at nine a.m. local time. A car will pick you up, so look for your driver, who will be holding an Atavos sign, in the arrivals lobby."

Pointing to the binder, she added, "That's a copy of your itinerary and hotel arrangements. Behind that, you'll see my research on Mr. 'Michael' Wong Wai Kay. While Mr. Wong is Chinese, his Cantonese habits and customs are dominant. He's a master negotiator, but in the slow and methodical way that is common in Asia. Punctuality is expected and respected, so, Mr. Big Shot, don't be fashionably late like you generally are in Europe. Mr. Wong is notoriously detail oriented. Be prepared to discuss the finer points of the deal. You'll be drinking a lot of tea during the day. No sugar or cream. At night, you'll switch to something much stronger. Mr. Wong is a traditionalist, which means you should expect at least one lavish banquet. Be prepared to reciprocate."

At the last, Ethan sat forward in his chair. He automatically held out his hand, into which Susan placed a second folder bearing the insignia of The Peninsula Hong Kong. "I have, of course, made arrangements for a hosted banquet at The Peninsula, where the team will be staying. The banquet is scheduled for Tuesday night, and Mr. Wong will be a distinguished guest. Invitations were sent a week ago. Mr. Wong has accepted. I suggest you study the event details prior to Tuesday"—she inclined her head toward the folder —"to make a lasting impression. The banquet will round out the visit on a high note."

"Anything else?" Ethan asked as he flipped through Susan's research. She'd conducted the investigation with her usual devastating thoroughness. He'd soon know more about Mr. Wong than the man's own mother.

"Yes."

Ethan looked up, waiting for the punch line.

"You're not the only one courting Mr. Wong and his company for an exclusive arrangement. Last week he met with Nokia. He's scheduled to rendezvous with Apple, Sony, and HTC in the coming weeks."

With that, Susan rose and strutted from the room, leaving him wondering how the hell his executive assistant was privy to the *confidential* negotiations of the international business elite.

At the door, she stopped. Without turning, she added a parting shot. "Bring your A-game, Ethan."

As usual, it sounded like a threat.

CHAPTER 4

"So Hong Kong busted. Big fucking deal." Ethan sipped his single malt, sinking further into the cushioned sofa in his office. "We offered the best package. The schmucks that paid more lost out."

"Correct," Billboard replied without any real enthusiasm.

"We're shifting focus. Looking to Denmark." *One* required a camera module that was miniscule, yet capability-rich. With the Chinese officially off the table, the Copenhagen-based Optik Scandinavia offered exactly what Ethan needed, taking better, faster, cheaper to extremes.

Not missing a beat, Billboard switched tracks. "It'll be prohibitively expensive to purchase from Optik. The Danes bring superb design, not affordable manufacturing."

"Not buying *from* Optik—"

"Good." Billboard's expression conveyed both pleasure and unease. Over the years, he'd retained the smooth movie-star persona, but otherwise little was left of the defense lawyer Ethan had known. These days Billboard was the silver fox of corporate sharks, one that looked ready to unleash bad news.

Instead of prodding him, Ethan sat back. Eventually, Billboard would spill, but that was just it. Only *in time*.

"Look," the other man drawled after several moments of tense silence, leaning forward to rest his forearms on his knees. "You want Optik?"

"That's what I said."

"Then we need a different team. Our guys don't get it. Think about Hong Kong—all coulda, woulda, shoulda." Ron downed the rest of his own whisky in a single gulp. "I know of a lawyer based here in New York— a woman who asks the right questions and gets the right answers. Her

31

clients don't end up eating billion-dollar mistakes. We need her."

"Fine." *And?*

Billboard raised his shoulders in a graceful shrug Ethan didn't buy for a second. "It's Scarlet Leore." A pause. "And before you ask, yes, she's *your* Scarlet."

The hairs rose on the back of Ethan's neck. His most trusted advisor had the gall to suggest he hire *her*. *His Scarlet.* The woman who, within a day of his discovering her unconscious form, within twenty-four hours of his saving her life, had accused him of trying to take it.

The arresting officers had been caustic when he'd questioned their cause. "*Any idea why she might think* you *robbed and then stabbed her twice?*" Both uniforms, one for each arm, had jerked him away from the cold brick of his Brooklyn apartment building, neighbors gaping at the spectacle. "*You have the right to remain silent… If you cannot afford an attorney, one will be appointed for you…*"

God, the indictment. His prints had been found at the scene, prints he'd laid down while seeing her to safety. Her mace spray had been recovered from his apartment, a bauble haphazardly collected when he'd found her crumpled, unresponsive body. And the crown jewel—Scarlet's damning testimony, swearing *he'd* cornered her in that parking lot, threatened her, stolen from her, and then slammed a blade into her body before dumping her car and calling the police in either an attack of conscience or a diabolical attempt to cover his tracks.

Why the hell would he have outed himself like that?

Bathed in cold sweat, Ethan swiped at his brow before Billboard could note the mental flailing. Seeing Scarlet's look-alike in the train station had been one thing. Working with her, trusting her to act in his best interest? Whole 'nother fucking show.

Funny how quickly the mind could travel through time and space. One moment he drank barrel-aged whisky in his posh office with an old confidant. The next, a gavel rapped against a judge's bench. "*Bail is set at five hundred thousand.*" It might as well have been ten million. There'd been more handcuffs, a different jumpsuit, and then a wrenching blue-and-white corrections bus.

Finally, *Rikers Island.* To await trial in style.

And all for the bargain price of two words: Scarlet Leore.

Surging to his feet, Ethan grappled for his two fingers of scotch. "Hell, no." The harsh words brooked no argument.

Billboard lifted his hands. "Easy."

"Fuck easy." Desperate to move around, Ethan prowled to his desk and picked up a discarded suit jacket ready for the cleaners. Billboard remained splayed out on the couch, looking ready to stay awhile, and the distraction beat violence. "I won't place myself in that path of destruction again."

Because *try* to destroy him she had. Not even a full day had passed in Rikers before his first test. He'd stalked onto a concrete basketball court, sweat dripping between his shoulder blades, heedless of the flurries cartwheeling from an overcast sky. Several men had tracked his movements, not bothering with subtlety. They'd hung back, likely contemplating whether his fight could match his size.

Ethan had propped a hip against a concrete wall, watching and waiting, forcing any strikes to come from the front. Sure enough, the initial reprieve hadn't lasted. Three men had broken away from the pack and prowled forward. The first taker had brandished a screwdriver. The tip had been filed to a point, with the other end swaddled in dirty strips of linen to form a makeshift handle. The guy had advanced with an uneven gait, throwing the shank in the air like a juggler's pin.

Forcing a show, the guy projected his voice. *"This here?"* He rolled his head on his shoulders, indicating the surrounding court. *"It's mine. You wanna play? You pay."*

Ethan crossed his arms over his chest and stared.

"You deaf?" the guy said, creeping closer. This time when the asshole flipped the shank, he skipped the acrobatics and caught the weapon by the handle. Still grandstanding, he added, *"Don't fuck with me,"* then sank back on his rear leg and adopted a dagger-hold on the weapon.

Arrogance like that—the kind rimmed with something to prove—didn't take a talk down, so Ethan waited, perfectly still. *Let him wonder.* After a moment, the man advanced with a smirk, gearing up for a lucky strike. *Keep telling yourself that, asshole.*

At the last possible second, a scant moment before the sharpened tip of the screwdriver sank into flesh and bone, Ethan reverted to type. He flashed a hand out and thrust his thigh high on a skyward jump, a disarmament he'd perfected years ago. No man, however lethal, could defend against an attack he failed to anticipate.

Bone crunched, giving way to Ethan's up-thrust knee. The man's shank arm overextended backward from the elbow. The joint cracked, and the weapon thudded to the ground seconds before its owner. A low moan drifted upward, the big man on campus reduced to a wounded animal, fumbling in the dirt.

"Think about it," Billboard snapped, dissolving Ethan's memory in his refusal to leave well enough alone. "She's young. Hungry for success. Ready to run circles around the goons we've overpaid for years."

Ethan cracked his office door and tossed the jacket at Susan. "Clean," he clipped, unable to voice more. Whirling on Billboard, he said, "You presume she'll come cheap." Like hell. Scarlet wouldn't be bothered to get out of bed in the morning for less than his first born child. These days, probably more.

"Not even close." Billboard flashed his shark smile. "And, by the way, I'm told she's still stunning."

Of course she would be. After his release, the only thing more disturbing than how much he'd hated her had been how much he'd wanted her. The years hadn't dampened either emotion.

He pictured her gorgeous, upturned face near a private elevator in a garage lined with luxury cars. Their single kiss and its aftermath had gone deep, *years* deep. Even now, he could detect her sweetness over the burn of the whisky.

Ethan clapped his teeth together, biting down on his cheek, close to lashing out at one of his few true friends, not to mention the man who'd given him his life back after Scarlet had done her worst. "I don't need your fucking advice on this. The last time I tangled with Scarlet Leore, you extracted me from a prison cell."

Cursing, Ethan rubbed his jaw roughly. Before she'd thrown him to the wolves, his desire had mingled with a curious tenderness. Despite her outward confidence, there'd been a hesitance about Scarlet, a subtle vulnerability that had shone through her worldly, gregarious persona. Or so he'd thought.

The want that spiked in him now had nothing to do with kindness or caring. He resisted a surge of erotic heat that only amplified his disgust.

And prodded him about his promise of revenge.

Billboard paused long enough for a plan to slink into Ethan's conscious. By the time the man snapped, "You're getting my fucking advice anyway," Ethan sat pensively behind his desk, brooding in silence while Billboard droned on.

"…plus Copenhagen is a hip, modern city, a perfect environment for a woman like her…"

The red-tinged need for retaliation had long since faded to gray, but since she'd figuratively fallen into his lap…

Ethan dragged twitching fingers through his hair, recalling each run in with Scarlet in detail. Her apology had been too easy for a rich girl. She'd offered cash, of course, and it had been money he'd needed but couldn't take. Acceptance had looked a lot like forgiveness at a time when he'd been burning through anger like fuel, craving the fire as he did food and water and air. Scarlet hadn't been allowed to steal his only energy source to ease her conscience.

As her client, he could work her too hard, bending her to his will and beyond. She'd be entirely at his mercy, all nice and legal like. Perhaps she'd mended her calculating ways, in which case she'd be safe. But if she fucked up, he'd be waiting.

The first glimmerings of a shrewd smile strained Ethan's tight cheeks. His head snapped up, and he crossed the span to Billboard in three strides, not bothering to mask the unholy light he knew gleamed behind hooded lids. "Do it. Get her."

Come to me, Empress. Time to pay my way.

He stalked out, quietly pulling the door closed behind him and leaving Billboard to ponder his abrupt change of mind when there obviously hadn't been a change of heart.

******

Scarlet pressed a shaking palm to her lips, hiding behind her office door. Rocking back and forth on her kitten heels, she could practically hear the music—*I am the champ-ion, I am the champ-i-on, of-the-world.* Today would go down in Scarlet history as the day she rose up and fisted her full potential.

And what potential it was.

Perhaps swaying to imaginary congratulations from Queen delved into delusions of grandeur. A tad. But she did have a new client. A big fish. She would get to say, "*My* client needs you to…" and "That's not good enough for *my* client…" Until now, she'd always said "So-and-so's client wants this…" and "The firm's client requires that…" Fine, but not earth shattering. Or particularly wallet-enhancing.

She'd received a call that morning from the President of Parlann Technologies, a Mr. Ron Michael. He'd requested a same-day conference call and had said that, if possible, Parlann wanted to retain JTS as outside counsel in evaluating and negotiating the acquisition of a Danish optics company. If it worked out, Parlann would throw more work her way.

Ron had done his research. He knew exactly what she and her firm could offer and was comfortable with JTS's astronomical rates, so with that, the pressure ramped. Fine with her. She was prepared to bring it.

Descending on the conference room, Scarlet couldn't help but reflect on the years of work and compromise that had brought her to the doorstep of success. In the months following Ethan's release, she'd come up hard against her father's aloofness. The struggle to heal what she could had knocked against injuries—the invisible kind—that wouldn't mend. Any sense of bravery had proved elusive.

Ethan had come up during one of many stilted calls with her dad. After explaining that Ethan would never *forgive* her mistake, she'd wondered aloud why her father had insisted she accuse him so quickly. No doubt she would've gotten around to it—at the time, the cold whisper of "Empress" against her throat had echoed through her nightmares—but Tripp had demanded an immediate accusation, as in schlepped NYPD's finest to her hospital bed for the gory details.

Her father's answer had been cryptic. "*Because money has its perks, and we needed closure.*"

35

LIBBY RICE

What kind of man leveraged monetary clout to send a possibly-innocent person to prison, and why the hell had "they" needed closure? She'd needed it, sure, but not at Ethan's expense. Her father had never *needed* anything.

Confused, and desperate to forge a meaningful relationship with her only relative, she'd asked whether he believed Ethan would overcome adversity to live a full, satisfied life despite her error. Foolishly, she'd shared her hopes that he would.

His response? *"Time to grow up."* And the phone had gone dead.

The next day, a Cartier wristwatch had arrived at the penthouse. A red box with no note—nothing at all to indicate the giver of such a fine gift— but of course her father had been the source of the sophisticated timepiece.

Time to grow up, the cold metal had silently admonished. *Let go. Move on.*

Staring at the watch, the price of the Leore fortune had crashed in, suffocating her remaining desires to beguile a man who preferred not to be won. Financial backing certainly hadn't brought the family together. Worse, had Leore not been a household name, her accusations of murder and mayhem might have been better vetted before Ethan's arrest. Her true lie had miscarried justice because of *who* she was, despite the fallibility of *what* she'd said.

Flip.

Ethan would never take her apology, but she'd taken herself off the payroll. Tripp Leore had gotten the watch back, and aside from keeping her other personal property—which she admitted was far from paltry—she'd never taken his money again. Through a combination of her own income and the sale of her old life, Scarlet had cobbled together an upper-middle-class existence. Independence had morphed into her new normal.

Now, walking the halls of JTS, Scarlet beamed with each step toward cementing her status as a pseudo-self-made woman.

Twenty minutes later, she surfaced for a breath. Some nameless in-house attorney at Parlann talked fast while she wrote slow. Already, lines upon lines of notes swam before her bleary eyes as the basics of the upcoming acquisition rattled through the call speaker.

In the middle of a lengthy monologue, a deep voice cut in. "No, once the acquisition is complete, Atavos, or most likely Parlann, will maintain the Danish design team in Copenhagen. We'll manufacture elsewhere, possibly in Brazil or Malaysia, so we'll need the Danes' expertise on the manufacturing side only temporarily."

At the mention of Atavos, Scarlet's heart lurched and then sped up. *Atavos was Ethan's.* There hadn't been time after Ron's initial call to research Parlann's corporate structure. Major projects got off the ground in no time at all, and she knew only that the conflict check had come back clean. It occurred to her now that Parlann could be a division of Atavos. And she'd have to be blind, deaf, and illiterate to be unaware of Ethan's ascent as the

36

founder and CEO of Atavos International.

The grapevine—and the media—dubbed her once-upon-a-fling a gifted engineer and a brilliant business strategist. Also, if the newspapers and magazines were to be believed, much of his success was attributable to the fact that few could resist his charm… when he chose to exude it.

No surprise there.

Taking herself in hand, Scarlet breathed deep. She stared robotically at the blinking red light of the call console. Despite Ethan's reputation as a micro-manager, it would be highly irregular for the CEO to get intimately involved in the day-to-day details of a single business division. Ethan would be asked to weigh-in at a higher level. Surely he wouldn't even know about today's call.

Scarlet considered the comment about separating the design from the manufacturing. "What's your timeline for making the transition to independent manufacturing? I ask because once we have a letter of intent in place, we may need to begin looking for manufacturing facilities in your target countries to ensure a smooth conversion over a short time window." She kept her tone mild despite her inner *holy-shit*. Just another lawyer getting the facts.

"Who's speaking?" That low, rough voice returned, reminding her that she hadn't introduced herself upon jumping in.

Only one man had a chance in hell of seducing her over a speakerphone. She felt a twitch or two where she shouldn't, and her hopes took on a frantic litany in her head—*Ron, Ron, Ron.* "I apologize," she began. "This is Scarlet Leore. I'll be the JTS project lead."

"Of course, Ms. Leore."

The reply that eased from the speaker was cold, devoid of all welcome, a rare attitude for an initial project meeting centered on developing positive relationships between people who would be working closely for the duration. Scarlet looked around. Her colleagues darted glances at each other, then back at her, perplexed by the animosity communicated in those four short words. Suddenly, it became a challenge to maintain her calm façade. Keeping her eyes trained on the speaker, she strove to ignore the dread that accompanied her escalating heartbeat.

"Am I speaking with Mr. Michael?" she asked, again keeping her tone light and businesslike. *Pleeeease be Ron.*

"No. This is Mr. Blake. Ethan Blake."

She'd known. Yet her eyes slid closed, and her hands flattened over the glossy conference table, sliding back and forth in a quest for physical affirmation that the world she'd inhabited only moments ago was still with her. The indomitable optimism of the morning crumbled with the knowledge that this couldn't be a coincidence.

"I'm sorry I came looking for you… you weren't worth it."

Ethan had been honest all those years ago when she'd tried to apologize, and his words had crawled into a locked chamber of her heart, only to be let out when she wasn't strong enough to maintain the barricade. She'd wanted to soothe whatever scars he bore from the experience. *Impossible.* So she'd tried to repair the logistical damage. To help him get back on his feet. Into school. Moved to a new apartment. But the slide of a check across their café table had been greeted with a killing look and snarled condemnation. In her book, regret over saving her life wasn't far from wishing her dead.

And now she'd put herself at his mercy.

JTS attorneys were held to high productivity standards. She'd risk her career by refusing to serve a plum client like Atavos, especially after coming so far—thousands of dollars of time poured into the first call alone—and for something so adolescent as *personal reasons.* Nor could she afford a break in employment or to burn bridges at her firm. She could hear her explanation to the partnership now. *You see, one time, when I was young and stupid, I was attacked while strolling the darkened streets of Brooklyn, outside a fight club no less, all alone. Well, long story short, I was kind of stabbed and almost died. And the weird thing is, I blamed the would-be founder of Atavos. He wasn't my attacker, of course. He'd actually saved my life. But he still went to prison for a time. Maybe we should throw this fish back, yes?*

Desperate to look normal, Scarlet let her pen scribble nonsensical gibberish onto her notepad, taking care to appear deep in thought, the whole time reminding herself of who she was and what she'd become. *A damn good lawyer and a consummate professional.* Ethan had hired her to do a job. Nothing personal. No vendetta. He'd be the first to say she didn't warrant a second of his attention.

"Hello, Ethan." Speaking slowly, her voice didn't crack, and it was all she could ask for. Barely wincing, she added, "Now, about that timeline?"

Because there was only so much jewelry left to sell.

CHAPTER 5

Ethan saw Scarlet first. She sat at their flight gate, flipping through a magazine while a smartphone buzzed in her lap. How fitting. If he were to e-mail and say, "Jump," she could reply immediately to ask, "How high?"

She perched in the middle of a row of Naugahyde-and-steel chairs, each flanked by its mirror image to the rear. Her pencil skirt and button-down blouse were no doubt meant to impart competence, but the getup was pure schoolmarm fantasy.

If one were into that.

The years slipped away under his examination. Billboard had been right. She looked flawless, her body petite and perfectly curved, as he'd known it would be. Her blond hair gleamed from a soft chignon at her nape, and her stiff posture screamed, *"Look but don't touch."* When she glanced up at the clock, those honey eyes were apprehensive.

A nice start.

Entering the area near their gate, he bit back angry words. Threats would only amplify her anxiety and have her watching every move. An abundance of caution wouldn't do.

He circled around behind her and sat, his back to hers, and breathed her feminine scent. With his head only inches away, her light floral fragrance worked like a fairy's lasso to the torso, invisibly pulling him into her realm. He'd never recognized the unadulterated power in a well-tailored skirt and the right bottle of perfume.

The rockin' body beneath doesn't hurt.

Ethan shifted uncomfortably in his seat. He hadn't predicted the sharp pangs of longing that threatened his smug self-righteousness at how their lives had changed. Word on the street whispered that her poor-little-rich-girl status had swirled down the drain years ago, and from the looks of it, she'd descended a few rungs on the social latter. A little less heiress and a little more working woman.

For the millionth time, he squelched his curiosity. Despite every instinct, he'd never allowed himself to check up on her or to garner even the faintest awareness of the trajectory of her life. He wouldn't start now.

Whatever her issues, Billboard's recent comments had been telling. A hotshot lawyer at a respected New York firm was a woman who'd picked up the pieces. And someone with obligations. When he'd given Billboard the go-ahead to contact Scarlet, he'd known it would be difficult for her to turn Atavos away, and he'd relished the idea of holding her perfectly-manicured hand to the fire.

Now, not thirty seconds after spotting her in the airport, Ethan entertained thoughts of wiping the unease from her features. He ached to reassure her that he sought nothing more than her expertise and that he hadn't set out to wound.

Such reassurances would not be forthcoming, however, because both sentiments were of questionable truth.

Ethan glanced up to see Billboard and Susan making their way to a nearby seat, and he gave a subtle jerk of his head. For now, his people needed to keep their distance. Ethan wanted to confront Scarlet personally, without an audience. Knowing time was short, and the crowd would only grow, Ethan began with a clear message.

"It's been a while, Empress." He said the words to her back, knowing it had to be a shock since she hadn't noted his arrival.

No, Scarlet, I haven't forgotten.

The day she'd stammered her insincere apology, the title had provoked a telltale flinch. It still did.

Her head rolled back over her shoulder. "Ethan," she began. Pausing, she seemed to choose her words carefully. Most likely, she contemplated how pleasant she *had* to be to her biggest client. Finally, she continued, her voice patient as though she were a bank teller explaining a new ATM system to an elderly customer. "I could have refused you. Come to think of it, I still can."

"And what happens when you get back to the office and tell your colleagues you left me sitting at the airport, counsel-less no less, on my way to complete a business deal you were hired to investigate and negotiate?"

"I tell them you're an ass and remind them that an ass is a malpractice risk."

"How so?"

She spun in her chair to face him. "You don't actually want me here. You'll be looking for problems. Glitches are easier to find—or to manufacture—when one is looking." Then she mimicked his deep voice. "Scarlet didn't do this. Scarlet should've done that. Any *reasonable* attorney would have—"

"What makes you think I don't want you here?" Not wanting her had *never* been the problem.

Her nostrils flared. Then she shook her head slightly, averting her face and shutting him out. She looked weary when she murmured, "Life's too short, Ethan." She placed her magazine in a legal-sized shoulder bag before she stood, turned on her delicate kitten heels, and strode away.

Leaving. Just like that.

Ethan's mind shrank with fury at the childish stunt. Was this some kind of joke? A game? The Copenhagen deal could make or break a key Atavos product, and she was his fully-contracted ace in the hole. Supposedly the best.

Ethan didn't let her get far. Splicing through the boarding line to follow behind, he reached for her upper arm just as she would have stepped onto the escalator, bringing them both to a sudden, and less-than-gentle, halt. "You were aware of my identity and our mutual history when you took Atavos on. You'll do the job you've been hired to do, Scarlet, or I won't sue you, I'll destroy you. I'll exploit every weakness you have, and I have a feeling I'll find plenty." He gentled his tone, but only slightly. "Don't doubt it, *Empress*."

******

Though his grip didn't hurt, Scarlet stared at Ethan's hand. Touching was fine. *Wanted.* The days of flashbacks and phantom pains at the slightest human contact were behind her. Yet unsolicited touches remained challenging and angry ones unbearable.

The appendage wrapped around her arm was strong and calloused, with blunt fingernails. A bruise marred the tanned skin of his forearm, calling attention to the raised veins that still tracked from beneath his sleeve to his thick wrist and then across the back of his hand. Looking up at his face, she took in the strong lines of a tanned throat that bisected impossibly broad shoulders and the hard, uncompromising profile it supported. His was the face of a man who, no matter what else, won.

Ethan may have given up fighting for his supper, but everything about him screamed that the boxer was still in there.

"You're crowding me," she whispered, knowing he could feel her arm quiver beneath his fingers. The involuntary tremor only increased as she stiffened against it, while a chaotic fog filled her head like a balloon. *Breathe, goddamn it. In then out.* She followed her own instructions, managing a long, ragged inhale. *Again.*

"You okay?"

The question sounded fuzzy, like he'd yelled it through a mile of cardboard tubing. His big body was over-the-top, and she wasn't used to letting people, even the smaller ones, so near. She shook her head, and as soon as she could project her voice, she added, "Let go, Ethan, please."

His hand slid away immediately, and when she looked up, she saw concern banked in the obsidian of his gaze. Worry he didn't want to feel warred with the anger he did. She realized that, for very different reasons, neither of them wanted to recall the events that had torn them to pieces. Yet the memories were like living, breathing beings hovering between them. Their very own ghosts of Christmas past.

"I'm sorry," he said, albeit reluctantly. This time he was the one who appeared to search for the right words. "This may have been a mistake—for both of us—but what's done is done, and we're booked to leave in fifteen minutes. If I don't show up in Copenhagen, someone else will. Atavos can't afford to lose Optik, especially for the wrong reasons."

His hand smoothed over her blouse where he'd touched her arm, gently pulling the fragile fabric straight. "You'll board that plane, through persuasion, blackmail, force… whatever it takes."

Drawn to his lighter, now almost hesitant touch, she let him stroke her while her vital signs returned to normal. "You're right on one count," she said sadly. "This is a mistake."

The smile he gave her was cold, but the soft stroking along her arm didn't stop. "Probably won't be your last."

She shrank back. Abruptly, her chest ached. Not because he was being an ass, but because she'd allowed herself to indulge in tormented fantasies that he wouldn't be, and now she reeled with the backlash of disappointment. Wanting him to be different didn't make it so, and between them, bygones could never be bygones. If she were honest—something she'd decided *not* to be with herself until this was all over—she'd wanted much more. Now, she saw the project for what it really was.

A trap.

Rubbing the exposed skin at her sternum, she said, "If you don't mind, I'd really like to get some water. That's all, Ethan. I wasn't leaving."

"*Hell*," he muttered under his breath. "I'll see you onboard. We're in coach since we booked last minute."

"Fine." She stepped onto the escalator, relieved to be beyond his reach. "Optik awaits."

Minutes later, Scarlet settled into her seat, anticipating her first glass of wine from the flight attendant. Never much of a drinker, she planned to rock a slight buzz to sooth her tattered nerves. They would fly direct to Frankfurt before hopping a second flight up to Copenhagen. She situated her lap blanket and headphones and focused on relaxing before what she hoped would be a seven-hour nap.

The previous night had been restless. Ethan had teamed with her troubling finances to occupy her thoughts until dawn, crowding out all possibilities of sleep and leaving her exhausted for reunification day, as she called it.

Their reunion had definitely started with a bang. But the debacle had been more her fault than his. She'd been so prepared for a confrontation she'd unwillingly caused one. Worse, Ethan was right about her limited choices, and for all her denials, he was dead-on about her so-called ruin-ability. Yet only a fool would fail to seize the career-defining opportunity he offered. And her new motto, *carpe diem*, didn't allow her to let life-altering chances pass her by.

Ethan Blake had her over a barrel. He knew it, and he wasn't afraid to exploit the advantage.

The realization hit as the man in question sauntered down the aisle and slid into the adjoining seat.

CHAPTER 6

Ethan watched through slit lids as Scarlet ate her in-flight lasagna with all the fervor of a beaten-down Emily Post. While the table manners of her past had sent him into carnal orbit, today she was delicate and controlled, lifting each small bite to her lips and chewing—he swore exactly twenty times—before swallowing. The marked joy was missing from each forkful, but at least she ate.

The wine? Now that she drank like a woman intent on forgetting all about her seatmate and lulling herself into an alcohol-and-chronic-fatigue-induced coma. Like the timid eating, her obvious lethargy was an unwelcome realization. At least he could pinpoint the source of her nerves. *Him.*

Susan had made sure Ethan shared a row with Scarlet and an empty seat, a request she'd grudgingly but efficiently granted. Despite the clear opportunity to catch up on years spent apart, neither he nor Scarlet spoke a word. Their seat screens sat dark and headphones stayed stowed. Ethan silently observed—and she did, too, if he wasn't mistaken—learning preferences, noting mannerisms, even matching the cadence of breath.

Like foreplay.

His body tightened at the thought. Only after Scarlet had slumped into sleep did Ethan's focus shift from the strain of having her near—all that inviting warmth imminently accessible—to the research he'd long-denied himself. Accessing the on-board Wi-Fi, he trolled the Internet for all things Scarlet Leore.

Most of the last several years had gone undocumented. He found only brief blurbs announcing her graduation from Yale Law and her decision to join Jahn Tremane & Spellman shortly thereafter. Her firm bio included a professional headshot along with a synopsis of her legal experience and publications, a slew of speaking engagements, and an impressive list of previous deals she'd negotiated. Scarlet exuded "accomplished professional" on paper, but any idiot could craft a brilliant résumé. Whether she was worth her salt, and his money, would prove out over the next few weeks.

Apparently, she wasn't a fan of social media. *Good girl.* The deal was highly confidential, and foregoing hourly updates didn't gel with the Facebooker set. Ideally, the world wouldn't know Atavos had hired Scarlet, or that his legal team had descended on Copenhagen, until the deal was dead or done. Pre-closure knowledge bred too much deal-tanking speculation.

Continuing his search, Ethan noted a brief mention of the relationship between Scarlet and her father. A *Times* society article dated about seven years prior called Tripp Leore and his only child "distanced," though it didn't go so far as to say estranged. The piece must have been written around the time Scarlet had finished undergrad and returned to New York from Stanford. She would have been searching for a suitable philanthropic opportunity, or possibly work in the arts, something that required beautiful clothes and regular appearances in the society pages.

Surprisingly, she'd gone straight to law school. He wondered who footed the bill for the former debutante's three years at one of the country's most exclusive—and expensive—private institutions. Perhaps they weren't *close*, but Daddy had surely gone all-in for that one.

Scarlet shifted next to him, and a small, distressed sound floated through the silence of the cabin. The window shades were drawn to emulate night as they floated above the Atlantic. Most of their fellow passengers were either sleeping or trying to behind eye masks and noise-cancellation headphones. Glancing over, he saw Scarlet's unfocused gaze latch onto the only light available—his glowing computer screen.

"You're reading about me while I sit here," she said dully. "How tactful." The words expressed surprise. The tone said she'd expected nothing less.

He ignored her look of woozy disgust. "What happened with Daddy Dearest?"

"You *know* what happened," she answered with a hint of a slur. "You've read all about it."

Okay, he thought, not entirely sober. He handed her a chunk of cheddar leftover from his own meal. As he reached out, the back of his hand lightly grazed the giving flesh of her right breast, shooting a killer buzz up his arm. Before he could draw back, she crooked her neck, absently searching her chest for the source of the sensation.

"Eat this," he ordered. "And maybe I want the story straight from the horse's mouth. You two were tight when you took me down."

Snickering. Then, "Horse's mouth? You think that kind of talk gets you what you want from a woman?" She looked truly appalled that he ever got anything he wanted. From anyone.

"Always." It was never *conversation* that he, or they, wanted. "Let me rephrase. I want you to tell the story of your life. Not the *New York Times*." He ran the back of his hand down her upper arm. "Tell me, Scarlet. How did my Empress fall from her throne?"

Drunk or not, her eyes shuddered. "We passed on the stairs, remember? You were going up as I was coming down."

She merely played with the cheese, pulling the piece apart and laying it bit by bit on his tray. Finally, he reached out to still her busy fingers. Breaking off a tiny bite, he held it up. "Eat. You need it."

Sighing heavily, she said, "I'd rather have fermented grapes."

"Tough." He brought the tangy cheese forward toward her lips. "Eat the cheddar, Scarlet." When he reached her mouth, he couldn't resist. His fingertips brushed over her bottom lip for the briefest second before she pulled back. Her softness burned like a brand, and it was all he could do not to slip a finger inside her warm mouth, just to see what she'd do.

Bite me, most likely.

"Feeding me now, are you?" she scoffed, chuckling low. Yet her eyes dilated, and he didn't think she could blame the low light.

"Did you lie to him?" he asked abruptly. *Betray him like you did me?* He needed her to shoulder the blame for the rift between father and daughter. To have shown herself, once again, for the manipulative bitch he could easily set from his mind.

Her mouth went slack as she ate. Only ten chews this time. "Excuse me?"

"It's a reasonable assumption given your tendency to use and abuse." In that moment, he wanted to be away from her almost as much as he wanted to be inside her.

"Never. I—I—" Her mouth opened and closed like a fish floundering out of water. "What happened to you?" she asked suddenly, staring at the yellowing bruise that snaked along his forearm.

"Battle wound." As if she gave a shit about his Monday night fight, but he let her change the subject. For now. "You should see the other guy," he added with a wink.

Scarlet scooted up in her seat and brought his arm into her lap, massaging the soreness and tracing the bruise with her soft fingertips. Her touch jolted across his skin, a torch's sizzle. They made a combustible combination, one that could burn them both to cinders and leave them standing bereft and beyond repair. At the same time, not even his practiced loathing lent the will to resist.

The raw silk blouse she wore had shifted with her movements, and in the computer's glow, he could see the outline of a lacey bra. The shirt and the bra were so delicate he could picture the outline of her nipples. He knew what they'd look like… shell pink, a shade darker than her pale skin. They'd be small and sensitive to his touch. *To his tongue.*

He hardened at the thought. Fuck, he *ached*. For a woman he refused to want or trust.

"Do you contact him? At least often enough to keep yourself knee deep in those big checks you're so fond of?" He knew the question would be a cruel reminder.

The soft touches against his arm stopped, and he almost took the taunt back. Anything to keep her fingers on his skin. When she looked up, her eyes had gone wide, but her jaw remained set. "*Especially* not that."

"Sounds intriguing," he mocked.

This time when she answered, her musical voice was low and hesitant. "Why do you care? You never even knew him—"

"Wrong." He let the "g" vibrate against the silence of the cabin. "We've met several times. He even fucked me over on a land deal a few years back." When Tripp Leore had backtracked on their signed contract and invited Ethan to sue if he wanted to do something about it, Ethan had pulled out. Nearly getting burned by another Leore had opened old wounds, seconding the fact that the name was poison.

"You're not alone in that, I'm afraid." She sat sideways in her seat and rested her temple against the headrest, staring at her fingers as they curled around the air above his arm. He sensed her hesitance to touch him again, yet she didn't tell him in no uncertain terms to fuck off.

She was softening.

"That kind of money," she continued with a brief squeeze of his wrist. "*Your* kind of money. It can be dangerous."

Yup. That freaky money gets me every time. "My kind of money is the only way to live, sweetheart."

"Until you're crushed under the weight of it. Or realize neither you nor those you hold dear can see past it. Maybe you even hurt someone with it—"

He clucked his tongue in the dark. "And how would one do that?"

She reached for the remaining cheese he'd set aside, her movements languid. "Maybe you need to apologize for wronging someone you care about, and money becomes your tool because it's the only emotional currency you know."

What was this? An excuse for her seven-figure apology? Pointing the finger at him had destroyed his reputation, delayed his business launch, and gotten him evicted from his apartment and expelled from school. For months, he'd slept with his eyes open in a place where balled fists hadn't meant prize money, but survival. When proven wrong, she'd waltzed in with a little regret and a lot of cash, expecting him to fall at her feet in gratitude.

"Money could never compromise my humanity," he said. And anyone who gave her fortune that kind of value could never voluntarily part from it, no matter what she said now. The number of zeroes before his decimal may have surpassed hers, but she obviously remained entrenched in the good life. These days he knew the worth of those massive diamonds winking from her ears. Quite the business casual for a woman who suddenly shunned wealth.

"Leave off, Scarlet." He registered the scathing scrape of his voice as he reached out, tracing a fingertip around one of the stones. "We both know you didn't willingly part with that kind of money. You wouldn't. More like *couldn't*."

His hand slipped to her neck, and she inched away. Sober again, her face had lost its dreamy tranquility. "Here's the interesting thing, Ethan. I don't owe you or anyone else a play-by-play of my checkbook balance. Contrary to what you obviously believe, I don't owe you anything."

He let a slow smile spread across his face. "A pity, that." A rush of pride at her defensive posturing swirled into the potent desire he'd stopped denying.

Mute, she blinked at him, chewing almost violently at her lower lip until he brought his fingertips to her mouth. "Don't." His emotions yo-yoed. One minute, he welcomed her worry. The next, he couldn't bear to witness it.

Jerking away from his seeking fingers, she burst out, "No." Her eyes widened in shock before she added, "I'm not for *you*."

"Really?" he asked silkily. "Then who are you *for*?"

He didn't think she'd answer. But after a second, a reply too raw to be fabricated slipped out. "Maybe no one."

Her honesty stripped his defenses. "I disagree. You're too..." *Beautiful, alive, real.* "You can have anyone."

"Except Ethan Blake."

"*Especially* Ethan Blake." Or at least parts of him.

She turned away without another word, her petite form huddling under her lap blanket, curling into the seat toward the window. The posture showcased her slender neck and a few pale tendrils that had escaped her updo to curl invitingly against her flesh.

Grinding his teeth in frustration, he fought to kick-start lungs that refused to function properly. The tension inside him grew to an excruciating pitch until his breathing tripped, and he barely resisted the urge to drag her to him.

Then his willpower gave him a big "fuck you." He shoved his laptop beneath the seat, stowed his tray table, and reached for her. "Scarlet, let me—"

"Leave it." The words were harsh, signifying an end to his inquisition, whether he liked it or not. "I told you—"

"Hush." He dragged a hand from the nape of her neck, down her spine, and up again. "Shh." He kept stroking, occasionally switching to knead the tension from her slim neck and shoulders until he felt her relax into the seat. Anticipation leapt in his chest when she accepted his touch. Leaning in, he placed a lush, closed-mouth kiss against her nape, her delicious floral scent coiling in the back of his brain.

Purposefully avoiding anything threatening or overtly sexual—for now—Ethan used his hands and mouth to first relax and then to gradually arouse, saying nothing for long minutes as he continued the gentle massage. Finally, her body went lax in his arms, and he traced the shell of her delicate ear with his tongue, marveling at his first taste of her skin.

It was like he remembered. One feel, and he would do anything, forgive anything, for another.

"Can I touch you?" He prayed for a *yes*, doubting his ability to tame the need that steamrolled in through his fingertips.

"You *are* touching me," she answered, her voice husky but uncertain as she flattened her hands over the window shade. The motion caused her to rock back into his arms as though she were unsure as to why she responded to him the way she did, but was *really* interested in finding out.

He arched into her, silently pleading for her to take more from him. "Scarlet? Can I make you feel good?" *Use my body to pleasure yours?*

She moaned softly, and the effect was intoxicating. The low sound stole through his veins, the ultimate *attaboy*. His hands surged under the blanket to brush against her breasts, massaging them like he had her back and stomach. Straining to get closer, he came up hard against the armrest that separated them, smacking his jean-clad erection against unforgiving plastic and metal. With an impatient tug, he arced the offending blockade out of their way, his movements stirring the air around them. Beyond the fresh scent of woman and exclusive French perfume, he detected the barest hint of feminine arousal. His brain stuttered at the thought of her body getting ready.

Ethan closed his eyes and imagined them going beyond what the confines of the plane cabin would allow to a place of mad lust, where the only thing that mattered would be him pounding out the ache he knew pulsed between her thighs.

Making her come until he was lost.

He slid his hand into her silken hair, close to the scalp. A few pulls released her ladylike chignon and arched her spine forward, thrusting her gorgeous breasts up to beg for his touch.

He lowered his mouth to her ear. "I'm so fucking hard, Scarlet."

As her head slammed back against his shoulder, her lips parted in a soundless moan. The sight of her arousal had him hardening further.

"Ethan, I—oh, *God.*" She peeled her torso away, again pushing against the window shade, though this time, they weren't separated by the intrusive armrest. Her backside twisted frantically against his cock as he sat turned in his seat, the friction of his clothing nearly burning him alive. Rearing back, Ethan tried to shake the intensity, but the feel of her pert ass grinding against him had his skin prickling all over, like his whole body was an extremity being awakened after going to sleep.

Then, without his permission, her low, desperate cries triggered an elemental need to see her satisfied.

Reaching around again, he slowly unbuttoned her silk blouse and spread it apart. He swallowed the incoherent sounds that bubbled up when he flattened his hands over her warm stomach and slid them upward over the demi cups of her lacy bra, fascinated by the way her breath sawed in and out in desperate gulps.

It would take nothing to release her nipples. The flick of a wrist.

He couldn't resist, and with his next move, he reached inside her lingerie to cup her, gently pulling the mounds from their confinement before rasping a forefinger over each distended nipple.

This time there was no suppressing the guttural moan that vibrated his chest.

******

Hunger settled in Scarlet's middle in a scorching, insistent ache. Ethan's large hands palmed her breasts all too knowingly, his hardness sliding forcefully against her rear.

One part of her demanded she stop him. *Now.* Another niggled that she'd always known Ethan wouldn't hurt her. She'd *known*, deep in some silent, unrecognizable corner of her heart, and yet she'd made unforgivable accusations. Perhaps he deserved a little trust even though he'd threatened, insulted, and then laughed at her in the space of a day. Because despite the war cry of her every last instinct for self-preservation, her traitorous body cried *hell yes.* She wanted to hate him for his disdain, but the hate part refused to cooperate.

All she got was the *want.*

She'd become the mouse after a baited piece of cheese that might well kill her, and she didn't have the strength to resist. He offered pleasure at a high price—*a trap*—but she'd grown so damn hungry she was willing to pay.

"More?" he rasped behind her, and she felt her body heat in answer. Not one touch without at least implied permission. "Scarlet?" he asked again.

Go ahead. Trust the lightening not to strike. "Please," she said on a ragged sigh.

With warm fingertips, he nudged her nipples into hard points. When she arched forward into his hands, one disappeared, his fingers returning *wet* from his devious tongue. The combination of moisture and cool air on the tip of her breast brought an uneven demand to her lips. *"More."*

"Turn for me, Scarlet. Let me see you."

"The others…"

"No, sweetheart, everyone's asleep." While Ethan's voice was barely a whisper, she knew any concern for being detected had flown long ago. For both of them, the risk became part of the attraction.

She let his hands ease her around in the seat. Instantly, his head bent, and one nipple—the shiny wet one—disappeared into the hot depths of his mouth. When she hissed at the shocking heat, a low *twirling* in the back of her throat, he sucked at her for a moment before pulling back to alternate puffs of blown air with assuaging licks over the swollen peak.

Scarlet clutched at his shoulders with her nails, sinking into the pleasure, watching his hand trail around the curve of her knee at the edge of her skirt. His voice came in a dark whisper. "Will I find you wet?"

She nodded tightly, ready to drag his hand to where she needed him most. But those fingers kept stroking in place, only inching upward after several moments. The ascent was agonizing, but he finally reached the apex of her thighs and the lace nestled between.

"Answer me, Scarlet." He stroked her cleft through the material, pushing in slightly, teasing her blind.

"Yes." She whimpered. "Wet. *Too hot.*"

"Oh, sweetheart, you're definitely both," he said hoarsely. "Can you part those beautiful thighs for me?"

Barely. But she did her best, easing her thighs as wide as the seat and the skirt would allow.

He moaned around her swollen nipple. "That's it. Ah…" Soothing her inner thighs, he murmured his appreciation. "Smooth. Soft."

Sneaking beneath the lace to the flesh beneath, his finger was a soft stroke right up her center, blitzing her nervous system.

He raised his head from her breast and looked at her, his eyes glittering with intensity. "Fuck, Scarlet, *you're ready.*"

Forget the lightning. Let it strike.

"Please, Ethan." The words were a hoarse demand. Her hips rose to meet his hand, to press against him as he brushed right where she ached, just hard enough to intensify her need, to merge it with madness.

Without another word, two thick think fingers sank into her, and she convulsed at the sudden sensation of being filled. Looking at him, she caught a glimpse of his pink tongue swirling around her nipple. Letting her eyes rove lower, she watched the erotic dance of his muscled forearm as it disappeared beneath her skirt in time with the warm pulls of his mouth.

Her world shrank to the point where his fingers caressed her in a thick slide—in and out. When his thumb swirled gently around her swollen clitoris on the downward stroke, she couldn't stop the words that tumbled out. *"Oh, how I've wanted this,"* she panted, realizing she was going to come. Knowing she would have to do it silently. Barely understanding she might come to regret her candid, passionate words.

He knew. Pulling away from her throbbing nipple, he growled, "Tell me when, sweetheart. Give me everything."

"Now, Ethan, now." The words had barely left her lips when his mouth covered hers for the first time. He ate at her, a sensuous stroking of lips, teeth, and tongue, swallowing any noise she might have made, or even thought of making, as the pleasure crashed in voluptuous waves. His fingers didn't stop. The powerful, surging advances and slow retreats continued through the storm, teasing out every trace of release.

When the surges ended and she stared at him, mute and horrified, he withdrew his hand from between her legs in an unhurried motion and smoothed her panties into place, stroking over them before he inched her skirt down beneath the blanket.

After he buttoned her shirt, he placed a chaste kiss to her forehead.

His lips skimmed her ear. "It seems that you, Empress, are going to be worth the wait."

CHAPTER 7

July—Copenhagen, Denmark

Adjoining suites. That minion of Ethan's, Susan What's-her-name, had booked them into connecting rooms at the Hotel d'Angleterre, a two-hundred-and-fifty-year-old throwback to the days when grand hotels were called things like, well, the d'Angleterre.

Scarlet sauntered into the space, her eyes drinking in a host of eighteenth-century furnishings that popped with lavish fabrics in varying patterns of ice blue and cream. Surprisingly, the subtle melding of paisleys, stripes, floral prints, and an occasional solid created a sumptuous sanctuary, not the tacky chaos she would have expected. Maybe this would be the hotel room that let her sleep.

While the bedroom exuded Victorian haven, the bathroom eschewed the vintage theme for the full Scandinavian spa experience. A round ceramic tub beckoned from the corner, complimenting the bowl sinks that perched atop a mirrored vanity. Plush white rugs lazed upon a warm stone floor that, if she desired, could be heated from below. Ultramodern conveniences overlaid the otherwise classic elegance of her suite.

Knowing her team had assembled downstairs, she peeled back the door of an antique armoire to reveal rows of satin hangers. Breathing in the scent of cedar that emanated from beyond the mirrored panels, Scarlet pushed Ethan from her mind long enough to stow weeks of business clothing. Fitted pencil skirts falling at least to the knee should have been a practical choice, but after the incident on the plane, she wondered if even they were too sensual. Ethan had made quick, delicious work of her conservative attire.

When she wore clothes that fit, her curves came knocking. Baggy clothes meant to tone things down lent her the look of an unprofessional slob. Stowing a particularly lovely silk blouse in mint green, she pictured the gray linen skirt she would pair it with. Like a second skin around her hips, it fell to a sublime, but slight, flair at mid-calf. She rousted the skirt from her luggage and hung it next to the blouse, running her fingers over the material, momentarily transported.

"*Worth the wait,*" he'd said. Her wardrobe choices were moot. A showdown was coming whether she showed up in Channel or a gunnysack. Might as well look good.

Only partly unpacked, Scarlet drifted to the room's crowning glory, an oversized picture window framing what had to be one of Europe's most striking public squares. Placing her hand against the cool glass, she looked on as walkers and cyclists ruled street and square alike. Most of Copenhagen's inhabitants couldn't justify owning a car, which made for a true pedestrian city that beckoned her to join the bustle.

A young mother pulled her toddler from a low fence that separated a ring of weathered cobblestone from an inner plot of lush green grass. Intent on reaching the flowers beyond the barrier, the child rushed back, only to be thwarted by his watchful mom once again. Nearby, a couple, probably in their seventies or eighties, commandeered an iron bench facing her hotel. Every few minutes, their clasped hands would separate, reaching in unison for a bag of seed before taking turns throwing food to the pigeons at their feet.

Leaning in, she could hear the tinkling of bike bells as they overtook meanderers along the sidewalk. Even her nasal passages prickled at the ocean's salty tang drifting through an open window, further taunting her about the piles of work that awaited downstairs.

Backing away from the cloudless day that invaded her room, Scarlet turned her focus to a door behind her carved breakfast table. She *wished* mere doors separated her from Ethan. On the plane, she'd thrilled to his touch. Against her better judgment, she'd allowed herself to believe— though only during those scalding moments—that his reverence hadn't been about power or proving that despite her anger and distrust, he could rule her body.

She wandered to the wall she shared with Ethan, then cracked a door that, sure enough, led to another door she knew opened into Ethan's suite. Staring at the gateway from her room into his, she prayed a few inches of wood could keep them from destroying each other. Because she secretly ached for another go, only this time with equal access to Ethan's muscled torso, his ribbed abdomen, his… everything.

Worse, she knew that like his presumptuous statement on the plane, the room arrangement sent a message. Susan the Minion did exactly as her master ordered—to the tee, and if possible, with a cherry on top. Ethan had gone out of his way to orchestrate their particularly close quarters.

And you, Scarlet, are the cherry.

With a dismissive shake of her head, she scooped up her computer and made her way to the designated conference room for a scheduled rendezvous with her team. Tomorrow would bring an initial meeting with Optik. The two sides would volley back and forth until she had what she needed to report to Ethan regarding the legitimacy of Optik's asking price.

As she strode into the conference room, Scarlet acknowledged her colleagues seated around an antique mahogany conference table that must have weighed a thousand pounds. A huge vase, overflowing with yellow daisies and azaleas, anchored the dark expanse of wood, while crystal chandeliers hung low over a careless smattering of laptops and coffee mugs. The ravenous wolves she called coworkers had eaten all the damn Danishes.

Adopting a smooth air of indifference, she prepared for knowing looks, maybe even perceptive comments. She couldn't expect her in-flight closeness with Ethan to have gone undetected. Even if their little foray into PDA had flown under the radar, someone must have noted that their spat before boarding contrasted against Ethan's attentiveness in getting her to the hotel and checked in after they'd landed in Copenhagen.

Plus there was the matter of the adjoining suites.

Yet when she looked around, ready to take her medicine, the group collectively noted her entrance with disinterest. After a round of quick *hellos*, heads re-bowed and fingers re-engaged. And, yeah, it was occasionally a lucky break to be surrounded by people who were simply too busy to worry about anyone or anything besides themselves and their own obligations.

She walked around to Brian Wentworth at the far end of the table and began setting up shop. While the rest of the team had let her off the hook, Brian immediately stopped flirting with the big-breasted associate to his left. The sudden break in conversation emphasized his eyes on her as she plugged into a gilded socket. Theirs was a friendship forged in the trial by fire of the young-lawyer trenches at JTS. They'd been pulling document review all-nighters and orchestrating three-in-the-morning pizza runs for years. Now Brian's sly grimace let her know he'd sensed the Ethan-Scarlet dynamic, *whatever that was.*

"How's your room, Scar?"

Scar. Her second-worst nickname. The more she reminded Brian not to use it, the more he "forgot" not to liken her to a partially-healed flesh wound.

"Room's fine. Don't you think?" she replied in a monotone, not bothering to look up as her computer booted.

"The view?" he asked, pretending she hadn't injected a question of her own.

"Fantastic."

"Your neighbor?" Now his eyes sparkled with ill-suppressed glee.

Looking up, she met Brian's gaze and simply licked her lips. Slowly.

His eyes went wide and his voice drifted into sing-song. "*Knew it.* Nobody looks that dreamy after hours on a plane. Not even me." He muted his outburst, but it still garnered attention. "I mean, no one pulls off long trips like you, Scar. Really, you're a natural traveler. Such *stamina.*"

Brian cracked his knuckles and began typing furiously. His instant message came fast. *But be careful, honey. Not sure of his plans for you. Can't tell whether he wants business, revenge, sex…*

Scarlet swallowed and gazed at Brian over their screens. She nodded silently in answer. *Most likely all three.*

******

Mentally grappling with a plan to turn the tide, Scarlet wandered the corridor outside her room, dressed for dinner alfresco but feeling like saltines in bed.

Ethan opened his door with suspiciously impeccable timing. "Can't get my mind off the flight," he murmured, falling in step.

No kidding. "Try harder."

"Harder," he said solemnly, "is an interesting choice of words."

She stopped, needing to clear the air before their dining with Optik's top players. "Ethan, you know this can't happen."

"This?" He looked around in mock confusion. "I'm walking down the hall. Not exactly untoward."

"We cannot happen." *Even though I want you so badly.* "No flirting." *Because then I'll let "us" happen.* "No touching." *Because we want each other for different reasons.*

"Tell me why." Ethan didn't sound angry, exactly, more like tense.

Hello chest squeeze. She swallowed hard, eyes darting around the corridor, stalling everywhere but his questioning face. The motivation behind his tenderness on the flight and his lingering interest couldn't be noble. They may have delved into the personal on the plane, but they'd avoided the elephant in the room. Her accusation of violence and his subsequent imprisonment weren't going away.

They'd also ignored the little fact the he was her client and a big catch for her firm. Ethan was off limits no matter how many past demons they overcame.

"You know why," she said, finally responding to his demand for an explanation.

With that, she resumed her trek to dinner, intent on ignoring how well he filled out his designer suit. Most men couldn't work the classic cut of Dior Homme, but the midnight wool of the suit and the equally dark silk shirt, tieless and barely open at the throat, only combined to make him look bigger, sleeker. Equal parts dangerous and erotic.

And Ethan *was* a danger to her. So much so she feared she couldn't handle his brand of hurt.

"Bullshit." He towered over her, his voice at once sensual and menacing. "We're both attracted, and you have neither a meaningful nor convincing reason as to why we can't enjoy each other."

More like use each other, she thought, startled by his revealing choice of words. But how utterly tempting.

"Then let me spell it out." She came to an abrupt halt, her need to understand Ethan's motives driving the whole sticky scenario from her lips. "I accused you of trying to kill me, an accusation that landed you in a notorious prison for months and shattered your livelihood and future plans. I tried to reconcile. You made it clear any apology from me was both unwanted and unacceptable. You hinted that revenge would be sweet. Fast-forward nine years. You drag me unwittingly into your now-luxurious corporate world, bent on executing a plan only you understand. What is it, Ethan? What *is* your plan? What must I endure for you to feel better? I've paid my dues."

Her heart worked in painful beats. The simple act of verbalizing her fears initiated great rushes of emotion that left her floundering. All the pent-up suspicion and worry had provided a framework of almost physical support, a tension she hadn't known she'd come to rely on.

Without a word, Ethan snaked an arm around her waist. Like on the plane, his other hand went to her face, her hair, stroking in that way of his that both comforted and aroused. He made low, whirling sounds in the back of his throat, and within moments, her heart no longer squeezed in painful lurches and her breathing returned to normal.

When she peeked up at him from within the embrace, he refused to meet her gaze. Evading her barrage of questions, he focused on her lower lip, rubbing at it with his thumb.

"I'm not that complex. No tricks," he said darkly. His voice dropped and his head descended to nuzzle the base of her throat when he murmured, "You know exactly what I want, Empress."

The calm evaporated. He'd momentarily lifted the fear of being ground under his heel only to throw it over her again. To him, the name "Empress" functioned as a weapon. He used the mock endearment to maim. On the plane, when he'd touched her with such care, he hadn't called her that. Instead, he'd called her "sweetheart," his voice low and reverent, as though she were a treasure, not a piece or three of heart-shaped candy he badly wanted to eat.

Battling a tide of emotion, she pushed at his chest. Rather than displacing him, the shove sent her reeling. Quickly, he reached for her hips, steadying her heavy sway before trailing his hands across her stomach and dropping them to his sides.

"I don't want the same things you do." She didn't trust herself to say more.

He straightened carefully, then turned to pluck a rose from a vase situated on a nearby sideboard. He snapped the stem and slid the flower behind her ear, all the while looking as cool and unaffected as she was shattered.

Panting, she met his amused stare. "Dammit, Ethan," she whispered, frustrated that her honesty hadn't reached him. "I can't be casual about us." The low entreaty didn't halt the perusal that meandered along her body from flower stem to dress hem, and she snapped her mouth shut.

Stop baring your soul to someone who doesn't care to see it.

"Then don't be," he said enigmatically, leaving Scarlet standing stoically against the wall of the corridor, chest heaving and hands fisted at her sides.

CHAPTER 8

Dinner impressed everyone but her—an evening garden party on the terrace of the Restaurant l'Alsace. The patio blazed with candlelight. Beyond the fringe of the glow, handsome half-timbered, ochre houses peeked over a border of raised flower boxes.

After two days of negotiations, both sides felt that despite slow progress, the acquisition held promise. Five courses and a tide of red wine later, folks were primed and ready to relax and enjoy a more personal affair.

Scarlet hadn't arranged the meal, which meant Ethan at least understood the art of adding a social dynamic. The only way to really get through to people—stressed-out business types especially—was to reach out on a human level, generally with food in one hand and booze in the other. The Optik lineup had to like Ethan and his team. Achieve *the like*, and an agreement would be infinitely more attainable.

Raw from their encounter at the hotel, Scarlet studiously avoided Ethan throughout the night. He'd made it clear he wanted her, *and God*, she wanted him, too. But his desire was purely physical, whereas she also wanted forgiveness, friendship, acceptance, even caring. All needs that wouldn't be met by the simple sex he offered. Scratch that—the anything-but-simple, mind-blowing, spine-out-of-alignment sex he offered.

The feast was winding to a close, and she glanced up to see Ethan studying her intently. He averted his gaze, but not before she caught a glimpse of feeling seething through the candlelight. There was lust, yes, intense and violent. But she also detected curiosity, even craving, in the way his eyes continually crept back after their reluctant desertion.

She leaned forward to reach for her wine, her movements slow with exhaustion. When her fingers closed around the delicate stem of her glass, she heard the chime of fork tines ringing against crystal. Looking up, she watched Ethan rise to his feet, easily commanding the attention of his guests. "I'd like to say a few words. A toast"—a leisurely survey of the audience brought his eyes to hers—"to our *team* and to the coming weeks."

The collective focus shifted in her direction. Tipsy office workers who'd dutifully awaited a message from their fearless leader now peered at her with scandalized interest, *her* people included. She sipped her Bordeaux before carefully setting it aside, maintaining a casual appearance despite the beginnings of an inner chill.

Ethan continued to speak as though directly to her, his head tilted at a mocking incline. "May our hard work here in Denmark bear fruit. If all goes as planned"—a deafening pause—"it will result in our *joining*. A satisfying endeavor, I'm sure."

His meaning hit like a furnace blast. Yet she knew to show nothing, not the resentment, certainly not the hurt. Finally, when her nerves stretched to the breaking point over whether another humiliating innuendo would follow, he raised his glass and said, "To us." The crowd joined him, shouting "Skål!" as they downed their drinks like a rollicking clan of conquering Viking assholes.

Several people didn't bother to subdue their amused cackles, and she swallowed the growl that rose in her throat, hardly able to comprehend he'd made her the target of his jest. Alone, the toast would have been fine, but combined with his intense stare and the marked tension radiating between them, the double entendre hadn't been lost on their colleagues.

She clung to the fact that, by and large, Europeans didn't suffer the fool of sexual repression. Optik's people would view Ethan's comment as a legitimately funny and lighthearted joke, something to giggle over and no more. To her own colleagues, however, she'd lost a great deal of face.

Ethan had declared war. In so doing, he'd set out to undermine her professional integrity and competence, knocking her down with his insinuation that she was nothing more than a plaything.

He'd succeeded. Glancing around, her cool look didn't last. Soon her face flamed at the knowing smirks directed her way.

And now, despite the fatigue pulling at every limb, she couldn't leave. Bolting after a show like that would play right into his hands.

She summoned her strength along with a practiced smile. *Focus. Don't let him win.* Letting her face fall into an unconcerned mask, she homed in on Susan, The Minion, who at least in her mind, was responsible for the repeated and sure-to-suck hall encounters she would undoubtedly endure over their stay at the d'Angleterre.

Likely in her early forties, Susan was attractive in an efficient sort of way. Tonight she'd dressed conservatively in a dark business suit and hose set against dated pumps with that trying-to-be-leather sheen and slightly roughened texture.

Even though others had begun to shuffle seats or head inside to the bar or to the restroom, Susan sat still, chain smoking and looking damned unapproachable as she eyed a discussion between Ethan, Ron Michael, and Optik's CEO, Arland Magnus.

Personality-minus, Scarlet thought.

Taking a deep breath, Scarlet scooted into a seat next to the ash tray. "Nice job with the dinner, Susan. May I call you that?" *Or should I stick with The Minion?*

Susan exhaled smoke, not *in* Scarlet's direction per se, but also not away from it. "If you'd like."

"Do you always accompany Ethan on business trips?"

"Usually. Ms. Leore—"

"Scarlet, please."

"Scarlet, then. I police the distractions." Her eyes inched over Scarlet's emerald cocktail dress, making it clear she considered Scarlet to be one such distraction. Ethan's speech hadn't helped, and Scarlet fumed through a fresh wave of resentment.

Striving to remain aloof, Scarlet added, "I'm sure there are many demands on Ethan's time, not all of them legitimate."

Susan's look intensified, and Scarlet could tell the woman didn't appreciate her inability to ruffle Scarlet's feathers. "*Always.*"

Cocking her head slightly, Scarlet considered Susan as she sat there smoking and watching. Why the dislike? Even if Susan knew about Scarlet and Ethan's past, Ethan had done nothing to outwardly indicate his people should harbor hard feelings. This was his show, and therefore, he set the tone. And here Susan did her best to alienate his lead counsel, an odd move for their little cruise director, a role that generally involved bringing the smiles and rainbows.

Perhaps Susan took subtle cues from Ethan, and after that toast, she'd decided Scarlet was along purely for Ethan's entertainment. In that case, Scarlet almost couldn't fault the woman's aloofness. Ethan had made it quite clear *he* didn't take her seriously, so why should his minion? Scarlet now faced two options—try the feminine bonding thing or skip the bull and make it clear she was higher in the food chain and that, yes, shit did flow downhill.

Though the latter held great appeal, Scarlet grudgingly opted for the former, at least at the start, saying, "So how many deals have you and Ethan worked?

Susan's response was sharp. "All of them."

"Wonderful. You know the ropes."

Susan turned her gaze to Ethan and spoke in a low, almost carnal tone Scarlet wouldn't have believed she possessed. "You could say that."

Okaaay. Secretary-plus.

"What do you think of Optik?" Scarlet asked, hoping to guide them to more comfortable ground.

"The price is too high."

And your basis for that is? Oh yeah, nothing. "How so?"

Ignoring Scarlet's question, Susan stood and stretched. "Great chat, Ms. Leore, really. But mine is an early morning." Susan listed toward Ethan with a small, insolent smile. "And yours is likely a late night." With a meaningful look, she lit another cigarette and walked off the terrace in the direction of the hotel.

Scarlet stared after Susan, sure her WTF look had taken firm root. Ethan's assistant/taskmaster/friend/*maybe one-time lover* had given her the slip, right after blatantly accusing her of sleeping with the enemy.

With Susan gone, Scarlet succumbed to the creep of stress and fatigue. The endless days of the Scandinavian summer encouraged one to forget the time. The sun had finally faded around ten p.m. hours ago. She'd lingered long enough, she hoped, to show Ethan's little toast held no particular significance, at least not to her. With any luck, his audience would begin to question whether they'd imagined his intimations.

Rolling her head on her shoulders, she acknowledged her body's demand for sleep, however unlikely a full night's rest might be. Even the best hotels differed significantly from her overpriced urban fortress in New York, with its twenty-four hour, specially-trained security personnel. Yet, perhaps her mounting exhaustion and the sheer luxury of her bedding would lull her into a much-needed nap. Tension throbbed at the back of her skull, and all the neck rolls in the world weren't siphoning the ache from her protesting muscles. Looking around, Scarlet assured herself the remaining revelers were entertained.

They wouldn't miss her.

******

Ethan's weren't the only eyes that followed Scarlet when she stood to leave. He watched her acknowledge a few appreciative glances before adopting her brand of a thanks-but-don't-ask smile.

The emerald dress ended just above the knee and swirled around her body like water. A wide black belt showcased the curve of her waist and the gentle flare of her smooth, rounded hips. Instead of a vee, her neckline fashioned a loose oval that shifted when she moved, displaying the creamy skin of her collarbones and the barest hint of pale cleavage.

His double entendre had hit its mark. The look on her face had reflected a woman condemned—part dread, part acceptance, even a dose of shame. In aiming the jibe at Scarlet, he'd come out the loser. The pinch in his chest could only be regret.

She didn't trust him, and frankly, she was wise to be wary. Ethan couldn't predict whether he'd seduce Scarlet for revenge. Even if his conscience reared its ugly head as it was apparently wont to do, he could easily—almost subconsciously—be careless with her, staging a high-stakes game with her affections.

And judging from her sweet, hot response on the plane and her subsequent attempts at self-preservation, she didn't know how to play.

Scarlet had damaged him, not only with the time in Rikers, but also the desperate crawl from the black void after his exoneration. His subsequent successes didn't dissolve the past. Yet each time she showed even the faintest glimpse of distress, admittedly in response to something he said or did, he panicked. There'd been moments when he would have done anything, *everything* to sooth her. It dawned on him that he might not be capable of intentionally causing her a moment of true pain.

Despite his preconceived notions, Scarlet had proven smart and strong. Likable. And what a glorious lover she would make. Images of voluptuous curves rocketed through his brain—Scarlet undulating beneath him, sucking a breath as he stroked her breasts, tongued her sex. Sitting there, he could feel her hands all over his body. His cock jerked violently, and he broke into a sweat.

Looking through the terrace doors, he watched Scarlet approach the maître d', her squeezable ass swaying slightly as she strolled on strappy nude heels. She spoke with the host briefly, and after a moment, the man smiled and picked up the phone for a short call. Scarlet waited patiently, giving Ethan a chance to admire her profile and contemplate what she needed. A cab? With the hotel a block away?

After a few minutes, Scarlet peered out the front doors into the night. When she turned to retrace her steps, Ethan saw her lips were drawn into a tight line. She raised a hand to unconsciously rub the base of her neck, a move he'd seen her make repeatedly throughout the night, and his hands itched to massage away her soreness and tension. He clenched them in his lap, resisting her pull.

Pacing now—and clearly unaware of being observed—Scarlet's anxiety grew palpable. *What's wrong, sweetheart?*

When a black Mercedes cab pulled up a few yards from the door, Scarlet's gaze eased to the now-empty host stand. The man had left to seat a large group, and noting his continued absence, Scarlet hesitated. She glanced around the restaurant, rooted in place. When the maître d' didn't appear after long moments, she took a deep breath as though preparing for a daunting task. Then she darted out the door and into the waiting cab, whisked away into the night.

Ethan's hackles rose. Scarlet hadn't mentioned having friends in the city or wanting to visit any favorite nighttime haunts. Yet she'd left the gathering in a cab, alone and at midnight. He recognized nerves when had saw them. Scarlet had embarked on a venture that made her extremely uncomfortable.

She'd looked guilty.

Ethan's pulse quickened with the doubt that crept inward. Too many competitors would love to get their hands on Optik. A leak could kill the acquisition while both sides sat gauging a reaction in Atavos's stock price. Inside info about the deal could also encourage another potential buyer to blatantly interfere.

The market had been curious about *One*. Rumors flew. Negotiations needed to progress quickly—if a deal was imminent—before news broke that Atavos courted Optik. Ethan's own marketing machine would spin the story if, and when, it hit the media.

Surely Scarlet wouldn't risk so far a fall. But then, why would she sneak away in a cab at midnight in a strange city without a word about her plans? He wrapped his discussion with Billboard and Optik's CEO and trotted over to the hotel.

Ordering a martini in the lobby lounge, he took a seat in full view of the hotel's entrance, planning to intercept Scarlet upon her return and ferret out whether her little foray involved business or pleasure.

If pleasure, she might have a valid reason for rebuffing his advances, which was a *bso-fucking-lutely fine*. If business, then despite his inclination to soften, maybe he wasn't against seeing her suffer after all.

Unfortunately for her, Scarlet never returned.

CHAPTER 9

The hit reverberated from Ethan's wrist to shoulder. Waiting as pain lanced through his arm, he gritted his teeth and focused upward, tracking a grimy maze of piping and ductwork that mottled the ceiling of the basement gym he'd found near the hotel.

On a greedy inhale, he tasted dust and sweat. If the gym had made efforts to filter and condition the air, they'd failed. A drinkable musk floated around him.

Pulling his head together, he refocused with proper stance. Otherwise, he'd come away with injuries from a fucking leather bag. Throwing a second jab, and then a third and a fourth, Ethan repeatedly slammed his fist forward, letting the frustration flow from his gloved knuckles into the swinging target.

In between punches, his mind rehashed the possible reasons for Scarlet's late night. Perhaps she had a love interest squirreled away in Copenhagen. He wouldn't put it past her to keep a Nordic princeling full of European money on a vacation leash. Yet she hadn't behaved like a taken woman on the plane. Instead, he'd sensed a tantalizing lack of practice in her passionate, yet hesitant response.

Knowing he might have read her wrong, that she could have played him with those innocent gasps and her bewildered shock after that staggering orgasm, brought a rush of violence. He swung with abandon, rounding on the bag with a brutal kick that sent it swinging.

Right now, Scarlet knew more than anyone about the deal, even him. She would provide a status report later in the morning, and he wondered if the document had already been sent to another executive or, worse, a media outlet willing to pay her price. A lover was possible, but a better explanation of her midnight foible involved an anonymous Internet café from which Scarlet could send messages about the mediocre status of negotiations between Atavos and Optik. She'd never risk her own or any other traceable computer.

He'd been so focused on his own motives for hiring Scarlet he hadn't acknowledged the possibility of her having an axe to grind. The "why" wasn't yet clear, but life had dealt Scarlet a significant financial blow. People betrayed loved ones for less, and there was little love lost between them.

Betrayal burned in his gut as he worked in four-minute rounds, repeating a series of punches. The repetitive motion—left, right, right, left, right, right—gradually diffused his temper, and his pace slowed with each progressive blow. After endless hits, he adopted a steady rhythm that allowed him to consider a measured approach with Scarlet. She'd be questioned. He'd learn from her responses. And God help her if she lied.

For a moment, he considered letting Billboard deal with her. Billboard wouldn't be swayed by how badly he wanted to fuck the woman.

Then again, maybe not. Most men were susceptible to her brand of curvaceous, sex-on-a-stick perfection. In fact, the majority wouldn't see past it. They lacked his... personal experience and wouldn't believe such an innocent facade capable of unparalleled duplicity.

After his Scarlet-induced stint in maximum security, he knew otherwise.

******

Scarlet's inner bitch roared, not in a power play, but because she was really pissed off.

Ten people, five each from Atavos and Optik, gathered in Optik's conference room. Scandinavian to the core, the dark and pretentious mahogany and leather furnishings of her New York office gave way to clean, modern lines done in light woods. Optik excelled in the school of Norse simplicity.

In fact, Optik might have been too successful in its quest for minimalism. Overdoing it had apparently impaired Optik's ability to store records, or so Optik would have her believe.

Stalemate.

Insecurities rang in her ears while she planned a great save, mentally flailing for a compelling argument that would bring Optik around. Tongue tripping over the words, she heard her father's last bit of vitriol. *"I built your mother from the ground up, just like you... Without me and the money you carelessly throw away, you'll crumble."*

He'd been wrong. She hadn't dissolved in self-doubt. But she walked a knife's edge. One wrong move and she'd tumble from either side into an abyss, sans safety net.

While Ethan watched, laughing his ass off.

The king of her personal hell sat diagonally across the table. Undeniably *hot*, he said little, but each time she looked in his direction, his gaze struck like a coiled snake. That cold fire pinned the lack of cooperation from Optik squarely on her shoulders. He shifted impatiently in his seat, probably mentally sticking with last night's theme that she made a better Barbie than barrister.

Swallowing, Scarlet slid a chart across the table to Arland Magnus, her movements quick and efficient. "This list reflects Optik's portfolio as you've represented it. We haven't been able to verify the existence of over *fifty percent* of the entries on the list. You'll need to provide copies of each of the noted patent applications, along with autobiographical information such as serial number, file date, and status."

Grumbling in low tones, Optik's CEO grabbed the list. Small companies often prided themselves on their ability to react quickly to the market, but they lacked necessary personnel and sophistication. They moved fast, but their moves were messy. Then the so-called small stuff drowned them in the transition between the baby pool and the deep end.

Arland clearly viewed Atavos's due diligence efforts as a waste of time. He thought he *knew* the worth of his company, and that, eventually, he could find a buyer to accept his take-it-or-leave-it strategy. A damning blow might do him some good.

Scarlet's looked to Ethan with raised brows, expecting him to mirror her concern. Instead, he sat back, twirling a pen around his middle finger in rapid beats. At her curious glance, his eyes narrowed with ill-concealed menace.

His disappointment speared *her*, not Arland.

Sickness settled in her gut. Ethan had his own imaginary reasons to be displeased. Providing him with real ones would court disaster.

With a deep and, she hoped, imperceptible breath, she shut Ethan out and leveled a glacial stare on Arland. "Let me be clear, this process involves an *independent* analysis of the value of Optik's technology and whether it would behoove Atavos to own it. We don't take your word for it. If you do not, or cannot, provide the information we seek, this deal *will* fail."

"Ms. Leore, our asking price is fair, low even. Numerous buyers would love to be in Atavos's position at this very moment."

The implied threat couldn't be ignored. Scarlet leaned forward, balling her fists below the table. "Might I—"

"Remind you," Ethan said, jumping in with a scathing retort, "that we are operating under a signed letter of intent that requires Optik and Atavos to negotiate *exclusively* and in good faith." His voice flat-lined and he stood, slowly circling his chair before settling the bulk of his forearms across its leather back. "There will be *no other buyers* for Optik until those guidelines are met. As for other interested parties? Give them this shit"—he leaned over and rattled the incomplete chart that lay on the table—"and they'll slip through Optik's fingers like Atavos is about to."

The words were clearly directed at Optik. The rage behind them, however, arced toward Scarlet like a live wire.

Arland sat rigid in his seat, refusing to rise to the bait, so Scarlet simply let Ethan's outburst sink in before moving on.

She cleared her throat, shifting attention from Ethan's rising hostility to the agenda. "I also wanted to cover raw materials. We need to see the purchasing agreements with your suppliers to determine whether they're assignable to Atavos upon the sale of Optik."

This time Arland's answer was immediate. "We have the contracts." His lips lifted in a smug smile. "In Danish."

She responded after giving him a moment to gloat, offering an easy grin of her own. "We can get translations within twenty-four hours." *Always a step ahead, asshole.* "Looking at the material lists, we haven't identified any other bottlenecks…"

The meeting droned on until they touched all the salient points. Optik would again have time to drum up the requested information and documentation. Then her team would analyze and crunch more numbers.

Worn from long, stressful hours and a lack of sleep in the hotel room she'd had such high hopes for, Scarlet rose and doggedly packed the papers shuffled about the table. The sun beat through the windows, announcing a perfect day to explore the city on foot. Dragging or not, she'd take advantage of the lull resulting from Optik's delay. The first order of business would be to remedy a grave oversight—she'd been in Denmark for days without gorging on European chocolate.

Ethan's light grasp on her shoulder interrupted visions of dancing cacao beans. "Let's talk," he ground out, features tense.

She stiffened but didn't pull away. "About?" The negotiations were spiraling downward. She didn't need him to point out their increasingly inevitable failure. Perhaps Optik wasn't interested—or interested enough—in selling. If that proved true, an angry pep talk from Ethan wouldn't salvage the project. It would destroy morale. Jerking from his grasp, she rushed to stuff the last spreadsheets into her briefcase, feeling an inexplicable need to escape the tension with the rest of the grunts.

He trailed after their departing colleagues before closing the door behind the last straggler. Still gripping the handle, he didn't turn around when he said, "Have a seat, Scarlet."

If anything, she stood taller, snapping her bag shut with a smart click. "Again, why?"

"Sit." When he finally turned, his rigid stance said any argument would be futile. Letting her gaze travel up his body, she instinctively stepped away from the fire burning in his onyx eyes. Heavy lids descended to shut her out, like he didn't trust himself to look at her.

Wary of the violence emanating from a man she barely trusted, Scarlet obeyed, but rather than sink into the nearest chair, she balanced on the edge of the seat, poised for immediate flight. "What can I do for—"

"An interesting question." His eyes opened, and he reached for the back of a second chair, rolling it to the space in front of her. "And one with many answers."

He sat, too close, with his knees bracketing hers. Her smaller body responded to his massive one like a chemical reaction, her core instantly warming. The moment she detected a slight tremor in her thighs, his eyes went heavy-lidded. The man knew the effect of his proximity. And he enjoyed causing her discomfort.

"Why are you here, Scarlet?" The rumble of his voice scraped across raw nerves.

His chair-back faced an internal window spanning the length of the conference room. Even though they sat in a fishbowl, Ethan and the furniture hid most of her body from view. True to form, Ethan took advantage of their makeshift privacy. His knuckles traced the length her arms, skimming toward her fingertips until coming to rest in her lap. His hands were warm against the tops of her thighs, the gentleness of his touch at odds with the viciousness in his stare.

Apprehension prickled beneath her skin. His question *should* have been rhetorical. "I guess I don't know what you mean." She was an open book. The project would help build the legal practice she desperately needed to pay the bills, plain and simple. In theory, she'd get in, get out, and get paid. *He* was the one who'd been dishonest about his motivations. Sure, he wanted Optik, but he also wanted a piece of her.

"Of course not," he growled, squeezing the pliant flesh above her knees, not causing pain, but with enough force to get her attention.

The touch didn't work in the way he might have imagined or even the way she would have expected. Instead of putting the fear of God in her, her body went warm and lax. "Fine. You want to know why I'm in this room specifically?" she purred. "Or why I'm in Copenhagen? You know the answers to both questions." Last night, he'd made his attraction plain, announced it to the world. Perhaps he wouldn't like finding out the feeling wasn't mutual. If she could muster the lie.

"Do I?" His hands began to move back and forth over her lap, caressing each leg through the soft linen pulled tight over her thighs. "I don't think so."

"Because you don't think at all," she snapped. Unlike him, her sleepless nights left time to examine her ill-conceived decision to come to Denmark. Crossing her legs, she rid herself of his roving fingertips. "You hired my firm, and me specifically, to negotiate the purchase of Optik. That's what brought me to Denmark and that's what has me here this morning."

Looking at his hands, she damned her yearning to have them back on her legs. "Did you want it to be something else? You perhaps? Maybe a long-felt need to please you or beg for forgiveness?" She slid to the edge of her seat, masking the truth of her words with a hard look. "I already tried that. Didn't work, remember?"

"How could I forget?" he sneered. "Guess the guilt's worn off. Now you're willing to sell my company out to the highest…"

Ethan kept going, seething, flaying her alive with cruel accusations of corporate betrayal that she could neither absorb nor understand. She heard him but receded into herself, wondering vaguely what brought this on.

Some lawyers put up with aggressive, borderline abusive shit from their clients. Too many in her opinion. Reminding herself she wasn't one of them, she stood to leave, cutting Ethan off mid-tirade.

But when she rose, his long, muscular legs kept her bracketed between his big body and the chair. He reached around to snug the edge of the seat behind her knees, forcing her down onto the cushion.

She wasn't going anywhere.

******

"We've established you didn't come to Denmark to make amends, though if I were you, I'd reconsider." Ethan cleared his throat, but all the gravel refused to smooth out. She'd deceived him. Used him. *Again.* A muscle in his jaw began to twitch with barely suppressed fury, and he held up a warning hand. "I'm not an enemy you want, Scarlet, and you're well on your way to making me one."

Pain crossed her face briefly, but anger quickly replaced it, and then finally, a convincing rendition of bewilderment. In a smaller voice, she said, "I don't understand, Ethan. Get to your point."

"This *act* is beneath even you."

Ethan watched her grapple with which persona to present. Apparently strong and confident won out over seductive and surprised or innocent and confused, for the time being. With a defiant toss of that golden mane, she shifted out of her bemused mien.

"You're wrong," she said, drawing the words out, "about whatever offense you imagine I've committed."

Really? So tell me where you go during your midnight haunts. "Where did you disappear to last night after dinner?"

She passed an unsteady hand over her forehead, abruptly looking less comfortable, more on edge. "You're talking in riddles." Her eyes darted away. "I went to the hotel."

Eventually. "That so?" he prodded, allowing his voice to reveal *all* the disbelief and skepticism coursing through his system. Grasping the armrests

70

protruding from her seat, he began moving Scarlet back and forth by her chair, bringing her knees into contact with his and then rolling her away as far as his arms would reach. To an outsider, the movement would appear to be a lazy sway, maybe even a gentle flirtation. But between them, it was a pure demonstration of control. He had it. She didn't.

When she stayed quiet, he pressed, "You called a cab to travel one city block on a hot, crowded night?"

A heartbeat passed before she answered. A mere moment, but glaring. "I made a detour," she rationalized, head rising and chin jutting forward. Her hands tightened and released her quads, right over the spot he'd squeezed. "I... needed things from the drugstore, then..."

Disappointment ripped through him like an acid wash. Ethan had wanted to be wrong more desperately than he'd realized, and facing her deceit nearly sent him to his knees. Even now, with the lie fresh on her lips, he wanted to kiss her, to drag her to the carpet and drown in pleasure. But the two of them weren't to be.

She hadn't detoured to the drugstore. Ethan would have intercepted her return to the hotel after a mere shampoo run. He'd waited for hours. And if she'd been gallivanting about on a romantic tryst or some otherwise legal endeavor, she'd have owned up to save her ass.

"You *lie*," he snarled. Grasping for control, he released his grip on her armrests and rolled his chair away, needing some distance from the tired, wan face that made him ache to apologize for his harshness. "And that's one thing you don't get to do. You won't be needing those *things from the drugstore*, Empress. You're through."

In every way I can manage.

Blinking at him, her expression went blank. She hadn't expected this. He could see that much. The surprise made her appear even more bewildered and vulnerable.

Ignoring her subconscious appeal, he spoke in a bored voice calculated to be heard beyond their private room. "You're fired. Susan will see to your flight. Coach. Hell, the cargo hold if she can arrange it." He paused for a long, impatient breath. "And let's hope this farce doesn't permeate the JTS team." Little chance of that. Selling him out had been personal, the exact thing he'd vowed to watch for in his decision to bring her onboard.

Ethan stood and stared at her in disgust, refusing to react to the flash of pain and disbelief Scarlet couldn't hide and hardening himself against the continuing urge to comfort.

Save it. You've been fool enough.

"Expect an investigation." After turning toward the door, he stopped. Rather than look over his shoulder and tempt himself to take it all back, he stared out the internal window to where their colleagues pretended to go about a normal day.

Then he nodded, more to himself than her, only now recognizing that fate had dealt a certain poetic justice.

"Perhaps I won't be the only one of us to see the inside of a prison cell, Empress."

CHAPTER 10

The trap had sprung.

Scarlet hunched over the edge of a park bench, entirely numb except for the diet soda that slipped down her throat to join the melee of nausea coiling in her stomach. The laughter of nearby children and tourists reminded her the day was a beautiful one. With any awareness, one could smell the tang of iodine and salt as it spread over the city from where the sea thrust itself inward through winding canals. But little of the splendor registered, not when, as Ethan had said, *she was through.*

Careful years had preceded this, her most egregious mistake since the night she'd decided to walk alone after dark in a shitty neighborhood. This time, her error hadn't taken the form of refusing help. It had been an act of accepting it. *Never* should she have trusted him.

Swallowing, her throat spasmed in indecision over whether she'd be sick. A trash can beckoned from across the cobblestone walkway. If worse came to worst...

Ethan's offer had been too good to refuse. But, *dammit*, she'd known it was also too good to be true—a plum, well-paying, and well-respected client that would rocket her toward partnership and, with it, a greater measure of financial security. While she'd been rightfully leery, Scarlet had trusted him to relegate any revenge to petty annoyances she could handle.

Jokes at dinner? Doable. Single-handedly dismantling her legal career? Not so much.

Denmark had been a grave miscalculation. By bathing her in bright, comforting light before plunging her into darkness, Ethan had left her not only fearful for her future, but also completely disoriented.

Shivering in the evening sun, Scarlet sat back against the scratchy wood of the bench and closed her eyes. Fishing her mobile from her purse, she reminded herself the bastard had planned this from the beginning. She'd played right into his hands. At the airport, when he'd threatened her with ruination—a punishment she now knew he'd planned to carry out at the first opportunity—she should've laughed in his face and left him high and dry. Yet she'd taken the high road, which, like in any tragedy worth its ticket price, had been easily usurped by the low one.

A text from Brian buzzed in. He recommended waiting Ethan out, even offered up his own suite as home base.

Sure. Run straight from Ethan's accusations to Brian's room, where the two of them would get shitfaced and watch romantic comedies. Every few months, Brian made a casual suggestion that they'd do well "as more than friends" because "hot people belong together," or some such gibberish. The co-worker thing aside, Brian's sky-is-the-limit metrosexuality put her on edge. He liked women and maintained a tight ship on his "chick calendar," but he also liked manicures and pedicures and midi rings. Scarlet just couldn't *do* that.

Contemplating a career in peril had her absently raising chilled fingertips to her ears. The earrings were her only remaining valuables worth enough to sustain her lease and other necessities for any length of time. The unemployment Ethan threatened might eventually demand their liquidation.

Feeling carefully, she detected the scars the large stones adeptly concealed. A plastic surgeon had repaired the wreckage left in the wake of having the studs ripped to freedom through protesting cartilage and skin. Now only thin raised lines hinted at the trauma.

She pictured herself ordering a pair of cheap, cubic zirconium monstrosities to cover the scars in the earrings' absence. In this, Ethan would ultimately, even if unwittingly, hand her dad the last laugh. She'd have proven him right, showing herself to be completely incapable of making it without his backing. "*I'll see you when the money runs out,*" he'd said.

The jewels would go long before she'd bow to Tripp Leore.

Shaking her head dizzily, she saw the hotel beckon in the fading light, and she trudged across the street to the safety of her suite. She hadn't contacted Susan for a return flight. No doubt Ethan had sounded the alarm about her imaginary attempts to sink the deal, so little more than scandal awaited her in New York. She could see it now—yellow tape blocking her office while men in black poked around her desk, reviewing her every e-mail and running a forensic analysis on her computer.

Good luck with that.

She relished the idea of making Ethan pay when the facts became clear. But that dream would go unrealized. She'd been the one to teach him that innocence could be meaningless. That it doesn't matter what you did, only what your betters think you did, or worse, *want* you to have done.

You're a fast learner, Mr. Blake.

Inside her room, she slid her back down the door to land on her rear, legs folded in front of her. With arms locked tight around tucked-in shins, she laid her forehead on her knees, forcing her mind to flee her worries. Breathing slowly, she concentrated on the voice warm-ups that had lived in her brain since boarding-school choir—*one, two, three, four, five, four, three, two, one.* In her mind, her voice raised a note with each number between one and five and then descended again. Over and over, she sang in her head, never allowing reality to intrude, until finally, she drifted off for the first time in days.

She dreamt of an elusive sea of money when a violent pounding shook her into awareness.

******

Scarlet hadn't left.

Ethan raised a fist and pounded on her door, prepared to drag her bodily from the d'Angleterre if need be. He didn't care how late it was. The little traitor wouldn't spend another minute in their midst, plotting and scheming.

An answering knock sounded through the wood in the vicinity of his knees. Something had obviously hit the door from the inside. *Kicking me in spirit, are we?* The immediacy of the response said she'd been near the door when he strolled up.

Crashing an open palm against the wood, he warned her through the barrier. "You've overstayed your welcome, Scarlet."

As the last word left his lips, the door cracked and then slowly opened. While Ethan remained quiet, shock flitted down his spine. She wore the same clothes she'd had on earlier in the day, but they were rumpled, like she'd slept a night in them.

Loose blonde curls had been carelessly scraped off her pale forehead, and her raised hand rubbed at the base of her skull. She winced with each stroke, hinting at the source of that answering thud.

Her groggy eyes were dry, but they hadn't been. He'd never seen tracked mascara look so tragically beautiful, and he realized the last thing he should do was confront this woman—a vision he could barely resist—in her room. *Next to her bed.*

"What do you want, Ethan?" she croaked, letting the hand that massaged her scalp fall limp at her side.

Pushing the door wide, he prowled into the suite, searching for packed bags and finding a lived-in space. A skirt and camisole draped carelessly over a chair. A service tray, probably from breakfast, perched on her nightstand, boasting a half-eaten bagel and a mini tub of cream cheese. Shoes littered the floor in front of the television, and he was momentarily struck dumb by her array of high heels in every color and style. At the sight of one of his most sensual obsessions, he froze, imagining her walking toward him, wearing nothing but sky-high heels.

When she reached him, he would press her legs apart and lower himself to the floor in front of her. He would lick into her lush heat until she came, over and over, no longer able to balance on the stilettos. Then he would...

With a low hiss, he pushed the fantasy away and jerked the armoire open. After grabbing her suitcase and garment bag, he laid them on the mattress, a mattress with a perfectly even coverlet smoothed over its surface. The bed clearly hadn't seen a body since the maid. Had she been sleeping in front of the door? It would explain the noise, the tender skull, even the midnight perfection of her bedding.

Ignoring the pang of remorse that accompanied the realization, he spoke in a dull voice. "You're still here," he said, as though stating the obvious would fill the stillness of the dim space. Then he threw the suitcase open with every intent of seeing her packed and gone.

"So I am," she said mechanically.

Had she yelled it, he could have ignored her. But her voice was calm, soft, and when she spoke again, she reached out to still his rushing hands. "I don't have a plane ticket or a reservation at another hotel. I can't leave, Ethan."

He shook her off. "Not my problem." Back at her closet, he ripped clothes from their hangers and returned to the bed to stuff them inside her baggage.

"Ethan," she said, her increasing alarm radiating outward, "it's too late to go tonight." Her pause pulsed in the air, and he wondered what she wasn't saying. "I'll go to the airport first thing tomorrow morning. I promise. Tonight, I'm staying in this room. I'll pay for it."

The last brought him up short. "You think I give a damn whether you pay for the room? This hotel is Atavos's negotiation headquarters, Scarlet. You shouldn't even *know where we are*. Whipping out your credit card? Not quite the point." Stealing himself, he gathered her shoes from the floor, tossing pair after pair carelessly on top of the clothes he'd retrieved from the closet.

She moved to stand in front of the door, a sentinel prepared to barricade him from leaving with her things.

With her floor and closet clean, he stepped into her bathroom to grab her night cream and body lotion and all the other shit women hauled everywhere. When he flipped on the light—

His mind shorted, totally blank. "What the fuck is this?"

He couldn't believe what he was seeing. Her bathroom dripped in expensive lingerie. The towel bars, the tub, the shower curtain rod, practically every available surface sported something scorching—bras, thongs, lace panties, translucent negligees. While nothing screamed Letters to Penthouse, neither could her choices pass for demure. And he'd purchased enough women's intimates to know high-end when he saw it. Everything looked to have been set out to dry.

Nearly doubling over with the sudden force of his erection, he heard her whisper behind him, from her post by the door. "Out," she said. "Now."

He whipped around, examining her pallid face. "Well, well. An interesting find, to say the least."

"Laundry services aren't good with fine lingerie," she said breezily, her expression anything but. "Get out of my bathroom."

He sauntered toward her, full of caustic scenarios. "Quite the haul for a few days. Do you change and hand-wash your underwear three times an afternoon? Some kind of phobia? A kinky fetish?" When he reached her position by the door, he added with a leer, "I know. I've had you *really* hot and bothered, so drenched you've gone through a bucket of Woolite." He placed his arms against the door on either side of her head and whispered against her temple. "You get more captivating by the *second*."

Her arms tightened against her chest as if she were struggling to protect herself against an oncoming physical blow. She'd sold his company down the river without a twitch. Now, when he stumbled upon her silly hoard of drying undies, she worked herself into a high lather. Her posture positively transmitted... fear?

Whoa. Not what he'd expected. His arms dropped from the door, and he stood up straight. Despite the roiling bitterness, he'd never intended, or even understood, that his aggression might scare her. Yet, looking back, their previous encounters had been in public spaces and during polite hours. Now he had her backed against the wall of her private suite in the dead of night.

"Would *never* hurt you, sweetheart."

Then it didn't matter as the lust and guilt and anger coalesced in his chest. In that instant, his body took over. One hand gripped the back of her neck. The other stole around her ass to press her against him. When his lips met hers, blood sizzled along the insides of his veins. After a heartbeat, she opened to him with a low moan, and their tongues met in a hostile dance while his cock throbbed against her soft stomach.

He pulled away just as suddenly. "You make me crazy with your scheming ways and your fearful eyes and your hot fucking mouth and even hotter underwear. *I want you gone.*"

"Then take me."

Take me. The permission he'd longed for.

She went on, destroying the moment. "It's the middle of the night. I'm exhausted. I don't know the city and have no idea where to go, so if you want me somewhere else, take me there."

The words were logical. The desperation in her plea was not. Neither was her bathroom nor her combination of cool, if calculating, professional confidence and extreme personal vulnerability. He couldn't figure her out and was tired of trying. "Perhaps you should go wherever it is you went around this time last night."

Her lips quivered slightly before she rolled them over her teeth.

He groaned at the sight. "Noon. Tomorrow. Beyond that, no force on Earth could keep you in this room, Empre—"

She reared back, her shoulder blades slamming against the door as tears took hold, shocking him with their sudden onslaught and violent force. "Don't you *ever* call me that again. A man called me Empress as he *stabbed* me. A man I thought was *you*." The torrent of words wrenched out between heartbroken sobs. "Do you have any idea how it feels to be called that name? When you say it, the world seizes, and I can barely stay sane knowing you're using it to hurt me. Goddamn you! I don't want you, or this awful job, or even your apology when you figure out how wrong you are."

Once the storm passed, her eyes closed, releasing the last of her tears. On a shaky breath, her small hand lifted, and she braced her weight against his chest before her forehead bent to rest between his pecs. He flinched, not at her touch, but with the knowledge that she'd later regret seeking comfort from her tormentor.

After a charged silence, she sniffed and murmured, "I'm sorry, Ethan." And then nodding in what looked like a gesture of internal acceptance, she looked up, straight into his eyes. "I'll go tonight."

Stunned, he stared at the roots of her glossy hair, not knowing whether to confront or comfort and marveling at her innate ability to make him care whether he got it right. Here he stood in the grasp of a woman who'd fucked him over at every turn, and all he wanted to do was ensure those tears never returned on his watch. He'd had a front row ticket to a lot of feminine meltdowns. Scarlet's had been the first to reach him. Perhaps because at the end, she hadn't begged him to stay like all the rest. Not in her life. Not even in her bed. Instead, she'd agreed to go.

He backed away with a hand out, palm up in a silent offer, sensing he shouldn't touch her again without invitation. She'd made terrible choices, but unless her acting skills merited an Oscar, she neared the end of her rope. When he felt a feather-light contact slipping over his fingers, he eased her toward him, gently, slowly, just enough to get the door open behind her.

"Stay tonight, Scarlet. Go tomorrow. Please." Then he stepped around her, careful to avoid further contact, sure it would lead to a landslide that would bury them both.

CHAPTER 11

Ethan needed answers. Brian Wentworth could dish out or go down with her.

Scarlet joked around with the guy before and after meetings. From what Ethan could tell, they were buddies of sorts. On the group's first day in Copenhagen, Ethan had passed by the d'Angleterre's sunny dining room on a quick trip to his suite after morning conferences. Seated at a round two-top, Brian and Scarlet had handed their menus to an eager waiter, obviously placing their lunch orders. Then, sipping sparkling water and gazing out a bank of windows to the park across the street, the two had sat in companionable silence, appearing relaxed and well-acquainted.

In a conference later that day, when Scarlet had summarized Atavos's expectations for the negotiations and rattled off a list of information she needed from Optik, Brian had watched with guarded, yet keen, interest—the intense perusal of a man for a woman, not the respectful attentiveness one colleague for another. Ethan couldn't blame him. Scarlet only got hotter when she talked shop.

A burn settled in his chest. Who was he to care whether Brian's yearning remained wholly one-sided or whether Scarlet *occasionally* reciprocated? He did know she wasn't in an exclusive relationship with any man, or at least she hadn't been when he'd had his hand up her skirt on the plane.

He approached Brian from behind, both of them melding into the chaos of Copenhagen's bustling car-free zone, Strøget. Men manned gourmet hotdog stands that beckoned passersby with the smell of sizzling meat. Crowds of tourists gathered around street performers who perched upon makeshift podiums, providing a smorgasbord of entertainment options in exchange for a bit of spare change. Ethan watched a young girl amble by a life-size bronze statue. She jumped three feet in the air when the statue reached out and brushed her arm. Laughing, she threw five krone into a bucket that peeked from behind the "statue's" legs.

A messenger rushed his bike into a packed rack before disappearing into a nearby building with a stack of manila envelopes. Ethan chuckled to himself when a woman standing nearby glanced at her husband who bent under the weight of too many shopping bags to carry. She pointed to the kitchenware displayed in yet another shop window. Before he could stop her, she bounded in that direction, leaving her beleaguered spouse to lumber behind, shaking his head.

When Brian made a move toward Birger Christensen—no doubt on the prowl for a designer man purse and more V-neck sweaters in lavender wool—Ethan shouted from several steps back. "One would think you'd have more on your mind than fashion."

Brian stopped, and Ethan added, "After the mighty Scarlet falls, doesn't her lackey—*you*—have to pick up the slack? That would certainly be my hope and expectation, poor swindled client that I am."

Without breaking his fluid stride, Brian pulled an about-face, the air around him veritably cackling with tension. A few strides brought them chest to chest, and Brian drawled, "I'm gonna go ahead and assume, probably to my detriment, that you have something useful to say."

Brave man, Ethan thought. Few dared to antagonize him. He hadn't expected lip from the guy in skinny jeans. With a dark look and a grim sweep of his palm toward the street ahead, he *invited* Brian to tag along for a stroll.

They moved with the sea of people in silence, giving Ethan time to mentally re-run the state of affairs. Scarlet's betrayal had slowed progress, but nothing in the papers or online indicated the negotiations had gone public. Given Arland Magnus's progressively uncooperative behavior, she'd most likely solicited another favorable buyer behind the scenes, causing Arland to lose interest in Atavos. A sweeter deal waiting in the wings would explain the procrastination. The arrogance.

Optik would slog along until Ethan and Atavos grew weary of the process and threw in the towel, conveniently leaving Optik free to entertain the other offer.

In that, at least, Scarlet hadn't sunk the deal. Ethan could weather a lot of feet-dragging before growing weary and allowing negotiations to collapse.

Lifting his chin a notch, Ethan slid his gaze to the brooding lawyer that reluctantly matched him stride for stride. The show would go on until he decided otherwise, maybe with Brian at the helm. "Tell me about Scarlet's plans." *And maybe throw me a bone about the woman herself.*

Brian shrugged but didn't pretend to misunderstand. "I overheard that showdown in the conference room yesterday."

"And you knew nothing before?"

"You've got this all kinds of wrong. And my comparably meager money says you'll regret it."

"Does it now?" Ethan snapped, preparing for an unsolicited earful from Scarlet's second-in-command. *Perfect.*

Brian jerked his head toward Ethan. "You think I haven't been watching you? You might be a cold bastard, but in this, you're easy. You want her. Probably care for her. That scene at Optik was as hard on you as it was on her."

So his adversary not only knew the Scarlet-Ethan backstory, the man had serious intuition. "Bit sure of yourself. Despite everything," he bit out, refusing to meet Brian's intrusive gaze.

"I'm probably as emotionally close to Scarlet as she's ever allowed a man to get. All the shit that went down eons ago? I've watched it haunt her. Now I'm watching it peel you both."

Ethan would have laughed if the situation weren't so un-fucking-funny. Why did everything come back to nine years ago? Yeah, he was pissed and untrusting. Maybe he did want to see Scarlet pay for her mistakes. But passing his deal to the highest bidder had nothing to do with that.

This was all her and all new. "Neither Scarlet's actions nor this conversation have anything to do with Scarlet's attack."

Brian gripped his sleeve, jerking them both to a stop and earning anonymous glares as the foot traffic surged around their path. "You arrogant son of a bitch. They have everything to do with it."

The guy had mastered—invented?—the prep-school-boy-band look, but his height and obvious dedication to the gym lent him a bulk that probably got him taken seriously despite all the pastels.

He sized Brian up, gauging whether listening would be time well spent. When a pair of ice-blue eyes met his in unwavering challenge, he decided it might. "Enlighten me," he demanded, crossing his arms and waiting for Brian's epiphany, thinking if the story wasn't good, he'd take two JTS lawyers down with one roll. *Lucky strike.*

"No," Brian said bitterly, stepping away and slipping both hands into his pockets. "The mighty Ethan Blake is so goddamn untouchable he acts first and asks questions later. You sleuth things out, badly, get it all wrong, and then have the nerve to act affronted when you don't get the girl. I won't tell you shit." Then, raising both precision-tweezed brows, he added, "Maybe *I* get the girl."

Over my dead body. "I don't fucking want the girl. I want to know what she's done to my deal."

Enunciating every word with a bland smile, Brian said, "You asked Scarlet about the cab, *and she lied.*"

"Yes," Ethan bit out, fighting the urge to put Brian through a shop window. The lawyer explained it clinically, as though he accepted her lies as easily as she told them. Fresh anger tore through Ethan, leaving behind mutual twinges of illness and invincibility. Last night, when she'd fallen apart at being called "Empress," her panic and hurt had ripped at him, shaming him for his black nature and for all the things he'd said. Over and over.

In the light of day, after hearing Brian's breezy characterization of her dishonesty, he welcomed his rage back to the fold. This time, he wouldn't set it aside.

Brian set off again in hard strides. Ethan could either keep up or give up, and he wasn't sure which option held greater appeal. Scarlet's colleague had a thing for her, and he no doubt offered a relationship free of career complications and the bitter taste of past bad blood. A smart man would let his lingering curiosity about her life slide. Scarlet had been dishonest. Time to cut the cord.

But the defeated look on her face when he'd accused her of lying and the feel of her trembling against him in the wake of his eviction rampage through her suite wouldn't shake. The vacillations between hot and cold and from self-assured businesswoman to anxiety-ridden lingerie hoarder tied him in knots.

"How much do you know about Scarlet?" The question interrupted Ethan's inner debate, and he glanced up to see Brian talking over his shoulder as he strode away.

Ethan kick-started his legs. "Not nearly enough." Much of his success grew out of being an adept judge of character. Yet Scarlet had easily deceived him. With too-little thought, he'd put her in a position capable of impacting his business. His lifeblood. The bright side to her betrayal lie in the fact that his coming down on her with the force of an anvil wouldn't be mistaken for petty revenge.

"Any sense of the impact the attack had on her life?" Outwardly, Brian appeared contemplative, but Ethan swore the man enjoyed the squirm-worthy question.

"I know it was a long time ago. And that she's recovered."

"Physically? Not quite. Emotionally?" Brian's words ground to a halt. Ethan followed the man's intent gaze to a group of school children in gray-and-white uniforms. A young woman led, holding the hand of the first child, who held the hand of the second, who led the third, and so on. With the kids in sight, Brian momentarily went silent, but when his attention swung back to Ethan, his face shuttered with regret. "Dream on, lover boy."

The words elicited an unwelcome pang in Ethan's chest. Probably because he didn't enjoy being called her lover. That was *totally* it. Because he wasn't. Never would be.

He swung away. Brian could follow him this time. "I need a drink."

******

Ethan downed a British cask ale in four gulps. Slamming the glass to the solid wood table, he saw the other man looking on with cool detachment from behind a glass that appeared long-empty.

The pissing contest had morphed into a drinking one. *Game on, hipster.*

A bent man with a scruffy salt-and-pepper beard flanked a yuppie couple in front of an impressive polished cherry bar. Beyond them, the sight of a bank of genuine hand pumps threatened to bring a tear to Ethan's cynical eye. Proving they were really used, the ceiling was littered with discarded pump clips showcasing the brews that had flowed through those pumps at one time or another.

From their dim booth in the corner near an unlit hearth, Ethan scoped out the Danish micros on offer, contemplating his next entry in the who's-dick-is-bigger challenge.

As though Ethan weren't there, Brain got up and wielded his way to the bar through a hodge-podge collection of tables and chairs, returning with one beer. He took a long drink while Ethan watched.

"As far as I can tell," Brian said, "knowing about Scarlet will only make you realize what a fuckwit you are. Then you'll run as fast as you can to sweep her off her feet. Feet I enjoy *massaging*, thank you very much. No replacement needed."

Clasping his hands and staring into the beckoning froth of the fresh beer he'd managed to finagle from a passing waitress, Ethan clung to his patience. Brian couldn't know how close all the insinuation brought him to the edge. The chorded muscles in his neck strained at the thought of Brian touching *any* stretch of Scarlet's skin.

What else of hers did the bastard enjoy massaging? Ethan chuckled softly and reached across the table. He snagged Brian's wrist in a death grip. "One more fucking word—"

"For years after the attack, Scarlet suffered from anxiety… nightmares, flashbacks, panic attacks, you name it. She saw a therapist, which gradually diminished her symptoms. She rarely has trouble these days, but I've seen her flip in some run-of-the-mill situations."

Strategic or not, the interruption shut Ethan up. This was the intel he'd come for. After a warning squeeze, he threw the imprisoned arm back at its owner. "As in?"

Brian cradled his wrist, rubbing at the spot where Ethan's thumb had left a slight impression. After a moment, he smoothed the cuff of his pretty shirt into place. To think Scarlet had actually let this guy touch her feet.

Brian kept both upper appendages close to the chest when he went on. "We were on a business trip like this one. Singapore. The life drained out of

Scarlet over the duration of our stay. She started out fine, and then with each day, she grew paler. Withdrawn and jumpy. Toward the end, I realized she wasn't sleeping. At all. It's happening again here."

Ethan had noticed. Nothing in particular, Scarlet merely grew a little less *Scarlet-y* with each passing day. And last night, he'd swear she'd been hunkered down on the floor in front of her door, physically blocking it with her body to get some rest.

Tipping his glass, Ethan flicked an impatient glance at the clock above the bar. "I'm hanging on every word. Really."

Taking the bait, Brian went on. "On the last day of our stay—after we'd closed the deal—one of the other lawyers came on to Scarlet at the closing party. Out of the blue, he put his hand on her waist and whispered in her ear. She jolted, hard. Her drink fell to the ground, totally shattered. When the guy tried to usher her away from the glass, she stared at him, frozen in some silent out-of-body experience. Several minutes ticked by. I'll never forget the look on her face."

Ethan stilled and then nodded. He'd experienced his own share of flashbacks. Rather than re-living the physical violence of Rikers, he'd seen himself locked in a tiny cell, contemplating his failure to climb out of the hole he'd been born into and despairing where that failure would leave his mother. He didn't have waking flashbacks anymore, but sporadically— when he couldn't wrestle reality into the mold he'd configured for it—he weathered waves of uncontrollable anxiety. The dreams reminded him there were aspects of life even he couldn't control. Scarlet was turning out to be one of them.

Seemingly lost to the story, Brian continued, "I'll also never forget what she said, so quiet, yet panicked."

"What?"

"Most of it was incomprehensible—things like 'cold' and 'no.' But then she said, 'Ethan, don't.'"

Jesus fucking Christ. "Not possible."

Brian's face went hard. "*Happened.* I walked her back to her room. She let me lead her along, totally listless, and she admitted that she doesn't sleep well in hotels. That's an understatement. She doesn't sleep at all."

Ethan thought his chest might explode. The faraway look on Brian's face hinted at how difficult the episode had been to watch. And while Ethan wanted to kill the guy over his closeness to the woman who was driving him slowly insane, he was grateful Brian had been there, had helped.

Yet as much as he disliked what he was hearing, he didn't get how Scarlet's frailties justified her present betrayal, one that wasn't playing out in the vacuum of a flashback where she apparently still thought him a killer. "So Scarlet doesn't like hotels or people sneaking up on her. Two extremely rare afflictions, let me tell you."

"You demand info and then mock it?"

"That's how I roll." Stroking his wrist as though he were petting a trusty dog, he sent Brian a pointed look. "Get on with it. Now."

"You were right. Scarlet didn't go to the drugstore."

No. Shit. Projecting his voice like the loudspeaker at the circus, Ethan wailed, "Ladies and gentlemen, prepare for Brian Wentworth's shocking exposé." His tone shriveled. "Oh, wait…"

Brian was so fired along with his little massage-ee. Ethan pushed off, making to exit the booth. He'd been on this merry-go-round long enough.

"She went straight to the hotel."

Eyes flaring at Brian's upheld hand, Ethan sank back down.

"Before you go off half-cocked about how no one would get a cab for a block, think about what I've been saying."

Ethan gritted his teeth. "Scarlet came away from her attack with baggage."

"She hides hers well—"

"Who doesn't?"

"She's afraid she'll be hurt. *Physically*, Ethan. The type of thing that leaves a person bleeding in the street, a car, an apartment, a *hotel room*. Alone and with no one to help."

Ethan stilled, a queasy feeling piercing his insides. *That's why you don't sleep in hotels, isn't it, sweetheart? No trust in the security.*

With each word, the accusation in Brian's tone climbed. "Think about the cab, you son of a bitch."

She'd been attacked walking alone at night. "She blames herself? For going out alone?"

Brian nodded. "She regrets accusing you, of course, but also for being so irresponsible as to put herself in danger in the first place. I don't think she's repeated that"—he raised his fingers in air-quotes—"*mistake* ever since, no matter the location or the distance."

Ethan drained his beer, wishing it'd been sixteen ounces of whiskey. Not even that could have prepared him for Brian's coup d'état.

"*That's* why she lied about the drugstore. She finds the truth embarrassing. Fact is, she's afraid of the dark."

A dull ache pulsed at Ethan's temple. "You're saying it's feasible she waited for the cab *much* longer than it would've taken to walk one block along a well-lit, crowded street, and then she paid the cabbie to trace the same path to the d'Angleterre."

He pictured Scarlet's expressive face at Optik when he'd accused her of scamming his company. If her lie about the drugstore hadn't catapulted him over the edge of his anger, he might have recognized her genuine confusion and then embarrassment.

"I'm saying she *did* do that." Brian leaned forward in the booth, still keeping his hands tucked away. "When I left dinner, Scarlet was talking to Susan. The timing of their conversation, the cab ride, and my walk must have coincided. When I approached the hotel, I saw the doorman assist Scarlet from her cab. She beat you home, asshole."

Ethan's exhale came in a rush. *Scarlet was already in her room when I set up camp in the lobby.* She *had* lied about the ride, but for very different reasons than he'd assumed. He'd trampled all over her real fear and anxiety, not feigned, and he'd scoffed at her hesitant efforts to make him stop.

Hitting Brian with the dead stare he typically saved for the boxing ring, he asked, "What have you had, other than her feet?"

Brian smiled darkly. "More all the time." Then he hesitated the briefest second before adding, "And I don't suffer from a lack of trying."

Already half-way up, Ethan froze. "*More all the time* better mean *nothing.*" Then he reached out, his finger straying to the developing bruise peeking from beneath the man's lavender cuff. "And stop trying."

At Brian's uproarious laughter, Ethan saw why Scarlet trusted this particular colleague, who could both take it and dish it out with the best of them. "I'd tell you to make her make me, boss, but the fact is, you can't have her." The man still shook with humor.

Ethan merely arched a brow.

The mirth cooled quickly, and Brian grew serious. "She's your lawyer. There are rules. Number one? Don't fuck your clients."

Sitting up, Brian leaned in, wrists and all, as if to share a secret. "I think I'll actually up my efforts."

*****

Scarlet kept her end of the bargain. Bright and early, she found Susan's room on the third floor. The woman answered her door before Scarlet's fist could hit the wood a second time.

Silent, Susan stepped aside to let Scarlet into her lair.

Before she could open her mouth, Susan held out a folder. "Your itinerary. An E-ticket. Your flight leaves at nine a.m. A car will fetch you at seven. I can't get you out of here till tomorrow." Crossing her arms over her chest, Susan added, "Unfortunately."

Unwilling to take yet another person's shit, Scarlet nodded brusquely. "Thanks. It's been a pleasure." *Yeah, and I'm looking forward to my next pap smear, too.*

Schedule in hand, Scarlet spun on her heel, intent on leaving the way she came—fast and without a fuss.

"He's not what he seems, you know."

Susan's voice sounded so grudging Scarlet almost didn't believe she'd heard correctly. "I do know," she said over her shoulder. "He seems like a well-respected, well-mannered businessman. He's actually an evil genius bent on my destruction."

"Maybe. Maybe not." Susan took a seat and poured a cup of coffee from a silver pot. She didn't offer Scarlet a chair or a mug. "He can be hard. Controlling. Being thrown in prison without provocation changes a person. So does the hill climb from a reputation-maligned boxer to one of the country's leading minds. Everyone he meets wants a piece of him."

"I don't."

Susan took a sip, then added a sugar cube and stirred. "I met him right after he got out." She threw Scarlet a speaking look. "Of Rikers."

"I know. We spoke briefly after he was released."

"When you tried to pay him off?"

Yes. Scarlet nodded at a chair opposite Susan. "May I?"

Susan gifted her with a regal incline of her head, and Scarlet bit back a sarcastic thanks as she sank into the cushioned seat. More and more, it appeared Ethan and his minion shared a rapport that went far beyond dictation and travel plans. "You know a lot about your boss."

"I know a lot about everyone," Susan provided, skewering Scarlet with an unapologetic glare. "Even you. I figure people out for Ethan. Along the way, I've learned about *him.*"

Scarlet could banter with Susan all day, but why bother? In her kindest pre-cat-fight voice, she said, "Not that I don't enjoy an early-morning chat, but do you have a point?"

Susan wagged her head, not rushing to expound. Once Scarlet began to squirm in her seat, Susan sipped her coffee again and set it aside. Seeming mesmerized by her porcelain cup, she started to talk.

"A few years after I started working with Ethan, I went through a divorce. The situation got nasty, and I was spending all my resources—money, time, energy—fighting my ex for our kids. After six months of hell, my lawyer called out of the blue. My husband's attorney had suddenly offered a reasonable deal. One might say too reasonable. To this day, Ethan hasn't admitted involvement, but my ex was bitterly open. Ethan had made it clear that absent my husband's quick cooperation, he'd use whatever clout he had at the time to sink the man's contracting business. Capitulate, or never get another customer."

What a gem, Scarlet thought uncharitably. *He also probably saves kittens from the streets.* "Ever wonder if Ethan wanted to test his own influence?"

"Maybe he did. That doesn't change the fact that he used the test to help me escape a bad situation. He didn't even know how terrible things had been. A test also fails to explain why my sons attend private colleges on Ethan-funded scholarships. I'm not supposed to know about those either." She picked her cup up again. "Ethan has a habit of doing what he thinks needs done. Perhaps he can be forgiven for only sporadically asking permission."

Scarlet eyed Susan's coffee pot, reminding her fingers to sit still in her lap and not reach for a cup. Minion's story sounded good when you said it fast, but only because nobody was all bad. Not even Ethan.

"Are you familiar with Ethan's charitable contributions?" Susan asked.

"Laying it on a bit thick, aren't you?"

"I write the checks. He keeps it private. You won't be reading about the twenty million he's given on CNN."

Scarlet felt her brows crawling up her forehead, but she gave her watch a pointed tap.

Susan responded with a look that said *like you have anywhere to be.* "He can be loyal, even selfless, but he's ruthless when warranted. You've abused his trust. This reaction to you is the exception, not the rule."

"I didn't—"

Susan held up a hand. "Frankly, I don't care whether he likes you. But I won't watch you wallow in your self-righteous dislike for him."

The information was helpful even if the source wasn't. Ethan might be into silent acts of mercy for the good, but he preferred blunt force trauma for the bad. Simple, controllable, effective.

"I get it," Scarlet conceded, her voice bored and flippant. "He's got an isolated cold spot in his warm, fuzzy heart for me. Thanks to you"—Scarlet held up the folder containing the details of her escape—"I can leave him to it."

Because divorces and college tuitions and charitable donations aside, Ethan had *her* on his trauma list, and she'd given up dangerous places a long time ago.

CHAPTER 12

No extravagant gifts. Bust out the diamonds—and, oh, how he wanted to—and Scarlet would liken him to her father in two seconds flat. Feeling entombed in the ornate hallway, Ethan walked toward her room with a single white tulip that, if he'd found a competent florist, stood for forgiveness. He would also offer three handmade truffles, straight from Peter Beier's chocolaterie.

No alcohol. Not even a bottle of champagne. He didn't want her to believe he asked for more than a truce. He did, of course. He wanted that and much more, but his gifts were a peace offering, and champagne, when combined with the decadent chocolates and the flower, might be misleading, or worse, frightening.

No *Empress*. That rule trumped the others. He would never call her the name again, not in anger or frustration or under the influence of any other emotion. He'd known, at least subconsciously, that the endearment had ceased to function as such long ago. As Scarlet said, he'd used it cruelly, as a reminder of a painful past she'd worked to forget. Never again would he deliberately use her fear against her.

Scarlet's plane left early the next morning. Susan insisted she'd been unable to get Scarlet on a flight any earlier. His girl was still in residence.

He'd dressed carefully. While he couldn't do much to subdue his size, the worn jeans and T-shirt didn't scream money or power. His stocking feet left him as short as he could get, and he hoped the stubble on his jaw conveyed casual. Just a regular guy bringing a lady some chocolates. Nothing to be worried or upset about. Happens every day.

At her door, his whole body clenched with nerves. Hopefully one day he'd look back and laugh at how badly he'd fucked this trip up. Right now, Scarlet would likely kick him in the stones before tossing him to the curb. If that happened, he'd have to respect her wishes and stay away. It was that or succumb to the inner stalker that couldn't leave her be. Not back then and not now.

His first knock was tentative, a light tapping. He stood sharply to the side, hoping if she couldn't see him through the peep hole, she might actually open the door.

When she didn't respond, he knocked a little louder.

Still nothing.

Scarlet hadn't checked out. Considering the distress she'd endured the night before, combined with the fact that darkness approached, overwhelming odds favored her being holed up in her room. He slammed the curled edge of his fist against the door. When she still didn't answer, he did it again. This time, the door rattled, threatening to vibrate off its hinges.

He heard her as he pulled back for another blow—a series of soft footfalls that came in fits and starts. She was moving around in there, and frantically, he'd guess. He waited… but still she didn't open up.

What the hell?

She might have seen him though the viewing hole despite his efforts to stand aside. Or perhaps she'd made an educated guess and thought he'd come again to drive her out. Bellowing through the door wouldn't go over well with the neighbors, so he opted for knocking louder.

Then rattling the doorknob.

After several minutes, Ethan stared in mutiny at the barred door, breathing heavily. Thinking to startle her into a confrontation, he returned to his own room. He stalked to the door that connected his suite to hers, intending to raise such a racket she'd be forced to face him. From inside his room, he could yell and beg and coax her to hear him out. If that didn't work, brute force would.

Desperate times call for desperate measures, sweetheart.

But when he jerked his own internal door open to reach hers, he jumped aside. A silent and violently trembling form tumbled backward to his feet. Scarlet. She'd obviously wedged herself between their connecting doors, clutching a nasty-looking steak knife.

The tulip hit the floor behind the truffles when, through a part in her robe, Ethan spied blood dripping from a nasty slice along her delicate ribcage.

CHAPTER 13

At the first light knock, Scarlet surged to her feet. An unexpected visitor at the door was, for her, one of life's little trials. The evening's goal had been to pack so she could get the hell out of Denmark and away from Ethan. Once home, she'd await his next move and piece things together in spite of the destructive swath he'd cut through her life. Lissa was on standby with a slew of bad ideas, most of which involved tequila or going out in public in a state of partial undress.

Brian would step onto the Optik frontlines. With any luck, the deal would come off without a hitch. She wondered what kind of a fool still wanted the best for Ethan and his company when he planned to engineer the exact opposite for her.

The repetitive thump outside her door grew more insistent, echoing through her ears at a volume that couldn't possibly reflect reality. Tamping down her alarm, she crept to the door and peered through the eyeglass embedded at its center. The standard look-before-you-leap protocol usually brought her fevered imaginings of violence to a screeching halt.

Her breath caught in her throat. Rather than a face or a torso, she saw an elaborate flower bouquet so common within the hotel. The blooms sat unobstructed upon the table across the hall.

Yet the banging continued. For a moment, she allowed her head to fall back. The ceiling blinked into view as she stood, frozen and unsure, feeling the door jolt beneath her hands.

Her unanticipated visitor wanted, quite badly, to both enter her suite and to mask his identity. No one she knew had a reason to stand aside like that.

Sick adrenaline flooded her bloodstream when the doorknob joined the fray, rattling in time with the hammer of a fist against wood. While her mind raced, her body refused to cooperate. Glued in place, barely daring to breathe, she stared at the twisting brass knob. She could jerk open the door leading to Ethan's room and bang on it until he took pity on her and let her in. But over the past few days, she'd become attuned to his movements in the adjoining suite. Unwittingly, he made his presence known via the shower, the sink, even the television. There'd been nothing but silence from that direction all night.

She had one exit. One *blocked* exit.

Forcing lead feet to lift from the floor, she lurched across the carpet to pick up a knife that rested on her dinner tray. The meal had been a lonely, solemn affair, but she thanked her inner hermit for keeping her sequestered for a good mope. Room service had left her some modicum of protection.

Knife in hand, she lifted the telephone receiver and hit "zero" for the front desk. An automated machine answered the call, droning through a list of assistance options in a paced monotone. She pressed "one" for English, but the urgent hammering at the door soon reverberated in her ears, drowning out the robotic desk assistant.

She didn't know the 911-equivalent in Denmark. *Fool, why don't you know this?*

Scarlet's pulse stuttered and the receiver slid from her grip, dropping to the floor beside her feet. The intruder *had* to be on the cusp of bursting through the door.

Unable to cower—never again would she willingly play the victim—she killed the lights and slipped between the flanked doors that connected her room to Ethan's. With his door at her back, she pulled her own against her cheek. There she waited, knife clutched to chest, staining to hear above the hammering of her heart.

The banging tapered off, then stopped, and her fist tensed around the knife's handle. Not trusting the lull, icy panic slid down her spine. She waited, her body shaking with strain as she fought to catch her breath. *Do something. Get back to the phone.*

When seconds dragged on in silence, hope sprouted. He might have gone.

Possibly.

Probably.

She strained to detect action in her suite over the blood roaring in her ears. In a sudden rush, Ethan's door peeled away from her back. Her legs crumpled without the rear support, sending her reeling into his room.

Flailing, she hurtled backward through space. The blade tasted her skin when the floor jarred her body on impact. Stunned, she stared up into Ethan's horrified face. The color drained from his features and he bent to lift her high against his chest. Then, cradling her close, Ethan carried her into her suite, laying her upon the familiar coverlet before switching on an antique lamp and bathing them both in soft, yellow light.

His forehead trembled when it met hers, and he gently pried the knife from her fingers, setting it aside. "Jesus, Scarlet, what's going on?" With a stroke of her cheek, his expression darkened. "Don't answer that."

She struggled to slow her breathing while he fumbled for the telephone receiver she'd abandoned to the rug. After he managed to dial, she watched his features tense at the pre-recorded message from the front desk. Ethan slammed the receiver down and tried again. This time, his fingers tapped out a room number. The curt instructions that followed brooked no disobedience. "Ron, I need a first aid kit in Scarlet's room. Yesterday."

He hung up and lowered himself to the edge of the bed, pulling the softness of her robe away from her body. His eyes slid past the pale satin of her matching bra and panty set and settled on the cut along her side. Swallowing, he rose and disappeared into the bathroom, returning with a warm, soapy towel.

She twisted her head to see the stinging gash. While the streak of blood looked menacing, the wound wasn't deep. Had Ethan not arrived, the injury could have been much worse. "Someone was here. Trying to get into my suite. I—"

Ethan froze. In that moment, everything changed. Cupping his palm behind her head on the pillow, he turned her face to meet his gaze, his body leaning over hers like a protective cage. His mouth worked open and closed, twice, but no words came out. She realized he was surprised. He hadn't fully understood why she would have hid between their doors with a weapon.

"What if he's still—"

"Hush."

"No, Ethan. Someone could—"

"Shh. I know, sweetheart. He's gone. You're safe. Let me tend to you, and then we'll talk." Pulling back, he brought the hot cloth to the neat slice that marred her torso.

His jaw clenched when he pressed the towel against her skin, leeching her pain away through the wet cotton. As the rampaging fight-or-flight reflex receded, she relaxed under hands that roved quickly over her body, soothing her side, stroking her jaw, touching her face.

"Ethan," she murmured finally, reaching out to thread her fingers through the silken strands of his black hair. "It's a scratch. I was more scared than hurt." He'd been callous, yet she couldn't stand to see the pain—guilt?—in the stark set of his features.

He glanced up, his face hard. "I don't like *scratches* on you Scarlet. I don't like tears either. Or tremors wracking your entire body." He bent and pressed a closed-mouth kiss to her injured side, gliding his fingers absently along her ribs. "All that has to stop. You're never to bleed again. Ever."

She nodded, forcing a straight face despite his ludicrous demand.

"Promise," he croaked, hell-bent on the impossible.

A brisk knock interrupted her bewildered refusal and sent Ethan to the door. After a few low words to Ron, he returned with a first aid kit and dropped to his knees beside the bed. With the practiced care of an athlete who was no stranger to flesh wounds, he efficiently cleaned, disinfected, and then bandaged the cut.

After patting the gauze into place, he glanced up and spoke quietly. "No sudden movements. You should probably take it easy for a couple days. And don't get this bandage wet because—"

"I'll be fine." She stilled his hand over the medical tape, putting an end to all the fuss.

He blew out a breath, and she felt it puff across her chest and neck. "Scarlet," he said, looking both hesitant and resigned. "Sweetheart, you're not going to like this."

Too late. She already didn't like it. None of their dealings since reunification day had suited her. And he'd started calling her sweetheart again, which in her experience signified an increase in unpredictability, as though their mutual existence wasn't, in and of itself, sufficiently volatile.

His fists clenched the lapel of her splayed-out robe. "I'm so damn sorry, for yet another thing now." He lowered his head and blew soothing air over her bandage, then nuzzled into her side. "It was me at the door."

She stilled in confusion. He'd scared her on top of everything? Frightened her in the worst possible way?

"Before you say anything," he went on, his mouth slack between each attempt at forming the words, "I came to apologize. For jumping to conclusions. For... everything. There's too much to even repeat. But I was wrong."

Her world narrowed to his apologetic face. She'd been right. *Guilt* pinched between his eyes. Facing away, she could only utter, "Why?"

He rose and sat on the bed, tracing patterns over the smooth skin of her stomach. "I didn't realize you'd think what you did." Swallowing convulsively, he rushed on. "The last thing I'd want to do is scare you. There's a lot I'm learning. All I've ever assumed or thought I understood about you, your life, or who you might have become... it's jumbled. Mostly off the mark." His eyes slid shut, his voice thickening with regret. "And now I'm paying for my mistakes by inadvertently making more of them."

The low baritone wound through her conscious like a beloved song, entrancing her, begging her to believe its sincerity, and she fought to remain withdrawn. Hers was a losing battle. The recesses of her mind whispered that he knew little of her ridiculous fears. He didn't know that when it came to personal security, she wasn't like other people.

"Why couldn't I see you? I looked out. You weren't there."

"I thought you would think I"—he paused and stood, walking to her picture window— "that I came to kick you out. Again." Resting his shoulder against the glass, he pinched the bridge of his nose between two fingers. "But I didn't. I came to tell you I know you'd never purposefully hurt me or my company. To ask you to stay. I didn't think I'd get past the door if you knew it was me. And I couldn't risk not talking to you, not apologizing, before you left."

Her chest tightened when he opened his eyes. She'd seen him run the gamut of emotions. Tonight she saw regret and sorrow, but most of all, she recognized soul-shattering truth mirrored in his shuttered gaze.

"How did you figure it out?" At his questioning glance, she added, "That I wouldn't sabotage you."

"Brian." He ambled back to the bed, sitting next to her hip. "Can I hold your hand?"

She slipped her chilled fingers into his strong ones. They enveloped her like a mitten, suffusing her whole arm with glowing warmth. Her breath caught at the innocent contact.

He squeezed. "I realized much on my own after thinking things through. Then Brian confirmed that he saw you get back to the hotel that night."

"I see," she whispered. He'd needed confirmation from someone else. But he'd made an effort to figure out the truth.

Shocking, but true.

On a wistful sigh, Scarlet slid her free hand down the bunched muscles of his arm. She kneaded until she felt the tendons relax under her caress, releasing some of the strain pent up in his big body.

At her subtle advance, his lost look stirred with relentless heat. "Help me do something right, Scarlet. Please."

CHAPTER 14

He couldn't stop examining her. Tousled and shaky, she looked unsure whether to believe all the soul bearing. She was right. The cut wasn't deep and would heal. He, on the other hand, faced a slow recovery. Seeing her on the floor, wide eyed and in pain, had stretched his skin over his bones like it was two sizes two small.

He'd made Scarlet bleed.

Her hand felt tiny and limp within his. Even her nails had gone pale, and he wondered if he should worry about shock.

With the tip of a finger, he traced a T shape across her forehead and down her nose. From there, he feathered light touches over her cheeks, ending with a soft caress along the fullness of her bottom lip. "You're beautiful." The words came without thought, but she didn't flinch away.

Instead, when he let his hand drop from her face, she peered up with eyes full of liquid-gold hope.

He momentarily forgot how to breathe. "You really thought it was me didn't you?"

"I had no clue who was out there, Ethan. That was the problem."

"No, the attack. You really thought *I* hurt you that night after the fight." No subterfuge. No punishment. Those shameful explanations were figments of his own tortured, vengeful mind. Fear at the caliber he'd witnessed tonight couldn't be faked. And it didn't lie.

Especially not to the police in a fit of pique after a near-fatal attack.

She winced as she pulled herself up against the headboard. Rushing to ease the way, he plumped a pillow behind her lower back before she brushed his hands aside. "I *knew* you were the one. Until you proved me wrong."

And you got side-swiped by a Mac truck of guilt. The answers he'd needed were so fucking simple. They'd both been victimized, and when Scarlet had reached out in comfort and consolation in the only way she'd ever known—offering him money—he'd pushed her way. Threatened her with retribution.

Christ, he'd told her he regretted saving her life.

And, after all of his selfish railing, she'd had the courage to follow him into this debacle, trusting him not to hurt her as he'd threatened to do. And her reward? No sleep. Public mockery. A dressing down undermining her professional integrity and threatening everything she'd worked to build. A gash in her side. A scare that had probably taken five years off her life. And now a brute with an erection straining not to pounce on all that ethereal beauty.

Ethan exhaled on a ragged sigh. *Nice and easy, lover boy. Fuck this up, and it's well and truly over.*

"Can I stay?" His voice cracked, and he wondered if she'd revel in throwing him out. Would never blame her if she did.

With a solemn nod, she slid over and made room.

******

Scarlet buzzed with mild surprise when he removed his shirt and slid behind her in socks and jeans.

"Are you comfortable in all that?" she asked against the sheets with a twinge of hesitation. She wasn't sure she wanted him to remove any more clothes. At the same time, she really, *really* did.

He pressed his mouth to her nape, and she felt his smile against her skin. "I'm as stripped as I'll get." He chuckled, pulling her close. "As comfortable as I deserve."

"What if I want more? Don't *I* deserve it? I mean, what if all that rough fabric and those pointy buttons chafe me in the night?" She was playing with fire, but it felt delicious. Like a normal woman flirting with a gorgeous, half-naked man. That happened to be in her bed.

"Oh, you deserve everything you want," he replied, a bit of strain entering his lackadaisical tone, "but you can't have it. Not tonight."

"And if I can't take the rejection?" She pushed her backside against his groin.

"I'll have to make it up to you some other way." As the words left his mouth, his knuckles found a sore spot between her neck and shoulder and rubbed, working their way down the length of her back.

"Oooh, you're forgiven," she breathed. *This is better than sex.*

"Not with me." His voice stroked down her spine with the same force as his roaming fingers.

Shit, just say no to not-so-inner thoughts.

His thumb eased into a particularly tight muscle at the base of her spine.

"I refuse to scare the crap out of a woman and then take advantage of her while she's trying to process numerous life-altering revelations, all discovered within the last thirty minutes. I do have a *few* standards."

"M'kay." Whatever, as long as he kept touching her.

He did, and after working out all the major kinks, he fell into a rhythmic caress, beginning at the tips of her hair and ending at her hips. Again and again.

She sank into a blissful daze, neither awake nor asleep. Floating in that warm, relaxing void, she heard his voice from far away. "Brought you something. Fetched them when I got the towel."

As his hands left her back, her nose detected a hint of sugar and cream. Opening her eyes, she spied two dark chocolate truffles on the pillow next to her head. They twirled in her vision like sugarplum fairies, calling her name.

Scrambling to her knees, she plucked the first piece from its paper half-wrapping and popped the whole thing into her mouth. The candy melted evenly, soaking her tongue in sweetness until she hit a chewy caramel center. Moaning, her eyes rolled toward the ceiling. "You win, Ethan. I'm your slave."

He propped himself up on an elbow, watching her devour his gifts with a slightly glazed expression. "I like the sound of that."

"You can have anything"—she snatched the second truffle and held it to her chest— "except this."

Suddenly serious, he said, "I'd hoped to get your forgiveness."

When she didn't answer right away, mostly because her mouth pooled with gooey chocolate and caramel, he upped the ante. "There's more where those came from. As I said, *whatever* you want, except…" His back arched in a long sensual roll.

She groaned. "As if I would succumb to bribery."

He reached out and swiped a bit of chocolate that had escaped her greed to end up on the edge of her bottom lip. Bringing the sweet treat to his mouth, he winked. "You just did."

******

Morning came swift on the heels of his tender words and simple gifts. Surprised to see light flooding the room, Scarlet stretched back on her knees into child's pose, rocking sideways to stretch muscles sore from both her fall and his thorough massage.

She'd slept. A full, uninterrupted night.

Crawling to where Ethan dozed, she studied his face and chest above the faded jeans he'd refused to remove. Sleep hadn't softened him. Despite the steady rise and fall of his chest, his features retained their hard angles.

While the thick muscles of his arms and shoulders remained still, they were clenched, ready for action.

She looked on in fascination, and soon detected his subtle awareness of an external presence. He might not know exactly who watched, but he subconsciously sensed an observer. From the way his breathing sped into a sharp staccato, the intrusion wasn't welcome.

Easing forward, she sought to soothe the tiny grooves that fanned outward from his eyes. Laying her pinky against his temple, she skimmed the side of his face, starting near his dark brows and lashes, past his ear and along his clenched jaw, and finally down the tendons bulging in his neck. When she lifted her hand to start again, the world exploded into motion.

His body bucked upward on a violent growl, and she scrambled back. Then came a savage demand. "Get the fuck away from me," he heaved. "No cage."

Stunned, she crept back. When his head rebounded on the pillow, his eyes remained tightly closed. Hands fisted at his sides, he strained away from an imagined threat. Without warning, he lashed out with a violent swing at whatever or whoever invaded his dream, and she barely dodged a blow that would have swiped her across the chest and sent her flying over the edge of the mattress.

"Ethan!" she shouted from beyond arm's reach, afraid to get close enough to jostle him awake. "You're dreaming, Ethan."

He responded with a thrash of his head against the pillow. "You'll pay," he snarled. "I'll see you in hell—"

Climbing from the opposite side of the bed, she grabbed a decorative cushion and fired it at his head. The knots of numerous blue tassels whipped at his face.

He struggled on, still spewing venom. "Goddamn you for locking me in here."

Locking me in here. He was reliving Rikers. *She* had put him there.

This time she threw a shoe. Not at his face and not hard, just a ballet flat lobbed at his six-pack. It hit with a thud, and he jerked upright on a roar, searching the room frantically.

"Ethan?" She stood to the side, shrinking away from the wildness in his eyes. "Ethan, look at me."

His gaze flew to hers, but his dark stare remained blank, unrecognizing. Gradually, she shuffled back toward his side of the bed. His breathing slowed and she saw recognition creep inward.

He knew her again.

In a tentative voice, almost sounding afraid, he asked the question she should have. "Are you okay?"

She nodded.

"I didn't hurt you?"

She shook her head, not knowing whether the news would make him mad or glad.

Bringing a shaking hand to his forehead, he exhaled through his mouth, punctuating the overblown sigh with an audible swallow. "Thank God."

Looking up, he said, "I'm sorry you saw that." Then slipping from the bed, he reached for his shirt. "I'll leave you in peace. We can—"

"Stay." She came forward and placed her hand against his chest, and his heartbeat slowed to a normal tempo beneath her palm. After days of speeding him up, she relished the ability to slow him down. Gripping his shoulders, she pulled him into a sitting position on the edge of the bed. From her stance between his legs, she pleaded, "Tell me about it. Was it prison?"

He encircled her waist with his arms. "Yes." His voice was lifeless.

"Were you fighting against"—she smoothed a lock of hair from his eye and took a breath—"me?"

His shoulders tensed, but at last a glinting humor pushed the disappointment from his face. "Those aren't the type of noises I make when I dream of you." He traced her lips with a questing finger and a suggestive grin. "And while I certainly make provocative statements, they're different."

"*When* you dream of me?" Warmth settled in her chest.

"Often."

She was torn between getting the truth about the nightmare and demanding delicious play-by-plays of their midnight romps through his mind.

She curbed an answering smile. "Do tell." He could decide which path to travel, memories or making-out.

His smile broadened. She'd never seen a look of genuine joy cross his harsh features. His forehead softened and his eyes sparkled. He appeared... approachable. More petals and fewer thorns.

Good choice. She gave herself a mental shake. Rikers later. Sexy reveries now.

"To start," he began, "I never yell. Though when I'm touching you, I usually can't hold back groans as I say things like 'smooth' and 'taste.' Sometimes I whisper in your ear, but only the words you respond to. You like it when I say 'luscious' and 'nipple.' In my dreams, I love your nipples. I lick them, bite them, and you reward me with little gasps."

His words pooled between her thighs. She allowed her eyes to drift closed as he told her of fantasies she'd thought were hers alone.

"When I can tear myself away from your round, perfect breasts, I roam your body looking for other delights. Sometimes I suck your fingers. Other times your earlobes. Because they're my dreams, I *always* get to kiss you here." His hand briefly feathered over the material covering her core. "And when I do, I tell you how good you taste. Like honey. Like life."

She bit her lip, not trusting the legs his words had turned to mush. "Ethan, could you—"

He leaned in until his mouth rested against her throat, his lips barely grazing her skin as he spoke. "Could I what? Tell you that after I worship your body with my hands and mouth, you writhe in my arms, begging for more, and that I always give it to you? Tell you that in my dreams, I slide inside you gently, again and again, while you plead for harder strokes in a hoarse voice? Should I tell you those things, Scarlet, or do them?"

She stayed in the circle of his arms, her head falling back on her shoulders. She could do this. She could ask for what she wanted like a woman in charge of her own destiny.

"Do them," she croaked. "Please."

CHAPTER 15

Ethan melted at her shy demand. But when he jerked in a flare of need, the bandage at her side brushed against his ribcage, reminding him of how he'd ended up in her bed in the first place.

"Does it hurt?" he asked, worried that any kind of intimacy would bring pain.

"No, Ethan, no," she answered, that sweet little curvy body of hers trembling against him.

Her clear desire to receive what he offered had him lifting her from the floor in seconds. Standing, he slipped his arms around her in a careful bear hug. Then he whirled around and settled her on the still-warm sheets.

Climbing on the bed to straddle her slim hips, he eased over her until his chest barely brushed the satin that still stretched over her breasts. Curling his fingers under, he tugged her bra low to reveal both of her peaked nipples to the light of day.

Bathed in the morning sun, he could see all he'd missed in the darkness of the plane. Her nipples were the stuff of dreams, a dusky pink, blending perfectly into her milky complexion. "Pretty," he breathed, bending his head and swirling his tongue in small circles around one, and then the other. As her skin heated, he tuned in to the scent that was uniquely Scarlet. She smelled of soap and flowers, and now, a spiced arousal that drummed in his brain, demanding his complete attention.

Her hands roved from his back to his hips, skating over his bunched shoulders and down his torso, touching, learning, driving him crazy. When she reached to unfasten his jeans, he stilled those busy hands with one with his own. "Not yet, sweetheart," he said with an easy smile. *Not until I've had my fill.*

Thwarted, she traced the length of his erection through his jeans, and he got a glimpse of how difficult it would to be to hold anything back. The taut denim barely shielded the base of his shaft, and when she squeezed gently, he strove not to buck violently into her grip. "You're killing me."

"I can't stop," she whispered, and with those three short words, his reservations died. They were both desperate for this. He would let them have it.

Ethan settled over her in a wave, stroking her face as he captured her lips in an insatiable kiss. Licking at the seam, he stroked inside, tasting the sweetness he'd known awaited him. Pulling back momentarily, he brought her free hand to his mouth, swirling his tongue in lazy circles over her fingers before returning them to the nipple he'd left behind. At her quick inhale, he whispered, "Touch yourself for me, Scarlet." *God*, he wanted to see that. Then he could re-imagine it always.

When she did, when she squeezed her nipple and sucked at her lower lip, his eyes riveted on the pleasure she gave herself. He knew then that, though he should never have taunted her with his callous prediction, he'd been right—Scarlet was worth every last agonizing second of the wait.

******

Scarlet toyed with her breast, watching the desperation rise in Ethan's expression as a sense of feminine power stole through her. Closing her eyes and arching her spine to enjoy the erotic brush of her own fingertips, she felt him kiss along her proffered ribcage, nibbling around her bandage before licking his way lower to her navel. Ethan's soft, wet tongue lapped at the slight indention before wandering even lower to the satin of the bikini boy briefs she'd donned for the trip home.

Expecting him to pull the whimsical panties from her hips, she jolted when he delivered a long lick through the thin material. "*God*, I've wanted to taste you, Scarlet." When he looked up and traced his tongue over his lips in a visibly moist caress, she stifled a whimper, feeling a warm rush at her center.

"You're going to be *mouthwatering*," he rasped. "I know this."

He bent and nuzzled the satin with his lips and tongue, his hot breath heating the damp material, driving her mad. "Do it, please," she panted, rippling beneath his ministrations, inviting him to take more.

"Do what?" he asked in mock innocence, his thumb stroking her clitoris through the satin while he delivered slow, saturating laps below.

"*Really* kiss me, Ethan. Taste me," she breathed. Was that her? Pleading with this man for more?

His thumb dipped below the fabric, dragging once, then twice through her wetness. He sat back slightly, and she watched in mute fascination as he sucked his own finger. A leisurely pull. His enjoyment at the evidence of her need was palpable, the shared wanting hurling her anticipation to new heights.

The panties were gone in an instant. And everything stopped. His eyes trained on the two scars that marred her lower abdomen. Squeezing her eyes shut, she berated herself for not showing him earlier, for allowing him to discover them in the heat of the moment. Neither terrible nor beautiful, the marks were mostly jarring, adept at making men wonder what she'd undergone and whether she carried too much emotional baggage for fooling around.

Unfortunately, she knew Ethan possessed the answers to both questions. She'd been stabbed, and she staggered beneath the weight of more baggage than any sane man would take on.

She reached to cover them, hoping to roll away without a scene. He stilled her hand. With an encouraging squeeze, he pressed a soft kiss to each scar like he had her bandage the night before. "So strong," he croaked.

His acceptance lent an ease to her obsession with the long-hidden imperfections and even the failings they'd shaped. He'd seen the scars—no, more like adored them—and then let them go. Straining to see him crouched between her thighs, she saw he waited, his jet gaze searching hers for permission. With a flick of her wrist, she waved him on.

When he licked into her heat for the first time, she shuddered, wondering if pleasure could kill. Or maim at the very least.

An answering growl reverberated against her skin. "*God*," he said shakily, delivering quick brushes of his tongue between words. "You're fucking *delicious*."

Exploring her deeply, thoroughly, his fingers joined in. As his clever tongue snaked over her clit, making her shiver and writhe beneath his mouth, he slid two deep inside, adding a gliding friction that, within a few lush surges, threatened to send her over the edge.

"Ethan." She gasped in surprise when her body clamped down. "Don't stop. *Keep. Going.*"

"I've got you." He worked her urgently, ushering her through the clenching orgasm, initially maintaining a pounding rhythm before tapering off to a languid pulse that drew out the pleasure until she lay trembling and dazed, bathed in a sheen of sweat.

Though the storm had passed, Scarlet couldn't contain the low keening that flowed from the back of her throat. Like the continuing lashes of Ethan's tongue, the sounds wouldn't stop. They came automatically with each exhale, each lick, finally drawing him upward. Crawling over splayed limbs, the muscles of his torso rippled when he reached for her, capturing her mouth in a violent takeover. Caught in the onslaught of raw lust, she could taste the mint that lingered on his tongue, mingling with her own arousal. It was the hottest moment of her life.

He devoured her with lips and teeth and tongue, and lifting her in a gentle series of movements, he settled her on top of him. His body was huge beneath her, the granite slab of his chest and abs like contoured concrete beneath her slight suppleness.

Breaking from the kiss, Scarlet stared down at him. "Thank you," she said simply before looking away, embarrassed to be expressing gratitude for that kind of gift.

Ethan tapped her chin tenderly, returning her gaze to his. Only fire and understanding burned in those black eyes. No judgment. "You can't possibly imagine how much the *pleasure was mine.*"

She reached down, unfastening the jeans beneath her before delving inside to feel his steely softness. "Mmm," she whispered, tugging the jeans away. "You go commando all the time?"

His eyes sparked. "I can…"

She stroked along his shaft lightly, purposefully, just enough to make him want it harder, before reaching to cup the tightness of his testicles. "I may have to insist."

Again, she squeezed to the point of making him groan and roll upward, thrusting into her grip.

After two more slow pumps, he stilled her hands. "I need inside, Scarlet." His head rebounded to the pillow and his whole body roiled beneath her. She swore she heard him mumble something along the lines of *so deep, never leave.*

"Condom?" She said it hesitantly, not wanting him to think she didn't trust him, but also not wanting to get into why a condom was imperative. "I need—"

"Shh. Of course, sweetheart. Right here." There was that look of understanding again, but this time it went deeper, told her he knew there was more to her request than a healthy respect for using protection. He reached for the pocket of his jeans, extracting his wallet and from it, two shiny foil packets. Looking up at her, he purred, his voice a low buzz from the back of his throat, "For unexpected miracles…"

Guessing at the pleasure only Ethan could provide with those two condoms, Scarlet snatched one away, relishing the rigidity in his hard body as she jerked his jeans to his ankles and rolled the latex over his straining cock.

When she sat back, he lifted her again and settled her over him. "You do it," he hissed. "You control the depth. The speed." His expression pierced her, said he didn't trust himself to be in control, not yet. She was about to look away from her glimpse into his mind, at the vulnerability she'd once refused to believe he could feel, when he reached out and touched her cheek.

The gesture spoke louder than any words. Finally getting what he'd claimed to want all along, he slowed the action, touching her in kindness rather than desire, even though she could plainly see the arousal thrumming through his body.

With her face cradled in his hand, she positioned him at her center and began a slow slide onto his erection. She whimpered as he speared deep. Breathing hard, she opened her eyes and looked at him. Sweat beaded on his lip and gleamed on his chest. His hands went to her hips, and he gripped her hard for an upward surge, biting out, "*So tight. God, Scarlet, so fucking good.*"

He'd ordered her to take control, but she gave herself over to him. Holding her with seeming ease, he lifted her body almost completely off his penis before simultaneously wrenching her down and thrusting into her. The motion brought him so deep that with each thrust, her clit brushed against his pubic bone, sending pinwheels of sensation up her spine.

All too soon, her thrumming nerves ascended to a peak, and as she neared the pinnacle, the backs of his fingers delved into her soft pubic hair, where they rasped over her slick clit, sending her careening.

"Please, Ethan." Her plea was soft despite the hard sex. As soon as the words escaped, the walls of her channel began to compress around him, physically demanding more of the ride through her climax.

"Fuck," he gritted, his heavy thrusts going wild. "I can feel you, Scarlet. Feel your body squeezing me. Sucking at me."

"Yes." As the single word escaped, he stilled and went completely rigid, crushing her to him.

She flattened herself against his chest, waiting for the world to right itself, her body flowing up and down in time with his lurching breaths. After hazy moments, she lifted her head and met his bewildered stare.

"Holy shit."

They said it in unison.

Filled with an overwhelming sense of drowsiness, she dozed with him curled around her back. When she awoke, stirring beneath the cool sheets and rousing from a deep, rejuvenating sleep, she realized Ethan was positioned behind her, barely wedged inside the soft, sensitive tissues at her opening. With her body hot and swollen and infinitely ready, the one or two inches he'd given her weren't nearly enough.

His hands roamed, massaging her breasts, her stomach, skimming over the bandage at her side. He pulled her leg further up and over his hip, opening her, but refusing to move, forcing her to wiggle as though she were skewered on a hook. She clamped her inner muscles, trying to physically drag him deeper, but he merely chuckled at her body's clutch.

"Ethan?" she said in a dreamy murmur, turning her head to lick at his lips.

"Yeah?"

"Deeper?"

Quietly he said, "Maybe." His tongue traced the shell of her ear, and she shivered, causing her body to pulse softly around the hardness she *needed* to coax further inside.

Still nothing.

After a few additional minutes of torture, he exhaled and began a slow forward surge, so controlled she closed her eyes and prayed for mercy. Finally fully seated, he withdrew with equal care, and then returned again, and again.

In the midst of the gentle fucking, her noises came back. The ones she couldn't stop or control. She apparently moaned in the third person.

Ethan's low voice soothed her worries. "I love the sweet sounds you make, Scarlet. I love that you can't help yourself, even though"—he finally thrust, deep and rough, causing her to cry out in sudden delight—"you want to so badly."

It was too much. She tipped into a long, undulating climax that dragged them both under.

CHAPTER 16

Ethan accepted a tray from room service and turned to see Scarlet stir from her long, post-coital slumber. She perked up like an actress in a Folgers commercial at the scent of their fresh-brewed coffee.

Sex and sleep had worked wonders. Already she looked capable of kicking the shadows beneath those expressive eyes. More of the two S's for her.

Setting the tray down, he took in her rumpled, sleepy perfection, thinking her attire should forever be limited to skin. And those flawless diamonds flashing from her ears. Maybe a pair of the strappy heels she owned in abundance. Thigh highs if he was feeling generous. He'd thought the same thing years ago. But their time had run out before his fantasy could become reality. He'd renewed it this week tenfold, but seeing her now trumped anything he could have imagined.

He wasn't in a hurry to break-up their cozy morning of, but reality would intrude eventually. Contemplating how to best broach their issues, he pulled back the sheet and traced a hand over Scarlet's rump, delivering a playful slap to spur her to flip over. When she complied on a high squeal, he held out a mug and let his gaze stray to the scars he'd discovered earlier. Two jagged marks texturized the creamy skin above her light, downy pubic hair. On first sight, he'd nearly come undone, but he'd sucked it up to keep Scarlet's mind far away from that awful night during the first time they'd made love.

He sank to the bed and reached out, tracing the scars one by one. When he looked up, he saw his own sadness mirrored in Scarlet's gaze, but not fear or anger. She stared at his hands, her expression initially grave, while he explored the most vulnerable part of her. Then her smile dawned in a slow reveal that brought a radiant happiness to her face. And he understood. She regretted their past, but she shared his immense relief that perhaps that past would no longer be a wall between them.

"Talk to me, sweetheart." A tender invitation.

Scarlet froze, then turned her face toward the window. The steaming cup slipped from her fingers, whether by emotion or inattention, he couldn't say. Not mentioning the spill, he made a grab for her mug before more of the hot liquid soaked into the bedding and dripped onto the floor.

"Will it help?" she asked, her voice choked, disbelieving. He knew she saw little point in rehashing the wounds that had caused such strife.

She didn't have to explain her trepidation. Beginning with the day she'd offered that check in apology and ending with the night he'd nearly thrown her bodily from the room they now inhabited, he'd been an utter bastard. A bevy of arrogant assumptions had paved his road of sanctimonious coldness and mockery. He'd given her every right to be wary, even after the incredible night and morning they'd shared.

Setting his coffee aside, he used his free hand to cup her chin and slowly return her focus to his face. Stroking her silky cheek, he said, "I think telling me will help. And in return, I'll talk about Rikers."

At the last, she started. Her expression didn't change, but he sensed a ferocious interest in her. She wanted him to unburden himself as well.

"They said I was lucky," she began quietly, without preamble. "The bleeding wasn't terrible and no vital organs were hit."

Ethan flinched when she said "vital organs," reminding him of the gravity of her injuries. While she spoke, he petted her scars in slow, peaceful circles, letting her know he listened, but refusing to interrupt.

"I missed a semester of school, but recovery went... as anticipated." Her breath whistled out between pursed lips. "I healed. No infection. I talked to my father on the phone, but I never saw him again after he left me in the hospital. When we went our separate ways about a year after the attack, he handled the logistics via phone, letter, even e-mail. Now I see him on television."

She glanced down at his tawny hand moving against the alabaster skin of her abdomen, and a tendon began to tick visibly in her jaw. "I can't get pregnant," she blurted, but when his scrutiny jerked to her face, her features were serene, revealing none of the anguish he knew must accompany such a prognosis.

Surely her situation wasn't medically insurmountable. He conjured up the names of fertility and reproductive specialists within his many social circles. She was young. Healthy. Deep pockets could give her a baby.

Despite his hopes, he remained silent, not wanting to undermine her explanation. Instead, he trained his attention on her face—hearing her halting story, no matter how difficult—all the while continuing to stroke gently over the light scars.

"That's not true," she corrected after several moments. "I might be able to get pregnant. I can't stay pregnant, and alive, which means I have to take precautions."

Over the next half-hour, Scarlet told him of the dangers an accidental pregnancy would pose. "Abdominal wounds often lance the kidneys or the liver," she explained. "Mine bypassed all major organs, so the blood loss wasn't catastrophic." She said it like she was *lucky*. His beautiful girl felt grateful for an in-tact liver.

"But my female organs were in the direct path of the blade. Both my uterus and an ovary were punctured."

He swallowed, already knowing the answer. "Does that mean…?"

"Debilitating scar tissue. Even if the blockage let sperm reach an egg in my fallopian tube, I'd almost certainly end up with an ectopic pregnancy. Without surgery to remove the fetus, I'd die."

Finally understanding that any attempts at conception would risk both her life and the life of her child, he opened up, alarm over what they'd done—*twice*—overruling any personal demons her injuries invoked.

"What if the condom had ripped?" He heard the panic in his voice and remembered the blood on her side the night before. "That would violate the number one rule, Scarlet. Remember? No more bleeding, for any reason—"

"I'm on the pill." She paused, sounding embarrassed. "Chick reasons. Hormones, you know." He did. "I haven't been very *active*, so to speak, so I've never considered getting my tubes tied. I dislike hospitals—really hate surgeries—and that's not a fun one. But the condom's only a backup. I'm religious about the pill."

And Ethan was religious about condoms. Many a girlfriend had claimed to be careful about the pill over the years, but he'd never left protection to his partner. Not as a young boxer, and definitely not after his bank account had declared him a walking paternity suit. Funny, he trusted Scarlet to protect them both, to be religious about oral contraceptives, but the stakes were high and her health too precious. He'd be as diligent as ever.

Leaning in, he trailed his hand from the scars on her stomach to the skin between her breasts. Comforted by the steady thud of her heart, he said lightly, "You can get some unique condoms in Europe. Wanna stock up on mint chocolate chip?"

"Tempting," she said, and he loved that even after the most serious of discussions, she could still see the bright side.

"Good. While you were out cold, I took a little field trip to the *drugstore*." He dew out the sensitive word, hoping Scarlet still felt charitable about his mistake. Perhaps repeatedly acknowledging he'd been an insensitive ass would put her at ease. And save her the trouble of a reminder.

With a low whistle, Ethan held up a box of condoms from World's Best and dangled it in front of her nose like a carrot. "Now we can do it like the

Danes."

******

Severe, dominating Ethan equaled sexy as hell. Playful, vulnerable Ethan escalated to utterly irresistible. Charmed, Scarlet tucked the box of condoms away, determined to get the answers he'd promised. "Later we'll do it like the Danes. Now? You tell me your story. What happened to you, Ethan, after I—"

His index finger pressed against her lips, halting her words before she could blame herself. "That's not how I see our past, at least not anymore. Rikers is just another thing that happened in my life, maybe for good reason."

"Tell me," she said.

He leaned in close and licked along her collarbone. "Can I be inside you during the telling?" His palm trailed over her sex to press against her in unhurried pulses that had her legs parting and her hips rising within seconds.

By all means. "No," she said on a fatalistic sigh.

Ethan moved his hand away, though not before allowing his fingers to glide lightly through her sensitized cleft. Without any further sexual advance, he crawled into the bed and pulled the sheet over them.

"Ron," he began, snuggling her spine flush against his chest. "He was my public defender. We had a rocky start, but Billboard came through in the end."

"Billboard?"

"He looks like one—the sharp-looking lawyer suspended over the freeway with a question transposed over his face. 'Hurt in an accident? We can help.' A total pit bull. He figured out that if I was innocent, and Club Rancor's security footage showed *me* backtracking to your car, then it also caught your attacker. After that, life became a game of whack-a-mole. Lots of heads popped up, and Billboard investigated each one before smacking it down. Finally, one last name couldn't be set aside."

Expelling a long breath, he pulled the mass of her hair over her shoulder and away from her face. Then he began a rhythmic stroking from her scalp to the ends of her mused curls. Always *touching*. At the airport, on the plane, in the hall, in this room… each time, Ethan had initiated some kind of gentle contact. Even when he'd accosted her at Optik two days before, his hands had stroked along the tops of her thighs in a way that brought pleasure, contradicting the fury of his words, his threats. Initially, she'd been sure he merely toyed with her, rather like offering a pet a treat before pulling it away. Now she wondered if perhaps he couldn't help himself.

"After the indictment, they moved me to Rikers to await trial since I couldn't make bail. The island was rough at first, but there are virtues to my background that quickly became... apparent." The thick biceps and forearms surrounding her tensed, and his chest and abs hardened along her back. She waited, though for what she didn't know. Finally, the tension drained away into the ether, and he continued. "I handled it. I was made for that kind of thing." His hand wandered over her waist to the scars on her belly. "You weren't."

Scarlet heard the finality in his last words. "You won't tell me more, will you?"

"Nothing to tell." She felt the tightness coil again, though he never squeezed. A slight tremor in his imposing arms hinted at the restraint he used to keep his reactions confined to his own limbs, rather than letting the pressure bleed into his grip on her. "The hardest part was not knowing whether it would be permanent. Wondering whether life as I knew it, had planned it, had ended."

"The dream?"

"The guards," he explained, "locking me behind the bars, taunting me, mostly with the disbelief that my presence in the cell block could be a mistake."

"I'm sorry, Ethan."

After a pause, "I know."

"You never let me tell you that."

"I know that, too," he said, and she understood the low appeal for acceptance in his flat statement. "I couldn't hear it then. And now I don't need to."

Sensing the cost for him to confront the memories of violence and desolation, she changed the subject. "How did you end up here, at the helm of a technology empire?"

"I kept boxing after my release, initially for my mom. She'd gotten a job as a food checker during my time in Rikers, but the pay didn't cover the expenses on the quiet house I'd finally set her up in. She was determined to find a cheaper place, so I hit the clubs hard, looking for the money to make her stay put."

Scarlet reached back to tousle his short hair. She got the impression any significant movement would break the spell and end his story. Ethan had mentioned family only once and in a few stilted sentences she'd never forget. When she'd asked where he'd learned to box, he'd said, "*Home*." The terse words that followed had told the story of brutal training that hadn't been about father-son bonding in the garage. In true Ethan-style, he'd "*learned to hit back*."

The mention of his mother told the rest. Scarlet's accusations had pulled Ethan away from a life devoted to protecting a woman who hadn't been able to protect herself.

"You were successful?" She pushed the question past the sawdust coating her throat. "She was able to stay?"

His nodding chin tapped the top of her head. "I was a big draw, for both fans and other boxers. It turns out spending time in an infamous prison is good for fighting PR, just like rappers and Martha Stewart. The intrigue alone got me fights. My rage ushered in wins. Those successes brought a glut of prize money. I used the appeal of Rikers to rake in cash on the wrong side of the tracks, while I allowed the disgrace of my arrest to dissipate. Playing both hands, I eventually finished an associate's degree at Kingsborough and then moved on to NYU with a great deal more money at my disposal. Mom never bagged groceries again."

He could write the book on the American dream. "You were always going to make it, weren't you?"

"Yeah." He dropped an absent kiss between her shoulder blades. "I started Atavos before we met, but it took off after I'd been an engineer with a small consulting firm for a couple years. Ron was there on the capitalization side. We raised a hell of a lot of seed money in a short time and, ultimately, made a break."

I'll say. "You should be proud. Of everything."

The praise went unacknowledged. "You, too."

Ethan's observation came as a surprise. Throughout much of her life, she'd been seen as the lucky one, the girl born with a silver spoon in her mouth. *"Sure, it's easy to stay fit when you have a personal trainer." "Yeah, I'd get good grades, too, if I didn't have to have a part-time job." "Must be rough, being born too rich, too thin, and too beautiful."*

Over the years, she'd succumbed to others' opinions of her shallow worth as an autonomous individual. Yet maybe, just maybe, they were wrong. She'd overcome adversity to achieve independence. Stood up for herself. Fought for her way of life.

He's right. Her lips parted in surprise. *Badasses come in all shapes and sizes and backgrounds.*

"Back to you," he said, his hands beginning to wander ever so slightly as his voice dropped to a low, rumbling pitch. "Tell me about the lingerie." Quickly, he added, "Don't get me wrong. *I'm crazy about it.* I'm using your bathroom from here on out. But I'm also curious." His mouth found a sensitive spot behind her ear, and he licked. Then he blew on the moist strip of skin.

Scarlet felt her face flame to the roots of her hair. She could explain or let him figure it out on his own because, while she needed to kick the habit of showering en déshabillé, stopping would be like an addict tossing away smack. She doubted she could accomplish the feat cold turkey.

One of his fingers rubbed over a sensitive nipple, rolling slowly, then pulling. "Don't be embarrassed," he reassured, continuing to tongue the spot behind her ear. "Like I said, *I like it*. Very arousing scenery."

She swallowed past a lump in her throat that not even Ethan's caresses could repress. *Spit it out.* "The shower," she began, hoping he would understand her small quests to feel safe. "I wear the lingerie when I bathe."

She felt the tension seep back into the bunched muscles bracketing her, but he only said, "That's okay." The calm gentleness in his tone began to dissolve years of resistance.

"I shower in at least a bra and panties, sometimes more. A teddy or a negligee. Only things that soap through, so I get clean, but that also provide some kind of coverage. I know it's weird, but since the attack, I've never gone bare. If caught off guard, I've needed at least that protection. An illusion of protection, really, because I know it's nothing. Silly—"

"No," he interrupted. "Never that. You're scared, and you've done what you can to be careful, to feel safe. Have you taken self-defense?"

She nodded. "My skills are mediocre. And my bathroom is consistently peppered with drying lingerie."

"We'll do more training," he offered with a surge of his massive body. She could feel his growing erection slide along the seam of her ass. "You can beat on me till you're a pro." The drop in octave said he couldn't wait.

Scarlet breathed easier after the confession. With a few words of easy acceptance, he'd diffused years of anxiety. "I'll do that." She parted her thighs slightly, landing the next thrust of his hips right where she wanted it.

"Listen," he groaned, rippling against her in a wave that traveled from her rear to her shoulder blades. "I know you want to get over this... shower thing. But not yet."

His cock prodded her through his jeans. "I can't imagine anything more gorgeous than you, in the shower, the water streaming over lace at your breasts, molding to your ass, sliding between your thighs." He slipped a hand from her breasts to the pale globes of her rear, eventually inching around to rub slow and hard over her pubic bone. "I have to see it, Scarlet. Now."

******

Pulling her with him to the bathroom, Ethan went straight for a sheer, sea-green thong and matching bra that had drawn his attention when he'd first seen the display two nights before. No wonder she'd looked so stricken. Unwittingly, he'd stumbled upon her secret and laughed in her face.

Another mistake.

The gossamer cups of the bra would be nearly transparent in the shower, showing him both everything and nothing at all. Before, he'd wondered why Scarlet's bathroom could double as a lingerie shop. Now he simply treated it as one, pulling the filmy confections from her towel bar with shaking fingers. "These," he breathed. "Stand still for me. Let's get you dressed."

On his knees, he held the panties open at her feet. Rising, he skimmed the lace up over smooth calves, then along sleek thighs that curved in all the right places, barely kissing in the middle. Finally, he smoothed the delicate fabric in place over the sweetest spot in his world.

With a low sound from the back of his throat, he gave each nipple a rough suck before drawing the band of the bra around her back and slipping her arms through the straps. He snugged the lace over her plump breasts, and then hooked the front clasp before continuing to mouth her hardened nipples through the flimsy barrier. The taste of her fired in his blood, like sipping the finest champagne after waiting eons for the double fermentation.

Guiding her to the mammoth tub in the corner, he adjusted the temperature and drew the hanging curtain in a full circle to create a steamy haven for exploration. When he pulled it aside, revealing an inviting sliver for them to slip though, Scarlet maintained her stance with an evil little grin.

"You have to earn it, Ethan. I don't wear these"—she splayed her arms wide, showcasing her jaw-dropping getup—"in the bath for just anyone." Then her voice fell to a softer, more hesitant modulation. "That's been the whole point. I've been alone in there, the rest of the world at bay."

Ethan seized. "I know, sweetheart, and it means"—he cleared his throat—"so much, everything, that you're willing to show me."

God help him, he knew where her thoughts headed. Struggling to control his labored breathing, he knelt to trace his fingers from her toes to her navel, dragging the back of his hand across her mound with a good bit of pressure on the ascent. His mouth watered to have her again, but he couldn't rush her though the doubt written all over her face. "Anything."

"Stand up, Ethan. The plane. This morning. You've been greedy." Her lips curved as she pulled him upward by his triceps. Okay, *somebody* was discovering her inner dominant and far be it from him to discourage.

"*My* turn," she whispered as his ear passed her lips.

Her words set off warm implosions all over his body. If possible, he grew even harder at the thought of her mouthing his cock. He rarely surrendered complete control over his movements. But Scarlet? She could tie him to the tub and suck him for hours if she wanted. So long as she understood that if he so chose, and he *would*, the torture would double on the turnabout.

Nodding simply he let his hands fall to his sides, waiting. Without a word she sank to the woven rug beneath their feet, but she didn't touch his straining erection. Instead, she kissed around his groin, moving ever closer to and finally finding his unguarded testicles.

When he was sure he would die from the wait, her small hand encircled his cock. *Finally*. With a light squeeze—*harder, please*—her tongue found the head of his penis and flicked. Slow and steady and for long, agonizing minutes. Then, without warning, she engulfed him in the hot slide of her mouth.

A ragged groan tore from his chest. "Fuck, yes, Scarlet. Like that. Take me as deep as you can."

With her eyes closed, she swallowed him deeper, moaning her enjoyment around his shaft and sending a buzz prickling up the base of his skull. Then, in an exquisitely delivered message, she skimmed him with her teeth, letting him know she, not he, would decide the depth.

Trying not to thrust, to do anything that would make her shy away, he slid trembling fingers into her hair, refusing to apply force but dying for more. Need intensified when she let him pulse against her tongue before beginning to move in earnest. But when she did... *What is she doing to me?*

Ethan pressed forward, and then pulled back. His movements were involuntary. Instinctive. So was his grip on her skull. He knew he'd regret letting her sweet mouth steal his control, but as he fucked her, she mewled against him, telling him it was all right, that she liked it as much as he did.

"I can't last. *Goddammit*. Scarlet, I'll come."

She pulled away suddenly, looking up at him with a dreamy grin. "No, Ethan, you won't." Her glazed eyes lowered quickly, as though she'd surprised herself and would examine her boldness later.

He stared at her, shocked, until she returned to suckling him with a vengeance. Then all thought fled.

On it went, until he vowed he'd either die or kill her with equal pleasure. When she finally let him come, the world imploded inward. He lurched on his feet as she took his semen down her lovely throat.

When he got her into the shower, he demonstrated that drenched lace did nothing but magnify the sensations—from his fingers, his palms, his tongue, even the top of his thigh. He tormented her aroused flesh. Only when she writhed for release, literally pleading for sex, did he don one of the condoms he'd set by the tub and shove the lace aside, lifting her to sink deep.

Coming home.

CHAPTER 17

Scarlet learned a lot about Ethan over the next two weeks. Days passed in a blur of meetings, nights in covert splendor.

Negotiations hobbled along, maimed, but inching forward. Along the way, Scarlet confirmed that Ethan's arrogant, distrustful, almost misogynistic attitude had been a front. Now he routinely sought her advice, affording her opinions the weight they deserved. Disagreement proved inevitable, but when they found themselves at odds, each presented a rational case. Scarlet occasionally let him win their debates.

After a string of days scorching Arland Magnus and his cronies beneath her microscope, Ethan told her to dress casually. Finally, an afternoon off.

She stood behind the wooden door of her armoire, pretending to ignore the fact that Ethan watched her every move in the mirrored panel at her back. "How long do we wait before we throw in the towel and head back to New York?" Her whole team had gotten noisier about the deal's dead end. "There *are* other optics companies."

"Soon," he said. "But not..."

He trailed off when she bent at the waist, slipping one foot and then the other into the legs of a pair of white trouser shorts. Practically kissing her knees, she grinned through the pregnant pause.

He falls to the rear-view mirror.

"Do you trust your team?" he asked suddenly. The question came out of nowhere and hit too close to the suspicion she thought they'd addressed.

"Yes," she replied, straightening and doing nothing to mask the wariness that crept into her tone, "without reserve. You?"

"My people have been with me for years. Some for nearly a decade."

Time didn't necessarily equal trust in Scarlet's book. Ethan had every right to believe in his tried and trues, but not at the expense of hers. "Cagey much?" After all, he'd gone so far as to accuse *her* of working the deal from both ends. "If you're right about this whole inside-job thing and the leak isn't one of mine"—she peered around the closet door and pointed at his chest—"it's one of *yours*."

A swift tug slid the shorts up her legs and over her ass. She turned and made a show of zipping her fly in front of the mirror.

Show's over.

They left the hotel hand-in-hand. A nagging voice in the back of her head—one she'd been working harder and harder to ignore—whispered that their date-like departure wouldn't go unnoticed. The voice fought valiantly for her reputation, but ultimately fell to her great reserves of denial.

A stroll through the city brought them to an arched gate, a curious juxtaposition of gothic architecture and cute Danish flags. White lighting scalloped the stone's edges, illuminating the sign at the peak of the arch. "Tivoli," it read.

"*Pleasure* gardens," Ethan murmured close to her ear. "The world's oldest."

The massive gated entrance opened to a wonderland of blooms and fountains. Ethan ushered her from one amusement to another amongst structures done in the exotic-style of an imaginary Orient. The sweetness of thousands of flowers melded with the heady scent of spun sugar wafting from sidewalk confectionaries.

Scarlet kept a watchful eye on their idyllic surroundings. A public garden was a far cry from squirreling away in one of their rooms. Scarlet hadn't hidden their involvement. Not technically. She also hadn't hung a metaphorical sign around her neck that said, "Come and get me, big boy." Today, any colleague with a hankering to see the city might spot them and connect the dots, realizing she entertained more than a passing fascination with her client.

Ethan lifted her to the back of a wooden stallion on an antique carousel, toying with her calf while she floated up and down to the tinkling music. The longer they lingered on the ride, the higher his touch drifted. When he reached the cuff of her shorts, her knee jerked with a mind of its own. He paused, looking up in sharp question, but she couldn't stem the instinctive wiggle and screech that dislodged his grip.

Later, when the tiny compartment of a toy scenic railway afforded some privacy, Scarlet latched onto his waist and held. On the final bend in the track, she straightened, ready to pull away.

"It's all right," he murmured, stroking over her cheek and down the side of her neck.

Her eyes slid closed at the tempting sweetness of his words. *Enjoy now, deal later.* But the worry wouldn't wait another day. She'd delayed all sense of self-preservation far too long, knowing that allowing their affair to begin and then grinding it to dust was anything but fair to him.

"I can't." The right words refused to lend themselves to an explanation of what she couldn't do. *Have you. Be with you. Love you.*

Silence fell, and Scarlet glanced up. Ethan's face appeared set, a bronze statue glinting in the afternoon sun. Another moment passed, and she saw a flash of understanding chase across the stillness, registering all the reasons she might pull away and burying them deep. He seemed to decide that unacknowledged walls couldn't come between them.

Scarlet frowned in the face of his stoic certainty. She knew better, knew she couldn't stay on in Ethan's bed and his boardroom, but Ethan wasn't one to do things in halves or pieces.

Ethan the client would have to go. She wondered whether she could orchestrate the transition without losing the man.

******

Ethan steered Scarlet through a commons of eateries serving everything from Argentinian beef stew to German sausages to pickled herring. Settling on Italian-inspired, they swept into an ornate enclosure with curved iron railings that swung outward toward a small, glassy lake. Pure, take-no-prisoners kitsch.

Watching her gorge on meatball sandwiches and cheap red wine, Ethan gradually relaxed into his chair, answering her questions about Atavos's early days. "We ran out of a warehouse in Brooklyn, not far from Rancor, actually. Totally cramped, dirty."

Like clockwork, water spurted skyward in an elaborate show from the manmade lake skirting their terrace. Scarlet shook her head and chuckled. "And look at you now."

Waggling his brows, he said, "Yeah, these days there's no end to the amusements I can provide." Letting the suggestive remark settle, he sliced off more of the sandwich and slid it her way.

"For me," she began, staring at the now-still blackness of the lake. "Yale was perfect, with its ambience of old-world scholarship. It's corny, but the land, the buildings, the environment itself, seemed to breed knowledge. I felt… peace."

Curiosity got the better of him. "How'd you pay for the top-shelf law degree? Loans?"

"The car." She spoke quietly, but without hesitation. "The stolen Maserati had been replaced with a top-end Porsche. I sold it and voilà, I had an independence my father never counted on. In that sense—in more ways than one—I'm not at all self-made. And still, my education, my career, even being here exceeds all I ever thought to accomplish on my own."

An "on her own" he still didn't completely understand. "Why the rift between father and daughter?"

Her chin went up, but her smile didn't break. "I stopped taking his money."

"And?"

A blank look. "That's all."

A pinch gathered between his shoulders. She'd thrown away a lifetime of stability, of opportunities others would kill for, without a backward glance. "Any regret?"

Tension stole across her torso. "I didn't wake up one day and decide to kick him to the curb, you know."

A response caught on his tongue, held back by a reoccurring weight that settled in his gut. Her hesitance to explain the rift with her father couldn't *just* be about Tripp Leore. Like her hesitance to embrace what they'd found in each other—a feeling she failed miserably to hide—couldn't *just* be about her career.

Luckily, she began without further prodding because he was fresh out of inducements. "He came to the hospital two days after the attack. That's the last time we met in person. I was hopped up on drugs and literally five minutes before, I'd found out my girlie parts had been mangled beyond repair. Yet he talked of delaying college tuition and directing the household staff, not a word about the prognosis."

No. He squeezed her knee beneath the table. He'd dwelled on his own experience in the days following the attack. Anger hadn't let him picture her, dwarfed by a hospital bed, trying to wring a smidgen of affection from her father's callousness. "Not like that."

"Exactly like that." Her expression remained calmer than the high-intensity words. "Dad had spoken with the police and knew I suspected you, though at that point I hadn't made my accusations formal. He told me I avoided my duty to do so because I had childish designs on you. '*Not a dating game*,' he said. He pulled some strings and before long, I was inundated with NYPD. You were arrested that very day."

Her explanation echoed against the hard walls of his head. Her father had pushed and pushed. "You accused me because of him?"

"I knew you'd think that. It's why I haven't talked about the estrangement. For what it's worth, no, I blamed you because I thought *you* attacked me." Her eyes glazed, and her voice dropped to a pained whisper. "Sometimes, when I don't have the strength to be rational, my subconscious still thinks *you* were *him*. It's like facts don't count, and I'm only allotted visceral responses that got the wrong memo ten years ago."

Ethan didn't budge. When the authorities had finally gone after the right man, he'd been ready to thank the guy. Now he could easily kill him. And Scarlet's father? Why wouldn't she have obeyed? She'd been young, terrified, injured. Her dad had played on those weaknesses.

"Why do you think Tripp cared?"

She shook her head on a shallow shrug. "I may never know. I only know it killed me to think I might have allowed my father's manipulation to punish us both. That I rushed and ultimately did something unforgivable because I depended on his fortune."

Leaning his head back, he swallowed, trying to clear his throat. Now he knew. When she'd handed him that check years ago, then in the airport more recently, even after his mocking toast and when he'd fired her in Optik's conference room, she'd been hiding more than guilt. She'd accepted his censure out of a deep sense of self-loathing, a belief she had penance to pay. *Fuck*, leaving behind the money and privilege and making herself vulnerable to a harsher world hadn't been about her dad, it had been about *him*.

And he'd ridden the wave, agreeing with her scathing self-assessment. "Tell me," he demanded gruffly, "what do you want most?"

Her answer came fast. "What I've always wanted—you."

The response humbled him. "You can have me." He lifted his glass for a toast. "What else?"

Their glasses met, and her eyes regained some of their sparkle over the rim as she drank the sweet varietal in a smooth swallow.

He watched her throat undulate. Then, in a voice that barely cleared the surrounding tinkling of forks against dishes, he asked, "Parenthood?"

Her head snapped up. "*I can't.*"

"You could adopt." *They* could adopt. Or use a surrogate. Their child, but carried by a woman whose body could withstand it.

Delight suffused her features, her face slowly coming to life. "I never thought I'd hear a man suggest such a thing. You know, that whole biological imperative to spread one's seed and all."

Many men did feel that way. He had, before. "We live in a brave new world."

In roving sweeps, he drank in her classic beauty bathed in nothing but the joy of a long-awaited revelation. She'd dressed simply in pleated shorts and a pink sweater with three-quarter sleeves. Chunky strands of freshwater pearls, glittering with silver accents, caressed the cashmere at her collar bones, popping against the brightness of her clothing and the paleness of her skin.

She tilted her head, watching him watch her, and a flush crept upward from her décolleté to suffuse her face with a delicate color that matched her shirt.

Ethan spoke without thinking. "There's nothing you can't have or be or do."

She stilled. "You work fast, Ethan Blake." Apparently she didn't mind too much. Her lips spread wide, into a teeth-revealing grin that spread over him like a spotlight.

Taken aback by his own sentimental fawning, he pulled her from her chair in search of a distraction. Near the main gate, Scarlet halted their trek out of the park. Silent in concentration, she lifted her arm to gesture across the street.

Beyond the tips of her fingers and the arched entrance, he saw his assistant dart from an anonymous-looking building to a waiting car. Private, not a cab. Susan wore one of her nappy business suits and carried a briefcase as though she'd been working. Yet her role on these trips involved managing his and his employees' comfort and convenience—a traveling do-it-all concierge.

He generally knew her every move, and Susan had no need for evening bouts of work today, when his team did little but await info from Optik.

Personal outings deviated from Susan's M.O. She never ventured far during business trips. She smoked in stretch pants, watched American satellite television, and restricted her professional activities to meeting his requests, all while impatiently awaiting the green light to return to New York. She'd asked him three times this week when their Danish stint would end.

His eyes narrowed.

Billboard's first victim.

******

Shifting on her feet, Scarlet watched Ethan's expression shrink from heavy-lidded contentment to slit-eyed suspicion. The Minion. A woman who'd made it clear she shared more with Ethan than work.

His hand tightened on hers as they tracked the black sedan down the street. When she tried to slip away through his fingers, he glanced down as though he'd forgotten her presence. She watched his face tighten and refused to fault him for his feelings, but his anger struck her as *personal.*

She felt helpless in the face of his mounting fury. "I'm sorry." *That it might be Susan, someone you've trusted, helped.* The words went unsaid, but a single nocturnal voyage did not a traitor make. She wouldn't let Ethan make the same mistake twice.

"Such a long time," he said, still staring across the street. "With her."

"I know." She didn't, not exactly. She reached up and trailed her fingers through the silk of his hair. "Who is she to you?" *Why are you so wounded? Why isn't business just business?*

"My assistant, since the day I founded Atavos. More often than not, my secret weapon." His laugh was bitter, as though he finally got the shitty joke.

"Nothing more?"

His head swiveled toward hers, nostrils flaring with each breath. "What are you asking, Scarlet?"

"Exactly what you think I am."

"Whether I've fucked her?" She stepped back at his coarse response, but he kept coming, prowling in her direction, sounding *aroused*. "Whether I fuck her still?"

Refusing to back down, Scarlet pressed on. "Yes," she managed, holding Ethan's searing stare. "Have you? Do you?"

"No," he said, and the fight visibly drained away. "I haven't been an angel." *Surely not.* "But neither have I been boning my secretary over the desk." A wry grin accompanied his answer. "Not exactly my type."

His taste had occurred to her. *Remember all the models? The actresses?* Not that she'd tracked him—okay, she'd totally tracked him—but his liaisons never featured fading chain smokers in, shudder, nylon stockings and open-toed shoes.

Lost to her musings, she barely registered the movement before he leaned in and drew her to him. Her mind catalogued his many publicized affairs with breathtaking, sought-after women, surely in thigh-highs—the really sexy kind with thin black seams running up the back of the leg—when his deep voice cut through the mental chatter. "You're the woman I'm fucking, Scarlet. The only one I want."

The words should have shocked her. Instead, she shivered in the warm air, wanting him to prove it. Over and over again.

CHAPTER 18

The come-to-Jesus moment came sooner than Scarlet had anticipated.

"What the *hell* are you thinking?" Brian flushed an unhealthy fuchsia as he waved his hands in excitable circles, cutting through briny sea air. The brightness of his face countered the darkness of the sky. Heavy clouds gathered over the city, and after a run of balmy summer days, a storm appeared imminent.

Despite the growing breeze, Scarlet faced him across an outdoor lunch table, his grim recrimination obvious in the severe cant of his head and, once he lowered his wildly gesticulating arms, the press of his fists into the crisp white tablecloth stretched between them.

Their little café fell into a trippy row of old sailors' quarters that had been converted to colorful bars, bistros, and jazz clubs. Looking away from Brian in embarrassment, she gazed past other patrons enjoying open-faced sandwiches of marinated herring and roast beef to observe sailboats gliding through the harbor canal.

Most of the little boats were leaving, and she wondered how they'd fare against stormy seas.

Brian motioned to a waiter and ordered a lamb burger, medium rare. Then he looked on, shifting every few seconds in his chair while she asked about the breads on offer for sandwiches. After choosing a ham and cheese on soft rye and a Tuborg beer, she sat back, intent on appearing disinterested in whatever burning issue had Brian's panties in a bunch.

As if she didn't already know.

"Spit it out," she chided. She kept the comment nonchalant. He'd never know she burned with curiosity over how he'd broach her taboo involvement.

The answer came quickly. Cringing, she focused inward, letting her longtime friend blast her with his "disappointment" and "surprise" at her "uncharacteristically irresponsible" and "unprofessional" behavior.

Looking over the crowd, she spotted their server. In near desperation, she made a c-shape with her fingers and, with the flick of her wrist, pretended to down a drink. The man appeared at her side in an instant, notepad at the ready.

"Aquavit, please." Served icy cold, the pale liquor went down fiery hot, a bracing chaser for Brian's conniption fit.

When the server turned to Brian, he dismissed the man with a sharp wave of the hand. "The whole team's talking about you."

Of course they'd figured it out. She could hardly believe how long she and Ethan had flown under the radar.

Brian's lips thinned, and he turned flippant. "Not sure how you'll backtrack."

"Is this something one backtracks from?" she asked, all innocence and light. She couldn't resist a little goading. "Am I supposed to *un*-fuck him?"

He looked at her full shot glass the moment the waiter set it on the table. "Are you drunk?"

When she didn't answer, he hissed, "You're talking like he *literally* fucked your brains out."

Oh, maybe he did.

Reaching out, he snatched the glass and downed *her* aquavit, taking something she wanted, at this juncture, quite badly. Without so much as a distinguished cough, he straightened his paisley tie and pinned her beneath a hard stare. "If word spreads you've jumped into bed with Ethan—your most important *client*—it'll end your JTS career, if not your legal career altogether. Shit, Scar, what you've done violates the ethical rules for lawyers in all fifty states *and* Puerto Rico."

Hearing the black-and-white facts finally jarred her denial loose. The justifications and excuses she'd hid behind over the last two weeks crumbled around her.

She'd done this—Ethan to be exact—with her eyes open. Now she'd pay.

Staring into her beer—at least Brian hadn't gotten ahold of that—she swirled the gold liquid and pictured the previous evening, envisioning Ethan's rippling shoulders hunkered between her thighs as he pressed his tongue to her center in an offer of outrageous pleasure. Her cheeks heated at the thought, and she looked away.

"And worse, this is my fault. I—"

"It's *not* your fault, Brian." A sick feeling lurched in the pit of her stomach, and she raised a palm to her forehead, rubbing in slow circles in a futile effort to conjure up a solution to her wholly self-manufactured problem. "I knew the rules."

"I told him things to soften him."

Her hand dropped to the table, reaching for a long pull of her Tuborg. "Like?" Battling a gust of wind, her fingers wrapped around the glass before it tipped.

"Ethan tracked me down. He wanted answers." Brian's eyes flashed with belligerence as he watched her struggle with the pint. "Now he understands you would never, ever betray a client."

Nope, only sleep with one.

"And you conveyed that how?" *God*, she already knew. He'd made her sound like a brow-beaten wimp. Disclosed every weird quirk...

Ethan had told her he'd talked to Brian. She'd just assumed the info transfer had been limited.

Brian's ruddy color heightened again. "I told him you took that cab straight to the hotel." With a hesitant, yet triumphant smile, he added, "And why. We discussed your... shall we call it a 'darkness complex?'" Leaning back in his chair, he settled in. "In fact, I think he came out of our little chat seeing you as some sort of fragile angel in desperate need of a man like him."

Ethan had extended the olive branch after being made to feel sorry for her.

I blew everything on a pity fuck. Correction, many *pity fucks.*

"You went too far." She hurled the words with lethal finality.

After a pronounced pause, Brian spoke. "So you'd rather he believe you headed off into the night to rendezvous with an alternate Optik buyer?"

"Not your choice."

She blew out a breath, gulping her hard-won beer in pulling surges that weren't taking the edge off. The thought of exposing yet another weakness to Ethan made her queasy. He knew she couldn't bear children and that she'd inexplicably parted ways with billions in support and inheritance. He'd witnessed her panic at not being able to positively identify a visitor at her door and how a few days in a foreign bedroom had worn her to the bone. He even knew she showered partially clothed, as though flimsy, wet cloth could save her from an intruder bent on destruction.

While she'd developed the various eccentricities over a period of years, Ethan had discovered most of her secrets within days. The fact that she practically feared the night—that she categorically refused to brave it alone—iced the cake.

Even if undeniable professional issues didn't stand between them, could an international playboy bazillionaire really desire a meaningful relationship with goods as damaged as hers?

Guilt and sympathy. Both were powerful motivators, and not the kind of emotions she wanted fueling her chemistry with Ethan.

With the barriers to a healthy relationship crashing through her mind, she watched Brian's eyes shift to and away from her in a tentative bid for understanding. Sinking into a slouch, he crossed his arms over his chest and propped a well-heeled wingtip over his knee, hostility and concern radiating outward in equal measure.

"I'm not sorry." He grimaced. "If I hadn't talked to him, he would have taken you down before you knew what hit you."

"He would have *tried*."

"And succeeded, Scar. He really believed you were trying to sack the deal, and he's an 'act first, ask questions later' kind of guy."

The truth didn't make the situation easier, just angrier.

She sat forward slowly, plumping her lips. Nice Scarlet was out. Nasty Scarlet was surfacing, faster and faster. "Now that your intel set Ethan and I on a path of no-holds-barred sex, intimacy that you and everyone else working this deal knows about, what do I do?"

Bullshit, her mind cried. Brian had nudged Ethan in a forgiving direction. Seizing her good fortune, she'd been an all-kinds-of-eager participant in her own downfall. She and Ethan would have found the mattress without Brian's help. And the floor. And the shower. And even that secluded troll-land ride at Tivoli.

She *did* know the rules. They were breaking her heart. The fight drained away, and she blinked, distracting herself from the stinging behind her eyes. She looked across the table with mute appeal. "I can't afford to be with him, Brian. The price is too high."

The last spewed forth in a rush, and she forgot all about pinning the fault on the friend who'd gone out of his way to help.

Blame wouldn't save her from the grief coming her way.

CHAPTER 19

Scarlet inhaled the burst of lilies and gladiolas, their rioting fragrances tingling in her nose. No simple bouquet, Ethan extended a portable Danish summer in her direction.

"Hi." The low rumble enveloped her like a pair of chorded arms.

"Hi, yourself," she said, wishing she could summon a welcoming smile. "They're beautiful." She reached for the creamy, etched porcelain. No smudged glass from Ethan.

The blooms weighted her trek to the nightstand near her bed. They felt like a parting gift. Ethan didn't know it, but they were. Facing the wall, she stalled, blindly positioning each stem.

"What's up?" Concern edged the curiosity in his deep voice.

When she didn't answer, a charged silence descended on the room. She felt, more than heard, Ethan's measured approach from behind.

Anxiety clamped around her chest like a vice. *Show time, that's what.* Procrastination was rarely her poison, but before her sit-down with Brian, she'd welcomed it in. With each passing second—every look, gift, conversation, *orgasm*—she'd sunk further into Ethan's quicksand.

"Can we talk?" she managed to ask.

A wary note crept into his tone. "Have you slept?" Along with his "no bleeding" and "no fear" rules, he dogged her incessantly about getting more rest. One yawn and you'd think she hadn't slept in a week.

She'd miss his protectiveness. Her very own version of the mated vampires she devoured in her romance novels, albeit corporeal and thankfully lacking in the blood-drinking department. A few tastes hadn't been enough. It took all her strength not to wave a white flag and scream *mine, mine, mine! Fuck my career!*

Unfortunately, she wasn't immortal. She could be hurt without the expensive protective mechanisms only money could buy. Like guards with guns in her lobby. Gainful employment wasn't optional. She simply couldn't risk digging in with Ethan.

For now.

Time—weeks, maybe months—would let the storm vent its wrath. She'd shuffle Ethan to another attorney within the firm. After that, being with him wouldn't risk all she'd worked for.

Resolve surged through her system. This would *not* be the end. She reared away from the flowers, needing distance from anything bearing his stamp.

Two steps brought her ass up hard against Ethan's thighs. An arm encircled her from behind, and his breath skated along the side of her neck.

"Good idea," he murmured, turning their bodies in unison and gently pressing her, chest down, onto the mattress. He caged her exactly where she wanted to be. "Sex relaxes. It's the warm milk of exercise. You'll be asleep in no time after I'm through with you."

As he spoke, he straddled her lower back and spread strands of her hair across the velvety duvet, tugging his fingers through her curls.

Like always, his words warmed her against her will. Three little sentences and she was ready to throw caution to the wind for a bout of good-bye sex.

Except it would only be good-bye sex to *her.* She knew he suspected, but he didn't know.

Which would be too cruel.

"Ethan, I want you—"

"I know, sweetheart," he groaned on a subtle forward thrust of his lean hips. "And I can't wait for you to—"

"But I can't have you."

The thrusting stopped. "Oh, but you can," he said in a voice dripping with innuendo. His hands landed on her ass and slid to her sides. She stifled the urge to groan and surge up from the bed. With a cheek pressed to the mattress, she concentrated on the footboard, willing herself to stay still.

"Everyone knows," she whispered in defeat, hoping it would be enough.

His caresses slowed, but didn't stop. "You thought they wouldn't?" He kneaded her lower back before tracing the seam between shirt and skirt.

"I didn't think at all." *Liar.*

"I didn't want you to think."

His weight lifted, and a sigh broke from her lips at having reached him. The relief was short-lived. He merely gripped her sides and rolled her over before settling above her again. Before she could react, he plucked at her top button, then the second.

With each fastener conquered, he smoothed his knuckles over the revealed skin. "I wanted you to feel. Should I tell you want I want you to feel now?"

Yes, but lean close to make sure I get every word. "Please, Ethan, lawyers don't get to *feel* their clients. What I've done with you. To you. It's not allowed. I could be disbarred."

"Mmm hmm." Another button fell under his tender assault. He stroked between her breasts. She shivered when he nudged the scalloped edge of her bra, brushing back and forth, a physical promise to delve beneath if she asked nicely.

Desire clogged her throat and robbed her of the will to resist.

"Have I mentioned how I worship these skirts you wear?" Her blouse had fallen to his ministrations, and he shimmied backward to stand between her legs at the edge of the bed. Before she could utter a word, his hand slipped beneath her skirt. "So proper. Yet"—he squeezed her inner thigh— "not."

"Wait." Her legs went lax when he slipped two fingers beneath her panties, running them along her slick folds. "Stop," she rasped.

"If I stop, I can't do this." He pushed one finger in, deep, the way she liked. "You get so damn wet. Like magic."

He did it again, this time filling her with two fingers. Leaning over her splayed limbs, his tongue dipped inside her mouth to stroke in time with his hand below. She was too close. On the edge. Yet rather than enjoy the slow slide, anxiety gripped her mind's periphery. The more she said, the more lazily seductive he became.

"Scarlet?" His forehead pressed to hers and he panted, "You look like you'll splinter apart if I don't get inside you."

I will.

Sweat bloomed over her chest. She couldn't do this again. Hips bucking, she tried in vain to dislodge him, growing more agitated with each lurch. "Get off me. *Now.* Don't, Ethan, please—"

He rolled away in an instant, looking too sexy in his state of arousal and confusion and concern. "Sweetheart?" Rising to his full height, he held his hands out in surrender.

Sitting up, she reworked the buttons on her shirt with clumsy fingers before pulling the covers around her to block out the cold that lingered in his absence. Her heart hammered in a fierce staccato she feared he could hear, maybe see.

The desire had faded from his expression before she finished erecting the soft barrier between them. They faced each other in silence. Shoving his hands into the pockets of his jeans, his voice turned bland. "I'm listening."

Ethan studied her with a horrible detachment. He'd gone from the height of need to bored disinterest in the span of seconds, while she struggled to pluck a coherent thought from the cinders of her blazing arousal.

Make him understand. Her chest heaved. "Like I said, our colleagues know

I've…" An accurate description escaped her. *Fallen?* "That we've—"

"Fucked, Scarlet. Say it."

No, she didn't want his anger. "How you love that word," she said softly, grappling with her body's demand for the return of his touch as her heart cracked with the realization that rage might be all she'd get. "But yes, they know we've… fucked. And they don't like it."

Never breaking eye contact, he twined his arms across his chest in an impressive display that pulled his shirt tight over powerful biceps. She saw her fears enter his mind, disappointment that tightening the corners of his mouth. She'd managed to hide nothing. Still, he demanded, "Why?"

The harsh bark pegged her like a shot, rolling his sharp disappointment into one unforgiving syllable.

Through his rigid jaw, he gritted, "This is between us. You and me, no one else."

"I'll lose my job. If a grievance is filed with the state, I could lose my law license."

His eyes narrowed and he came closer, almost to the bed, but not quite. "I won't be filing a grievance, sweetheart." The mocking purr flowed from his throat. He'd already considered her arguments and found them lacking. "Sounds like overkill over two consenting adults having a little fun."

She sucked in a breath, her optimism wilting beneath his apathy. *A little fun.* "Easy to say when our affair costs you nothing."

"Think again." Balling his fists, he seethed, "Wanting you caused me to turn my back on the very thing that propelled me to the top. You asked me how I got here. Let me spell it out. I made it through a burning desire to watch you eat your apology, or more aptly, your pity. *Your check.*"

With a heave, he rattled a thick, wooden bed post, jostling her on the mattress. "No matter how misplaced, that loathing was a powerful motivator. Don't tell me that welcoming you into my life costs me nothing. I *liked* hating you."

And now you can't.

She clung to the fragile thread. "Pardon me for f'ing up your world view, but you're looking back. I'm looking forward. The latter is harder." Desperation spurred her on, made her careless. "Loving you requires me to surrender my livelihood."

He stilled, and she realized the wrong word had surfaced without her permission. *Loving.* He couldn't *not* use the truth against her, especially when she admitted her depth of feeling to push him away.

"'Love' now, is it?" His voice grew husky. "You're like a bad country song. All love and loss, but never your fault."

"No, Ethan." *I take it back.* "I don't want to part like this, fighting." Scarlet rolled onto her side, needing him to understand, to say he'd wait. "I can't be your lover *and* your lawyer."

He stood stock still, a muscle ticking in his jaw like clockwork. For too long, he said nothing, seeming to adjust to the fact that she wasn't bluffing and that he couldn't sway her with pleasure or logic or even anger. Then, without warning, he leapt onto the bed, close enough to hold her and tell her he'd be there when the time was right.

But he didn't.

He leaned in close, his black eyes flashing with dangerous emotion. "How long will it take?"

She managed not to flinch. "I don't know."

"We finally get a chance, and you're picking your *job*. For an unquantifiable amount of time, I'm to stand aside with a smile so Ms. Scarlet Leore can have it all." His face darkened, impervious to the pain his accusations caused. "Why does this whole Scarlet-knows-best routine feel like déjà vu?"

His fury filled her with a nameless dread, like the feeling she got when something terrible was about to happen, but she couldn't place the danger.

Only she could. She'd rediscovered Ethan at the wrong time. She'd lose him, and he'd choose to believe she wanted it that way.

Flopping onto her back, she stared at the patterned ceiling, shivering in the void of his emotional withdrawal. She took a deep breath. "I have to eat, Ethan." *And have a roof over my head, and security, and drivers…*

His eyes went wide on a vile curse, and he busted up, laughing in her face. "Yeah, fuck you, *counselor*." Then, with inexplicably tender movements, he rolled the covers around her to form a protective bunting, tucking them in until only her face peeked through.

"I'm not buying it," he forced out. "The women in my life don't generally suffer reduced circumstances." His disdain was all the more hurtful for the certainty in his voice. So many people had needed him at one point or another. Now he couldn't accept that she could only come to him whole, by choice rather than necessity.

Frustration swelled in the back of her throat. "Am I to become a kept woman? A few great nights"—*and shared secrets and yearning and trust*—"and I should throw caution to the wind because, wait for it, you've got money, so who needs mine?"

"Yes." The finality of his decree smashed into her. No exceptions. No talking it out. Just let him take care of everything, a black and white vision of the world and their places in it.

She bolted upright. Money had once torn them apart. "I can't, Ethan. Don't you get it? I was wrong when I accused you of hurting me, and you were arrested *on my word*. For anyone else, one young woman's accusation wouldn't have been enough. For Tripp Leore's daughter, it was plenty. And when I tried to pay you for all the ugliness, you hated me."

Her heart pounded in the aftermath of her outburst. "I'm not your mother or your hard-luck assistant or the empty socialite on your arm." Harsh breaths tumbled over each other as she fought to calm down. "I can't *need* your money like they can. Like I did *his*."

He leaned over the cocoon he'd fashioned, eyes bleak, empty. "And I'm not your father. What happened then wasn't about Daddy's money, and what's happening now isn't about mine. Our problem isn't your job or my wealth. It's that you won't trust me. You're afraid. There's a word for people like you."

She recoiled into the blankets. He spoke of the thing she'd spent the last ten years convincing herself she wasn't. Despite the memories, the lying awake at night fearing—knowing—someone was in her apartment, the lingerie hanging in her bathroom even now, she'd told herself it was all to be expected. That she wasn't a coward.

"Says the man who'd forfeit nothing more than the joy of hating me."

His head snapped back. He slid from the bed to stand over her, and then backed toward the door. "I say it because I'm willing to weather the storm. You aren't." Each step widened a chasm between them until it was much more than physical space. "You don't want us bad enough."

The accusation sent ice sliding down her spine. "Don't go like this. Talk to me, Ethan. You know I would…"

The begging shamed her, but she couldn't stop. She didn't trail off until the door shut quietly behind him.

What had she done?

******

Ethan could think of many reasons to end a relationship with him. Money wasn't one of them. He stood, rhythmically clenching and unclenching his fists in the hall outside her door, drinking in deep, measured breaths, damning her willingness to cast out their chances.

A decade of longing had gone into their charged encounters. Yet she questioned his investment. Sure, sex with Scarlet had been exceedingly entertaining, he had to admit, but only because he'd wanted her with every fiber of his being.

She'd turned him away, unwilling to take even a calculated risk with her precious career. In a stroke of naiveté he hadn't expected, she'd forgotten business economics 101. So long as the Atavos checks rolled in—and they would—her colleagues would turn a blind eye to what happened during Scarlet's personal time. No grievances. No reprimands.

Case closed.

With a disgusted look at his bulging jeans, he acknowledged he'd had this coming after a lifetime of not giving a shit. How many women had he wished well after a few good nights? He'd sent them packing, knowing all they sought resided in his pants—his wallet, primarily. Ironic that Scarlet ran from his affluence like a gold digger from a prenup.

Poor, he'd had no chance with her. Rich, same story.

He slammed into his room, flinging his shirt onto a high-backed chair. Then, unzipping the fly of his jeans as he moved, he practically hopped into the bathroom, yanking the denim from his heels and kicking the constraining cloth away.

Arousal threatened to overwhelm him. Despite the harsh words, he throbbed with the need to slide inside her warmth, to remind them both that their desire for each other couldn't be shelved for the sake of convenience.

Hard and aching, he stared at his erection, contemplating the separation she demanded. He needed her with a desperation he couldn't have predicted, wanted to hate her for the ease with which she pulled away. She'd tantalized him with a glimpse of happiness, only to snatch it back.

No matter what she'd claimed, she didn't love him. Not when a hiatus would obviously bring her little more than relief. Yet she was right. He'd be a fool to cast her aside over a delay, no matter how long or how indefinite.

The knowledge that she'd been less affected pounded between his ears, ridiculing the depth of his feelings. While she'd been plotting her escape, he'd been planning ways to give her the child she wanted but couldn't have.

While she used the *word* love, he welcomed the *reality* of it.

Scarlet hadn't been another fling, a pleasurable lay. He *would* wait for her. But he'd be damned if she'd know it.

Groaning, he stepped under a frigid fall of water. The instant he realized the cold hadn't withered him in the least, he gripped his erection without mercy. Stroking his hand up and down in brutal swipes that had him sucking air, he pictured the perfection of Scarlet's porcelain skin, imagined that each thrust coaxed another moan from her lips.

He dragged his thumb over the seething head, then froze at the music of an indrawn breath. Jerking his gaze toward the door, he saw Scarlet's blurred features through the shower curtain. Her lips parted in a silent "O" as her wide eyes traveled the length of his body, settling on his straining erection and the hand that eased it. Before he could move, she licked her lips and drifted forward.

"Here to help?" he asked, regretting his decision to leave his internal door unlocked. He'd hoped for a hell of a lot more from her ability to move freely between their rooms.

At his clipped question, she backed away, never tearing her attention from the show. "I—we can't leave it like this."

Further aroused by her hot, unrelenting stare, even though she uttered all the wrong words, he barked, "Scarlet, either join me or get out. Now." He refused to *perform* for a woman who'd put him on the shelf. If he recalled correctly, he wasn't to provoke intimacy between them until further instruction.

Fuck. That.

She turned and fled, and with a groan, he pumped his fist ruthlessly until an empty, meaningless release boiled over. The whole thing left him feeling tight and twitchy, completely devoid of the relief and relaxation he'd sought.

Exiting the shower, he wrapped a towel around his waist and stalked into his suite, only to come up short at the sight of her. There she sat on his settee, an accidental professor fantasy in a slim tweed skirt and a fitted button-down with a crisp collar. If she would just chew daintily on the end of a No. 2 pencil and murmur, "You've been a very naughty pupil, Mr. Blake."

He'd lied to himself at their airport reunion weeks ago. It turned out the schoolmarm look was, without a doubt, his *thing*.

"I said get out."

She shrugged, her golden gaze locking on his chest like a heat-seeking missile. "I thought you meant the bathroom."

"A creative interpretation."

If possible, she sat up straighter. The unconscious shift thrust her breasts forward, magnifying the reel of images playing in his mind. *Somebody get this woman a scarred writing desk and a ruler.*

"Maybe," she conceded, crossing smooth, bare legs at the ankles. "I won't stay away. Not when you're furious with me." She paused, seeming to look at anything but him as her voice fell to a strained whisper. "I can't, Ethan. This wasn't... You weren't supposed to—"

"Your whole point has been to 'stay away.'" He kneaded the back of his neck. Fresh off his decision to concede to her wishes, he doubted his ability to withstand the seduction routine.

Finally, her eyes shifted—round and panicked—over his damp body, which responded whole-heartedly to her visual caress. Hating his uncontrolled reaction to such a vulnerable perusal, he lashed out. "Here to finish what we started? Because if so, I'm all ears, among other things."

"Yes," she answered, never looking away. "But *after*... Please at least try to understand."

Yes? He blinked, sure he hadn't heard right. She'd pushed him away in her suite. Now she sat in his, thwarting her own career-saving plan within minutes of putting it in place.

Alarm rose up, winding its way to his conscious in a sharp realization that killed the anger. Scarlet remained convinced she needed distance before she could be with him, that without it she'd be ruined. Yet here she was, blatantly initiating sex, unable to heed her *own* demands for space.

"Ten minutes ago you put us on hold. What are you offering, Scarlet?"

Her face flooded with rich color, an answer that spoke louder than words.

Equal parts aggression and uncertainty spiked in his veins. He didn't fault her, not really. But that blush, her very presence, meant that despite her demand for distance, she would come to him over and over again if he agreed to her fake separation. Scarlet had subtly kept them on the down low from the beginning. That much was now clear. Yet, despite her efforts, everyone knew. As smart as she was, she lied to herself in imagining a clandestine affair could slip by.

His mouth watered to *take*. Decency would only let him if it helped her fight her own demons.

If he let her sabotage the steps she viewed as crucial to their being together, she'd be *right* the next time she came to view him as her downfall. God, they *did* have to part, not only for her, but for a long-term *them*.

And it had to be believable.

He breathed harder. To be believable, it had to be *real*.

Act I of the next hour would be easy. He'd have her nice and deep. Act II might kill him.

He hit the floor between her knees. "Glad you came to your senses."

This time, he didn't have the patience to slowly unbutton her blouse. Gripping its edges, he jerked the fabric apart, scattering silver buttons across the plush carpet. Ten seconds later, her bra went the way of the buttons when he flicked the clasp between her shoulder blades and pulled the supportive lace from her outrageous breasts.

"Look at your sweet little nipples," he breathed, reverent. Circling each one, he pushed her back against into the couch. "Do you want me to suck them?" He pinched one wicked peak, harder than usual. "Maybe this one?"

She nodded, eyes drooping, body going lax. *Yes, this is what you need.*

Sliding his hands to below her bent knees, he toyed with the soft flesh of her legs, watching her writhe beneath his hands. When he skimmed calloused palms over her smooth calves, a whimper tore from her throat, and she began to slowly saw her legs back-and-forth against each other.

Enthralled with the way her impatience swayed the plump swells of her breasts, he focused a light caress over her moving feet, withholding the tonguing he knew she craved. A flush stole over her face and her undulating chest. He felt her tense as she moved beneath his hands, under his burning scrutiny.

"Relax, Scarlet." *Enjoy it while it lasts.*

Her smooth muscles gathered, and she uncrossed her ankles, wiggling her toes into the sides of his towel in silent command.

He released her delicate arches. "You want me bare?"

She nodded adamantly, and he obliged. With a swift tug, he released the towel and crawled up her splayed body, biting back a low moan as his cock met the soft skin above her skirt. Bending his head, he flicked his tongue over the fragile pulse that fluttered at her jugular. When she whimpered for more, he licked from the base of her throat to the smooth globe of her breast. Latching onto a nipple with quick tugs and releases, he blew soothing breaths over the straining peak.

While he sucked, he rubbed his shaft over her skirt, then snaked his hand between their bodies to press against the tender spot that always welcomed him. Fisting the material, he rasped, "Do you want this gone, to be open for me?"

On an expelled breath, she reared beneath him. "More than that. Impaled." Her face went hard, and he saw a flash of resentment break through her desire. "*Fucked*," she grated.

He *did* love that word. Loved saying it. Imagining everything it entailed. But hearing her put her need in basic terms—even when she didn't want to, *especially* when she didn't want to—snapped his control.

"Count on it," he growled, unzipping the side closure to her skirt before tugging the garment from her body. He stood to toss the skirt away, glancing down—

He stopped cold.

No panties. She'd come to him, exposed and ready. His gaze slammed into hers. "Guess you took me for a sure thing."

She conceded the point with a jerk of her head.

He could smell her excitement. Dropping to his knees on a low groan, he delivered a slow, wide lick up the center of her wetness.

So ready. "Always like this." He nibbled and licked before stiffening his tongue and pushing into her with a leisurely thrust. One, two, three times. Then again because he couldn't stop.

Above, her moans spurred him on. Draping her thighs over his shoulders, he settled in, massaging her lower abdomen as he had her with lips and tongue. It wasn't enough. Her taste buzzed in his skull like a full-on addiction. How could he give this up? Even for a little while.

He pushed all second thoughts aside. He could do without anything in the short term. Yet a smaller voice echoed in his head. *Not Scarlet.*

As he curled his tongue around her swollen, sensitive clitoris, she rose to meet his mouth. Gasping, she pleaded for what they both knew he could give her. "It feels so good. I can't... Ethan."

When his name left her lips, her sex begin a wet clenching, and he drove two fingers into her demanding channel, answering her body's call to be filled. With each pull, she whimpered, "Coming. *Ethan.* Can't stop."

He pushed roughly, keeping time with the heaving pulses of her body. "Never stop. I feel you clutching me. Perfect."

After her orgasm ebbed, she looked at him with still-frantic desire glinting in her gaze. "Need you," she said, pulling him upward. She squirmed to the edge of the settee, meeting his cock halfway. And when she used her own hand to open herself and rock her wetness against his engorged shaft, his mind whited out. No force on earth could have stopped him from pulling back and thrusting to the hilt.

"Oh, Jesus, don't move, Scarlet." If she stirred even a fraction, it was game over. With a performance like that, she might be glad to see him go. Probably would be anyway.

He held her still, bracketing her in place while he licked her neck, then traced the flawless diamond at her ear with his tongue.

Finally gaining control, he began a slow, shallow thrusting. Before he could delve deeper, she pressed down on his shoulders, pulling herself up and *off* his erection with a command that he "sit." With a grimace, she weighted her body to the side in a futile attempt to clamor her way to the top.

Understanding the gist of her instructions and sensing now wasn't the time to ignore her commands, he stood and sat on the couch with her cradled in his lap. Immediately, he lifted her over his straining erection.

She pulled back. "I once read in a magazine that men like to *alternate*." Her voice sounded low and scratchy, like she hadn't used it for a while.

Alternate? This time he had no idea what she wanted. Her drenched folds hovered a mere inch above his dick, and she wanted to talk about a Cosmo article.

"You know, alternate?" she prompted, low and harsh.

No fucking clue. "I know if you sink down, you find something we've discovered you *like*."

She leaned in and purred in his ear. "I'll help you." She shifted and slid down his erection, inch by inch. When completely seated, she pulled up and did it again.

Yeah, baby, help me. Just like this.

Torturously slow, but over and over, she rose and then fell, gliding over his shaft. She moved as though fucking him was a top priority and a job she took very seriously. Tables turned, she hijacked his lesson with one of her own.

After long moments of drawn-out pleasure, he leaned back, observing through slit eyes as she rode him. Gritting his teeth, he clenched his abs so hard each ridge shadowed the next.

With her flushed features and swollen nipples and wild blond curls, she personified sex. "Look at you, Scarlet. See your hot little body taking me in."

He reached around to palm her ass, but when his hand touched the smooth globe of one cheek, she snapped her hips, wringing a surprised gasp from his scratchy throat.

Glorying in the fact that she might be ready for harder play, he placed his hands on her hips and bucked into her in quick, sharp thrusts. "Like that—"

She pulled up—all the way up—literally leaving him moaning the loss. "I take it back, I'm dying."

"We're trying something, remember?" With that, she slid down over his body and sucked him into the warmth of her mouth, her hot lips engulfing him without warning.

Alternate! He was *so* renewing her magazine subscriptions when this was all over.

"Your article was right," he hissed when she feathered her wet tongue over his dick like a carnival treat. "I *love* it." *And you.*

Fear that he might lose both set the fierce pleasure against the urge to be sick.

Again, just when he thought he'd explode, she pulled back, this time to inch back up his body and slide him inside her once more.

Sweat beaded on his chest. He let loose with a long, low growl. "How many times did your article tell you to do this?"

She flashed a wicked grin. "Lots."

Half an hour later, Ethan had gone mad. She'd enslaved him, not that he hadn't seen it coming. She finally rode him hard. As an insurance policy, he slipped his thumb between them to rub her slick clit on each downward stroke. In less than a minute, he felt her tightening. His ears devoured the sound of her helpless mewling, those innate sounds of pleasure she couldn't hold back.

"Come on me, Scarlet." His voice had gone guttural. "I want to feel you squeeze me when you let go."

"Anything—" Her body convulsed in waves. He met her, letting loose into the reaching depths of her body.

Slowing down and breathing hard, it hit him too soon that he'd literally bathed her womb with his seed. *No condom.* The thought had him scrambling away in panic, the worst scenarios imprinting on his mind.

Scarlet in pain. Losing a child.

"Wait." She reached out, tethering him.

"We didn't use protection," he said, hearing the desperate edge to his voice. "Shit. I wasn't thinking."

"It's all right." She clamped her knees to the sides of his thighs, holding him in place beneath her. "Ethan, we're okay. You know the condom's a safety net." Stroking his cheek, she added, "We're fine."

Yeah, *he* would be fine. *He* didn't risk his very life with conception. The thought of Scarlet facing an ectopic pregnancy—any kind of threat whatsoever—had his teeth playing bumper cars. "Never again."

Her face went sad, eyes distant. "Not as long as that, but not for some time. We have to be convincing."

Like this had been? Bitter laughter welled up. *Yes, we have to be convincing, and I hope you'll forgive me for making sure we are.*

Even knowing what he had to do, his throat closed at the sight of her earnestness. *Now or never.*

Lifting a sensitive nipple to his seeking tongue, he drawled between licks, "You said you can't be my 'lover and my lawyer.' Seems you just chose 'lover' in a pretty big way."

"No," she said, sucking her lower lip. Oh, how he wanted to do that for her.

He tilted his head, considering, then stated the obvious. "You're still choosing 'lawyer.'"

The accusation hung between them like he knew it would. Scarlet would be fine, was getting what she wanted, what she believed she needed. For his sake, he hoped she got it fast.

He stared at her wordlessly, preparing, and then gently wound an arm around her lower back to chain them together for the harsh road ahead.

******

Ethan clasped her chin between his fingers, urging her head around to face him. An hour ago he hadn't been hearing her. In a move more desperate than she wanted to admit, she'd come to him again, determined to show him, in the most basic way possible, the emotions he'd refused to believe.

Her relief at having reached him dissipated when she saw his expression. The passion from moments ago had fled, leaving his features cold. Utterly remote and unyielding. Even the muscles beneath her bunched, going taut.

"You didn't think to manipulate me with a bout of *really* acrobatic sex, did you sweetheart?" His voice was smooth, satin easing over blown glass. "Certainly you're not that naive or that stupid."

She froze at the accusation. Pain hit, then expanded in her chest. *No, not this.*

Mute, she squirmed on his lap, trying to break loose.

"You knew," he rasped out, "that I'd think you'd changed your mind, that I wouldn't touch you otherwise. In your suite—before, when you were intent on leaving me behind—you were *desperate* to avoid my touch."

She shook her head, frantic to change the loathing that distorted his features. "I wanted to show you—" She swallowed the admission. "I thought once more wouldn't make a difference." But she'd only considered whether her colleagues would find out about an extra round, not what it would do to them when, afterward, parting remained a reality.

"Honesty didn't work, so you pranced in here without underwear. What, did you think making me come would make me more malleable? Make me agree to your temporary split?"

Her limbs shook, but her eyes remained dry, aching in their sockets. Hurt like this felt too immense for tears. Like her skin would rip apart at previously unknown seams. She tried to rise off his lap, but he anchored her in place.

"Please let go," she whispered.

"With pleasure." But his grip didn't ease. "You know what, Scarlet? All kinds of women have tried to rule me with sex." A sensual glint entered in his gaze. "They've used dirty, wet, sucking sex, like you, to bind and control. It hasn't worked. It never will." His body went pliant beneath hers, lids lowering. "But let me tell you, I enjoyed the effort. And if you ever feel like trying again, you know where to find me."

"I see," she whispered. But she only "saw" his mocking expression, laughing at her for giving him everything.

"You got your 'once more,' Scarlet. Now I want my 'get out.'"

He'd asked her to leave the suite when she'd interrupted his shower earlier, and she clung to hope a saner person would have abandoned. "Of your room?"

The arm binding her relaxed, freeing her to go. "Of my life."

The three words wound around her heart, squeezing in her chest until air became scarce. She had gambled and lost.

Sucking in a breath, she pushed herself up, then began to collect her discarded clothing, first her skirt, then her bra from behind the couch. Her lovely blouse lay crumpled next to him on the sofa. She decided to abandon it since most of the buttons littered the carpet. Another thing destroyed.

Pulling herself upright, she resisted a last look in his direction, afraid of what her face might reveal. Then, with his stare burning into her retreating back, she walked through the connecting doors left ajar upon her arrival. On the other side, she shut hers quietly behind.

Seconds later, his followed suit. A deadbolt slid into place with a low thud.

Unstable legs carried her into the bathroom. A harsh twist sent hot water streaming into the tub. Eyes darting around the room, she eased into a sitting position at the edge of her bath, bombarded with piece after piece of lingerie hanging from every available surface. Each bra-and-panty set screamed safety. Security. All the shelter Ethan had just taken away. Emptiness clawed upward and she fought to prevent herself from grabbing something, anything, to cover her body before she sank into the water.

But she didn't. First one trembling arm and then a leg, she braced herself against the porcelain and lowered her body into the steaming heat, forcing down the instinctive rush of the old habit that rose to greet her.

If he never gave her another gift, Ethan would at least leave her with this, the strength to push forward. Raw, scared, fractured. But less afraid.

Brave.

CHAPTER 20

So much for the valiant attempt to save her career and her love life. Instead, she'd overseen two slow deaths.

Scarlet shifted on the curb that fringed the d'Angleterre, gripping the handles of her rolling luggage and examining her cherry red manicure in mutiny. When that became a bore, all too quickly, she flashed Brian a tentative smile. "It's coming, right?"

"I called, Scar." He looked her over from head to toe. "Don't be scuffing those Manolos in your enthusiasm. We're taking our time, walking out of this shit show calmly, heads held high."

She regarded the glossy heels Brian so admired, red to match her manicure. They stood out against the silk of her fitted business suit, gray to match her mood. If she decided to sabotage the only bright things on her body, let alone her mind, she'd hurl the shoes at Ethan's thick skull.

Deceptively calm, she dropped her chin and let her eyes blur until she saw two rosy blobs silhouetted against an indistinct backdrop of hot concrete. Squinting, the splotches stretched wide, giving her designer clown feet. Her fashion fixation had grown involuntarily as the Optik deal had dwindled over the last several days. Each time her confidence took a hit, her compulsion to perfect business-chic consumed the lost ground, eventually overtaking her drive to usher Atavos and Optik, not to mention her and Ethan, into enduring partnerships.

Now she *looked* great, meticulously groomed, in control, and worth every cent of several-hundred dollars an hour. Yet the deal smoldered at her feet, and she was out a client. She refused to dwell on what else she'd lost.

Lissa would say she'd reverted to type. Stress did strange things to people. A few ate. Some drank. Still others slept. She shopped for things she technically couldn't afford, letting the thrill of the chase consume all the unsavory details.

Until the money runs out.

Ethan had told Arland Magnus to fuck off that morning. With one clipped obscenity, the deal had screeched to a halt. Atavos would go elsewhere, leaving her and the rest of the team on a sunbaked curb no less than two hours later.

Flights had been booked and cabs called. Now the fat lady sang a heart-wrenching good-bye in Scarlet's ear, and that imaginary farewell appeared to be all she'd get.

Other than an hour-old e-mail from Ethan, her dismissal had been largely silent. His initial message had been addressed to her but copied several JTS colleagues in Copenhagen and, unfortunately, New York. First, Ethan had extended a tepid thanks for her efforts. Then he'd gotten down to business. *Atavos will no longer require your services or the legal expertise of Jahn Tremane & Spellman.*

Flinching in memory, she mentally reread between the lines. She'd asked for time and space to figure out how the two of them could sustain an above-board relationship. In response, he'd cut her from his life with all the precision of a surgical knife. At the same time, his devastating message had severed their attorney-client relationship and technically opened the door to the possibility of a legitimate love affair.

A follow-up e-mail, this time to her alone, made it clear that Ethan didn't intend to pick up where they'd left off. *I wish things could have been different.*

Message number three had arrived hot on the heels of the other two, only it had come from a JTS partner who never minced words. The head of JTS's corporate group had requested to see her upon arrival in New York and rubbed the whole wretched story in her face. *An eventful trip, Ms. Leore.*

The smarmy insinuation lent Ethan's curt, professional set-down additional sting.

After sampling all she had on offer, Ethan had found her lacking, both the lover *and* the lawyer. Even her damn boss knew about her double-edged failure.

Snip.

"Scarlet?" Brian's voice jolted her out of the untimely obsession with her well-shod feet. She looked up to see him haul his luggage to a waiting taxi. On a steadying inhale, she gathered the tattered reserves of her pride and trundled forward, bags in tow.

A hand on her shoulder halted all progress. Feeling no trace of fear at the sudden contact, she whirled to face the only person who'd dare such high-handedness. Ethan towered above her with his back to the hotel and the summer sun bombarding his aviators. Not a telltale twitch or squint in sight, he stood in a loose stance that emphasized the sharp cut of his three-piece suit.

For the first time in their volatile history, Ethan didn't look at Scarlet when he spoke, as though he couldn't be bothered to tilt his head in her direction. "Ride with me," he said. As she'd come to expect, his low voice issued a command, not a request.

But she'd do it. Wanted to, in fact. Perhaps the simple act of yelling at him over the twenty-minute airport dash would prove cathartic.

"I'd love to," she said sweetly. Then, with a dazzling smile, she turned to The Minion at his side. "You can ride"—she gestured over her shoulder to Brian with a quick jerk of her head—"over there." Without awaiting a reply, she kicked the Manolos into gear and strutted past the two of them to slide into a black Mercedes that eased to the curb.

And screw you, Susan, for not sucking more. Sinking into the butter-soft leather seats, Scarlet acknowledged her standing reservation at the bottom rung of hell. But really, couldn't The Minion have shown herself to be slightly corrupt? Maybe an itsy bit of backdoor dealing to reroute all those fingers pointing straight at the legal team?

Ron Michael had staged a veritable inquest, and Susan had come out smelling like roses—an ordinary bitch, not a double-crossing one. And apparently one that enjoyed the occasional European tryst. Admittedly, given Susan's revealing little "pep-talk" over Scarlet's first return itinerary, the woman's enduring loyalty to Ethan hadn't come as a surprise. The news that Susan had most likely been getting laid the night she'd aroused Ethan's suspicion had, on the other hand, been the surprise of the summer.

Nope, parting ways with Optik had been a run-of-the-mill breakup. Like thousands of companies before them, Atavos and Optik simply didn't suit. The Danish company would move on to the next sucker, looking for a buyer with a different management style, fewer questions, and a higher— though completely unwarranted—offering price. While the same story played out daily in boardrooms the world over, this particular flop had run at least a week long and a hundred grand high, an easy failure to chalk up to Scarlet, the sub-par negotiator.

To boot, Ethan believed she'd used her body to coerce him into a sham breakup for the sake of her career.

The idea was laughable. She didn't possess the sexual confidence to manipulate a man like Ethan with her charms. From the insults still batting around the inside of her skull, Ethan agreed. *"Certainly you're not that naïve or that stupid."*

Ding! Ding! Ding! She knew her limitations well, and a man-eater she wasn't. But she *was* naïve enough to follow her heart into his bathroom to work at repairing the rift between them and stupid enough to follow her libido into his bed, or at least onto his couch, after seeing the searing way he'd touched himself beneath that sheet of water.

He also thought—and this time he was right—that she'd always choose a modest independence over turning to a man for a pampered existence. Even if the man was Ethan. *Because* he was Ethan. The only person her money had ever hurt.

If she *needed* something from him, how could offering love be considered anything but payment?

Staring out the tinted window, she saw a hint of a smile crack Ethan's face when he picked up her luggage and passed it to their driver. She'd left it there to piss him off, blatantly implying he lived to serve and mentally rubbing her hands together over the little indecencies men had to suffer when they pissed the wrong woman off.

And he found it funny.

Opening the door, he peered into the comparative darkness of the car's interior. In a slow drawl, he asked, "Anything else I can do for you, Ms. Leore?"

Tell me you can't live without me. Then take off your clothes and give me a real ride to the airport. "Not particularly," she said, busying herself with the seat belt.

With those and several equally uplifting thoughts, she pulled her attention back to the harmless peep-toe heels that, if she said so herself, totally elongated her petite legs. Another pair—same style, different color— might be in order.

She'd nearly coaxed herself into rock-solid indifference when he crawled into the back seat, resting his thigh a tad closer than necessary given the spacious quarters. That come-hither heat she'd come to expect from his nearness radiated between their bodies.

Despite the closeness, he didn't reach out. For the first time, his touch wasn't a sure thing. She ran a clammy palm over her legs, skimming the shoes, but it didn't do the trick. When *he* touched her, she felt a jolt of emotion—calmed, aroused, desired, cared for. When she touched herself, she felt like a pretender, a loser groping her own leg in an attempt to emulate her ex-lover's hands on her body.

And here she'd planned to rebuff the advance she'd "known" would come, to make it clear that while he panted after her, she'd grown immune to his charms.

Wrong again.

"I got your messages," she said quietly, staring down at the beautiful shoes.

"Yes." Paper rustled, and the dry sweetness of newspaper ink permeated the car's interior. "Now you're free."

Free to do what? Not sleep? Get fired? Want him more than ever?

She didn't turn. "You, too."

More rustling, then a gentle stroke swept along on her jaw until she turned her attention from her feet and looked his way. Like a doctor examining a patient, he trailed a finger beneath her eye, tracing the dark circle she hadn't been able to conceal with any amount of makeup. He gently turned her face a bit further, then traced around the other eye. "Not sure I'd call giving you up 'freedom.'"

"Then what?" she asked, refusing to let his meaningless banter matter. Ethan had been the one to cut her loose, after all. Veiled hints that he hadn't liked the role only engendered false hope.

"Giving in."

She leaned her cheek into his palm and closed her eyes. "Giving *up*."

"Call it what you want. This is exactly what you demanded."

"Right before I *un*-demanded it."

He pulled away. "And you have *such* a way with words."

She'd wondered how long he'd play civil. The back of her hand drifted to one cheek and then the other, preserving his fleeting caress.

"Like I said," he went on, "call me next time you feel like doling out that kind of convincing."

She flinched but forced her tongue to barb up. "Why bother? It didn't work."

"It worked," he murmured so softly she strained to her. "Only not the way you'd hoped." This time he was the one to look away.

CHAPTER 21

September—New York City

Law firm hallways sucked in general, not just Scarlet's. They made it impossible to get around without being subjected to either crappy, yet inoffensive, artwork or a fellow lawyer on the colossal-blowhard list.

And any lawyer who doesn't own up to such a list, lies.

C-Blow One on Scarlet's list swaggered down the hall, past a boxy, tan pedestal supporting a bronze statue of the scales of justice. Dreadful, both of them.

She slowed, glancing to a point ahead where the hall veered in three directions, wondering which route he'd choose. She hated to lose forty minutes to his vision of the business and how others simply lacked his drive and enviable ambition. He labored longer, thought more strategically, and earned more money than her little mind could comprehend. Obviously.

A door opened and Brian stepped into her path on the right, his body blocking a table of colleagues deep in discussion. No nameless client in sight. She lurched to a standstill, eager to use her friend as a human shield. Peeking around his shoulder, she wondered if she'd missed the memo. "Did we have a department meeting? Don't tell me I'm supposed to be in there."

Embarrassment flitted across his features. It fled fast, but she pegged it.

"No," he insisted, pulling the door shut and obstructing her view of the action. "Not this time."

A rare legal breed, Brian hadn't learned to lie. He couldn't even muster a convincing evasion.

Innate curiosity urged her to dig, but the distance she'd felt from everyone but Brian since her return from Denmark shut her up. She couldn't afford to piss him off. "Busy lately?"

She shot fidgeting hands into the pockets of her skirt and beat back an eye roll. At herself. "The busy" was a standard water-cooler question for lawyers, and one she fervently avoided. Inundated lawyers were good lawyers. They worked twelve-hour days, pulled all-nighters, and had a strong physical reaction to setting their mobiles aside.

Lawyers with time on their hands were bad lawyers. The ability to maintain a family or hobbies or friends meant they couldn't find enough work to fill the many, many six-minute billing increments in the day. Those attorneys found themselves out in the cold.

A colossal blowhard never failed to work "the busy" into casual conversation. Simply mouthing the question provided the asker with an opportunity to wax poetic about how buried with work he or she had been. So many daughters' dance recitals missed and spouses' birthdays forgotten, all because the asker was clearly a big fucking deal.

Guess she could add herself to her own list, even though recent weeks had seen Scarlet leaving the office earlier and earlier. Yesterday, she'd gone to a movie in the middle of the afternoon. She'd returned after, hoping to find a message from a colleague or a client in need of her oh-so-capable assistance. The work gods hadn't smiled on her.

Brian shifted on his feet. "Yeah, pretty busy. I'm stepping out for a client call."

An uneasy feeling took hold. Overlapping meetings went beyond "pretty busy," which meant the work dearth didn't apply to everyone. "Need a hand? I've got some bandwidth."

His fingers clenched around the doorknob brushing his hip. "We need to talk, Scar."

A lump of dread rose at the base of her throat. Too many small signs sent a big message. Management had expressed disappointment with the Copenhagen fiasco. She'd gritted her teeth through more than one "joke" about the "talent" it took to lose a corporate client within a month of signing the engagement letter. Usually, they said, such a feat took years. *Ha. Ha.* She also didn't have enough work to fill her days despite the fact that her colleagues were drowning and couldn't keep up. And now? She'd been excluded from a department meeting, and Brian looked ready to give her a hug over what must *not* have been an oversight.

Crossing her arms over her chest, she inclined her head toward the room he blocked with his body. "Is that meeting what I think it is?" *Out with Scarlet and in with a lawyer who either wouldn't screw her clients or would do it well enough to keep them.*

He nodded at the floor. "Give me time, Scarlet. Their search isn't going well. How could it? They've gotta find a young, vibrant personality with the mind and experience of a seasoned gray hair." The phone in his pocket buzzed, and he reached for it. "Fuck. I'm late for this call." He shuffled sideways down the hall, half in her world and half in his client's. *"Don't* panic. I'm thwarting them at every turn." He answered the phone and disappeared.

She stared after him, apparently too long, because as soon as Brian vanished, C-Blow took his place. Trapped, she endured a conversation made for one. He talked. She nodded, doing her best to suppress the worry that prowled out from the walls of her stomach.

"A law firm's money is made on the margin," he told her, "primarily when attorneys greatly exceed their billable hour requirements. Busy lawyers pay the bills."

Yep. She inclined her head slightly, enough to show she hadn't slipped into a coma. That little mathematical reality contributed to his immense, self-inflated value. It might be the death of hers.

Insomnia hit hard that night. After hours of silent, sleepless brooding, Scarlet caved to the sinking feeling Brian's words had left in their wake. She slipped from the bed, reluctantly making her way to one of the wooden stools she kept tucked beneath the overhang of her kitchen counter. Firing up her laptop, she navigated to JTS's "join us" page, full of flattering information about the firm and its people and policies. At the bottom, she clicked on a link that said "open positions."

The darkness of her kitchen only enhanced the glowing list that popped into view. Minutes fell away while she stared at it, unseeing, mentally instructing her sweating palm to return to the mouse. All those knowing-is-half-the-battle people were wrong. Knowing what she'd find didn't make finding it any easier.

Her hand curled into an ineffectual fist. *Do it.*

There, last on the list, was an entry for a "senior M&A associate." She jerked forward and clicked the title, her eyes speeding over the small print. The selected attorney would be based in New York City. He or she would represent JTS's business clients in "complex commercial and corporate transactions involving both negotiated and unsolicited tender offers, mergers, minority investments, leveraged buyouts, and proxy contests." The lucky winner's primary responsibilities would include working with in-house business teams to assess corporate valuation and negotiate contractual terms.

The time bomb ticking away in her skull exploded, and her forehead sagged over the keyboard. JTS's job posting represented everything she'd sought to avoid in her ill-fated attempt to pull away from Ethan.

Work had dwindled to a trickle. Efforts to rake in hours weren't panning out. And now, at a time when she had little to do, when she wasn't *busy*, the firm had officially launched a talent search for a lawyer with her same experience and skills.

Her replacement.

Wave upon wave of impending doom crashed over her. Another life lesson about carelessness. She didn't want to believe Ethan had planned this all along. That kind of betrayal would render his every caring word and touch an act, and paint her a gullible fool.

But wanting wasn't doing. "*I'll destroy you. I'll exploit every weakness you have...*"

Ethan was keeping his promise.

******

Ethan barely knew where he was going. In a bleary daze, he made his way through his darkened penthouse. "Scarlet," he growled, her name a benediction and a curse.

He ended up in his private gym, among the benches scattered between rows of free weights. Though the space was his alone, it could accommodate several men. Prowling past the heavy bag suspended from the ceiling, he approached a smaller speed bag hanging beneath a flat, circular plate. On the nights when life lingered too close to the surface, killing all thoughts of sleep, he sought out the rhythmic beat of the speed bag to silence the chaos in his mind.

Three strikes in, he let the ball fall still. For once, the sharp staccato of the bag rebounding against its backboard repelled rather than soothed. It wasn't a honeyed voice or a gasping laugh. Instead of cracked leather, his hands ached to touch soft skin, gently rounded hips and thighs.

Scarlet, dammit, where are you?

Abandoning the speed bag, he knelt before a mini fridge. His fingers closed around a half-empty bottle of gin he kept handy for guests. Skipping the mixers, he drank directly from the source, all the tang of a pine forest flowing down his throat.

The liquor burned a path to his stomach, but the anticipated feelings of warmth and escape eluded him. Life remained a bleak, faded version of the existence he'd inhabited with *her*.

His demand that Scarlet get out of his life hadn't touched her. That, or her relief at the opportunity to save face in front of her colleagues had consumed her regret. She'd collected her clothing with cool efficiency and left him falling apart on the couch in his suite, staring after her.

Alone in the cab after the deal had gone sour, she hadn't railed at him over the injustice of her firm's firing or pointed out that with him out of the picture as a client, the coast was clear for romance. On the plane, she'd moved—actually asked the attendant to shuffle her seat assignment—when he'd sat next to her. "*I really do need an aisle*," she'd said in a dire tone, as though she'd get leg clots if she couldn't easily pace the walkways during the flight.

After weeks, there hadn't been a single call. No e-mails. Not even a hand-written letter telling him off in style.

The forced separation killed him, but she wouldn't have carried through on her own. He should have let her thwart herself, let her destroy her credibility by seeing him right under their noses after swearing she'd ended the affair. He hadn't been able to let her do herself that kind of harm.

"Lawyers," he said on a sterile laugh before swigging more gin. "Fuck you when they show, and fuck you worse when they don't."

He sat heavily on a nearby weight bench, acknowledging he much preferred it when they—or at least she—showed.

Surely she'd saved face at the firm by now. *Drink.* Proven her eagerness to sacrifice. *Big drink.* How long did the woman need? *Fuck, bottle empty.*

He rolled back against the bench and examined the ceiling. No floating sensation. Not even a decent case of the spins. The booze might as well have doused a brick wall.

The weight bench and dry bottle kept him company for the rest of the night. His old plan obviously sucked. Minute-by-minute, a new one took shape. The next morning, he marched to the helm of a meeting at Atavos's headquarters, determination weighing heavy.

On his way in, he'd heard Susan whisper to Billboard conspiratorially. "*Ethan's on the brink.*"

She had *no* idea.

The team gathered to discuss more optics, this time from South Korea. Twenty-five of his best and brightest bellied up to a massive birch conference table. He looked them over, barely concealing his disgust. Each person appeared engaged. Some studied computer screens. Others contemplated charts or spreadsheets.

Multiple failed deals and here they were, a veritable beehive of activity without the parts or the capability needed to manufacture *One*. And whose fault was that? Fuck if he knew. Probably his.

Atavos's head of procurement looked particularly busy reviewing page after page from a ream of data. "Mr. Mertoy," he began, "You know we're here about a role-based, multiple application device—*One*. We've been in talks to purchase two different optics companies. Both times, negotiations have failed. Now? We can't acquire an optics company prior to *One's* release. We'll purchase what we need from an autonomous supplier. I need to know whether other Atavos components come from South Korea, which components, from which suppliers, and the pros and cons of working with those companies."

Mertoy brushed a hand over his balding head and cleared his throat. "Of course." After shuffling his papers into a neat stack, he began sifting through the sheets, setting one after another aside.

"Is the answer in those documents?" *Of course not.*

The man had the decency to look embarrassed. "Unfortunately, no."

"Off the top of your head?" If Mertoy had one to speak of.

His target offered up a placating smile. "I haven't been involved in direct purchasing for the past few years, but I can speak with our procurement specialists and include their experiences in a report to you later today."

Ethan locked a sharp retort between his teeth. They'd morphed into one of those upside-down pyramids with too many chefs and too few cooks in the kitchen. He'd gathered his top brass to make a clearly-defined decision, and he couldn't get any valuable information until they interviewed their underlings and readied reports.

Only Susan had arrived prepared. Looking inordinately pleased with herself, she sat still behind an untouched binder, a smile threatening but, of course, held in check. He knew the binder contained a host of her uncanny character studies.

In an alternate universe, outside counsel would have run this initial analysis. But Atavos no longer had outside counsel. He'd traded the old guard for a blond minx, and he'd fired her in a last-ditch attempt to keep her for himself.

He stilled at the thought. In one stroke of retrospective stupidity, he'd lost his counsel and the girl. Perhaps he'd get them back the same way, minus the stupid bit.

"Clear the room," he ground out, sending Ron a look that said, *don't even think about it.* Employees from the rank and file scattered like he'd thrown a grenade on the table. "You, too, Susan."

She huffed, clasping the binder to her chest as she rose from her seat.

"Leave your report, please," he told her blandly. He needed her intel, not her attitude, while he took the next step toward clinical insanity.

"You don't want to hear what I have to say?" Displeasure oozed behind her frigid tone.

He sat up straight and looked around the edge of the table at her *bare* legs. Usually, he got a kick out of letting her boss him around. And he'd been unspeakably relieved to discover her quirky habits hadn't morphed into something more sinister in Denmark, but enough was enough.

"Why, Susan, I do believe there is a run in your pantyhose." His devious gaze shifted to Billboard, shutting her out as he continued. "She's always missing the little details, don't you think?" Back to Susan with a smirk. "Might wanna run along and fix that. Such an unprofessional display might take me from *the brink* to *over the edge.*"

Her eyes flared, and a mottled red climbed from beneath her cardigan, flooding her cheeks. In an invisible cloud of smoke and eau de sugar cookie, she slapped the binder in front of him and marched away, never pointing out that she'd kicked her tan-nylon addiction post-Copenhagen.

Scarlet would be so proud of The Minion's legwear reformation. He smiled at the apt nickname he still couldn't get over.

With the cavernous conference room emptied save he and Ron, he clipped the two words he'd been holding back. "Rehire JTS."

Billboard didn't budge. True to his namesake, his face looked exactly the same before and after hearing the startling demand. Then, "You're an idiot."

He'd probably get used to the title before this was over.

"Get Brian Wentworth." The empty table reflected the sun streaming in through the windows, calling his attention to the so-called meeting he'd been forced to disband for incompetence. Palm up, he motioned to the vast expanse of wood that stretched away from his and Billboard's perch at table's end. Brows arched, he issued a challenge. "Unless you feel we don't need the help."

His long-time right hand nodded, but without fervor or even real agreement. "I'm sorry about what happened with Scarlet."

So was he. But Ron talked like she was gone for good. "Make sure Brian understands Scarlet isn't to touch us."

All rules would be strictly observed. She wouldn't get anywhere near him as his lawyer. But meetings with Brian at her offices would legitimately land him at her side. Repeatedly. He intended to be very demanding.

From there, nature would take its course.

Ron frowned. "What's your game?"

"Chicken." He hoped she didn't veer off a cliff when she saw him coming.

CHAPTER 22

Midnight had come and gone when Scarlet decided she'd had enough. Each night, she stayed at the tiny East Village apartment a little longer. A gradual weaning. In a month, she'd vacate her fortress and spend her first full night in the grimy studio she could actually afford.

With a thump, she plunked a scrub brush down on the side of the tub and sat back on her heels. An hour ago, the grout and tile of her shower had been *furry*. It would never look new, but the worst of the stains had faded.

On a slow roll, she rose to her feet, stretching through each cramped vertebra. A mountain of plastic bags sat on the kitchen counter. One held the final touch to her serviceable—yes, she told herself, *perfectly workable*—bathroom. Crossing to the sacks, she routed out a clear shower curtain. No design to obstruct her view from within.

Curtain installed, she surveyed her progress. Over the last week, she'd scrubbed every surface, from the linoleum covering the floor to the chrome rusting on the faucet. Between the shower-tub combo, the toilet, and the pedestal sink, she barely had room to maneuver. Yet she'd managed a fresh coat of taupe paint after grudgingly accepting the super's promise that the veins of brackish mold stretching upward from the water basin didn't present a health issue. A new chain lock gleamed against the back of the door.

The bathroom would serve as a safe room of sorts. If she had any problems, she'd retreat to powder her nose with her cell phone. The lock and the old sturdy, wooden door should last until help arrived.

Sixteen square feet down. Three hundred and change to go.

Bone tired and fighting the slink of a headache that moved between her ears, she could scarcely appreciate the rare privilege of having work due at the office early the next morning. Brian had begun funneling extra projects her way. So long as the work got done, no one noticed who did it.

JTS's search for a Scarlet brain-double progressed slowly through a series of meetings and calls that occurred under her watchful, but uninvited, eye. According to Brian's intel, the partnership "questioned her judgment," which might render her "a liability." She and Brian had chuckled over that one, given that the firm's managing partner had recently embarked on this third marriage, likely a short-lived paradise since he was less-than-discretely seeing a twenty-four-year-old associate on floor thirty-eight.

Her gaze fell to a wooden broom and a saw she'd picked up at the corner hardware store. One more project stood between her and a cab home to a secure bed.

Carrying the tools to the window, she aligned the broom handle with the top of the frame. Using the saw, she slashed a hash mark where the handle passed the sliding portion of the window below. Then, stoppering the end of the broom in a corner, she sawed away.

The cheap, dull blade gradually ate through the wood, leaving her with a custom rod she wedged into place. Functioning lock or not, the wooden stump compressed the window shut. An intruder would be forced to break the glass—both loud and slow—giving her ample time to escape out the front door or into the locking bathroom with her cell phone.

And just in time. A figure moved into the space beyond the age-waved single pane. Scarlet reeled back with a pained gasp before realizing Lissa stood, smiling and waving, from the rickety landing of the fire escape that snaked down the front of her new building.

Scarlet's hand flew to her chest, and she sucked in several mouthfuls of air. Gradually, her heartbeat slowed enough to stagger forward and free the homemade stump-lock with a melodramatic yank.

Lissa opened the window, exposing the already stale air of the apartment to the scent of Chicken Lo Mein rising from the Chinese restaurant at ground level. Cool as ever, she ducked into the room, sampling the pungent aromas of food and cleaning solvents in sniffs too mockingly delicate to be legitimate.

"What the hell are you doing? Trying to kill me?" Scarlet barked.

"I'm trying to freak you out so you'll move in with me."

"What part of 'I'm moving to this dump to avoid Ethan's handouts—oh, and also to avoid reneging on my vow to never rely on my dad's money again,' did you not understand? If I can't accept their charity, why would I take yours?"

"You won't be paying me with sex or blind obedience?"

Scarlet slammed the window shut and shoved her makeshift lock into place. "Exactly what would I *pay* to inhabit your recently-renovated Uptown brownstone?"

"The satisfaction I'd derive from your continued health and well—"

"That was a *rhetorical* question, Lissa."

Fists on hips, Lissa assessed the studio in a slow three-quarter spin that gave her the grand tour. "You could have said so. Besides, you'd be taking care of the place while I'm gone. I'll be in Colorado and then India for God knows how long. That's *payment*."

Excuse me while I go bang my head against the shower stall. "Look, Lissa, thank you. I love you for asking. But I have to do this."

"No, you don't," she fired back, and finally a creeping worry entered her voice. "But I'll let you if you swear not to hang on in the likely event this… *lifestyle* becomes too much. If you can't sleep or eat or work or shower—"

"Don't ever let anyone tell you your vote of confidence isn't inspiring."

"—or if you get really tired of Chinese food—"

"I don't plan to eat there."

"—or if you discover a rat the size of Punxsutawney Phil—"

"There are no rats!"

"Roach infestation?"

"*No.*"

"Fine. But if you ever discover a dead body on the landing, you're out of here. I'll hogtie your perfectly curvy ass and drag you home where I'll bury you under a mountain of priceless art—namely mine and perhaps a Rubens or two—until your money situation improves and you can afford a real apartment."

Lissa sidled to the door and began working the locks that crept up its back side. When the last chain hung loose, she turned. "Promise, Scarlet."

Scarlet smacked her chest. "Cross my heart."

A curt nod and Lissa slipped out.

Scarlet's head throbbed by the time the cab pulled up in front of her old building an hour later. The acidic stench of ammonia had taken up permanent residence in her pores. When she stepped from the car, her head rotated toward the convenience store on the corner. *Ibuprofen*, whispered an internal voice. *Take four and live to see the morning.*

Undecided, she shared a look with Andy, who stood as shiny and official as ever on the front steps. The elderly gentleman didn't open the door with his usual flourish. Instead, he lifted his chin in the direction of the store, a silent chiding. *Go on now. You can make it.*

Andy had manned the door for so long. After a thousand "good mornings" and "goodnights," he must have realized her habits didn't include late-night jaunts to the keepers-of-the-Advil. The shining mischief in his eyes rooted for her.

Hesitant, but finally willing, she nodded. With one sidestep, and then another, Scarlet worked her way toward the street corner, turning her head to keep Andy in her sights as long as possible. When she passed from her building's exterior lighting into the shadows, she whirled and ran.

She made it. Shuffling along the well-lit aisles, Scarlet picked up a bottle of pain killers and some half-and-half for the morning coffee she'd need to bury the remains of the headache that promised to linger. A pack of cinnamon bears also made its way to the counter. A reward for good behavior.

The walk home took her by surprise. Like a child's hesitance to ride a bike without training wheels, her refusal to venture out had stemmed from a well-worn fear rather than the danger associated with the task. At least in this neck of the woods. She looked around in wonder, swinging her bag of goodies back and forth.

People milled about even though the night entered the wee hours. A group of young women in hooker heels tottered along, laughing too loud and bantering about which greasy spoon should soak up their night of clubbing.

A couple walked hand-in-hand, heads close. As they passed, she saw they shared a dripping ice cream cone. A man on the corner sold honey-roasted nuts from a rolling cart. More than a few insomniacs waited in line for an early-morning snack.

Back at her steps, Andy chimed, "Good evening, my dear," and opened the door with a flourish, as faux-British as ever.

Scarlet let her lips flow into an easy grin, clutching her nighttime booty. *Good evening, indeed.*

******

Scarlet's trip to the corner store grew into a walk from the subway station across the street. Then from the office. Later a nearby restaurant. After the slow build, she tackled a stroll to and from nowhere for the sheer joy of walking a beloved city she'd let become a stranger.

She lingered in front of a backlit window display. The sun dipped behind the concrete cliff of Manhattan, stealing the reassuring glare glinting off the glass. At one time, she'd have hailed the nearest cab. Tonight she didn't mind the several blocks that separated her from home.

Besides, she couldn't tear herself away.

Behind the window, a child-size mannequin in a tutu danced on a rotating pedestal. Next to the ballerina, mechanical dummies in nylon jerseys batted a soccer ball back and forth. In the far corner, tiny boxing gloves draped over a miniature title belt.

She slid her palm along the cool glass. Would Ethan teach his son to box? Maybe his daughter, too?

Her hand fell away, and she stepped back, ignoring the slow turn of her belly. The Chelsea lease ended in a week. Pondering Ethan's future parenting practices wouldn't construct a more affordable version of her high-rise life or muster the frayed remains of her career to pay for it.

Packing would.

Casting a last look at the red gloves, Scarlet started down the sidewalk.

Her street offered the chaotic welcome she'd come to expect. Curbside vendors and dog walkers and neighborhood families made the most of the dregs of summer. The only stillness waited ahead. He stood in the shadows beyond the marble steps leading to her lobby. The man wore a hooded sweatshirt and propped a shoulder against the building in a familiar lanky pose.

She stopped short. "Ethan?" The note of hope in her voice revealed too much, calling her progress all kinds of a lie.

He shook his head within the folds of the hood.

The rush of recognition and euphoria withered. Of course not.

Unexplained sweat beaded along her spine, but she started forward anyway. Something about the man's presence, his unsolicited but undivided attention, felt wrong. Malevolence thickened the air with each step, and when her gut told her to run she tripped over her tennis shoes in a sudden burst of movement. Slowing, she focused on Andy and her building's secure entrance. They would come first. No need to pass him by.

The sense of familiarity lingered. His size and stance. The way she could feel his gaze track her every move even though the night cloaked his features. The crouching menace that pulsed in her direction.

She made it to Andy and started up the stairs. When he opened the lobby door to the guard waiting beyond, reluctant suspicion slithered past her defenses. She lived in a guarded residence for specific reasons, defenses mandated by a dark figure that, at least once, had meant her harm. The fine hairs on the back of her neck froze in retreat, and she whirled on the man who'd started forward with slow, methodical purpose.

Life transformed in a split second. She'd done this before.

"You," she croaked.

"We meet again, Empress." He reached up and pulled his hood to his shoulders, letting light flood over the triumph and challenge etched into a face she'd known for years.

A scream lodged in her throat. After single heartbeat crashed against her ribs, she stumbled backward into the sprawling foyer. The door clicked shut as she slid to her knees, fists against the glass. That face had taunted her from the blackness rimming a flashlight. Under the glaring fluorescents of a courtroom, she'd memorized its every detail.

That was years ago. At his trial for her attempted murder. Age had barely altered the brutality of his features.

Gerard Chamber was back.

CHAPTER 23

Compulsive shivering had a way of dispersing body heat. Despite the slick coating of sweat that soaked her clothing, Scarlet huddled further into the blankets the police had retrieved from her hall closet.

In the hour after her narrow escape, she'd thrown up several times. She prayed *that* storm had passed, but her stomach protested even the steaming tea the more sympathetic female officer had pressed into her hands with an order to "drink."

No denying it, Gerard Chamber had been paroled shortly after her return from Denmark. Thirty seconds on the state's inmate database had made it official. Why she hadn't known—?

An image seared through her brain. Her, crumpled on the floor, clutching the copper-plated receiver of her father's old-fashioned rotary phone. On the other end, the DA spoke gently, explaining why the charges against Ethan were being dropped. At first, she reeled, breathing only in pinched gasps, not understanding how this could happen. But as the DA went on, she began to see how wrong she'd been.

New evidence had surfaced, all of it linking another to her attack. After watching every second of security footage from Rancor that night, Ethan's public defender had discovered several peculiarities. Ethan's opponent hadn't disappeared to the showers after their scuffle. He'd headed in that direction, but then casually remained in the arena. The video had showed Gerard Chamber staring intently from a semi-darkened corner, still bloody and torn from the fight. Rather than watching the subsequent match between Lissa's man and yet another boxer, Gerard had scrutinized Scarlet's section of the stands.

Rancor's cameras had caught him again, this time leaving the club about thirty minutes before Scarlet and Lissa emerged to stand huddled under the front awning. And low and behold, a truck matching the one Scarlet had been thrown against in the parking lot had been registered to the very man Ethan had humiliated in the ring a scant hour before her attack.

The video, the truck, and testimony that Ethan's pet name "Empress" had received plenty of locker-room play had prompted a search warrant. The police had found a flashlight and a knife bundled together in Gerard's apartment. The knife had been cleaned meticulously, but it was the right size and type. Her lipstick had survived the plundering of her purse, along with the bag itself. They'd also found a pair of leather gloves with a single strand of long, blonde hair mottled into the lining. DNA testing had shown it was hers.

Beyond the direct evidence of Gerard's crime, the search had recovered a dwindling supply of a polypeptide protein hormone used to stimulate growth and cell reproduction, both illegal and expensive.

"You in there?" another officer asked from a distance, snapping his fingers in front of her nose and dragging her back to the present. This one, not so sympathetic, blocked the view of her stark kitchen with his bulky frame, his stance harsh and belligerent as though the steel of her appliances bled into his persona.

"We'll report the incident to Mr. Chamber's parole officer," he explained dully.

"Will it keep him away?" The question slipped out in a misguided quest for some kind of reassurance.

He stared at a notepad clutched between beefy fingers. Of course he had to answer, even if he wasn't inclined to make the effort. "Maybe. I'm no parole officer."

It was a far cry from the comfort she realized he couldn't, or wouldn't, give.

His attention lifted from the notes, and a mantel of burden settled over his shoulders. In a move she'd seen him repeat several times, he took in the antiques that graced her open-plan living room and the French doors that opened to spectacular city views. When his gaze landed on her bedraggled, blanket-wrapped form, she saw his disgust. Others out there actually needed his help, not a princess high in her tower.

Slightly above average could be a bad spot. Enough money—the kind that attracted the interest of reporters and camera crews—and the place would be crawling with cops ready to track her tormentor to the ends of the earth. She'd been there once before. A *little* money made her an undeserving drain on a system with limited resources. Apparently she was there now.

One corner of his mouth quirked. "I'm sure you'll be a top priority." The silent "dream on" practically echoed off the walls, cramming her fear past the closed muscles of her throat.

"I'm sure," she stressed, "you'll see to it." Gerard Chamber had nearly killed her before. She knew in the marrow of her bones he'd returned to try again.

A few more minutes saw the police say farewell, lifting the false sense of sanity that had accompanied their bombardment of questions and instructions. Adrenaline receded with the chaos, and where her insides had previously twisted into a strangled knot, now they fell hollow and cavernous.

She moved the blanket aside to see bruises darkening over her knees and shins. In her haste to flee Gerard's advance, she'd broken Ethan's no-bleeding rule. She bled on the inside, in more ways than one.

But that wasn't his fault. Ethan wouldn't have wanted this—a broken heart and empty wallet, surely, but never this. His alarm that night with the knife had been too real, utterly instinctive.

Her laptop and cell phone sat in her lap. Lifting the phone, she typed on the touchscreen—first an "e," then a "t," followed by an "h." That's all it took for Ethan's number to pop up. She stared at his name, eyes blurring at a picture she'd snapped at Tivoli.

How desperately she wanted to press the green button and hear his deep, reassuring voice on the other end. Even though he'd evicted her from his everyday life, his sense of chivalry would send him running. He'd wrap her in those solid arms and promise everything would be okay. Because the words would be Ethan's, she'd let herself believe them and pretend for a few hours that they shared a great love.

She closed her eyes and imagined their reunion. He would let her cry and tell her it was normal to be afraid. The hot brand of his hand would stroke over her back until she fell asleep, and when she woke, he'd still be there, watching over her with that oddly fierce, yet gentle, intensity.

She slammed the phone onto an end table. Tempting as it was to be the pathetic ex-girlfriend that called crying in the night, she could cry alone just the same.

Sleep continued to elude her as dawn streaked the New York skyline. She hadn't made it to bed. No, she sat still on the island of her couch, focusing on her apartment's two doors, thankful morning had finally arrived.

Showing up on her doorstep had shattered Gerard's parole. She could only hope he'd be re-arrested and imprisoned by nightfall, sparing her another all-night vigil over a change in custody status that should never, ever have escaped her notice. She'd diligently maintained her victim notification request with the state.

With unsteady fingers, she logged into her laptop. An electronic notification might have gone the way of the penis enlargement ads that piled up in her junk mail.

Sure enough, she found the notice of Gerard's impending release sandwiched between a message from "teens with sexy bodies" and another from an errant government official in Ghana. He needed her savings account number to distribute her $2.8 million in African lottery winnings.

Thinking on it, the post office had held her snail mail during her stay in Denmark. Most of the buildup had been trash—credit card offers, coupons, sweepstakes entries, mail-order catalogues. Rather like her e-mail, she'd carelessly tossed the pile and lost the most important communications of her life.

The day wore on in silence, the stillness growing more oppressive with each moment she didn't hear from the cops or Gerard's parole officer. Inch by inch, the walls of her spacious apartment contracted until they compressed against a handwritten list clutched between her fingers—a name, social security number, age, and date of birth. She also knew Gerard Chamber had been born and raised in New York City.

She swallowed audibly. Not an impressive sum total.

The authorities had offered little—scratch that, nothing—in the way of protection. Gerard had made contact, sure, but talking to her wasn't an overt threat. While his breaking parole justified an arrest warrant, a national emergency he was not.

Scarlet shuddered at the memory of his quiet rage pinning her to the steps, of his knowing tone when he'd called her "Empress." No matter the consensus of the powers that be, his presence was a big fucking deal. A warning she couldn't fail to heed.

At trial, the prosecutor had painted motives of greed and revenge. Gerard hadn't bothered to contradict the theory that he'd imploded under the weight of his damaged pride and a dependence on illegal hormones his wallet couldn't withstand. Back then, they'd assumed he'd worked over Ethan's wealthy new toy, solving *all* his problems while punishing his primary competitor.

But after ten years, why?

A long shot, but she pulled up Google and typed in "Gerard Chamber." The search resulted in over two-thousand hits, and when she scrolled through the results, most of the links pointed to sites or articles she could easily discount. Several people named Gerard apparently made chamber music. They popped up repeatedly since Amazon and other sites sold their CDs as "So-and-so Gerard—Chamber Music." Another guy named Gerard maintained a Facebook page for his store, "Chamber of Secrets."

At the bottom of the fourth page of results, she found a link that at least related to New York City. According to the synopsis visible on the search page, a teenager named Anna Chamber had died after a stabbing in a Chelsea city shelter about fifteen years ago.

The article originally ran in the regional section of the New York Times. It didn't take long to locate the full story in the digital archives. The piece highlighted a murder and pointed to the plight of victims of gentrification throughout various up-and-coming neighborhoods spread across the city's five boroughs.

> *Anna Chamber, 14, was found dead Friday night from apparent stab wounds inflicted while staying at the Good Hands Homeless Shelter in Hell's Kitchen. Cory Lossor, 39, is currently being held in conjunction with the attack and bond is set at $10,000. Diane Sutter, the shelter's manager, said "Lossor (had) suffered from substance abuse and mental illness for years."*
>
> *Anna's mother, Donna Chamber, claims her daughter's homicide is the result of the family's recent eviction from a rent controlled apartment in Chelsea after the city's Landmarks Preservation Commission neglected to stop construction of the Cora Tower Condominium Complex.*
>
> *Experts point to this as yet another example of the city's gentrification and displacement policy. Politicians have long sought to resolve residential displacement as a result of housing demolition, conversion of rental units, increased housing costs in rent and taxes, and/or evictions.*
>
> *"Those displaced without access to alternative housing in areas like Park Slope, Fort Greene, and Harlem often turn to the city's shelter system," says Antony Vavichie, Manager of the Urban Housing Authority. "Events like the Chamber homicide only highlight the severity of the city's affordable housing crisis."*

Cora. The word flared on the screen. Her own middle name, taken from her mother—Cora and Scarlet Cora Leore. After her mom's death, her father had developed a habit of naming things after his "beloved" wife and daughter, a clever PR stunt designed to make him appear the sentimental family man. Scarlet and her mother served as namesakes for Tripp Leore's Yacht, a golf course in Florida, a cattle ranch in Montana, and in the city, the Cora Tower.

Like Scarlet after her, Cora had been her father's possession, a woman to dress in fancy clothes, escort to fast cars, and trot to events like a show pony. Her beautiful mother had loved, but her generous gift hadn't been returned.

Scarlet closed her eyes and rested her head on the back of the couch. The year of the Cora's construction lived fresh in her mind. She'd been young—about the same age as poor Anna—and had dubbed the tower hers, telling teachers at boarding school, "The Cora's mine. For my mother and me." No matter the distance or death that separated her from her parents, the fact that her dad was building the city's preeminent high-rise in her mother's name had been pretty damn cool at the time.

The blanket slid from Scarlet's lap when she stood with sudden, jerky movements. Exiting through the glass door, she perched against the rails of her expansive balcony. For once, she didn't appreciate the city lights or her view of the Hudson, silent and sparking under a handful of burgeoning stars. Gerard waited out there, possibly watched her from below.

Her grip tightened on the railing, its metallic chill seeping into her skin. Scarlet didn't symbolize the Cora. She *lived* in it. When her dad had sold the building, she'd jumped at the chance to move into a complex with meaning, however small, and a connection to the mother she'd missed so dearly.

The choice had served her well. *Until now.*

Nauseated and trembling, the need to escape welled with a vengeance. If Anna Chamber was linked to Gerard, then his attack that night in Brooklyn had been bigger than a play for drug money, her Maserati, or petty revenge against Ethan. He'd done it to get to her father, retribution for the eviction of a vulnerable mother and child.

The railing slipped against her sweating palm, and this time she clutched it to keep from falling down.

He'll come.

But the Cora was the safest place for her. The building had served as her haven for years. Solid and faithful and guarded, it'd proven worthy. She couldn't leave now, costs be damned.

She pictured Ethan, secure in his world—probably sipping a glass of scotch over dinner with an underwear model—and wanted to scream over her endangered checkbook. Instead, she superimposed happy images of him over her spiraling reality. She saw him plying her with chocolate truffles in bed and kneeling before her on the bathroom rug in easy—more like eager—acceptance of her strange showering habits. She heard him suggest adoption and relived his distress in the moment he'd seen Susan exit that Danish warehouse, worried that his longtime friend had betrayed his trust.

She'd never forget the horror carved in his granite features after he'd caused her to cut herself with that steak knife. "*Let me tend to you,*" he'd said. And, oh, how he had.

God, Ethan, why did you go?

As if in a trance, Scarlet drifted backward until her shoulders bumped the glass of the French doors. *Enough dreaming.* The sudden solidness jarred her into action. She'd prayed this day wouldn't come, had gone to great lengths to avoid it. But she couldn't buy time with money she didn't have.

Eyes stinging, she deliberately retreated inside, compressing the door handle with a bone-white hand. The security backs of her mother's earrings came loose with a harsh twist. One by one she laid them upon the bare kitchen table with shaking fingers. The diamonds followed suit. Fighting the urge to give up, she made low sounds of distress as she reached for her phone and punched in ten numbers.

Two rings brought a gentrified inflection.

"Christie's auction house, how may I direct your call?"

CHAPTER 24

Pink was the new black for men. Even Ethan knew that much after his mom's most recent gift—a fuchsia golf shirt. But Brian's mauve cufflinks matched his tie. And his belt. As Ethan had come to expect, his new attorney brought valuable business insights, advice he'd do well to heed. So the irritating clothes didn't justify Ethan's lack of focus.

That prize went to Scarlet, who sat precisely six doors down from the conference room where he and Brian sat discussing Korean optics. The second he'd crossed the threshold of JTS's posh offices on the thirty-sixth floor, all thoughts of business had fled.

"…reasonable opportunity for a solid relationship… One thing Atavos might want to consider…"

He refocused on his lawyer with a harsh shake of his head. "Is Scarlet here?"

A slow grin spread across Brian's face. "Now why would you care about that? Might upset me if I thought you hired me to get to her and not for my unparalleled legal prowess."

"Fuck off. I hired you for both."

"What a relief." On a low laugh, Brian sat back and crossed his arms over his chest. "I don't know whether she's here or not. She hasn't had a lot of work lately, so her hours have been sporadic."

So much for chalking her silence up to being swamped. "Good. She needed to slow down."

"I don't think she'd characterize her status as 'good,' but hey, you're the expert." Brian's voice thinned to a low mutter he aimed at the table. "Fuck'em and fire'em, right?"

She'd practically demanded it. "This is what I get for six-hundred bucks an hour?"

Brian merely blinked, not even mustering the grace to look affronted.

"Yup."

Ethan opened his mouth to spread the firing around when, out of the corner of his eye, he saw a fall of blond hair sweep into view beyond the glass door.

Scarlet stopped at the lobby's reception desk. To compensate for her tiny frame, she heaved herself on top of the raised counter, feet dangling below, and swept her arm out until her fingers clasped... ah, a stapler. As she slid back to the floor, the receptionist returned from parts unknown and rushed to help.

Her body stood in the lobby chatting with the assistant, but her mind obviously dwelled elsewhere, someplace sinister and threatening. His girl had lost weight, too, though not enough to justify how small she appeared. Her tailored skirt hung low on her hips. Beautiful, but he missed the juicy curves that had filled out her clothes only weeks ago.

"What happened to her?" he asked through clenched teeth. Scarlet smiled at the woman—obviously explaining her successful pilfering of the stapler—and Ethan's breath caught at the sadness in the gesture.

Brian glanced over his shoulder at Scarlet. "Happened? Oh, you know, the usual. Hunting for a shitty apartment since she won't be able to afford her place at the Cora after she loses her job. Dodging violen—"

"She's not losing her job." He'd let her go to ensure it.

"Not now. Everybody around here knows your call back had her name written all over it. But before..." Brian trailed off, and Ethan's fingers curled into the table.

"Nice touch for your man Ron Michael to declare the project wasn't to tread near Scarlet's ground. It hasn't. She has no clue you're back on the roster." The smug bastard raised his hand and flapped it at Ethan, pulling his attention away from Scarlet. "Maybe you should wave."

"Why do I get the feeling you think this is funny."

"Because I think it's totally fucking funny. Not *her* situation, mind you, yours. For one of New York's most documented Casanovas, you haven't got a clue." Pointing a thumb over his shoulder in Scarlet's direction, he added, "Now, did you want to talk supplier agreements, or do you want to me leave so you can lick the window?"

Scarlet disappeared down the hall. Once she receded from sight, Ethan stood. "We need finished goods at our manufacturing facility in Singapore in two months. You've got the numbers. Handle it."

On his way out, he added, "I'm not paying for this hour."

Mr. Six-hundred didn't bother to turn around. Instead, his flat answer followed Ethan down the hall. "Did you know lawyers can fire clients? We call it 'inviting them to find new counsel.' *Nothing* is more freeing. I've had orgasms that were less enjoyable. So, yes, Mr. Blake, you will pay for every fucking second."

*****

To onlookers, Scarlet would appear engaged in the bogus Word document on her screen. After all, she sat at her desk, back to the door, fingers on the keyboard. Inside, her thoughts tumbled like clothes in a dryer.

No more delaying the inevitable.

With an unsteady hand, she reached for her office phone and dialed Gerard's parole officer. When she was about to hang up, Ralston King answered, sounding harried. Part of her had hoped the ringing would drone on forever.

At her request, Ralston reluctantly dug into Gerard's official file. The sound of shuffling papers drowned out the scratchy radio she heard in the background. As the seconds ticked on, she clung to the threadbare hope that Anna and Gerard Chamber weren't connected.

"I don't see a record of a younger female relation," he said.

Her chin dropped to her chest with the beginnings of relief. Unhinged stalking seemed preferable to the wrath of a man who'd plotted bloody revenge for nearly half his life. "What about his mother or some type of maternal-figure, maybe an aunt?"

Ralston fell silent, and the rustle of pages began anew. "His mom's alive. It looks like she was his only regular visitor in the pen."

"Can you tell me her name?"

"Looks like… Donna. Donna Chamber, now in her mid-fifties."

Chills skated outward from the nape of her neck. *No.* Despite a stern self-admonition, she felt herself sway in her chair. *Donna Chamber.* The woman who'd publically blamed Tripp Leore for the untimely death of her daughter in a homeless shelter fifteen years ago. The crossover couldn't be a coincidence. That woman was Gerard's mother.

Scarlet squeezed her eyes closed. *Sister.* The dead girl, Anna Chamber, had been Gerard's baby sister, a fourteen-year-old with her whole life ahead of her. At the time of her death, Gerard would have been nineteen.

The computer screen blurred. About fifty people walked by her office each day. In her precarious position, she couldn't afford a mid-morning breakdown. Regardless of Brian's reassurances, her behavior had to inspire confidence, not shred it. Pressing the receiver between her shoulder and her ear, her fingers randomly flew over the keys in an instinctive imitation of a normal client call.

Nothing happened when she opened her mouth to speak. After three tries, she forced out the crucial question. "And still no word on Gerard?"

"Not yet."

Her eyes squeezed shut. They wouldn't find him. *So long as I breathe he has a vested interest in remaining at large.*

She offered a feeble thank-you and hung up, wanting nothing more than a few moments of numbness. But the facts crashed through her mind with ruthless clarity. Tripp Leore didn't have a baby sister. He had something better—an only child who served as the namesake for the building that had displaced Gerard's family, the precursor to Anna Chamber's stabbing. A daughter Anna's age, who now lived a pampered existence in that same damn building.

Eye for an eye.

Bile rose to the back of Scarlet's throat. She swallowed hard, breathing in and out through her nose.

Focus.

She reached up and combed her fingers through her hair, scalp to tip in an outward motion, pulling slightly too hard. The strokes probably did nothing but frizz the curls, but they calmed her mind until, eventually, she could think straight.

The *Times* article revealed more than a familial link between a long-dead girl and Scarlet's tormentor. When interviewed, Donna Chamber had insisted that the city's Landmarks Preservation Commission shouldn't have approved construction of the Cora Tower. Like the Chamber family's rent-controlled building before it, the Cora sat in the Chelsea Historical District.

Her father's property empire hadn't been her only real-estate rodeo. Before narrowing her practice to corporate mergers, she'd worked a few big real estate deals—enough to know a building in a historic district was protected under the Landmarks Law and subject to the Commission's approval before *any* type of work could begin. Minor alterations were often rejected in the interest of historical preservation. Permission to demolish a historic building in its entirety? Almost unheard of.

An unwelcome dizziness returned as the chips began to stack. Gerard's mother had publically denounced the validity of Tripp Leore's demolition and building permits, an extraordinary focal point in the hours following the violent killing of her teenage child. She must have felt, and quite strongly, that Scarlet's father had done something wrong in his quest to build the Cora.

One explanation tumbled over another, beating against the inside of her skull when her office door clicked shut behind her.

******

"Can I help you?"

Ethan stood frozen in the doorway to Scarlet's office and, for once, unsure. Scarlet's question had started strong but faded to a budding quiver, like a violinist who'd saved the vibrato for the end of the note. She obviously didn't want her visitor to suspect a problem. After spying her in the lobby, he already knew she had one.

"Yes," he answered.

The busy tap, tap, tap against her keyboard went quiet at sound of his voice. After a few seconds, her chair began to turn. New emotions surfaced as each inch of her face was revealed. He'd expected the surprise and fury. But her sadness settled in his chest. The terror brought him up short.

"How did you get in?"

Definitely not happy to see him. "I'm back in the fold," he answered. Without awaiting an invitation, he took a seat in front of an L-shaped portion her desk. Studying her with care, he took stock of the purplish smudges below her eyes. They spoke of too many nights without rest.

"Your insomnia's back."

Her lip quirked, but the reluctant humor didn't last. "You look good, too."

"I didn't say anything about your looks." He gentled his tone, wanting only to calm her skittishness. "You're beautiful. But I'm right."

"As usual."

"What happened?" He burned to call her sweetheart, but one of her hands clung to the edge of the desk. The other gripped an arm of her chair, ready to push off and propel her around him and out the door. She wouldn't welcome his endearments.

She ignored his question. "I thought you'd sworn off this den of idiocy. What brings you back 'into the fold?'"

You. "Brian Wentworth is a damn fine attorney."

The last bit of color leached from her ghostly features. "That he is."

Ethan tensed. He'd said that wrong. "And he's not you."

Her eyes narrowed, and she shuddered against her seat. Almost imperceptible, but he noticed.

"Exactly," she whispered. "But surely you didn't come just to remind me I'm a shitty lawyer. I already know, so there's no need. Now if you'll excuse me—"

"I meant that Brian's not someone I…" He trailed off, searching for a way in. "Retaining him doesn't present any conflicts, Scarlet."

"Ah." She looked away. "Brian's your attorney. Not me. Is that honestly an invitation to pick up where we left off?"

Shit. He'd walked right into that one. "Would you say yes?"

Mirthless laughter bubbled up from her chest. Even that died quickly. "That's rich. You haven't been my client for weeks. *Weeks,* Ethan."

"You needed time to rebuild. To recover." *And then come back to me.* "I assumed you hadn't repaired the damage of our affair, and I didn't want to intrude on the progress."

"An impossible task," she said through her teeth.

A faint edge entered his tone. "What?"

"I can't *fix* the damage." Her palm slid over her forehead and rubbed in small circles as though the motion might appease a lingering ache. When she looked up, her eyes sparkled with unshed tears, like whiskey rimmed with the lighter edge of fire. "Ethan, I checked out of your life, just like you asked. We—Copenhagen was enough."

His gut flooded with an unnerving premonition that something had gone drastically wrong. His fingers fairly burned to touch her. "It'll *never* be enough," he said in a ragged whisper. "Scarlet, tell me. Why did Brian say you aren't busy? That you're not 'good?' You've—"

"I'm fine."

"—lost weight. You're not sleeping, and I can tell you're upset. Right now, you're anxious and afraid."

She didn't answer, and her silent suffering broke over him when she buried her face in her hands. "Go," she finally heaved between ragged breaths. "Leave."

"*No!*" he roared, panic blooming at the possibility of her slipping though his fingers. He barreled around the desk, landing on his knees at her feet. "I'm not leaving until you tell me what's going on. Hear me? I *won't* leave." *Ever again.*

She shuddered when his hands landed lightly on her upper arms. He saw a faint quiver of her lip in the space between her hands. Tears tracked down her cheeks. Afraid to make it worse, he burrowed through the flesh-and-bone barrier she'd erected and brushed each one away with the lightest phantom caress. "Look at me, sweetheart. Tell me."

"You," she choked, wiping furiously at her eyes. "You refused to wait for me. Fired me. I won't let you do that again."

His hand rested against her cheek. "No," he whispered. Leaving was supposed to have helped her. He *couldn't* have been that wrong. "You said we had to break it off. But you came to me right after. You wouldn't have stayed away."

He pulled her hair away from her face. "You left so stoically." More than that, she'd stood up and marched out without a backward glance. "I didn't know. I'd *never* hurt you this badly."

The thought of what he'd done punched him between the ribs. He'd bought into her strong facade. Yet she'd been suffering while he waited for her to relent.

Her voice dropped to a wounded whisper. "Never hurt me? You kicked me out of your room. Accused me of trying to manipulate you. I don't even know how to do that."

"But *I* do." He slid a finger under her chin, tipping her head back. "Don't you get it? You said you needed time, then proved you wouldn't take it on your own. I never intended to give you up. Not for a second. *I fucking lied, Scarlet.*"

She met his gaze, the molten hurt kindling in a flash of flame. *Finally.* He welcomed a million miles of her anger before one inch of sadness or hurt or fear.

"Where were you all this time?" Her voice took on a warning edge. "I trusted you."

He trailed his knuckles along her neck, then up to an ear—a bare, pale earlobe bisected by an even paler scar. He stifled the question that blinked in the back of his mind.

"Waiting. For you. Until I couldn't take it anymore. Then I hired Brian, and here I am, already at your feet after my first meeting with that prick." He let out a frustrated growl. "I lied about him being a good lawyer, too. Your friend's an asshole."

That coaxed forth a watery grin, a real one, however slight. "The best ones are."

"The best lawyers are assholes or the best assholes are lawyers?

"Both."

Relief poured through him. Jokes meant progress. "But not you."

He grew serious. Heartbreak explained some of her changed presence. Work-related stress might account for more. But that wasn't all. Scarlet's tentative smile was too forced. A terrible vulnerability simmered beneath the surface of genuine, but overblown, ire. She fought against owning up to it. "Scarlet, what—"

"Ethan, I still need—"

"Whatever it is, *yes.*" He dropped a kiss to her brow.

She stiffened at the intimacy. "Go. I need you to *go.*"

Anything but that. Carefully, he settled back, dropping to his haunches a few inches from her chair. His gaze searched her face, settling on her naked ears. And yeah, he deserved her see-through-you stare. "You should be angry," he conceded, "but I can't—won't—leave you like this."

"You don't have a choice," she said sadly. "You once said to me, '*I want you gone.*' Take your own advice, Ethan."

Copenhagen rushed in without an invitation. Not only her words. Hell, every one of her choices had shown she needed two things to thrive: safety and independence. He'd bet one or both of them had been threatened. The caveman routine probably wasn't helping.

"Easy," he murmured, rising and returning to the chair in front of her desk, prepared to launch a different, less-aggressive tactic. But as he folded himself into the miniature visitor's seat, a speculative gleam overtook her gaze. She tilted her head, then drummed her index and middle fingers against a lifted chin.

After several moments of assessment, she said, "You still box," as if his hobby were a revelation.

"Competitively. I never quit, though the winnings aren't quite as important these days."

She stared out the window. When she turned back, her flat look was heavy with decision. "I don't trust you."

He nodded, swallowing a coaxing retort.

"But you're smart. Strong. And though you hung me up emotionally, I don't think you want to see me hurt—physically, that is."

"An understatement," he said mildly. Hearing her describe his supposed feelings with such clinical calm nearly killed him. But he'd fix that later.

"I do need someone. A bodyguard of sorts. Nothing more, nothing less."

He stilled. A bodyguard? Scarlet needed physical protection?

Her gaze shot past him, blank. "Gerard Chamber is free, and he wants another stab—no pun intended—at me."

Breath abandoned him. After twenty seconds, he pounded on her desk to kick start the instinct to inhale. Then, bit by bit, he extracted himself from the damn micro-chair and inched back around the desk before gripping her head between both hands.

"Start talking."

******

Elbows to thighs, Ethan sat on the edge of Scarlet's spare bed with his hands clasped between his knees, waiting. Scarlet had alluded to loving him once. He'd laughed at her, implied she only said so in an attempt at manipulation. Now, when Ethan would give anything to break through her barriers, she took his help but kept herself locked away.

At least she trusted him to keep her body safe. It beat what he'd started out with.

A knock at the door brought Ethan to his feet. Scarlet stood in her bright hallway. Expression cautious, she held out a light summer blanket and several towels.

Guess he wouldn't be helping her shower this time around.

She'd told him of Gerard's release and that the bastard continued to evade arrest. In halting phrases, he'd dragged the entire story from her stiff lips. The Chamber family's eviction... Anna Chamber's murder... The perceived connection between Scarlet's father, the Cora Tower, and the girl's death. She'd even told him of a short-lived flight to cheaper rents—courtesy of finding JTS's advertisement for her replacement online—and how she'd broken her new lease in the East Village when Gerard had appeared on her front steps.

Through it all, he'd been waiting for her, thinking he'd done her a favor. In reality, he'd nearly gotten her fired, evicted, and killed. In that order. If he hadn't fired her, and with her JTS, she wouldn't have faced unemployment. If her job had been secure, she wouldn't have feared missing rent at the Cora. If she hadn't been worried about the money, she wouldn't have been traveling back and forth between her old and new apartments in the middle of the night, getting used to the exposure and eventually opening herself to a psychopath who wanted her dead.

No wonder he'd been relegated to the hired help.

For all the detail he'd coaxed out of her, the earrings had gone unmentioned. After the better part of a day, he'd realized her diamond studs, or lack thereof, had pricked his awareness in her office. When he'd caressed her face, they hadn't winked at him through the silken mass of her hair. Instead, he'd seen more scars.

No explanation necessary. Ethan knew exactly what she'd done in a last-ditch effort to stay at the Cora.

Remorse balled in his gut, spreading outward to his limbs like he'd inhaled anthrax. Yet it wasn't enough to torture himself with the knowledge of the hardship he'd caused. Forgiveness aside—*because she may never offer it*—he had to fix the damage.

Questions swirling in his brain, he moved slightly to the side and motioned her toward the bed with the linens, hoping little intimacies like close quarters—if only for a few moments—would reignite the spark.

Scarlet pressed in, careful to avoid physical contact, and set the supplies on the covers. "Do you need anything else?"

A dry swallow stuck in his throat. She wore a pair of black yoga pants that molded to every curve. Her baby tee fell to the waist, exposing a sliver of smooth skin between its hem and her low-rise waistband.

When he didn't answer her question, she spun around, first looking at him and then down at herself, no doubt noticing the sweat that dampened her shirt between her breasts. "I work out here in the apartment. Guess I've taken on some sloppy habits."

"No. It's"—*so fucking hot*—"fine. I want you comfortable. That's what I'm here for." *To please.*

Scarlet looked around him to the doorway he now blocked. Gerard's reappearance had taken a toll. She'd come out of her shell so much in Denmark, and as it sounded, even more here with her bold attempts to rent a more reasonable apartment and investigate Gerard. But her shallow breathing and the way her eyes darted around the room told another story. The drone of low-grade stress and fear had cost her.

Seeing it cost him.

With a casual sidestep, he propped a shoulder against the open door, clearing her path.

"Scarlet," he said as she flitted past, obviously eager to end the moment. She stopped next to him, eyes fixed forward.

He reached for her stiff shoulder but pulled back. "Gerard Chamber won't get to you." *But I will.*

In profile, her chin dipped in subtle acknowledgement. "Thank you."

Then she was gone.

CHAPTER 25

The aroma of coffee drifted into Scarlet's room with the sunshine. She rolled over, pulling her pillow against the crook of her neck on a deep sigh. Eggs hit next. Then cheese. Hesitant to leave the dream without a taste of bubbling cheddar, her eyes barely cracked. What she wouldn't give for eggs over toast, accompanied by a stream of scalding, nutty coffee.

A loud clank sounded from the direction of the kitchen—metal against her gas range—and she jolted upright. She wasn't alone. Her apartment really did smell like a bed and breakfast. Panic saturated her senses, and she dove for her phone on the nightstand. As her fingers slipped over the plastic casing, she remembered.

Ethan. In residence.

The tantalizing aromas had interrupted a deep slumber. Funny how Ethan had that effect on her when sleep was the last thing he brought to mind. After talking to him the night before in his room, she remembered showering, and then… nothing.

She snatched her hand to her chest and slid from beneath the covers.

In her closet she found an ice-blue satin robe. After securing the material with a tie about the waist, she set out to find the chef.

One step into the hall had her returning to her bathroom. She brushed her teeth and hair. Splashed cold water over her face and smoothed on a dab of moisturizer. And, hell, a tiny bit of tinted lip gloss never hurt anyone.

He'd practically admitted to tearing her down for her own sake, and she couldn't accept that kind of management. Yet he threw himself into protecting her without question or hesitation.

A little primping for a guardian like that had to be normal. *Surely.*

In the kitchen Ethan manned the stove. He slid something that smelled divine onto a plate. With the reach of a long muscular arm, he set what had to be a five-egg omelet in front of her place at the bar. Lips sealed, he took in the deep vee of her robe. When he looked up, his pupils had dilated, telling her exactly what *he* wanted for breakfast.

"Ethan, I'm not the entire first string of the New York Giants. I can't eat this."

He bent over the counter, fork in hand, and sliced off a corner of the omelet. Holding it to her lips, he enticed her to bite down. "You can try for me."

As she chewed, he pressed a steaming mug to her palm, never taking his gaze from her mouth. "Eat what you can. I'll handle the rest."

There was an edge to having such a big man in her small kitchen. Cooking for her. Feeding her. No doubt she sampled a winning omelet. But in worn jeans and a faded black T-shirt that emphasized the lean sculpt of his arms and torso, Ethan didn't look tame enough for domestic use.

A fork clattered against the porcelain of his plate. "That depends on the type of use you have in mind, sweetheart."

She choked on the food. *Not again.*

After a long, hard look, he let it drop. Still standing on the opposite side of her bar, his omelet disappeared with clean, efficient movements. Then he quietly ate half of hers.

"You mentioned Donna Chamber's preoccupation with the Landmarks Preservation Commission." His tone dripped suspicion.

Scarlet slurped a spoonful of coffee, wishing she could ignore his question. "I did."

"You know something," he observed smoothly.

She set the spoon aside and plunked an elbow down on the counter, cradling her cheek in an elevated hand. "Gerard's mother had a point. It would have been an extraordinary move for the Commission to approve the demolition of an entire apartment complex in a historical district, especially to be replaced with an ultramodern high-rise."

"A bribe?"

Bribe, payoff, kickback. "Maybe." She'd avoided saying the words, even thinking them too loudly, as though denial could distance her father from her attack.

Stillness fell over them, and she got the impression he played a hundred different scenarios out in his head, missing nothing.

"Business as usual for you today," he announced with a glance at his watch. "I'll take you to the office. Then I'll dig into it. Brian and Billboard have my affairs handled."

Wait. Instinctive gratitude flooded her system. But that wouldn't do. As late as yesterday, he'd sworn her off. Today he offered easy understanding, safety, breakfast, and now help making sense of it all.

Wary, she cleared her throat with a discrete cough. "Why are you doing this?"

The fork making its way to his mouth stopped in mid-air. "I wish you didn't have to ask."

Hearing the news from him might ease its sting, but letting him take over would send her tumbling half-way down a slope that still looked awfully slippery. She could find the answers, knew where to look.

"I'll handle the research. We settled on protection. Nothing more, nothing less."

He repeated the last along with her.

******

The trick would be ensuring Scarlet's safety while using her as bait.

Ethan picked Scarlet up at her building late in the afternoon. Brian walked her from her desk to the passenger door of Ethan's car while Ethan scrutinized the urban landscape surrounding her office. Satisfied, he drove them straight to the Cora. She obviously equated her building with safety, but he'd begun to think they should relocate to his penthouse, if not Bermuda.

His mood darkened. Leaving wouldn't draw Gerard out.

Entering from the secure garage, she checked her mail and they rode the elevator to the twentieth floor. Within an hour, dinner arrived in the lobby.

"Do you think it's strange he hasn't made a move?" Scarlet asked, eyeing a bite of filet mignon. "It's been days and… nothing."

He watched her slip the meat between her teeth. Chew. "Yes and no," he hedged, shifting in his seat.

Yes, because Gerard was no doubt watching and waiting and, if they were right about his motive, feeling a deep urgency to finish what he'd started.

No, because Ethan's sudden presence put a kink in the plan. Ethan couldn't be sure, but he sensed Gerard's commitment to coming after Scarlet with a knife. His sister had died from stab wounds, and a blade had been his weapon of choice in his first attack on Scarlet. Ethan also knew from experience that inmates had opportunities to hone their carving skills. Not so much with guns or other longer-range weaponry.

A knife meant Gerard had to get close, and Ethan made a hell of a barricade.

Pain flared in his palm. Looking down, he realized he'd done a number on the business end of his fork. Discretely turning his hand in his lap, he eyed several puncture wounds from the tines.

He almost wanted to squeeze a second one to catch another dose of relief the pain brought with it.

"And that means?" Scarlet prompted.

He topped her wine glass with the remainder of the Malbec they'd shared. "He might be down a rabbit hole."

She drank deep. It pleased him to see her fed, but as of yet, the food and wine had done little to liven her color. Weeks of gluttony might be required to restore the junk to her trunk.

A challenge. He pushed a warm loaf of sourdough bread toward her plate.

The temptation worked. She pulled off a chunk with her fingers. On the way to her lips, he swiped it from her hand and calmly slathered it with butter before passing it back.

"You really do like your women with curves, don't you?"

He looked her over. "I like them healthy. Happy. I know you appreciate good food. You should be eating it."

Staring down at the bread, she offered a bittersweet smile. Then the moment was lost. "What do you mean by rabbit hole?"

Steadily, he accepted the transition. Details might make her feel more at ease. And so far, she'd resisted anything that veered into the personal. "I'm afraid he won't be satisfied unless he can get close to you, until he can deliver whatever message he's burning to convey. He's biding his time."

With each word, her golden eyes went a shade darker against her white skin. "We let him make a move?"

He held her gaze, refusing to react but shocked at her suggestion.

"Never. We let him *think* he can."

******

Dessert moved them to the couch. Ethan's powerful frame took up most of the real estate, so Scarlet curled up near an armrest. She smiled inwardly at the progression of their evening. Eggs appeared to be Ethan's culinary specialty, but he ordered a mean five-star takeout.

She hadn't eaten steak in months. Or a buttered baked potato with real sour cream. The invading aroma of a hot charcoal grill had weakened her willpower to resist a lot more than food, and that was before Ethan had unwrapped the dishes, releasing a full-fat, carbalicious mayhem. Before he'd watched closely as she consumed every bite, encouraging her to enjoy the food with hedonistic abandon simply because it made her happy.

Now he spooned up her weakness. Never feeding her, but handing over bite after bite of decadent chocolate mousse that slid along her tongue and down her throat like silken heaven.

He didn't sneak a taste. Instead silent, anxious energy rolled off his stiff body each time he refilled her spoon. She wondered if he might splinter from within.

The pulsing stillness left her inexplicably nervous. "Tell me you like chocolate." The possibility that he didn't was rather appalling.

He shook his head and extended another dollop, "Never have."

Her hand flew to her chest in mock horror. *Sacrilege.* "You're like people who don't love puppies. If you don't like chocolate, I can't trust you." *Not sure I can anyway.* "And here you are with the job of keeping me safe."

The spoon in his hand twisted in front of her mouth, demanding attention, and she snaked her tongue out. The only thing more delicious was his deep voice when he said, "Perhaps I could be persuaded. To try it, I mean."

She looked up in question.

"I seem to remember enjoying a truffle or two in Copenhagen. Though I don't think I ate them directly."

The spoon floated away from her lips before landing in its empty dish. Ethan set the bones of the dessert on the coffee table.

"No, I suppose I tempered the flavor," she murmured.

Memories flashed through her mind. He'd brought the truffles in apology. She'd gorged. He'd watched. *Seems like a habit.* When she'd demanded a whole lot of Ethan to go with her chocolate, he'd refused and settled in for an undoubtedly uncomfortable night in his jeans.

Ethan hadn't given in until morning. In the hours between his gift and his capitulation, he'd kissed and stroked her not-so-naughty bits, no doubt sampling a hint of those delicious truffles along the way.

The reminder settled low in her stomach, burning. Smoke curled upward into her lungs, leaving her to function on hot, singed air. He made her... want. "How then?"

"How what, sweetheart?" The innocuous question didn't betray his thoughts, but the dark gleam in his eyes told her he could be more than a bodyguard. *Anytime, anyplace*, it said.

Shallow breaths barely eased inward. Ethan wasn't meant to be resisted.

"How can I persuade you to try?" she asked unevenly. "You can't continue on with a character defect of this magnitude." She twirled her index finger in circles around her ear. "Cra-zay."

Ethan jerked, chilling their light mood. He buffed his mouth and jaw roughly with his fingers. "I think you know."

Already overwhelmed lungs seized. *Yes, I do.* But she couldn't risk the devastation of watching him pull away again.

So they would do this the hard way.

Leaning forward, she forced herself to give detail, and not the kind Ethan obviously wanted. "Can you give me what you did that first night?" He knew the one. "Sleep with me but not *sleep* with me? With you, I fall asleep without any trouble. Sometimes I even dream. When you're not there, I—"

He threw an incredulous look her way, but heat blasted off his body. "You want me to help you sleep?"

"And"—*say it*—"kiss me. Touch me a little."

He jacked forward from the couch and bounced back against it hard. "Just so I'm clear, you want me to lie beside you. Kiss you. Stroke you *a little*. But no more. Only help you rest. Along the way, perhaps I'll catch a hint of that dessert as my reward?"

She looked away. He was going to tell her what she could do with her ridiculous needs, but she nodded regardless.

The room itself stayed quiet, as though waiting for his answer. The longer he took to respond, the more she gave in to embarrassment. Of course he wouldn't agree, probably considered her a tease. And now she knew exactly where they stood.

Slipping her legs from beneath her, she thought about toothpaste and started to rise. No chocolate for—

"Fuck yes, I will." He extended his hand in her direction, palm to the ceiling and fingers curled slightly inward. Waiting. *Inviting.*

Relief loosened the lock-down on her lungs. She clutched his thick wrist, and he pulled her up with him. Before she could strike out for her bedroom, he slung a hand behind her back and another beneath her knees, swinging her high against his chest.

"Solo chocolate is iffy, but did I mention how much I love a chocolate-flavored woman?"

******

Ethan walked smoothly with her dangling from his arms. If a comforting presence helped her shut out the world, then his hard-on could fuck off.

But her reticence still pricked. She'd been drawn to his silent offer to give her much more than peace. He'd seen it. The hitch of her breath. The way her warm stare slid along his torso, coming to rest on his groin. Scarlet denied herself because she still didn't trust him for anything more than his ability to knock heads.

Turning in her hall, he used his ass to nudge her bedroom door open. She already drowsed against his shoulder, so at the bed, he lifted a knee to support her legs while he threw back the covers. Dropping to a squat, he slid his hands from beneath her body and then stepped back.

"Thank you."

Her weary murmur drifted to his ears. She'd said the same thing last night after dropping the towels off in his room, like his renewed presence in her life was a favor for which she owed gratitude. In her eyes, he'd become the neighbor that mowed the lawn during an illness or the church lady that organized meal deliveries to an aging parishioner.

Performing a duty. Acting out of obligation. Here today, gone tomorrow. That's what she thought of him.

His hand went to the button on her jeans. "I'm not going to pounce on you, Scarlet, but can we get these off? You'll sleep better."

A nod.

Okay, she trusted him that much. He released the button, the zipper, and then slowly pulled the dark denim from her limbs.

Aaaannnd fuck. Welcome back to Scarlet's lingerie fetish. They were two see-through-panty lovers in a pod.

On instinct, he reached out to trace the peach lace that curved over her hip and between her thighs. Almost too late, he pulled away.

Throat dry, he pushed her a little harder, tugging at her shirt. "Can we ditch this, too?"

"Mmm hmm."

By the time her shirt had joined her jeans on the floor, he knew she fought against her arousal. Her nipples puckered against the delicate cups of her bra, demanding attention, and when he sat on the edge of the bed, her back arched up in a slow roll. Seconds later, she gripped the sheet and pulled it over her, straight to the neck.

Biology demanded a closeness he'd taught her to distrust. No wonder she fought it. He took a hand that peeked from beneath the cotton and began to trace slow circles against the impossibly soft skin of her slender wrist. The innocent touches seemed to remind her he wasn't there to get laid. Gradually, her body quieted.

"Did you believe me," he began, considering each word before he said it, "when I said I never meant to hurt you? That I pushed you away because, even though you didn't know it or intend it, I'd become your instrument of self-sabotage?"

She shifted under the sheet, giving him a glimpse of a satin collarbone. "I believe you *now.*"

The swift, sure affirmation surprised him. He'd expected waffling. "Do you believe I didn't suspect how you'd be affected?"

There was a pause, and her gaze darted to and from his face in indecisive intervals. Then a quiet, "Yes."

A little confliction, but she seemed sure. "Do you know I care more than"—he opened and closed his mouth several times, squeezing her hand—"a great deal about your safety?"

This time she nodded right away.

He reached out and carefully smoothed a lock of hair that had slipped over her eye. *Right answers. Zero help.* "You thought I'd used and abused, but now you understand my motives. And regret. That's not enough?" He cringed inwardly, hoping the last hadn't veered into blame.

She stiffened, re-tucking the sheet beneath her chin with the hand he didn't clutch like a lifeline. "You did what you thought was right." *No shit.*

"But that decision? You took it out of my hands like I wasn't capable of being part of a sensible solution."

"I'm not used to—"

"And I'm not a child," she finished.

Her unflinching gaze said *there's more*. "No matter your choices, or how angry or disappointed you made me, I couldn't set you aside for any length of time. That was the whole problem, right? I needed you, wanted you, too much to say good-bye. You didn't see it that way."

"*I* knew it wasn't forever." Otherwise, he'd *never* have let her go. "You didn't."

"It doesn't matter why or whether you thought you'd get me back. You were able to end it, which means you don't feel what I do."

No, I feel much more.

"And I thought you did." Her voice cracked at the last, and she rolled away from him. "I can't trust either one of us after being so wrong."

Guilt propelled him away from the bed. The wall looked pretty damn good in comparison to her accusations. He jammed his hands against the doorframe to her bathroom, stretching back and dropping his head between rigid arms.

"You're right," he said tightly. *Even though you're so goddamn wrong.* "I'm sorry. More than I can say. But know this. While you thought I was enjoying life solo, I tortured myself with images of you doing the same. In the end, I couldn't stay away. That's why I ran at JTS again. It's why I'm here now."

Louder than he'd intended, his declaration rang against the walls. The echo was the only response he got. Turning around, he saw she'd scooted to the middle of the bed and curled her arms and legs into herself. The defensive position jarred him out of his mission to make things right with a few words.

Her head poked up from the pillow. "Would you grab my phone from the living room?"

"Why?"

"I—I like to have it nearby when I sleep."

God, she thought he wouldn't stay, that after his outburst, he'd leave her to brave the night the way she usually did, apparently curled in a ball, clutching her cell.

"You don't need it." They'd hit another wall, but it wouldn't do for her to question whether he planned to honor his promise to sleep next to her. Returning to the bed, he stretched out along the curve of her back.

And what do you know, when he reached out and threaded a hand through her hair, she didn't pull away. Even better, with each combing stroke through the bright strands, she inched backward toward his chest until the tightness in his throat began to ease.

After long minutes, he barely heard her whisper against the pillow. "Thank you."

The unwanted gratitude grabbed him by the throat and squeezed. One breath in, one breath out. Again and again. Then calmly, "Welcome." *Because these things take time. They're earned, not demanded.*

With one last shift, he plastered his chest against her spine. Chocolate-flavored woman would have to wait.

CHAPTER 26

"I don't know if he habitually paid off officials," Scarlet grumbled. "My father and I probably spent a combined ten months under the same roof in all the years after my mother's death. I was young, and as you love to say, *spoiled.*" She dragged the word out until Ethan's pupils disappeared in a skyward roll.

It was mid-Saturday and Scarlet had finally attacked the mail piling up on her kitchen table. She painstakingly opened every single envelope regardless of its expected contents. While she considered each bill, each coupon, each advertisement, Ethan peppered her with questions that were becoming increasingly difficult to answer.

"I didn't care about his business dealings. He could've invaded a small country, and I wouldn't have known."

Ethan raked his fingers through cropped hair that spiked out in rebellion. He held up part of Scarlet's most recent research, a printout showing a mug shot of an attractive middle-aged man with a touch of gray at his temples. "About five years after your dad built the Cora, this guy"—he pointed to the photo—"pleaded guilty to two counts of conspiracy to commit honest services fraud and two counts of conspiracy to commit bribery. At the time of his arrest, he served on the Landmarks Preservation Commission. When your dad sought approval for the Cora? He was the committee's chairman."

An everyday asshole and a bona fide crook were two different things. "My father was never charged with a crime."

"True." He fell back against the couch, roughly palming his eye sockets. She'd dug up the info. Barely a day had passed before she relented and accepted Ethan's help deciphering it. Since then, he'd spent the better part of his nights reviewing and adding to her findings. Even Billboard had fielded a few requests for hard-to-find tidbits.

"There were several co-defendants in the criminal case," he continued, "all convicted of bribing this guy in exchange for priority in construction permitting—a hotelier, a restaurateur, another developer. Never your father. Yet I'm not so sure."

Scarlet's mail progress slowed. "George Rosono."

"Exactly. Looks like family money. He got involved in all sorts of give-back positions around town. The kind with more respect than pay. Guess he wanted the pay."

Busy plumbing the depths of her memory for dirt on Rosono, she reached for a manila envelope. The writing on the back warned, "Pictures. Do not bend." She pried the tape from the flap and reached in.

Ethan lunged up, suddenly pacing the hardwoods of her living room. "It's too much of a coincidence. Tripp Leore got the permit of the century. He demolished a historic apartment building in the center of a historical district. All this went down while the gatekeeping function designed to prevent such destruction was headed by a man who currently sits in prison for accepting bribes of the *exact* nature your father would have sought. I don't buy—"

Death. Real and inescapable. All Scarlet saw was a young girl lying in a pool of her own blood, eyes eternally open and mouth parted in a silent scream. The image scalded her fingers, and she dropped it, stumbling from her chair and falling to the floor.

"It's her, Ethan. Her." The litany reverberated against her skull and out her mouth as she crab-walked away from the photo and the offending envelope she knew would contain more of the same. "Her, her…"

Ethan crouched overhead. "Who? Scarlet, calm down." His hand streamed over her forehead and scalp until it cradled the back of her head. "That's right. Look at me. Breathe deep. Where?"

She couldn't answer. Easing her shoulder blades onto the spinning kitchen tile, she pointed a limp finger toward the envelope.

Violence registered on his features, and he spun for the table. He grabbed the top image first, like Scarlet had.

"*Fucking Christ*," he bit out. Gripping the table's edge, he flipped through the remaining pictures with his free hand. With each image, he lowered a fraction until he sat in the chair Scarlet had vacated.

Seconds ticked by. Finally, he ground out, "Anna Chamber bled out on the scarred linoleum of a homeless shelter." His attention snapped to Scarlet, now propped against the cupboard with her knees raised against her chest. "This is what I meant by Gerard having a message for you. As graphic as these are, we knew about Anna. *This can't touch you.*"

But Gerard could. "Now I see his plans for me."

Ethan tried to shove the pictures into the envelope, but they hit something, jamming it further toward the bottom of the pocket. He reached in and pulled out a folded piece of stationary. A note?

Cold seeped through every exposed pore on her body. In seconds, her limbs shook, and even though she forced a shallow pant, it didn't feel like oxygen traveled to her brain.

"From him?" She heard the question, knew she'd asked it, but suddenly she didn't care. The gruesome scene played out in another life and time, someone else's kitchen. From far away she heard Ethan unfold the paper and press the crease from its middle.

"No." The savage syllable ripped from his chest, and her mind registered that the message had been the game-changing element of her anti-care package.

"No?" she echoed faintly.

Her vision tapered to bright pinpricks of light through which Ethan moved like the moon in a solar eclipse. Close now, he reached out and gently felt along her neck with cool fingertips. "That's my girl. Take a breath, slow and easy."

Pervasive weakness unfurled, sapping her energy. She couldn't nod.

"I'm going to pick you up. Is that all right?"

She tried to say "yes," but her mouth refused, totally slack.

The floor fell away, only to be swiftly replaced with the soft pillows of her couch. A throw swept along her legs.

Ethan's hand settled in the center of her chest, a radiant heater against the ice block of her torso. "Keep at it, Scarlet. In and out, like clockwork. Focus on something good. When this is over, think beach. Nothing but Mai Tais, that waterfront yoga you chicks dig, and couples massages for a month."

This time she managed a small head jerk to let him know she was with him. There was an idea. *Sun and sand, yes. Mai Tais and massage. And, if I make it, all the sex I've been stupid enough to turn down.*

The weight of his hand lifted, and she heard him on the phone. Police. Of course. The night Gerard had approached on her steps he hadn't made an overt threat. Mailing pictures of a mutilated teenager took care of that formality. Maybe now she'd get a little love from the cops.

Out of nowhere, Ethan coaxed, "Your lips are blue. Drink this. All of it." He held a mug to her mouth and tipped it back until sweet warmth flowed over her tongue.

"As soon as you feel steady, we'll go down to the station. We're not leaving without a personal police shadow. Either that, or it's a security company." When she made a noise in the back of her throat, he snarled. "You just received a package containing ten photographs of a *dead child*. I don't give a fu—"

He froze, then started again, calmer, "I don't care about your money hang-ups. You *will* be safe."

With a frantic push, her voice finally debuted. "It's not that. Guards are fine." *Wanted.* "But I'll pay for them if it comes to that." The earrings had left her with cash on hand, and her job had taken an amazing turn for the better.

Ethan had done that.

"Don't make this about money." His jaw snapped shut with an ominous crack, and he shot up from the couch, stalking toward the kitchen table. Halfway there, he stopped. "Whatever you need, Scarlet. If you have adequate protection, I'll... deal." The concession came in fits and starts and ended on a tortured groan over his shoulder.

Jingling and slamming roared out of her kitchen. Finally, he came into view with a pair of tongs and a Ziploc bag. Using the tongs, he slid the note into the protective plastic, careful not to touch any more of it than he already had.

Bag in hand, he returned to her side on the couch. "How do you feel?"

She took in the tendons that stood in stark relief against his throat and the way his free hand fisted and released. His calm and rational routine needed work.

"Better," she lied. When he didn't budge, she reached out, fluttering her fingers. "Let me have it, Ethan. I'm steady."

"Not for long." He laid the bagged note in her lap. "Scarlet, I'm sorry."

The message was short and on her father's stationary. She would forever wonder how anything so chilling could look so innocuous.

She read it once, then again. Ten years ago, her father had stood by her hospital bed, unmoved. Because he hadn't been surprised.

Mr. Chamber,

The pictures of your sister sadden me. Really, they do. But to threaten my daughter? It only makes me thankful I don't suffer the delusional emotional entanglements that plague you. Scarlet is smarter than you are. So am I.

Good luck,

Tripp Leore

Sickness slithered in her stomach. She'd know her dad's strong, rigid handwriting anywhere. As usual, he'd printed the date neatly along the top, right-hand corner. Her father had written Gerard Chamber mere days before her attack outside the fight club.

All the twists and turns of the truth hit her fully formed. A hundred bullets at once. "I take it back. Tripp Leore bribed George Rosono for that permit," she supplied in a deadened tone. "The Cora shouldn't exist."

The cryptic message explained everything. Gerard had recognized her in Rancor as the daughter of his nemesis. He'd issued a graphic threat against her life, looking for... what? An admission of guilt? Money? An apology?

Instead, her father had wished him luck.

She hadn't realized it was possible to *feel* one's blood pressure nose-dive. *Wished him luck.* To do anything else would have opened an investigation capable of blowing the lid off the bribes she no longer questioned.

Her father had known about Gerard all along. How relieved he must have been when she'd uttered Ethan's name from that hospital bed. The stars had aligned, and he'd seized the chance to bury Gerard's suspicions, afraid they'd surface at trial and sink him and his schemes along with the man who'd tried to kill her.

"*We needed closure,*" he'd said by way of explanation. *Yes, Dad, you certainly did.*

Plain and simple, her father had placed the highest premium on his liberty. He needn't have worried. Legal retribution had never been Gerard's game.

Her gaze flew to Ethan's. Never mind that Tripp's silence before the attack had nearly killed her. His silence afterward had allowed the wrong man to go to prison. "He knew you were innocent the whole time."

"Yes." His tug pulled the plastic-wrapped note from between her fingers, and suddenly, he braced his hands on either side of her ribcage, his big body bristling above, daring her to take the blame. The warmth of his breath washed over her temple when he leaned in close. "And I don't fucking care."

Horror and shame cleaved into her chest. Copies of those tragic pictures of Anna Chamber probably rotted in her father's safe. If anyone could have helped Ethan from the beginning, it had been Tripp Leore. But what was letting one nobody take the fall for another? Speaking up would have provoked too many questions. New York might have stumbled upon the truth of its prodigy.

"I'm sorry," she breathed. "For all of it."

Other than a slight undulation across his tan throat, he could have been a statue. "Don't, Scarlet. Don't even think about apologizing for a man who almost got you killed. What he did to me pales—and I mean *glows in the dark*—in comparison to his crimes against you."

"Why didn't Gerard pipe up at his trial? Call attention to the permitting and payoff issues he and his mother suspected?" Either way, Gerard had been destined for a cell, but he could have taken her dad down with him.

"Because he never wanted to see your dad behind bars. He wanted— *wants*—a different kind of revenge."

To see me dead.

Ethan gradually eased away, settling next to her hip. "Publicizing his real motive would have complicated his end game. As it was, he bamboozled the parole board, secured his release, and walked right up to you on the street within days of clearing the prison gates. That wouldn't have been possible had he come clean."

Shock took a backseat to logic. Her jaw slackened incrementally when the last piece of the puzzle fell into place. "He's making it known now because he doesn't think there's anything we can do to stop him. He relishes my terror."

Ethan took both of her cheeks between his palms. "We *will* stop him."

Tripp Leore rarely paid compliments. Yet his letter to Gerard had boasted of her intelligence, as though he believed—or at least wanted to believe—her mighty intellect would save her from the clutches of a madman who thought nothing of using the bloodied images of his dead sister as a scare tactic.

"My dad got it wrong. Gerard's outsmarting me as we speak."

The light pressure on her jaw and cheek bones didn't ease. "No. That was the *only* thing your dad got right."

CHAPTER 27

Scarlet shattered the silence of the car. "Bloomingdales? Yeah?"

Ethan shook his head to clear out the fog, certain he hadn't heard right. "Have you lost your mind?" The police station faded into the cityscape, and Ethan eyed Scarlet's NYPD escort in the rear-view mirror.

"You'll be there." She gestured to their tail with a hitchhikers thumb toward the trunk. "He'll be there."

"The guy trying to kill you will come along," Ethan added helpfully. "It'll be a party."

"I can't stand this. I need something… A handbag that spurs positive thinking. Nothing red, like blood."

"A bag. We're leaving the precinct, a place we've spent the last four hours because you have an exceedingly violent and determined stalker, and you want a purse. Not red, of-fucking-course."

Officer Save-a-Scarlet would trail them both and post himself within whatever building she entered. The extra hand only slightly relieved Ethan's rampant mind fuck. Seeing those photos of Anna Chamber—really grasping Scarlet's reality and the symbolic demonstration of how little control he had over the situation—had physically hurt.

Daddy's added bonus hadn't helped. The statute of limitations had run on any illegal activity her father had undertaken fifteen years ago, but the evidence they'd collected was sufficient to prompt an investigation into Tripp Leore's more recent business activities.

If legal battles didn't take him down, the resulting public-relations nightmare would. Whatever remained standing after the press spit him out? That could fall victim to a little private entrapment. Let Leore rot in a cell next to the one Chamber would soon return to. See how well the two got along at meals.

"Fine," she replied in what he now recognized as a classically-deceptive surrender. *Lovely little liar.* "But look at this. It's all ragged." She held up a pristine bag with opposing, inverted "F's" on its oversized buckle. He'd shopped for too many one-month anniversaries not to recognize a Fendi. In red. "I put those pictures in here, Ethan," she cajoled. "I can't use it."

Do not turn around. Do not give in. "I know you've heard of online shopping. Today's your day to excel at the one-click-and-its-yours."

"Oh, yesss. Mine." With an expression of concentration, she tapped her temple and lowered her voice suspiciously. "You always were a thinker, you know. But it's not the same release, and it doesn't fulfill the same desire."

Release. Fulfill. Desire. He slowed the car and looked her over. That delicious mouth sounded serious, but a faint tinge of pink flooded her cheeks when she returned the perusal. Starting at his thighs beneath the steering wheel, she worked him over in an expressive visual examination. Around mid-chest, he jerked his attention back to the road when a horn blasted them through an intersection.

Jaw clenched, he drove on, eyes forward.

"Retail therapy," she cooed, low and sensuous, "is a great pleasure. Ever heard of it?"

The passenger seat reclined until she spread out next to him like a woman buffet. He swore he heard her mumble, "Must have with all those mercenaries you've dated." Then an afterthought, "Only the real thing will do."

Oh yes, real shopping. Like the demonstration she'd provided in Copenhagen. He'd gotten on a first-name basis with every high heel in her collection, and the cherry-red numbers she'd worn that last day had been a new addition. A well-loved one if her adoration on the way to the airport had been any indication.

Flexing her feet this way and that. Petting them instead of him.

He pulled into her parking space at the Cora, punctuating his "hell no" with a hard stop. "Not happening. Overnight the bag. My treat." Thinking of how touchy she remained about money, he added, "The shipping, that is."

His arm spasmed in her unexpected grip, which slid upward over his shoulder and down between his pecs. She had no idea what kind of bear she baited.

"Please," she begged. And she wasn't asking for the goddamn handbag.

After waiting and wanting and letting her set the pace, she spoke to him of desire? She knew nothing of it. Need, elemental and raw, stretched tight beneath his skin. Worry ate at him. Those sickening pictures, her ridiculous requests… Something in him stretched and—

Snapped.

Take. Control. This time her thank-you would be worth it.

With a low curse, he bit out, "Upstairs. *Now.*"

She extracted herself from the car and beat him to the elevator. On the ascent, she met his unbreakable stare floor after floor. They stumbled out into the hall, and after two tries, she keyed her apartment code correctly, and they wrenched into her entryway.

"*Release* is it?" He yanked her to him and pressed her back against the wall, trapping her dainty wrists overhead with a single hand.

"Yes," she squeaked, licking her lips.

Face-to-face, he memorized her. Blond hair streamed in disarray over slim shoulders. Wide, light eyes tracked him, giving both nothing and everything away. Against his chest, her breasts heaved and, with each retreat, he pressed closer, prepared to take all she offered. "So beautiful," he rasped. "You've *haunted* me."

If anything ever happened to you…

Her teeth clamped around the flesh at his collarbone, releasing the low groan trapped in his chest. Unable to wait, he reached down and rucked her skirt upward, hitching it around her waist. Ripping at his jeans, he managed the belt, button, and zipper one-handed, pulling his erection free.

He kicked her legs wide, feeling the head of his cock straining toward the hot shelter between her thighs, ready to plunge inside and take her furiously. Without mercy.

A viscous yank cleared her panties from his path. Dimly, he let his good side intrude long enough to squeeze her wrists. Once she focused, he growled, "Don't tell me no. I can't fucking stand it." And she'd *asked* for it, in so many ways.

"Never no, Ethan." Hoarse cries escaped her mouth. His favorite. They pulled him to her in subconscious invitation.

"Exactly." He lifted her against the wall and centered himself, then pushed inside with all his strength.

A surprised gasp sounded against the bare floors and high ceilings.

His hips stilled. "*No*, Scarlet. Jesus, I was too rough." Panic and regret welled from a hidden reserve he rarely tapped. Had he hurt her? "Sweetheart, let me—"

"'Ssss all right." Her purr slurred deliciously, and her inner muscles clamped around his shaft when she curled her legs around him. Looking at her face, he saw her gaze darken, burning with lust.

He fought the urge to pull back, and then slam in too hard. "I want this"—*you*—"but only if you're with me."

"'Mmm there. Ethan, *move*."

In answer, he shuddered and stirred himself inside her, dying in the heat, the wetness. Gently at first—he still worried his entrance had caused pain—and then with increasing force. His body pressed against her, muscles tight beneath his clothes.

The ridges of sinew that curved over his hips pressed her legs wider, more open to him with each rock. Impossibly, he surged deeper.

"Need to feel you come." Ditching his grip on her wrists, he moved his hand low on her belly to thumb her clitoris.

Slender arms wound around his neck, and with the first pass through her slick folds, he felt her nails bite into his nape. The sting shocked him, and he could scarcely grate in amazement, "*Mark me. I fucking love it.*"

Her head fell back, and he leaned in to lick at her throat, never slowing the pitiless thrusts. A responsive shiver shimmied along his cock. When her face swiveled upright again, his breath caught, and his mind emptied. She didn't look at him with acquiescence, not even with simple desire.

Finally, Scarlet Leore had fallen in love.

******

She braced her shoulders against the wall and reveled in every inch Ethan gave her. The day had been a nightmarish culmination of the last horrible weeks. To have him deep, clearly at the edge of his control, smoothed the rough edges. She'd let them go—Gerard Chamber and Tripp Leore, the cops and parole officers, the job and the money—and welcomed Ethan in.

Each plunge grew more powerful, making her scream in surprised pleasure. His wildness, the utter desperation, blasted through her secret dreams.

One strong hand gripped her ass, pinning her in place, while the other swept back and forth through her wetness. When he didn't kiss or lick her skin, his lips parted on a ragged grimace. Not once had his eyes closed. He zeroed in on her with infinite focus, missing nothing.

Ethan had totally lost it, yet he'd never controlled her pleasure to such a degree. Every move issued a fierce demand she couldn't deny. And didn't want to.

As her climax crackled at the base of her spine, he gritted, "Now," and ground himself against her in persistent pulses. She felt the hot splash of semen inside and cried his name, again and again, before she collapsed against him.

He snatched her to his chest and turned around, sliding down the wall until he sat on the floor with her seated in the cradle between his raised knees and chest. "Astounding," he panted quietly, tucking a lock of hair behind her ear. "You all right?"

"Better than that." Would he remember that *take me shopping* worked as code for *fuck me really hard?* "I needed that."

"Me, too."

"Ethan?" She considered how to tell him of her mind's very strange trip. *He'll figure it out soon enough.* She leaned in to whisper in his ear. "Give me your credit card."

His lips quirked at the edges, but he silently rocked to the side to access the rear pocket of the jeans he still wore. The move pressed his semi-hard cock against her womb, and she breathed through the overwhelming urge to rise up and slide down. Extracting a silver money clip, he pressed an American Express Centurion into her palm.

She blinked at the black card with titanium engraving. "I should have known."

"Now you do."

Like him, she still wore her clothes. Aside from a few patches of fisted wrinkles, her dress had fared well. The skirt remained wadded around her waist, but she assumed she could salvage her look with an iron. Only her thong hadn't survived.

Almost like an afterthought, Ethan's fingers smoothed down the front of her bodice. Circling her breasts in a wide arc, he toyed with the fabric, but he didn't reach around to the zipper that ran along her spine.

"Why now?" he asked.

"It's a long story."

A one-eighty sweep of their surroundings brought his gaze back to her. "I've got time."

On a deep breath, she started, "I learned a lot today. About you, yes, but more about me. Like you said, Gerard's hatred wasn't news. And believe it or not, my dad's letter to Gerard was"—she shrugged—"a relief."

"I'm following, but very far behind."

"He never loved me. Christ, he never even liked me. I came to terms with that as a child. After what happened with you and Gerard, my gut said his money was wicked. You've mocked me for refusing his help, at times questioned whether I'm a liar. But I haven't taken a dime from Tripp Leore in years because though I barely knew him, I sensed he and his mint were equally corrupt."

Seeing him hang on every word, she went on, her voice thick with emotion. "Today proved me right. Turning away from my only relative didn't make me crazy. Or eccentric. It made me smart. I had his number, which means I'm probably right about you."

His lips curved to showcase strong, white teeth in the widest smile. "I like how you think."

"Everything in me wants you. Wants to trust you. So, yeah, I'm going to put some wear on you—on your body and on this piece of plastic." She held up the black card. "Because *you*," she emphasized, "for all your posturing, are *not* a bad boy. You're the safest game in town."

"Don't tell anyone," he said, taking her revelation in stride. "Can you put some more wear on my body before you start in on the plastic?"

"Maybe."

"Or, better yet, *while* you work the plastic?" He nipped her lower lip. "You can describe what you're buying. In detail."

"What would you like?"

"Stilettos with slender straps that restrain the ankles." His hands stroked over her feet, stripping off the heels she still wore and then skimming from her toes to her knees. "Maybe with those ties that trail up the calves. And thongs. Lots and lots of thongs."

"You asked for it." And then she laughed with him—at him—on a day that could have been the worst of her life.

"A warning," she offered in challenge, "I'm a rather high-maintenance girlfriend."

CHAPTER 28

The afternoon had nearly passed when Scarlet retreated to her desk to review a client's non-disclosure agreement. She'd promised comments before the end of the day and figured she had time to squeeze in a peek while Ethan talked optics and Korea with Brian.

Life with three shadows had taken some adjustment. At work, Scarlet's police escort monitored the bank of elevators from the ground floor. Ethan milled around her office or worked out of an empty conference room next door. Brian was on standby via speakerphone. With the press of his extension, her voice flooded his office. No need to pick up the receiver.

Each night, Ethan escorted her home and stayed, while another officer stationed himself in the hall outside her apartment.

Work and home. The end. True to his word, her stress-related shopping trips involved Ethan's Centurion card and a computer mouse. True to hers, she now owned several pairs of four-inch heels that would never see the light of day and more underwear than a lingerie model could wade through in a year of photo shoots.

Anna's pictures had arrived days ago. Limbo wasn't a forever option, but any mention of added risk had Ethan frothing at the mouth.

"We're already using you to draw him out," he'd clipped the night before. "That's why we're still in the city. He'll make a move, and mucho-macho in the hall and I will be ready for the strike. Any more than that, and we'll have to arm wrestle for it."

The lull in excitement had left her brave enough to feel little more than exasperation over Ethan's hesitance to put her in danger. "I'm climbing the walls. We can't do this forever."

He'd dropped to a knee and rolled back his shirt sleeve, then propped an elbow on her coffee table, palm extended in her direction. Anchoring his bicep with his other hand, he'd looked up, ready for action. "If I win," he'd said with a wink, "you can climb *me*."

He'd won. The climbing had been fun, but she wouldn't go in for his distractions indefinitely.

Distracted by the memory, Scarlet took a seat in front of her computer, closing her eyes while she waited for the first inked page of the agreement to ease from the printer near the window. She daydreamed of the trip they'd take once Gerard had been "beaten to ground," as Ethan put it. The four-S vacation—sun and sand, the original requirements, plus sex and shopping, which she'd subsequently added to the list.

Mid-thought, she simmered with vague awareness. Her office wasn't quite right. All the clippings and sticky notes were missing from the bulletin board behind her monitor. Only one item remained posted, and it wasn't hers. An eight-by-ten inch piece of glossy paper dangled from the middle of the board. She could only see the word "Kodak" plastered across the stark white of the sheet because the picture faced inward.

More Anna. She knew it.

Blindly, she reached for the printer. Her fingers slid over a surprise. The paper was thick and smooth, like touching a photo.

Confused, she pulled the sheet free and took a look.

Anna Chamber stared back at her, alive and smiling, the words of a random contract superimposed over her face and body. Each new sheet showed a different pose, but in all, Anna appeared happy and healthy.

Her office door whispered shut and plodding steps sounded behind her. Before she could react, the edge of a knife pressed hot and sharp against the side of her throat. She knew who held it long before she heard the oily malice in his voice.

"One word, and I'll end this right now, Empress."

CHAPTER 29

Part of her—the rational side—understood what was happing. Another part floated above, watching the situation unfold like she and Gerard were actors in a low-budget horror flick. It took a while to reconcile the two and consider her options.

Gerard's free hand grabbed the armrest of her chair from behind, and he whipped her around so her bent knees met his shins. The knife didn't move along with her, and with each inch, the blade scraped over the skin of her neck, barely sampling blood.

Massacre wasn't a word she tossed around, but hope fled when she saw him. A well-cut suit gloved a massive wall of muscle, right down to the platinum cufflinks at his wrists and the buffed leather loafers on his feet. Had he worn a shoddy wig, a janitor's gray, or even arrived looking like a handsome woman, he might not have slipped by. But people weren't programmed to question an attractive, successful man heading to her office in the middle of a Manhattan afternoon.

The trappings of wealth had effectively camouflaged the beast within.

All the dapper contrasted the wrath that pulsed in her direction, sharper because he hadn't played the thug. She didn't know which was worse, his hatred or his intellect. A stupid killer would have been easier. But this man had schmoozed a parole board, identified and infiltrated her residence, evaded arrest for nearly two weeks, and managed to slip past her defenses to corner her with a knife. Again.

"Confused?" He waited, but she didn't respond. To nod would risk further damage to her neck. "I walked. You'd be amazed at how few of the floors in these buildings have locked or coded doors to the internal stairwells. Don't worry, though, I mentally waved to your buddy by the elevators."

Gerard spoke calmly, like he donned a three-thousand-dollar suit and held a knife to a woman's throat every day. The weapon slid around to the base of her chin and pressed up. No telltale sting. He hadn't cut her this time, only used the weapon to tilt her head back.

When her gaze climbed to collide with his, he tugged at the pictures clutched in her hand. "She should be here now, looking like that."

Her mouth went desert dry. "I know," she said in a smothered voice. "I wish she could be."

She recalled Ethan's theory about Gerard having a message. Until he got it off his chest, he might not do anything irrevocable. Once he did...

Keep him talking. More talking meant more time. "I'm estranged from my father, you know."

The pressure increased, forcing her head to her shoulders, until she could only see him through slit lids.

"I know what he did," she continued. "I hate him, too."

Amusement gleamed behind hard eyes that pinned her to the knife as effectively as the pressure against her skin. He liked her fear.

"Think about it," she went on, dying to reason with him. "You sent him Anna's pictures. An overt threat." She paused, sucking a shallow breath as though through a straw. "And he told you to go to hell."

Silently, she implored him to realize he couldn't use her to reach Tripp Leore. In this case, killing the daughter wouldn't amount to much in the way of revenge against the father.

"Mind games," he taunted through clenched teeth.

Leave it to her to have a stalker who'd over-thought his wayward plan.

The knife lifted, only to settle point-down against her abdomen. "Don't bother."

She jerked as the dagger bit through clothes and skin. A familiar agony swamped her senses, and wooziness flooded her. *No, not again*. The room began a slow spin.

Gerard blurred in her sights, nothing but a barrage of gray matter sent to make her hurt. The dots floating in her vision prevented her from seeing him clearly, but she could hear. Even so, the threats were buzzing now, and she couldn't digest the gist of his taunts over her firing pain receptors.

Words hit in slow motion, as though they traveled through water to her ears. He would kill her, he said. Right here. But first, there was something she needed to see.

Holding her in place with a twist of pain in her gut, he reached behind her, coming back with the Kodak paper she'd seen tacked to her board. Like before, she saw white. Now that plain backing served as a canvas for hundreds of dancing black orbs.

Eventually, he'd turn the paper. She'd see Anna, lying limp in her own blood. The knowledge should have shocked her anew, but it didn't. Her mind had drifted out of reach.

In the moment he took to view the image only he could see, she pictured Ethan, close by and on guard. Like the wisp of a dream, she saw their long road. The way he'd initially tormented her, then learned her and waited patiently for her to learn him. He'd forgiven her. Watched over her. He'd even done things that were terribly misguided, but only because he'd truly believed they were right.

She loved him for his miracles and his mistakes, and he'd never know.

Ethan wouldn't forgive himself. He'd view Gerard's success as his eternal failure.

The thought hit like a bucket of water to the face. To succumb would ensure the person who'd done everything to help her would be the one to pay. Gerard's vendetta had cost Ethan too much already. Maybe she couldn't beat this brute at his own game. But she might prevail in a different one.

The picture dangled in front of her face, then turned slowly.

Her heart scrambled and she stared, stared until her brain accepted she'd been wrong. Gerard *had* followed her logic. He *did* believe her death wouldn't faze her father.

So he'd killed him first.

The picture didn't show Anna Chamber in a Chelsea homeless shelter. Her father lay in the same position but against a much nicer floor, his limbs splayed out against gray slate. Like Anna, blood pooled beneath him and his vacant stare conveyed anything but peace.

"This morning," Gerard provided with cold precision, his eyes roving her face for a reaction she couldn't give. Certainly she'd never wanted her dad to meet an untimely demise, but he'd been a stranger, a far-away figure who'd done little but cause harm. Other than regret for what could have been, his death simply didn't pack an emotional punch.

Further proof of viciousness in the man who'd killed him did.

Gerard's mouth morphed into a cruel sneer. "You were right. Pops didn't give a shit. And now, you're nothing but *extra*." He let the photo go, and she watched it silently flutter to the floor beside them.

The knife pulled away. She knew what came next. The evidence lay at her feet. With a keening cry, she kicked out, using his legs as leverage to propel her chair toward the phone. A clumsy punch of five buttons, that's all she needed. Through the years, she'd called Brian enough to commit the path of numbers to muscle memory.

Narrowing her focus, she managed to hit the "speaker" button, then three-six-two-two, the twenty-second office on the thirty-sixth floor.

Ethan was with Brian. He would hear.

******

Brian's speakerphone screeched and Ethan quieted, figuring the man's assistant had a quick question.

He heard a high, muffled cry. Then, "*You fucking bitch.* That will—"

The chair beneath him jammed the wall with the force of his body propelling forward. He sprinted out the door and down the hall, heart racing too fast for an organ that had stopped the moment he'd heard her call out. Seconds later, he burst into Scarlet's office, only to see Gerard push her to the carpet, blood at her throat. The vision was a primitive shock—Scarlet bent on scrambling away and Gerard on inflicting harm.

Gerard Chamber hadn't changed. Still muscled and mean. The suit did nothing for him. *Lipstick on a pig.*

He turned to Ethan with a crazed light in his eyes. "Just like old times."

Watching in horror, his long-time nemesis fell on Scarlet's little body with a knife. All rational thought imploded with the first thrust, and he knew desperation for the first time. Keening low, Scarlet lay still beneath Gerard without a hint of struggle, white against the blood that smeared the floor.

A profane roar erupted from Ethan's throat, and he hurtled himself at the other man. Dropping his shoulder, he hit Gerard squarely in the chest. The man reeled into the desk, smashing Scarlet's monitor. The knife flew to the side. *Thank God, not lodged inside her.*

Wrapping a forearm around Gerard's throat, Ethan shoved him to his knees and dragged him away from Scarlet's prone form. Gerard cursed and gagged, struggling wildly against Ethan's hold. The continued force was all the excuse Ethan needed.

"Yeah," he gritted in a voice that didn't sound like his own, "just like old times."

When, off the books, I always fucking won.

He twisted past a sickening pop, then let Gerard crumble to his feet.

A crowd had gathered outside her office, and the cop on elevator duty rushed into the room. None of it mattered. He knelt next to Scarlet and lifted her limp form into his lap, flinching at all the red. "No, please God," he whispered, hardly able to speak past the huge knob in his throat.

"Ambulance." The plea was a hoarse bark at the horrified audience in the hall. "Please, help her."

Diving in, he felt for a pulse. She had one, thready but detectable. After a lifetime of rigid control, seeing this one small woman hurt left him utterly helpless, fragile in a way he didn't think he could stand. Dropping his head back, he clutched her to his chest, rocking and waiting.

"I love you, Scarlet. *Love you,*" he rasped. "Do you fucking hear me? Wake up so I can tell you how much for the rest of our lives." Each word came harder as he struggled around choked tears. "You were perfect, using the intercom like that when I know you were afraid."

He looked down at her, desperate for a response. *Too pale. Still as death.*

"Come on, sweetheart. Give me what I want one more time, and I swear I'll never ask you for another thing. Look at me, Goddamn it! Let me tell you I love you."

She couldn't hear him. Blood seeped through her clothes from wounds on her chest and abdomen. There couldn't be many. Gerard hadn't had time.

And her neck. More blood oozed down her slim throat from slices he thought—*needed* to believe—were shallow. When had those happened? How long had she been in here, alone with an animal?

He'd failed her, demanded her complete trust, and then thrown her to the wolf. Now he'd yelled at her when she was down.

Gentling his tone, he crooned near her ear. "If you don't hang on, you'll break my heart. So cling to something. Cling to those self-defense classes you're going to take, to how hard I'm going to let you hit me for not protecting you like I promised, to all the chocolate I'm going to feed you."

He couldn't stop. "Think about our vacation. The sex. I know you at least love that about me. Hang on so you can torture me with it."

He looked up at the frozen faces of her colleagues. None seemed phased by his lapse into TMI. They, like him, hovered in fear. One by one, they grudgingly shifted aside to allow access for the EMTs and the stretcher.

He tore himself away to let the medics see to her, but before he did, he felt it.

A squeeze. Light, like her pulse, but alive and aware.

She'd heard.

CHAPTER 30

Scarlet awoke to beeping machines and a sense of peace only prescription-level narcotics could provide. She thought on her surroundings and immediately landed on the answer. *Hospital.*

Hopefully two times would be a charm.

She'd been poked full of holes, so all the tubes and needles she detected weren't a surprise. She faced another mystery, something that caught her off guard. An object sat cradled in her hand, not the I.V. that protruded from a vein below her knuckles, but an item that weighed heavy against her palm.

Fisting it, she detected patterned metal with rounded edges, slightly bigger than a golf ball.

She jolted, would have sat straight up if a strong hand hadn't stopped her climb, gently pushing her back toward the sheets. "Shh, none of that. Nice and easy."

Ethan.

She opened her eyes and looked at him. "How?"

He smiled. "You're going to be okay. Your liver didn't make it out scot-free this time, so you'll be here until the infection risk passes."

How tired he looked. Hollows sank beneath his lower lids, and while a notably large torso loomed over the bed, he appeared thinner, haggard, which couldn't be possible. At most, she figured she'd been out a day.

She looked to one side, then the other in a slow headshake. She hadn't wondered about her health, though now she worried about his. "Not that."

"Ah," he said, extracting the box from her clutching fingers, "I bought them at auction the day after I saw they were missing. Lissa was happy to share all the details about your jewels, but only between threats to relieve me of mine. With a dull knife. She tells me your collection has impressed many a Christie's customer over the years." He parted the antique silver along its center seam to reveal her mother's earrings on bed of black velvet. "But not anymore, and not these. Never these."

He extracted a diamond and brought it to her ear with a languid stroke of stone against skin. "You once told me these had been your mother's favorites. That she'd loved you, and you her. It's fitting for me to return them to you because I love you just as much."

Her body shook all over. "Thank you for saving my life."

His voice didn't rise. He didn't stiffen or pull away. But when he spoke, she knew she'd heed his demands.

"Don't you ever, *ever* thank me for another thing. My carelessness almost *took* your life. I should never have left your side, not for a second." He slipped the second stud through her other earlobe. "You sold these earrings because I thwarted your career. I got them back because *I love you.* Never thank me for that."

She nodded, eyes stinging. "Fine. I'll just love you back."

EPILOGUE

November—New York City

"We're busting this popsicle stand." Ethan made the pronouncement three seconds after the doctor pronounced Scarlet fit to leave.

"Hallelujah," she chirped, slipping carefully from the bed after seemingly endless weeks of confinement.

He held out the weather-inappropriate sundress he'd swiped from her closet. He also offered—of course—a barely-there satin thong and a strapless bra that would work under the dress. "How'd I do?"

"Perfect."

She disappeared into the sterile bathroom he couldn't wait to leave behind. When she came out, showered and dressed, he pressed the edge of a binder between her fingers.

A frown crinkled between her brows. "This is one of Susan's rule-the-world folders." She looked hesitant to touch the damn thing.

"Yes."

Without opening it, she sank into a chair beneath the window and looked up at him. "You weren't here when I woke up. You went."

Guilty as charged. "I knew you'd want to know."

When she didn't speak, he elaborated. "To most, New York lost a visionary in your father, so the memorial was a grand affair by any standard. The world doesn't know what we do, Scarlet. Yet we talked to the police, so I wouldn't be surprised to see inklings of a scandal eke out eventually, but with both Gerard and your father gone, it'll only be conjecture."

She bowed her head toward her lap. "I prefer it this way. Despite everything, I didn't want to see him maligned."

"No explanation necessary." Now she could heal in peace. "But man, are people keen to hear from you. I hate to give him any credit, but Brian did a decent job with your statement at the press conference. He directed all questions to him via the firm. Guess what that means?"

She met his gaze with a catlike smile. "We win?"

"You're free. Of this hospital, of all the questions, of your career woes. Don't worry. JTS awaits your return on baited breath. Which brings me to the binder." He tapped the edge until Scarlet gave in and split it open.

"Oh," she breathed.

"You begin to see."

The pages were stocked with brochures for hotels, cars, restaurants, wine tours, beaches, shopping, theater, spa treatments, galleries, museums, and on and on. If the south of France had it, Susan had carefully filed the information away in this detailed master plan.

Pulling several typed, laminated sheets from the front pocket, Ethan asked, "Should I explain like she did to me?"

"Of course."

"She said, 'You'll arrive in Biarritz at one p.m. tomorrow afternoon. Look for a person with a sign that says Mr. and Mrs. Blake'—she's never been particularly subtle—'You'll be ushered to the Hotel Du Palais. You'll have time for a quick nap or a glass of champagne before dinner. Reservations are at eight sharp, so don't be late.'"

Ethan looked at his watch, mimicking Susan's moves. "She took a breather here to explain that though she's planned activities to fill our days—I stipulated we'll handle the nights—we can make changes by providing her with twenty-four-hour's notice. She'll handle the details."

He refocused on the itinerary, then deflated. "I don't think you want me to repeat everything she said. It took a full hour."

******

Happy tears blurred Scarlet's vision, and she merely nodded, struck dumb by the thoughtfulness. Guess she couldn't call the woman The Minion anymore.

Ethan filled the silence. "Susan's still pissed at me for siccing Billboard on her in Copenhagen, though I don't know why because I'm pretty sure I caught them making out in my private lobby when I stopped by to pick this up." He took a huge breath. "But I digress. As I said, she's pissed, so her services come with an extra stipulation."

He dropped to a knee.

Nearly blinded, Scarlet chortled, "Ethan, if you dare to propose because your secretary told you to, I'll throw all your clothes in the ocean when we get there."

"I didn't pack any, for either of us. Figured my personal shopaholic could handle that on site."

He held out a ring, just the ring, no box or other fancy accoutrements. After all the joking, his mouth drew into a flat line, his gaze tentative but pleading. "I bought this in Copenhagen, before all hell broke loose. I knew then." Looking at the ceiling, Ethan sank his teeth into his lower lip in a way that looked painful. "Susan tells me if this isn't on your finger by nine a.m. the day after tomorrow, then we aren't a couple and she's cancelling our couple's massage."

He took her trembling hand. "So, yes, I plan to do what she says. Because we can't let that happen."

Crying in earnest now, Scarlet whispered, "No, no we can't."

The stunning solitaire slid into place, a perfect fit. Catching an edge, the sunlight fractured around the room in a breathtaking display.

"You'll have me?" he asked quietly.

She nodded, unable to speak.

A shudder rattled across his shoulders, and his eyes slid closed. Bending his head, he kissed her ring finger. "Better late than never."

THANK YOU!

Thanks for reading *Love Me Later*. I hope you enjoyed the read as much as I enjoyed the write!

Would you like to know when my next book is available? You can sign up for my new-release e-mail list at www.libbyrice.com.

I post regular snippets from novels, pictures of character adventures, and other fun extras on my Facebook page. I also post tidbits about what's going on with me. Come join us at www.facebook.com/libbyrice.author.

Or you can follow me on Twitter at @libby_rice and/or Instagram at libby_rice.

Reviews help readers find books they'll love. I welcome and appreciate *all* reviews, whether positive or negative.

You've just read the first book in the Second Chances series. *Art-Crossed Love*, Lissa and Cole's story, will be available in early 2015. If you would like to read an excerpt, please read on.

ART-CROSSED LOVE: EXCERPT

Available January 2015

Lissa Blanc is a painter on a mission. She filters the world through a lens of color, line, and form and hides her past failures behind a delicate smirk that lets her critics think life comes easy. Behind the glitz of a prodigious upbringing, she's driven to emerge from the shadow of painful memories that insist she'll never be a renowned talent in her own right. When a gorgeous photographer suggests a partnership that will prove her worth but test every last one of her artistic ideals, Lissa longs to refuse his demands.

Refusal comes hard when she can't resist the man asking…

February—Boulder, Colorado

Cole set the prostitute's money on the nightstand, wondering if his wife's angel was laughing as hard as the living woman would have. Low light from an overhanging lamp highlighted Ben Franklin's sagging jowls, and Cole flicked his gaze toward the cash. "We agreed on four hundred?"

"Yes," she said. "Thanks." Her voice held the cultured tones of the upper class. This wasn't your average streetwalking hustler, but an expensive call girl living the good life. Boulder, Cole was learning, didn't offer much variety in the way of hired sex. For cheap love, a guy drove to Denver.

Ms. Jewel, or at least the woman who called herself that, reached across a foot of empty space separating their respective queen beds. The hotel might be respectable, but he hadn't splashed out for a suite. Most of her customers didn't, she'd told him, and he wanted the pictures to be representative of a normal gig.

Long, tapered nails scratched lightly over his thigh in a less-than-subtle suggestion. In her mid-thirties, Ms. Jewel looked to be a willing—more like

211

eager—twenty-five, but her caress didn't stir anything but mild curiosity. No surprise there.

Cole hadn't come to fuck.

He halted her progress with a gentle hold on her slim wrist. "Beautiful, definitely, but you know why we're here."

"Close-ups and conversation," she acknowledged with a sly smile. "But a girl can hope." Drawing back with a languorous pull, Ms. Jewel stretched along the edge of the bed before propping her head up with one hand. With the other, she stroked along the curvaceous silhouette her pose presented to great advantage.

Facing off against a preening whore who looked ready to pounce only added weight to the digital camera in Cole's lap. God, the fall from regular contributions at Time to freelancing for Boulder's local daily had been far. In slow increments, he raised his bulky equipment and snapped a candid shot of this evening's companion, from the neck down, as agreed.

The woman's presence in his frame proved that pimping wasn't nearly as rare in Mayberry-esqe Boulder as one might think. Five minutes on Craigslist could get a man—or a woman, for that matter—a wealth of by-the-hour entertainment. Yet paid or not, the camera couldn't help but love Ms. Jewel's creamy cleavage and healthy, smooth skin. While hookers might abound in this hotbed of high-tech employment, they were the consensual kind, not drug-addicted runaways or kidnap victims without other options. No, Boulder hookers drove fast cars and lived in sleek apartments, pandering to white, well-salaried, workaholic techies who paid the bill before the sex, cringed at physical force, and felt a desperate need for affection.

All in all, Boulder made hooking look pretty good.

Cole stood and began a series of photographs in rapid succession, almost like he was shooting the cover of Vogue, only he wouldn't Photoshop or airbrush or taint the photos in any way. What he saw, readers would get. "Tell me how you started."

He didn't have to ask the question. Cole was just the photographer. A journalist would write the words, while Cole would provide the pictures. But a talking subject relaxed, and a relaxed subject made for better shots.

So talk he would.

His model didn't hesitate. "I enjoy sex." There was that smile again. This time she rolled onto her back and cupped her breasts. They were covered—he'd managed to axe every one of her efforts to strip—but barely. A skimpy sundress skimmed the top of her areolas, and without a bra, her nipples might as well have been giving a dance recital on her chest.

"I suppose that's a good trait in your profession." Probably too glib, but she didn't notice.

"Yes. I'm also attractive." *And humble.* "School was never my thing, and after the fifth offer, I finally took the money and rode, so to speak."

Damn if she didn't get a smile out of him with that one. "And?"

Ms. Jewel didn't spread her legs. She also didn't clamp them together. The thin material of her dress made her lack of undergarments all the more obvious when she went limp and relaxed against the bed. "Since I liked the… physical aspects of the work, I let them make me rich. Lines of good-looking nerds at the door have secured my future." Her teasing look said, *want to be next?*

Cole took a picture of her long fingers. They thrummed her hardened nipples with no sign of fatigue. He really ought to put a stop to her little show, which hadn't been on the agenda, but he couldn't quell the curiosity she'd sparked with that touch to his thigh. How far would this sexpot have to go to turn him on? If she slid that hand down into her heat, would he finally get hard? If she moaned? What if she lifted the dress to her waist and went ahead with the spread she'd been threatening?

"Enough," he clipped. "Gorgeous as you are, this isn't Playboy, and I'm not interested." Because every last one of his wonderings had the same answer: nothing would turn him on. She could play and pant, even moan and masturbate for his eyes only, and he wouldn't respond. Pleasure had died along with Kate. In its place, he felt nothing good, only a burning desire to be close to the woman he'd loved, only a visceral need to visit her grave, only an unswerving willingness to sacrifice a rising career to accomplish those goals.

No matter how succulent the woman, a whore in a hotel room could never thaw the ice. Cole stuffed his camera and a few scribbled notes in his duffle. The evening couldn't be called photojournalism at its finest, but he had several decent pictures and enough information to cobble together semi-informative captions. Ms. Jewel had her cash. The local paper would buy this shit and assemble a story that wouldn't surprise anyone. Yes, the world's oldest profession made its home on street corners and casinos and the Mustang Ranch. But prostitution had also infiltrated lily-white bastions of education and accumulated wealth, granola moms with thousand-dollar strollers be damned.

When he touched the door handle, tasting escape, she posed a question with the barest hint of contempt in her voice. "And you, Mr. Rathlen? What are you doing here? You were one of Boulder's best-loved sons, traveling the world, having your photos featured in all sorts of fancy publications. I swear I saw your Tsunami shots in National Geographic."

"I was," he admitted. "You did." But they both knew what she meant. *Now you're photographing a hometown hooker for the local daily.*

No longer. Thirteen months and seventeen days had passed without a care for the fact that Kate wouldn't have chosen mediocre. Ms. Jewel, who sold her body for money, at least had the decency to excel at it. Perhaps she hadn't been forced into this line of work, but few made her kind of choices without glimpses of pain.

The woman mocking him from the bed hadn't jumpstarted his cock, but she'd done a number on his head. Cole would be making some calls come morning.

******

June—New York City

"You don't look like your headshots."

Cole paused his perusal of a painting that monopolized an entire wall of one of the Meatpacking District's chicest galleries. Though the disembodied voice came from behind him, he knew the smooth tones interrupting his study belonged to Lissa Blanc. He drew out his response, glancing between the canvas and the nearby placard that described it. "And this painting doesn't look like a park."

"Your pictures make you look friendlier. Smaller. Happier."

She didn't wait for his rebuttal before circling around to tap the crimson drywall next to her work with a matching fingertip. "What do you feel when you look at it? Not like you're in a park, but maybe you think of being young and carefree?" Her lips curled into a parody of a smile, like she was being forced into used-car sales at gunpoint. "Maybe you see something you want to purchase."

"You're kidding." Morning Park was more interesting for what it lacked. Chunks of the car-sized canvas had been left bare. Where she'd seen fit to add paint, serrated jags of black and green crawled out from the edges toward a thin seam of yellow that unevenly bisected the disarray. The mess had all the qualities—if you could call them that—of the prints his wife had framed.

Kate had loved her "Blancs"—not that Lissa had reached that lofty, last-name-only level of acclaim—while Cole had wanted to use them as bonfire kindling. Where his wife had touted Lissa as an up-and-coming genius, mark her words, Cole had questioned the mental faculties, let alone the artistic integrity, behind paintings that could potentially be copied by a posse of well-trained five-year-olds.

Lissa stiffened, all the welcome-to-the-big-tent theatrics draining away in an instant. "Unlike you, Mr. Rathlen, I don't consider my work a joke."

He bit his tongue. She flushed when she got mad. The pinkening of the smooth skin rising above her black corset held his interest more than the paint she'd thrown at the canvas. "I'm critical, Ms. Blanc. I have not called you a joke."

Mostly because circumstances hadn't thrown him the chance. He was a photographer, not an art critic, so other than becoming a bona fide Internet troll, he lacked a platform to rant about the "talent" his wife had so admired.

"Sorry," Lissa sneered, examining her nails. "I was having a gin and tonic in my mind just now and missed your point." Slender arms wound across her chest. "What gives you the right to criticize work you can't possibly understand?"

"A mouth," he said dryly, "and a rampant superiority complex." Might as well be honest. Certainly less had allowed fools to masquerade as fine minds.

Turning to the painting once again, he marveled at the blobs Kate would have called brilliant. "There," she'd have informed him, "where the green prowls toward the black but can't reach it for the yellow. That's the essence of disrupted nature—a park."

"What's interesting about you," Cole told Lissa casually, "is what you don't understand. Art is more than critical acclaim. If great, ordinary people connect with the work."

And pay for it. He let the undeniable thrust of his words hang between them. Lissa had wormed her way into a few of New York City's most hallowed show spaces, but a big seller she was not.

Her do-or-die smile receded. Inexplicably, Cole wanted that particular danger to return. But professional relationships, like all others, began best in honesty.

"I hear the highway business is booming these days." He paused, eyeing her famously philanthropic parents in the crowd. Together they ran one of the country's largest construction companies. "Rumor has it these swank gallery showings have more to do with your family's heavy machinery than your hand with a brush."

The red blooming on her chest darkened to an angry purple. He got his smile back, but only in the form of a tight stretch of lip set against clenched teeth. A shame because, apparently unlike him, Lissa Blanc was photogenic as hell. The pictures he'd seen had portrayed her looks with staggering accuracy. They'd highlighted the thick chestnut hair that now gleamed auburn in the light and revealed the dark eyes that assessed him with cool intensity, at odds with the delicacy of the surrounding bone structure. They'd even done justice to her skin, showcasing the exact shade of white tulips, at least when she wasn't flushed with anger or frustration.

Most of all, her pictures had hinted that Lissa Blanc would be magnificent were she to stretch those generous lips wide with the proper smile she withheld.

"So that's it. You don't like it." Lissa stated the obvious, probably still out mentally sucking gin and tonics. "You sought me out for an appointment, then traveled to Manhattan, all to share your—with all due respect—less-than-worthy disdain."

"No." Taking her in, he drifted closer and breathed deep. Notes of fruit and an unrecognizable spice hit like an apple orchard in August, one he badly wanted to explore. Kate had smelled like Chanel No 5.

He froze, rejecting the thrall of long-denied senses rushing to life. Betrayal started small. First an innocuous observation, then… a crisis. Had Cole not believed in the power of temptation so ardently, he'd still have a wife.

Shame lashed at the part of him he kept on lockdown, not for insulting Lissa's painting or for tearing a chink in her armor, but for enjoying the tease and wondering what color she'd turn next.

He cleared his throat. Yet Lissa's the one I need, the one Kate would have chosen. Choosing Lissa himself—no matter how distracting the woman or how virulently he disagreed with his wife's prematurely-silenced admiration—would pave a path to absolution.

Without uttering a single superfluous syllable, he made his point, "I want you to paint for me."

www.ingramcontent.com/pod-product-compliance
Lightning Source LLC
Chambersburg PA
CBHW050928120626
46552CB00001B/99